"Now what?"

Trace heard the unmistakable sound of metal rasping against metal at the same instant he felt cool air against his cheek.

"I'm going to shave you." Bellami clipped away the long hair on his face with the scissors.

"Oh, the hell you are!" Trace was half out of the water as he spoke. This had gone on long enough. It was humiliating enough when his own sister tried to shave him. He'd be damned if some New York spinster would do it. He'd had enough of being treated like a boy.

"Would you like a towel, Mr. O'Bannion, or will you dry in the air?" Bellami asked sweetly.

Instantly Trace sank into the water, his face flaming with heat. Damned woman riled him up so much, he hadn't realized he was standing buck naked in front of her....

Dear Reader,

When we ran our first March Madness promotion in 1992, we had no idea that we would be introducing such a successful venture. Our springtime showcase of brand-new authors has been such a hit, that it has become a priority at Harlequin Historicals to seek out talented new writers and introduce them to the field of historical romance.

This month's titles include *All that Matters*, a haunting medieval tale about an imprisoned woman and her unwitting rescuer, by Elizabeth Mayne; *Embrace the Dawn* by Jackie Summers, the story of a woman kidnapped by a highwayman and forced to play his bride; a Western from Linda Castle that features a blinded hero and the woman who helps him recover, *Fearless Hearts;* and *Love's Wild Wager* by Taylor Ryan, a Regency-era story about a penniless heiress and the rogue who wins her heart.

We hope you will enjoy all four of this month's books and keep an eye out for all our titles, wherever Harlequin Historicals are sold.

Sincerely,

Tracy Farrell
Senior Editor

Please address questions and book requests to:
Harlequin Reader Service
U.S.: 3010 Walden Ave., P.O. Box 1325, Buffalo, NY 14269
Canadian: P.O. Box 609, Fort Erie, Ont. L2A 5X3

LINDA CASTLE

Fearless HEARTS

Harlequin Books

TORONTO • NEW YORK • LONDON
AMSTERDAM • PARIS • SYDNEY • HAMBURG
STOCKHOLM • ATHENS • TOKYO • MILAN
MADRID • WARSAW • BUDAPEST • AUCKLAND

ISBN 0-373-28861-1

FEARLESS HEARTS

Copyright © 1995 by Linda L. Crockett.

Printed in U.S.A.

LINDA CASTLE

is a third generation New Mexican. She is married, the mother of four and the grandmother of two. She is a member of RWA, SWW, LERA and is seeking membersip in WWA, as well as verifying her lineage for membership in DAR. Linda teaches part-time at San Juan College. She is embarking on two new projects: dog showing and home teaching of her two youngest kids. She loves heroes with a past who meet heroines looking for the future. When she's "resting," she rides, swims and collects antiques.

For my soul mate, Bill—who taught me about romance, who never wavers in his passion, love and belief in my quest—and for my children's endless patience, I thank God.

Thanks, Denise, for the first book. I am eternally grateful to Fabio for luring me inside the cover, to Laura Kinsale, Marylyle Rogers, Marilyn Campbell, Judith Steele, Shannon Drake and Virginia Henley for enchanting me with their words while I lingered there. For Ann and Merline's advice; Margaret O'Neill's heart; Elaine Davie's conviction and all who encourage me daily. You know who you are, thank you.

Chapter One

New York City
November 1884

The woman's kid boots made crunching noises in the snow as she stepped out of the hansom cab. Slipping the money into the driver's hand, she readjusted the hat with the softly shirred veil that covered her entire face. Pure feminine mystery.

The driver, wearing fashionable livery, watched with interest, wondering what she looked like under the veil. He could just make out the outline of her face, but nothing more. He didn't try to hide his curiosity as he stared at her. The horse pawed the frozen ground, anxious to leave, as the driver watched her climb the steps. Someone, probably the old caretaker, John, had swept the snow from them recently. She gave him no indication that she knew he was observing her, and she walked up to the big doors of St. Michael's Hospital for the Blind.

The gray stones looked cold and forbidding as she placed her foot on the last step and approached the double doors. There was a bell rope, but she didn't even look toward it. Instead, she placed her gloved hand on the brass knob and shoved.

She inhaled deeply when the big door swung open. Odd, how the smell of ether, starched linen and strong lye soap felt so comforting to her. She walked down the long corridor. She smiled beneath the concealing veil, but no one who passed her could know. Nothing could penetrate the protection of her veil.

Nothing and no one.

A nurse wearing a stiff white uniform stopped and smiled warmly in greeting. The veiled figure hesitated for only a moment and nodded once before continuing down the Spartan hospital corridor. As she approached a battered door at the end of the hall, she began to unbutton her heavy gray velvet coat. She removed the coat and her matching kid gloves, but not the hat with the veil.

Just as one slender hand was poised and ready to knock, the door opened abruptly. An older man with sharp piercing eyes looked at her in annoyance. "So, it's you. You're late. Did the snow hold you up? Here let me have your coat and gloves." He spoke gruffly as he took the garments. He hung the coat on a worn coatrack, which tilted precariously under the weight of its burden. The kid gloves were dropped to the top of his scarred maple desk. The man's features were sharp and hard, his eyes penetrating. He bore a striking resemblance to an eagle.

The hat turned in his direction, and a clear voice came from behind the veil. "No, it wasn't the snow. Claire came to visit Mother at the last minute, and you know how they are. I couldn't get away any sooner."

"Bellami—" his voice grated with exasperation "—will you take off the damned hat? It's me. You don't have to be so uncomfortable with me." He never took his eyes from the figure before him.

A deep sigh issued from the female. She looked toward the worn chair in front of the old rolltop desk. Sitting down, she took out the hat pin. With one hand, she lifted the hat from her head and carefully placed it in her lap.

"Much better, Bellami." Dr. Malone looked at her and smiled. He saw her every day, and yet he'd never gotten accustomed to the color of her hair. After thirteen years, the sight of it still made him catch his breath.

Once, years ago, the Russian crown prince had come to New York. Doc had seen him at the theater in a tall fur hat. It had been this exact color. Sable. Bellami James's hair was pure, rich and dark. With her gray-blue eyes it made, without a doubt, the most striking combination Dr. Malone had ever seen. He felt a pang of sympathy for her. She'd been as beautiful and as vibrant as any girl in the city, before the accident.

"I got your message. Now what's this all about, Doc? There's not some problem with my work here, is there?"

She looked directly at him, and he saw an expression of apprehension and pain flit across her face. After seeing him daily, he supposed, she'd gotten as relaxed about him looking at her face as she would ever be. But that wasn't saying a whole lot. He accepted it, the same way her family did. But if this had been anyone else, anywhere else, the hat would've stayed on, and Doc felt sad just knowing that fact.

"I've had a request from an old friend," he said, pausing to look at her with his sharp bird-of-prey eyes, "in the West. My friend needs someone with experience like yours, Bellami."

"I see you've been meddling again. Please go on, Doctor." She leaned back in the chair and smoothed the folds of her heavy dress in her lap.

He ignored the hard edge to her voice. "There's been an accident involving my friend's son." He detected an immediate yet subtle change in Bellami. He knew it, he'd been right, by golly! Give her a wounded soul to care for and fuss over, and she became as easy to manage as an angel. "He's been blinded, and the prognosis is not good. Evidently he is not making the adjustment very well."

Bellami tried to keep the ironic grimace from her lips. How often she'd heard the same phrase used to describe her after the accident. *Not making the adjustment very well.* "Please continue." She tried to swallow the lump that formed in her throat as she imagined the scene. A young boy, full of life and energy, suddenly finding his world changed. Forever altered.

"My friend wrote and asked if I would suggest someone who might come to New Mexico to instruct his son. You know, the basics—dressing, bathing, getting around his home without his sight."

Doc paused and let the words sink in. He'd learned long ago that the best way to deal with Bellami was to let her absorb all the information before making suggestions. Usually she arrived at the same point he did, at the same time, even if they frequently took different routes to get there. "I thought of Richards, but he's not nearly as patient as some others I could find."

Bellami frowned. Richards. Dr. Samuel Richards— brilliant, but one of those people who thought any kindness or sympathy to someone who'd been injured only slowed their recovery. And the all-important factor—*the adjustment*. She clenched her jaw involuntarily, just thinking about it.

Richards would breeze in, giving orders like an invading commander. Then he would begin to preach about the full, productive life ahead, telling the boy to forget the past, as if it had never existed. Bellami knew the speech well. She'd been on the receiving end often, when she was first hurt.

She swallowed hard. "What would this mean, exactly, Doc?" She brushed her hand across her cheek.

Dr. Malone exhaled as he leaned back casually in his chair. He tried to keep the smile off his face. He knew Bellami very well. She was interested. Now all he had to do was reel her in like a fish. "Well, they need someone to come to the territory of New Mexico. To stay with the boy, teach him to take care of himself. The usual things, Bellami. Except this will all be done at home, and not in a hospital. There aren't any hospitals nearby. It's pretty remote, near a town named Socorro. My friend has lived there for years. He owns a large ranch. He's a widower with four—no, it's five children.'' Dr. Malone tented his fingers and stared at a crack in the plaster ceiling while he talked. "It would be quite an adventure for—" he raised a bushy graying eyebrow "—someone."

"It sounds like it. You'd like that someone to be me, wouldn't you, Doc?" she said evenly.

"Yes, I would, Bellami. You know I've felt it's been too easy for you to hide, at home and here in the hospital. Your family's position insulates you from the world. Of course, I'm just as guilty. The work you do here hardly forces you to get out. You're only twenty-six years old, Bellami, far too young to put yourself on the shelf."

"You know I'm already on the shelf. No man will ever look at me twice. Anyway, I'm content. My family doesn't spoil me any more than they always have. My work here, with you and the children, is enough for me."

"Your family has spoiled *and* protected you, but I don't want to get into that. I'd like you to consider this opportunity, if for no other reason so you can see a bit of the world besides New York. You're a bright, caring woman, Bellami. I'd like to see you get on with your life."

"What's the matter, Doc? Don't you think I've made an adequate *adjustment?*" A touch of bitterness could be heard in her voice, but she smiled at the old physician.

"Go home, Bell. Think about it. I told my friend I'd let him know before February fifteenth. He has sent funds to cover the tickets, food—every possible need."

"Doc, if I decide to do this, you know very well money won't be an issue. I'll talk it over with Mother and Daddy. I'll let you know."

She rose slowly and put her hat on. When she had secured it with the crystal-tipped hat pin, she reached up to pull the veil over her face and tucked it securely under her chin. Again an aura of mystery surrounded her. She shrugged her arms into the coat Doc held for her. Methodically, out of long habit, she pulled on the soft kid gloves.

When Bellami reached the office door, Doc spoke again. "I think if anyone can help the young man, Bell, you can." He took her hand and gave it an affectionate squeeze, and then she stepped past him into the quiet hall.

Dr. Malone watched her walk away, her back straight as a rod as she approached the door to the outside world—or at least the very small part of the world she allowed herself. It made him unbearably sad to know what went on under her veneer of genteel composure. It damned near broke his old heart.

The brownstone looked inviting even in the cold gloom of late December in New York. Bellami felt a surge of contentment as she climbed the steps to the door. Fat flakes of snow collected on her coat before she reached the shelter of the porch. The oval in the frosted glass framed a picture of domestic bliss and tranquillity. There they sat in the parlor, enjoying the warmth of a roaring fire. Her family, her anchor, her shield.

A board game was spread out on the low walnut table. Bellami smiled. It was Bulls & Bears, a Wall Street game. Her older brother, Rod, had surprised them all by bringing it home just before Christmas. The game pictured William Vanderbilt and Jay Gould, as Bull and Bear respectively, shearing investor sheep!

Bellami felt deliciously wicked each time she played the silly game. Having met both Mr. Gould and Mr. Vanderbilt at one of her sister's parties only served to increase her enjoyment. She stepped inside and closed the heavy door quietly behind her, not wishing to disturb them, but a gust of cold air announced her arrival.

They stopped their play and conversation as she entered the room. Tilly, the maid, appeared from nowhere and whisked off Bellami's coat and gloves. The girl stood waiting for her hat as Bellami removed the hat pin. Tiny snowflakes melted in the warm room, leaving droplets of moisture on the veil.

"Bell, we were beginning to wonder." Patricia James' silver-gray hair was piled high, in the latest fashion. She regarded her daughter lovingly with blue-gray eyes. Her dainty, slippered feet rested on a needlepoint-covered footstool near the fire.

"I was at St. Michael's, Mother." Bellami answered as Tilly took the last of her apparel and left the room.

Rod handed Bellami a crystal cup of eggnog. He was frowning. "I thought you took the month off, to rest after the holidays."

"I did. Most of the children are at home with their families for a visit. Dr. Malone asked me to stop by. He wanted to speak with me." Bellami sat down on the velvet sofa near the marble fireplace. Flames reflected off tiny cupids on the polished brass andirons, and she watched the play of color.

"How is the old bird, anyway?" Donovan James bit the end off a slim brown cigar and spit it into the flames. Before he struck the match he was holding, he glanced at his wife. He stepped to the fireplace and leaned toward the carved hearth so that the smoke would draw from the room. Patricia wasn't fond of the habit, but she'd never chide him in front of his children.

"He's fine." Bellami wanted to discuss the job offer Dr. Malone had mentioned, but something made her hold back. Unaccustomed to making decisions alone, she found the prospect both exciting and a bit intimidating. She felt reluctant to speak of it until she'd given it more thought. In truth, the idea of leaving home frightened her.

A handsome young man with sable hair and gray-blue eyes entered the room and sat beside her. He leaned over and affectionately kissed the tip of her nose.

"What's that for, Brooks?" Bellami raised her eyebrows in question. She felt that familiar tug at her heart when she looked at her brother. The manliness of his face—and the scar on hers—were the only things that kept them from being identical. Of course, those small details made all the difference in the world.

He grinned and winked. "Oh, no reason. I just thought I'd give my favorite twin sister a kiss. What did Doc want to talk to you about, Bell? Is he after you to get married again?" Brooks leaned back comfortably and patted the back of his sister's hand absently.

Patricia watched her youngest children. Even now, at twenty-six years of age, they liked to be near each other. There was a special connection, a private link, completely undefinable but quite strong. She found herself remembering that horrible day, and the accident. While Bellami had been under ether during surgery, Brooks had slept the same amount of time. Patricia had feared that if Bellami died, Brooks would perish, as well. It was one more reason she had tried so hard to protect Bellami and keep her safe ever since. The sound of Bellami's voice shook Mrs. James from her memories.

Bellami's lips curled into an affectionate grin. "We all know I am an old maid, Brooks. Please, don't try to be coy. Of all the people in the world I expect to be honest with me, I expect it of you the most." She lightly cuffed him on the cheek.

Brooks watched his sister's eyes cloud over. The urge to hold her overwhelmed him. Brooks never looked at his sister without asking himself why? Why couldn't it have been him, instead of her? On a man, it would've added a touch of mystery. He would've looked rakish, like some piratical rogue. Seeing what the accident had cost Bellami broke his heart. He wished he could find a way to draw Bell back into society.

The sound of Rod clearing his throat made them turn to look at him in unison. "Speaking of marriage, Brooks, when do you plan on getting around to finding one suitable girl?" Rod pinned his younger brother with a penetrating stare.

The subject of Brooks's many girlfriends had been coming up a lot this holiday season. The bills had started coming in from Tiffany's in early December. At the time, Donovan and Rod had started to wonder if they were harboring a Don Juan. Bellami grinned as her brother shifted uncomfortably. Brooks courted many different lady friends from New York's social elite. But these little baubles he'd suddenly taken to purchasing had sent her father into shock. Brooks had been ordering identical earbobs for all his romantic interests. The last tally hovered somewhere around two dozen, and the season wasn't over yet. Bellami suppressed the urge to laugh when Brooks blushed and adjusted his waistcoat.

Brooks spoke without looking up, while he plucked at a tiny bit of thread on his brocade vest. "Bell and I are too young to be married . . . in fact, we may buy a brownstone and be eccentric twins. Wouldn't Patricia's bridge group have a time with that?" He rolled his eyes expressively, imitating one of the matronly ladies his mother frequently entertained.

Rod frowned at his brother's humor. Bellami glanced at Brooks from the corner of her eye. She'd been wondering lately if Brooks could really be serious about remaining a bachelor. He'd been mentioning the subject a lot recently. She had the uncomfortable suspicion that she was the reason behind it. He felt responsible for the accident. It would be just like Brooks to think he should sacrifice his future happiness for her. She wished she could tell him what was in her heart. Of course, none of them ever talked about the accident. The whole subject made them all so uncomfortable—Bellami had never really talked to anyone about what had happened.

Donovan took a last deep draw on his cigar. He tossed the butt into the fire-grate with a flick of his broad thumb. The tobacco caught, flaring brightly for an instant, then diminishing to become invisible in the ash of burned logs.

Bellami thought about Doc's offer. If she left New York for a while, perhaps Brooks would not feel as if he had to worry so much about her and her future.

"Dr. Malone told me about an interesting offer this afternoon," Bellami blurted out. Everyone stopped what they were doing and waited for her to continue. Tilly entered the room at that moment to refill their cups with fresh eggnog. She glanced at the group self-consciously, suspended as they were in silence. Bellami waited quietly while Tilly hurried from one cup to the next. After the blushing girl left the room, she spoke again. "Doc has an old friend in the New Mexico Territory who has advertised for someone like me."

Rod pulled himself up an inch or two straighter. He took on a familiar stiff-necked, protective posture she knew so well. He'd been doing it since Bellami returned to school after her long stay in the hospital. Each time someone asked about her face, he would appear from nowhere to place himself between her and the inquisitor. She had the feeling he was doing that right now. Bellami felt a rush of love for her older brother, and it made her more determined to meet his steely gaze.

"Just exactly what is someone like you, Bell?" Rod acted as if the phrase had been meant as a derogatory remark.

"Someone with my experience teaching blind children, silly."

"I see." Rod obviously didn't see, but Bellami knew it had seemed like the sensible thing to say at the moment—so he'd said it. He'd never been happy with Bellami's choice of work. The fact that she worked at all disturbed him. *She didn't need to,* as he so often reminded her. Bellami had never been able to make any of her family understand that working with the blind made her feel useful. When she found herself wallowing in self-pity during her recovery she found another child, more needy, to care for.

"Do go on, dear," Patricia said, and moved to a large leather armchair near the door.

"Doc thinks I should go out West and work with this boy, until he's more able to cope with his injury." The last part came out in a rush of words.

"You can't be serious!" Rod whirled around to face Bellami. His face was a mask of shock. She looked at her father and saw the same outraged expression.

"Why do you say that?" Bellami hadn't thought Rod or her father would be enthusiastic, but she hadn't expected quite this reaction.

Rod paced a few feet back and forth in front of the fireplace. His dark eyebrows knit into a deep scowl. "New Mexico Territory? Why the idea is preposterous! Alone, unprotected? It's clear across the country, for God's sake!" Rod proceeded to give her all the reasons why she would be mad to consider it. He ticked off the dangers and disadvantages on his fingers, one by one. Bellami watched while her family discussed the idea as if she were not even in the room. She shifted uncomfortably as she looked from one dissenting member to the other. Only Brooks remained silent. He seemed to be waiting to hear what Bellami had to say. Donovan and Rod finally blustered themselves out, and the room became tense with silence.

"Bell, I'll miss you," Brooks said simply. Three pairs of eyes turned to look at Brooks and Bellami, sitting side by side on the velvet sofa. She felt their eyes on her face, and from nowhere a scrap of memory flitted through her head. A wave of nausea swept along with it. Her throat burned and she gasped for breath as she experienced a brief flash of the accident and the remembered pain. Wringing her hands within the folds of her dress, she tamped down the despised memories. She swallowed hard, forcing them back into the recesses of her mind.

"Doc is a wise old man. You said the man in New Mexico is a friend of his?" Brooks asked softly, trying to see beneath her carefully rehearsed expression. He tried to read her mind, but all he could see was her mask. A mask she presented to the people within her corner of the world.

Bellami took a deep breath and felt some of the tension leave her body. "Yes, his friend's son. Actually, a young boy—some sort of accident. I don't imagine I'd be gone more than six or eight months, at the most."

"Go, Bellami. I think you should go." Brooks gave her hand a squeeze before he rose from the sofa. He went to stand in front of the hearth.

"Brooks, have you lost your senses?" Rod asked.

"No, I don't think so. Bell's a grown woman. I think she should make the decision. If she wants to go, then she should go. We'll be right here when she comes back. New York isn't going anyplace."

"Bellami does spend too much time indoors," Donovan said. "A trip would do her a world of good. She's been looking awfully pale to me lately. In fact, I was thinking of taking her to the farm upstate."

Bellami frowned. Her parents meant well, but they never asked her what *she* wanted to do. The lure of independence and some time making her own decisions beckoned.

"Patricia, it's late. Will you accompany me?" Donovan helped her to rise, then took her elbow and guided her to the staircase. As he passed Bellami, he gave her a kiss on the top of her dark head. "Good night, dear. I'll give this some thought and tell you what I decide at breakfast tomorrow.''

Bellami could almost hear Doc's voice telling her this could be her last chance.

The sun slanted through the leaded-glass window across Bellami's bed. She stirred and stretched, and her eyes drifted lazily open. The lavender canopy on her bed seemed to be illuminated by the light. Bellami savored the tranquil picture for a moment before she slid her feet over the side of the bed and stood up. She'd never been one to linger abed in the morning. She prided herself on her discipline and self-control. She walked to her closet and selected a dress for the day, choosing a bright rose-colored velvet. The subtle shade made her light skin and dark hair glow.

After she finished dressing, she picked up her silver-backed brush. Her hair crackled as she pulled the brush through the heavy mane for one hundred strokes. Bellami's hair was her one true vanity. There were moments when she thought she should cut it, that it had become too much work, that it took too much time from the children at the hospital, but she could never bring herself to do it.

She picked up a set of tortoiseshell combs and walked to the highboy between the long windows. Wrapping the full length of her dark tresses around her hand, she wound her hair into a fat loop. Before she placed the combs in the thick coil to hold it in place, she looked into the mirror.

Bellami had grown accustomed to the sight of her cheek. It was the way people treated her that she could not adjust to. Whenever she met new people, their eyes focused on her face or they self-consciously looked away. Or, worst of all, they would whisper sad words of sympathy to their companions. That was why she'd retreated behind the veil. It wasn't for herself—not really. It was for the people she met. As long as she remained behind the veil she didn't make people uncomfortable. Her life seemed almost as normal as others'. Strangers didn't have to look away; they treated her as if she were just an ordinary person and not an object of pity. That was what Bellami wanted more than anything else in the world. She wanted to be judged on her abilities and accomplishments and not treated like a fragile china doll because of the accident.

Dr. Malone had tried. He bullied the family and suggested they all come to grips with it and let Bellami get on with her life. He'd always felt they should face it, as Bellami had done. They hadn't taken his advice.

Bellami had tried to talk about it, but her family had gotten so upset she finally gave up. Now it had been so long, she didn't know if she could talk about it. Her family was absolutely determined to keep her from having to examine her feelings about the accident and what had happened to her face.

Bellami sighed. She hid her face from the outside world, but she never hid it from herself. That was the reason she started each new day with a long look into her mirror. Bellami faced each new day of her life with no illusions. She knew what she looked like. She accepted the fact that her life would never be like other women's. She had no hopes, no dreams. Her life as it was now was the sum total of what it ever would be. Pretty women were loved and cherished. Bellami knew she'd never again be called pretty. When she looked at her face, memories of the old taunts and remarks echoed through the room. The cruel words of childhood still had the power to batter her ego.

"Ugly. Bellami James is ugly."

The words, spoken in a moment of surprise, were still like a knife blade ripping through her heart. Tears would still come close to spilling over. Bellami took a deep breath and willed herself not to cry. She hadn't allowed herself to shed a single tear since the day Dr. Malone took off the bandages.

Besides, what would be the point? Nothing would change. Tears couldn't erase the past. She was an adult now; she was strong. She had learned how to cope, and she had come to grips with her face. She had learned to find joy in giving to others, and it was enough.

"It is enough. Your life is good and full, and you should be content. Think of the poor children—think of the little blind boy." She admonished her own reflection aloud. She hardly noticed the jagged four-inch scar running from her cheek to her jawbone as she shoved the combs into her heavy hair.

Brooks looked up from the morning paper in time to see Bellami walk down the stairs. One slender, long-fingered hand slid down the polished wood of the banister. Her face was bathed in morning sunlight. He could see the profile of her straight nose, the soft mouth, the curve of her right jaw. Smiling unconsciously, he felt a surge of pride. Bellami had such grace and poise. If only he could make other people see what he saw.

He'd tried to find suitable bachelors, but they always said the wrong things. The one thing Bellami could not abide was pity. She'd hidden her face from their nervous stares and whispered words, and she'd been hiding ever since. But she had never cried. Brooks wondered if tears might wash away some of her pain, and some of his guilt.

She turned to him as she reached the bottom stair, and he felt the cold blanket of self-loathing rest heavy on his shoulders. It never changed. He felt this way every day of his life. First the pride, then the guilt when he saw the scar. He would always feel responsible for putting that scar on her face, and it tore at his soul.

"Good morning, Brooks, Rod. Where are Mother and Father?" Bellami planted a kiss on each of her brothers' cheeks. She walked to the oak server to select breakfast.

As usual, it held a nice variety of meat and eggs. This morning, the cook, Mrs. Wiggins, had fixed waffles—one of Bellami's favorites. She piled food high on her plate.

"Father took Mother out for a morning ride through Central Park," Rod replied from behind the morning newspaper. He never glanced up from the business section.

Brooks watched Bellami's back while she sniffed the blueberry muffins. "What are you going to do today, Bell?" he asked, grinning as a strand of sable-colored hair escaped the comb. It reached nearly to her hips and swayed gracefully when she moved.

"I think I'll send a message to Doc, then I'll start packing." Her voice was steady, but Brooks saw the tremor in her hand. He knew she was frightened.

"Are you sure you know what you are doing, Bellami?" Rod's attention turned abruptly from the stock market to his sister. He laid the paper down, his black eyes riveted on her.

She turned to look him straight in the eye for a full minute before she spoke. This would be her first test. If she could withstand Rod's gentle disapproval, then she could stand up to her parents. "No. But I think I have to do this."

Rod frowned, and his eyes darted to Brooks, who sat stiff. "All right, Bell, but remember, if you need anything, anything at all, send a cable and I'll be right there to take care of you." Rod coughed as he pushed himself away from the table.

Bellami knew he was close to giving her one of his bone-crushing hugs. She watched his straight back as he left the dining room, and her heart brimmed with love for him.

She sniffed and cleared her throat. "Well, Brooks, you've been awfully quiet." Bellami took her plate and sat in the chair beside him. She picked up a fork and began cutting her waffle into bite-size pieces.

"I don't know why, Bell, but I think you have to go. For both of us." Brooks frowned.

She stopped her fork en route to her mouth and turned to look at him. It was so eerie whenever it happened. Neither one of them had ever really gotten used to it. She'd been thinking exactly the same thing at the same time. Being twins gave them some odd insight into each other's thoughts and feelings.

Even though she was terrified of the unknown and of leaving the security of home, she felt it was somehow necessary. Why, she didn't know, but if Brooks felt the same way, then maybe it was true.

He stood up and planted a kiss on top of her head before he turned to leave the room. When he reached the door, he paused. "I'm sorry."

Bellami felt pain in her heart and a lump in her throat. If she could have gotten to her feet, she would have called him back, but her head was spinning as the old, hurtful memories engulfed her.

Eight trunks were being loaded into a dray. Donovan James clenched a cigar in his teeth as he surveyed the baggage. "I certainly hope those poor folks in New Mexico have an extra room. They'll need it just for your clothes."

"I'll need all this," Bellami said. "Spring is on the way, then summer. Either I take all this now, or I'd need new things made for the warmer months."

Donovan James had the reputation of being a most indulgent father with all his children, but most of all with Bellami. She knew he tried to compensate for her face by spoiling her. It only made her love him more. "Well, daughter, I guess we'd better round up the rest of the family, if we're going to get you to the station on time."

As if on cue, Rod appeared at the door, with Patricia. Brooks came running down the stairs, pulling on his coat.

He'd nicked his chin shaving, and he dabbed at the bloody spot with a clean linen handkerchief.

"What time did you say Bellami's train is leaving?" Patricia asked Donovan as they walked down the steps together. He pulled out his pocket watch and opened it.

"It's scheduled to pull out of the station in twenty minutes. I guess we better hurry. Bellami's train may leave without her."

The group piled into the enclosed carriage, and the driver snapped the reins, encouraging the horse to a brisk trot. The wagon full of trunks moved ahead of the carriage.

Bellami cradled her hat in her lap, along with her white fur muff. She nervously plucked at the veil as they swayed down the snow-covered street. She glanced across at her brother Rod, who frowned and looked away.

"Now, Rod, please stop looking like that." Bellami reached across the carriage and touched his arm.

He attempted to smile, but he resembled a man going to the gallows. "This is the first time you've left home, since..." His words trailed off self-consciously, and he went a little pale.

Donovan and Patricia sat in stony silence, and Brooks coughed nervously. They all turned to look out the windows of the carriage, suddenly interested in the frosty lampposts.

Bellami sighed. This scenario had been played out a hundred times before. Brooks saying he was sorry a week ago had been the closest that any member of her family had ever come to discussing Bellami's face or the accident. Dr. Malone had tried once again to persuade Bellami to force the issue yesterday at his office when she told him goodbye. His arguments made sense, and she really had intended to do it. But she found herself terrified of the prospect and overwhelmed by another emotion—guilt.

Bellami felt guilty about the accident. She realized she felt guilty for getting hurt—guilty for causing Brooks to feel responsible. Most of all she felt guilty for becoming ugly and being so imperfect she'd never be loved.

She sighed heavily and watched as the well-ordered streets slipped by. It almost seemed like a dream. She was really doing it. She was leaving home, leaving the loving protection of her family. Bellami thought she might be sick if she didn't think of something else.

She looked out the carriage window when they approached Grand Central Station. Train smoke billowed in dark gray clouds over the heads of sojourners. Milling groups of people crowded the station. Their breath made little puffs of vapor in the cold as they shouted and waved to departing loved ones.

When the carriage stopped, Rod stepped out first, then Donovan, who offered his hand to Patricia. Brooks got out the opposite side and waited patiently for Bellami. She shifted her muff on her lap and put her hat on. She stuck the hat pin through, then she pulled the veil down to cover her face. With her armor in place, she could meet the world.

A uniformed conductor walked through the crowds at the station, shouting train departures to faraway destinations. Bellami shivered and jammed her hands farther into her fur muffler when her train was announced. In a flurry of activity, she was soon on the train, waving at the shrinking figures of her family in the distance. She found herself seated next to a dour older woman dressed in black. The woman nodded briefly in greeting, then turned her face away from Bellami. Well, at least she wouldn't be forced to make pleasant conversation.

As the train clattered and rocked down the tracks, she let her head fall back against the padded leather seat. The motion of the swaying car and the endless snow-covered landscape relaxed her.

Images of a little blind boy filled her mind. He needed her. Bellami wanted to be needed. She looked forward to caring for the child and making his life easier. It was one thing she could do that had nothing whatsoever to do with beauty.

Chapter Two

"Well, Missy, is he in a better mood today?" Clell asked as he rubbed his hand over the gray stubble of his beard.

"No. In fact, he's worse, meaner than an old boar bear! He threw his breakfast tray at the door again." The dark-eyed girl looked out the window of the sprawling ranch house while she spoke.

Missy O'Bannion had lived in this ranch house all her life. She'd grown up riding, branding and cutting cattle, just like her brothers. She could handle just about anything, except what faced her now. "I just don't know what to do, Clell. When I help him, it seems to make things worse—and if I don't help him... He can't shave, he can barely dress. It breaks my heart to see him like this." The rowels of her spurs jangled as she turned to face Clell. Shotgun chaps, showing signs of daily wear and tear, hugged her body. A loose, long-sleeved plaid shirt with the tail half out made her seem younger than sixteen.

"Has your father heard any more from the doctor back East?" Clell handed Missy a cup of hot, strong, aromatic coffee.

As she turned to take the cup, her face brightened a little. "Yes. Someone's coming. A Mr. Bellamy James. I hope he'll be able to help Trace. Pa said Mr. James worked at a hospital that trains blind people—he's the best." It had been real hard for her to accept Trace's blindness. She couldn't even imagine how he felt.

"Did you see Becky Kelly when you went to town the other day to mail that letter?" There was ice in Clell's voice.

"I thought about beatin' the hell outa the bitch!" Missy's dark eyes snapped like lightning in a black sky.

"Yep, the thought crossed my mind a time or two. I suppose it wouldn't change anything, but we might feel a little better." He winked at Missy.

"You sure have been sending an awful lot of letters to New York lately, Clell. Have you got a sweetheart back there?"

Clell turned and narrowed his eyes. A slow, cryptic smile curved his mouth. "Now, don't you go poking your nose into my business, Missy O'Bannion. There's things I do that's none of your concern." He turned his back to her and sipped his coffee in silence. The set of his shoulders and the way he braced his legs told Missy the subject of his letter writing was over. There'd be no more discussion of it today. Clell was nearly as stubborn as she was. She smiled at his stiff back.

Clell cleared his throat. "I hope that—uh, Mr. James gets here pretty quick." He grinned at her over the rim of his cup.

She frowned. "Well, I hope he's got a thick hide, a quick mind, and a strong pair of fists. Any man who thinks he's going to be able to deal with Trace O'Bannion in the shape he's in now is going to have a fight on his hands." She brushed a loose strand of unruly hair back from her face and took a sip of the hot liquid.

"I've been thinking, Missy—" his brown eyes narrowed and he rubbed his stubbly beard with a gnarled hand and continued "—maybe I should take Trace back to his house. You know, sort of get him settled, before that fella shows up.''

Missy studied the weathered brown face. She thought about Trace going home. He finished the house over six months ago, for Becky Kelly. He'd barely gotten moved in before he was shot. How would he feel about going back there now? "What if it makes things worse?" she asked, her eyebrows knitting into a worried frown.

"Don't think things could get too much worse, do you, Missy? I'll talk to your pa. If he thinks it'll be all right, I can tend him—as much as he lets anybody tend him."

A crashing sound snapped their heads around in time for them to see Lupe scurry from the direction of the noise. "I guess that means he doesn't like lunch, either," Clell said dryly.

Trace O'Bannion threw the tray toward the sound of the closing door. He hoped like hell that it hit something.

No, that wasn't true. Trace didn't really want to cause his family grief or pain, but he knew that was exactly what he was doing with each passing day. He knew deep down inside they were only trying to help, but knowing it just seemed to make things worse.

Every time Missy or Shane showed him kindness, every fiber of his being screamed in rebellion. He wanted to lash out, to hit, to draw blood. He wanted to rail and roar at the unfairness of it all. He'd rather die than be living this half-life. He grimaced in pain. Trace saw the stars and lightning bursting through his head, and he remembered that day.

He'd woken up in his own bed at home. The doctor from Socorro had been there. At first he'd been relieved, damned happy to be alive, in fact. Being a deputy, he'd been shot before. As gunshots went, the one in his head had felt a damn sight better than some he'd suffered. The bandage across his forehead and eyes had felt almost comforting. Without thought, he moved his hand over his forehead. His fingers touched a scar at his temple, just like Becky Kelly had done that day when the wound was fresh.

"How are you feeling?" she asked as she stroked his face with her cool, smooth fingers.

"Fine, honey, just fine. In a few days, I'll be back on my feet."

"Well, don't you rush it, Trace." She had leaned close and touched her lips to his forehead.

"I'm tough as rawhide, Becky. Besides, there's something mighty important I want to ask you." He had taken her hand and held it against his lips, depositing soft kisses across her palm.

She had stayed with him for several days. He'd felt stronger every day. Things were going to be fine, just fine.

Trace fidgeted like a cat, waiting for the doctor to remove his bandages. If he'd known, if he'd had any idea what lay ahead—he wouldn't have been nearly so anxious to learn the truth. Bitter memories made him squeeze his eyes tight. But when he opened them, the unrelenting darkness remained.

Blind. Trace O'Bannion was totally blind.

Before he even stopped reeling from that bit of information, sweet Becky had taken the opportunity to explain a few things to him. Sort of the facts of life, you might say.

Bitterness and bile made him grimace. Her lilting voice had echoed through the room. "Of course, Trace, I know you'll understand my position. I mean—how can I marry a man...well, an unsighted man? After all, I'm young. I have certain expectations." Her voice had sounded so sweet, so full of remorse, as she pleaded for his understanding.

Heartless bitch! Yes, of course he understood, he understood only too well. He was half a man now. He'd be damned lucky if any woman ever looked at him as a man again. Trace O'Bannion knew that if any woman did look his way, there wouldn't be a look of love in her eyes. No, not even lust. It would be pity. Pity! The one thing Trace couldn't stand. The real reason behind his rage. The thing keeping him from allowing his family to help. No matter how hard he pushed or taunted, they put up with it. And the reason was that they considered Trace too weak and helpless to take it! If one of them, just one, would treat him like he was still a man...

God! It was too much. Even Missy, little Missy, for God's sake. He'd rocked her to sleep, taught her how to rope, how to throw and tie a calf! Missy wiped his chin now, and tried her best to shave him.

Shave him. Like an invalid. He'd been reduced to the point that his half-grown sister had to shave him. Trace O'Bannion covered his sightless eyes with tough hands. He wept like a baby. It wasn't the first time.

Supper at the O'Bannion house had always been a rowdy affair. The O'Bannions didn't eat peas with their knives, or bring live chickens to the table—nothing like that. It was just that when they all got together it turned out to be a loud, unruly gathering of Hugh and his five headstrong, independent, free-thinking offspring. No meal ever took place in the adobe ranch house without some difference of opinion being aired. Tonight, it seemed, would be no different.

The absence of two family members only made it a little bit quieter. Flynn was still in Albuquerque with Elfego Baca, while he awaited trial. Trace had holed up in his bedroom, refusing to take meals with anyone. Hugh watched the faces of his remaining children with a frown on his face. He'd known they'd react like this. He'd received nothing but sour faces and sharp words since they'd heard he'd hired a teacher for Trace. Each one of them seemed all-fired sure they knew what should and should not be done for Trace. Suddenly everybody in the O'Bannion family was an expert in the care and handling of a blind man.

Oh, just wait until the mysterious teacher arrived. Hugh shuddered, thinking about the rough road ahead of him. As soon as his little brood found out what he'd really done—yep, there'd be hell to pay for Hugh O'Bannion.

His feisty offspring would probably turn their full wrath on him. Life would be a fearsome sight for a while around the O'Bannion spread.

Hugh had fought nearly every tribe of Indian on the plains. He'd faced Comanche in Texas and Apache here in the territory without flinching, but his children made him damned nervous at times. Hugh hadn't told anyone, not even Clell, that Mr. Bellamy James was really Miss Bellami James. When they found out, well, Hugh could just imagine the donnybrook.

It wasn't something he'd intentionally planned, but when everyone just assumed Bellamy was a man's name, well, he'd just let 'em. He frowned and thought back to the first time Bellami James's name had come up in conversation.

Clell and Logan had made the assumption it was a *Mr.* James, as he recalled. He'd been smart enough to recognize a gift from God when he saw one. The Almighty was providing Trace with the only possible solution to his problem, and that solution happened to be showing up in the form of a woman. Maybe an older female would be able to do what the family had not. Trace needed to heal, to mend both heart and body. The rest of them had all failed dismally in their attempts to care for him. Maybe Miss James could try a gentler approach. She could mother him, and maybe, just maybe, Trace would let her. Trace had a real soft spot for grandmotherly types and kindly old spinsters.

Trace's recent behavior was no big mystery to Hugh. He was hurting and scared, and he was too damned much like

Hugh to admit it. Men in the O'Bannion family were taught early to fight against weakness. They were supposed to stand on their own two feet. A man in the territory might not have to stand tall, but he damned sure had to stand up.

Asking for help, or needing it, was a frailty—a weakness that couldn't be tolerated, especially not here. Weak men, or women, for that matter, didn't survive in this country for very long.

Hugh had been blessed with strong, smart, resilient children who had toughened their bodies and their minds. They could handle this country and the people in it. But this blindness of Trace's... Well, it had taken the starch out of the whole family.

No man would be able to handle Trace, not like he was now. But there had been a glimmer of hope when Doc Malone wrote. He mentioned the lady who had worked with him for twelve years. Hugh frowned, thinking about that letter. It had arrived from Doc Malone at just the right time—as if borne on the wings of providence.

Almost as if some unseen force had guided it. Of course, that was a silly notion. How could Doc have heard about Trace? It was a long way from the territory to New York.

Hugh hadn't hesitated a moment when he read that letter. Twelve years was a long time to dedicate to blind people. This spinster, Miss James, would have to be very dedicated and patient, downright devoted, in fact. She might be Trace's salvation...

A masculine voice broke into his musing. "Well, I don't want to be around when Trace and this fella meet," Shane O'Bannion declared, loud enough to be heard in Magdalena. "He's gonna be killin' mad. Trace ain't goin' to like no prissy Eastern gentleman teaching him how to shave and bathe and all." At twenty, Shane had reached the lofty pinnacle of knowing everything about everybody. Hugh couldn't wait for another year or two to pass, to show

Shane how ignorant he really was. Hugh knew time had a way of making young men stupider and old men smarter.

"Well, someone's got to teach him. I think it may be easier coming from a stranger." Missy looked Shane straight in the eye as she spoke. He might be her older brother, but he hadn't cornered the market on wisdom, by damn.

Hugh frowned, laying down his fork in exasperation. "Is it too much to ask for? Just once I'd like to have a quiet meal in this house. It's done. The teacher will be here in a couple of weeks, so let's say no more on the matter tonight. All this yammerin' is ruinin' my digestion!"

Logan O'Bannion smiled mischievously. It tickled him no end when Hugh used that tone with his older siblings. Logan, the baby of the family, was spoiled rotten. He admitted it—and he enjoyed it. Being the youngest had definite advantages. They were all guilty of indulging him, and had done it all his life. Missy was the worst, but they were all guilty as sin.

When he was old enough to sit in front of Trace or Flynn, they'd bundled him up and took him with them on the range. He rode better than an Indian, and looked like one, too. Logan had inherited the black hair and eyes of his mother, Sky. Deep dimples creased his face when he smiled, which was often. Now his eyes were twinkling merrily, with some undisclosed secret. That was another thing Logan had inherited from his mother. He'd go to his grave before betraying a confidence, or telling somebody's secret.

"Logan, you seem downright amused. Will you share with us?" Hugh asked, clenching his jaw and fixing a stern gaze on the impish face of his youngest son.

"Oh, nothin', just thinkin' maybe you-all would be doin' Trace a favor if you just left him alone for a while. He never did like people fussin' over him. I think he needs some time." The fourteen-year-old watched as his family chewed on that a bit.

Taking advantage of the unusual silence, he continued, "I saw Clell earlier, while I was ridin' fence. He said he spoke to you, Pa." Black eyes bored right back into Hugh's, as he defiantly waited for a response.

"Oh? And what did ol' Uncle Clell say?" There was icy sarcasm in Hugh's words. Clell was like a brother to him, but sometimes his meddling burned Hugh's butt. He acted like a damned old mother hen, clucking around all the time.

One black eyebrow rose as Logan tried to stifle a grin. "He said he talked to you about Trace goin' home."

Shane and Missy riveted disbelieving looks at their father.

"Now don't you go lookin' at me like that. It was Clell's idea, not mine! I sure ain't throwin' the boy out! But Clell's got a point. Trace needs to come to terms with this, to learn how to function. He wasn't living at home when it happened, so why should he stay here now? He's a grown man...." There was sorrow in Hugh's voice. Trace would have it hard, and it sure didn't help, that flighty Becky Kelly doing what she did.

Hugh had known from the start Becky was no good for Trace but he hadn't interfered. Young men didn't ever use their heads around women. They didn't take time to think, all they did was feel. Trace felt too damned much for Becky. She wasn't worth it, not in Hugh's estimation. But no man could tell Trace how to feel about Becky, or about his blindness. He'd just have to work through it on his own. Hugh wanted to help him, tried to help him, but in the end it was up to Trace to help himself.

Suddenly an angry voice cut into the silence.

"It's about damn time you-all came to your senses! When can I get the hell out of here?" The sharp, bitter words made all four people wince.

They turned in unison to see Trace O'Bannion, wearing only his Levi's, standing in the doorway. His lips curled back in a sneer as he spoke. His sightless green eyes held a wild, untamed look.

It chilled Missy to the bone. She adored her older brother. He could shoot, ride and rope. There wasn't a man alive tougher, except maybe Flynn. And Trace could be so gentle. She had watched Trace spend hours nursing a sick colt. The look on his face now was anything but gentle. He looked like he wanted to commit murder, and he was staring in the direction of his own family.

Abruptly Trace turned away. Feeling his way along the wall, he inched his way back toward his old room. Everybody seated at the long pine table groaned when they heard the sound of flesh hitting wood, and the oaths that followed. Trace stumbled noisily over the coat tree in the hall. If he couldn't navigate his childhood home, how would he ever get along in the world, blind?

Trace woke up in a cold sweat. It had happened nearly every night since he was shot. Terror made his pulse pound in his ears. Every muscle in his body knotted tightly against the nameless horror as his heart pounded in his chest. There was another sound, too. What was it?

Lying there with his fists clenched tight, he tried to shove the fear back in the perpetual darkness. Suddenly he knew what the sound was. Hooves, horse's hooves.

His gray stallion was raising holy blue hell—again. Every night since the shooting, the stud had shrieked and ran along the fence line. At first Trace had thought a mare must be in heat nearby, but now he wondered.

He'd raised Ghost from a colt. One cold spring some Kiowas had come through, leading the scrawny foal. Trace had felt sorry for the pitiful creature, so he'd taken him home. God knew how many hours he'd spent nursing him. The wild little devil had had such a wary look in his eyes.

Clell had said he'd never be worth a plugged nickel, but Trace had refused to give up on him. Clell always said Trace had a soft spot for sorry horses and lost causes.

As the sickly animal grew and filled out, he'd become magnificent. The big gray had a deep chest, a small head, and powerful hindquarters. He could go all day long without breaking a hard sweat.

Trace threw back the sheet and rose from the bed. There were times at night when he pretended he could still see. Pretty stupid for a grown man to pretend, but he did it. At night, in the darkness, it wasn't so different from the way it had been before the shooting.

Like when he was a boy. He'd wake up in the middle of the night and walk to the window. Trace did it now, and for a fleeting moment he did not feel the horrible, disoriented awkwardness that plagued him since the bandages had been removed.

Why was it so different at night?

Were some of his problems tricks his own mind was playing? He knew every inch of this house. Missy hadn't moved one stick of furniture, and she'd threatened to horsewhip anyone who did, so why did he keep running into things? Trace pondered the question as he stepped toward the window.

He felt the coolness on his face before he reached the glass pane. No one had bothered to pull the curtains. There wasn't any need. Trace's own place, the house he'd built for Becky, was five miles away. There were no other neighbors in between here and there. Nothing but miles of prairie grass and sage from here to San Marcial. It wasn't like anyone would be looking in the windows. Lupe and Maria, the only women around besides Missy, had seen the O'Bannion brood naked so many times, they'd most likely lost count. In the summer, the whole bunch swam buck naked in the creek back of the house.

Standing at the window in the darkness, Trace felt the vibration of the big gray's hooves through the wood floor. He closed his eyes, imagining himself on the animal's back, the wind in his face. He felt a surge of excitement as the stud gathered power. Muscles rippled beneath him as the horse's stride lengthened.

"Stop! Stop doing this to yourself!" he growled, raising his closed fists to his sightless eyes. "You're only half a man now. You'll never ride again."

Clell loaded the saddlebags with the rest of Trace's clothes into the wagon and tied Ghost to the back. It was heartbreaking to see the boy like this. Trace had always been so proud, so self-assured. Even as a child it had rankled him to need other people's help. Clell could see the toll it was taking on him now. Once Trace heard Clell's offer to take him home, he'd grabbed on to it like a drowning man grabbing for a rope.

Trace O'Bannion shuffled onto the porch of the big ranch house. He took slow, hesitant steps. His boots hovered in the air above the steps of the porch as he gripped the smooth cottonwood railing. Missy walked about a half step behind with her hands held up slightly to catch him if he stumbled.

Clell flinched inwardly when Trace did exactly that. When the proud blind man felt Missy's hands at his sides, he shrugged violently, to throw them off. His pride was hurting now, even more than the rest of him. Clell wondered if Trace would ever get the bitterness out of his system. Like the poison of a rattler, it worked its way through his body and his heart. Mighty powerful stuff.

Hugh stepped out onto the porch, with Shane and Logan at his heels. They watched silently as Trace stumbled toward the buckboard.

"Trace—" Hugh couldn't finish. He just hoped that his son knew what was in his heart.

The blind man turned back to face the ranch house, his emerald-green eyes staring blankly ahead. "I know you all tried to help." Saying no more, he swung up onto the seat.

Clell noticed that damn little of Trace's strength or agility was gone. He settled next to Clell on the narrow wooden-plank seat before the old man gathered the reins. With a snap of leather on the bay's rump, they headed for Trace's house.

Clell could feel the tension in Trace's body. He watched the play of emotions on Trace's face from time to time. It was obvious the man was being torn apart. Clell was glad Sky wasn't alive to see her son like this; it would've destroyed her.

The sun had dropped low in the western sky before they reached Trace's home. Ghost's head came up, and he let out a piercing scream. Evidently the horse missed his familiar stomping grounds. Clell saw a brief smile touch Trace's lips when he heard the horse. "Why don't you ride that gray devil?" he asked suddenly.

Trace flinched at the sound of Clell's voice. "Damn you, Clell. I'll never be able to ride again, and you know it." The words held a hefty measure of self-pity. Trace's mouth twisted, and his face hardened.

"Why? You rode at night, didn't ya? How much different could it be? The horse ain't blind." Clell spit the words at Trace as he wrapped the reins around the hand brake and swung to the ground. "You're just bein' plain ornery about this, Trace. There's still lots of things you can do."

"Such as?" Trace stepped to the ground. He stood beside the buckboard.

Clell walked to him and shoved a well-worn saddle into his chest, hard. "Like carryin' your own damn saddle." He grinned when Trace's hands came up instinctively to grip the weight. Trace's reflexes were still damned good.

The old cowboy turned away, grinning, and he took a good look at Trace's house. Solid and sensible, even pretty to look at. Built with a wife and family in mind. Thick adobe walls would keep it cool in the summer months to come. It was large, with a steep tin roof to shed the winter snow. Since the railroad had come through in 1880, things such as metal roofs had become common. Clell remembered a time when such things had been a luxury. Just like the balcony and railing running all the way around the upper floor. Mighty fancy place, and too damned big for a single man.

Metal against metal sang an endless song as the breeze turned the windmill. New Mexico was a desert, but where water flowed an abundance of living things could be found. The stream running through Trace's land was home to a variety of animal and plant life.

He'd constructed his house near the stream since the well brought water right into the house, and for the view Clell guessed. Cottonwoods grew in a line along the stream. The dusty pink blooms of salt cedar mingled with the fuzzy green-and-brown spikes of cattails. Geese stopped both in the spring and in the fall. Bobcats, coyotes and an occasional badger shared the water hole with deer and antelope year-round. Yep, it'd make a mighty pretty sight to see, if a body could see.

Clell turned back to Trace, who was still standing with the saddle clutched tight against his chest. His knuckles were white, and his face was a pensive mask as he stared toward the gurgle of the stream. Clell wondered what images and memories were flooding through the blind man's brain.

Trace bit down hard, clenching his jaw against the assault. The smell of damp earth and new growing things brought back a rush of remembered pleasures. Not long before the shooting, Trace had been restless one night. He'd stood in the twilight, looking toward that stream. A blur of fur reflecting in the water had turned out to be a lobo she-wolf. He smiled, remembering how she'd slunk, sneaking silently to the water. Amber eyes glowing, she'd completely ignored the antelope nearby.

An unspoken truce was in effect at the watering hole. It was the way of things here. Water meant life. Trace adopted a kind of live-and-let-live attitude right along with the critters who shared his backyard. If the local predators respected his space, he would respect theirs. So far, it had worked out just fine. He didn't figure he lost any more cattle to predators than any other rancher. Certainly no more than his share—and he'd the pleasure of watching the animals.

When he could see, that is.

The man clenched his jaw tighter. Another small joy in his life, now lost forever.

Trace woke to a harsh pounding on his bedroom door. He wasn't so sure this had been a good idea after all. Clell was meaner than sin, and, if possible, getting worse each day.

"Coffee's on the stove. You want it, git it yourself." His gruff voice faded as he walked away from the door. He was long gone by the time Trace managed to pull on his dirty pants. He rubbed his hand over his chin, feeling the long, thick beard. It felt at least two inches long. He wondered for a minute what he looked like. Snorting in disgust, he groped around the room, searching for a shirt. What the hell did he care what he looked like? Nobody'd been out since he and Clell had gotten here. Not even Logan or Missy. What the hell—probably for the best all the way around. The sooner everyone left him be, the better he'd like it. He raised his arms to pull on his shirt and got a noseful. How long had it been since he took a bath?

"Oh, well, the nice thing about being a useless cripple, is that people quit expecting anything from you, like bathin', or shavin'," he muttered to himself as he opened his bedroom door.

The smell of freshly brewed coffee filled his nose. Slowly, with his hand on the banister, he made his way, shuffling down the stairs. He could smell overcooked bacon and fresh biscuits, too. The kitchen was quiet as he crept in. Carefully he felt his way to the cups hanging on the wall. He closed his fingers around one, taking it from the little metal hook. Then he held his hand over the stove, testing for heat. When he located the wire handle of the coffeepot, he grabbed the tail of his unbuttoned shirt to grasp it with.

He managed to pour coffee into his cup without soaking more than the front of his pants with the hot liquid. It cooled quickly in the cool spring air, and he complimented himself.

"Pretty good...better than yesterday." He set the pot back on the hot stove. Again he let his hand hover above the stove, trying to locate the biscuits. He found them and a couple of brittle strips of bacon. Trace jammed the two together and took a bite. One thing for sure, no one could accuse Clell of coddling him. The old devil cooked, leaving just enough for Trace to survive on. If he wanted it, he had to get it himself. If he couldn't manage, then he went hungry. Trace shoved the biscuit in his mouth. Keeping one hand free, he felt the air in front of him as he walked, hot coffee sloshing over the edge of his cup with each faltering step.

Clell opened the back door and stepped inside. "Well, I see you managed to make it down today." There was not one whit of pity in his voice. He rode Trace hard, putting the spurs to him every chance he got. He saw Trace flare his nostrils.

Trace sucked in his breath. Clell should try to get around blind and see how he liked it. The least he could do would be to ease up a bit.

Trace took the biscuit from his mouth with one hand and set his cup on the table with the other. "Get the hell off my back, will you, Clell?" the blind man snarled.

"Oho, I see you still got a little fight left in you. Good. I thought the boy I helped raise was gone." Clell's words dripped with sarcasm.

"What the hell do you expect me to do?" Leaning with both his hands splayed on the table, Trace shouted plaintively in the direction of Clell's voice.

"I expect you to fight, boy! Not lay down like some whipped dog!" Clell yelled louder as he moved closer. "You smell like a dead buffalo, and you look like one, too, with that damned hair and beard. When was the last time you dragged a comb through that mane?"

"How the hell am I supposed to shave and clean up?" Trace asked, his voice ringing with self-pity.

Clell felt his temper rising to a dangerous level. No child of Sky's should act like this. Her proud, wild blood flowed through Trace's veins. She'd been a fighter till the day she died. "Damn you, Trace. Crawl to the stream, fall in the damn water and wash. That's what I expect! You ain't no damned baby, you're a man, so why don't you start actin' like one?" Clell's voice was brittle with rage. He'd seen men lose arms and legs, and much more, in the war. Trace had gone soft, and it made him sick to see it.

"I can't do it, Clell! Do you understand? I can't do it!" Trace slammed his fist onto the table, then turned away. He groped along the wall, feeling his way back to the stairs.

In a few moments, Clell heard the slamming of a door. He dragged his hand through his hair. Maybe he'd gone too far this time.

The old man sat down at the table, staring at the speckled cup of coffee. A tiny tendril of steam still rose from the hot liquid. He wondered if Trace would ever pull out of this. That teacher better get here soon. If something didn't change pretty damned quick, Trace would be beyond help. Clell felt disgusted with himself for chewing on Trace. It was all getting mighty discouraging. Rising from the table, he went outside to resume his chores.

As he threw scratch to the chickens, he caught the unmistakable smell of rain on the breeze. He hurried, trying to finish before the shower hit. The first rain of spring. None too early, either—he'd felt winter's chill to the marrow of his bones this year. He was getting old.

Chapter Three

Bellami enjoyed the trip. Rod made sure she had the best accommodations. The sleeping car on the train was wonderful. It provided the only sanctuary where she could remove her hat and veil, and she cherished those private moments. Little by little the train left the gently rolling land she was accustomed to behind. The woods became sparser, until finally they disappeared completely. The earth flattened out. Expanses of snow stretched on mile after mile as they crossed the vast prairie near Fort Kearney. She changed trains only once, in Independence, Missouri. This train would take her all the way to the New Mexico Territory. A sense of discovery raised its sleepy head within her. As the picture outside her window changed, so did she. The barrier she'd constructed to insulate her feelings thinned out a little. For the first time, Bellami found her lack of beauty mattering less. She saw men and women with tough, weathered faces in each town when they took on new passengers and water. Bellami watched in fascination as Chinese men, in loose clothing, boarded the train.

"Where are they going?" she asked the conductor when he walked by her.

"Bound for the mines in the New Mexico Territory. Laborers headed for a place called Kelly, miss." He touched the bill of his cap and continued up the aisle.

She felt a surge of excitement. They were all going to the same wild place! As the miles wore on, Bellami busied herself by trying to put a face to all the names Doc had given her. One in particular kept her occupied.

Trace O'Bannion. Doc Malone hadn't really told her much about him. Only that the poor child had been blinded in some sort of an accident. She imagined a small face with large brown eyes that would be full of sorrow. Bellami smiled when she thought of how happy the little boy would be when he could manage a little on his own again. She'd seen a lot of frightened children come to St. Michael's over the years. Her greatest joy—her only joy, really—had been helping those children. This case promised to be especially rewarding because she'd be doing it all alone, without Doc Malone to help her. Bellami sighed in deep satisfaction just thinking about it.

It would be nice to have a little boy's friendship and affection. Bellami liked being around children; they were so innocent and trusting. They gave their love unconditionally.

They never minded so much what a person looked like. It was what was inside a person that counted. She found herself saying a silent thank-you to Doc for persuading her to take this position.

The conductor walked ahead of Bellami down the narrow corridor. She hurriedly pulled the veiling down over her face.

"Socorro, New Mexico Territory. One-hour stop." He repeated tunelessly over and over. The Atcheson, Topeka and Santa Fe Railway depot was located at the east end of Manzanares Street in Socorro.

Bellami stepped up to the conductor as he pulled a shiny gold pocket watch from his coat.

"Is there a mercantile nearby? I need to buy a present for a little boy," Bellami asked the man as he flipped opened the watch with his thumbnail.

"Any of the storekeepers here should be able to help you, miss. Just head straight up this street to the plaza." He raised a muscular arm and pointed west. Bellami nodded her thanks and walked in the direction he instructed.

The beauty of the bustling town surprised her. She allowed herself a few extra minutes to look at the San Miguel Mission. Bellami had never seen anything like adobe. She found it hard to believe that bricks made of mud could be pretty, but they were. One of the priests explained how adobe was made. His deep voice and Mexican accent charmed her. Bricks made from the materials at hand, baked in the hot sun. Trees were scarce here, so the resourceful residents adapted to their environment. And they had done it so well, she thought. The church seemed to be a part of the country, it blended so well.

Thanking the priest, she resumed her trek toward the business district. Bellami needed to find a present for Trace. Several stores fronted the plaza, and Bellami found an amazing variety of goods for sale within walking distance. There were several Chinese laundries, and there was a very large building with a sign proclaiming the Best Beer in the Territory.

In a short time, her arms were full of parcels. She carried something for each member of her family but she had not found anything for little Trace yet, and the entire hour was almost gone. She was due back at the train depot soon. Bellami gathered her packages and hurried down the street.

For a long time, Flynn leaned up against a post at the plaza just watching her. He couldn't see her face, not with that contraption she wore for a hat. What a god-awful thing it was, too. Did all women back East dress like that?

How on earth could a man see what he was getting? He rolled a smoke and let his eyes follow her movements from one store to the next. She seemed to be buying anything and everything for sale in Socorro. Flynn admired the way her traveling suit hugged her shoulders and chest. A real looker, all right. As she walked, the fabric of her long skirt showed the contours of her legs, and Flynn felt his curiosity growing. He didn't usually spend much time admiring women. It was not something his line of work allowed. He usually just took quick action, you might say. When he saw something he liked, he generally went after it.

Every so often he took a ride up to White Oak to visit the whorehouse. During the Lincoln County Wars ten years ago, he had acquired a taste for what they offered, and he saw no reason to change. This woman, though, she could rein in a man. Mysterious, and appealing—probably the effect of the damned hat.

Flynn couldn't pass up an opportunity like this. He just had to see if her face was as pretty as the rest of her. He'd never been bothered by morals or guilt—that was his brother's department. Trace was the ethical one in the family. A grim smile twisted Flynn's mouth. He knew Trace had never made an improper move toward that damned Becky Kelly, and where had it gotten him? Jilted, that's where. She walked away from Trace, never giving him so much as a backward glance when he needed her the most.

Flynn stubbed out his cigarette and focused on the woman again. She flitted out of the store, nearly dropping her bundles in her haste. He stood away from the post, grinning. Maybe he could help the little lady out. The bundles were piled in her arms so high she could barely see over them. When she came close to losing her hold on the paper-wrapped packages, Flynn stepped in front of her with his arms outstretched. Just as he reached her, she stumbled and lurched forward.

Bellami's teeth jarred together painfully. She gasped and caught her breath, thinking that she must've run into a wall. The bundles tilted in her arms, and she struggled to keep the packages from falling. Suddenly strong hands gripped her arms. She took a peek through a small crack between the string-wrapped parcels.

A low bass voice washed over her. "S'cuse me, ma'am."

Bellami shifted her bundles and looked up to see where the voice was coming from. Through the veil she saw a pair of twinkling brown eyes in a tanned face. Heat flooded her cheeks. She was grateful she had the protection of the veiled hat so that the man wouldn't be forced to make stammering apologies as he stared at her scarred cheek but tried not to.

Flynn knew he should let the woman go, but he wanted to get a look at her face. He leaned closer, but couldn't see a thing; the veil was too thick. He heard her clear her throat.

"No, please excuse me, sir. It's entirely my fault. I can't see very well, I'm sorry." She stammered out an apology as she clung to the packages. He continued to hold both her arms—not tightly, but she wasn't going anywhere unless he released her.

"No harm done, ma'am. Where're you goin' in such a hurry? I'd be happy to carry those bundles for you," he drawled, grinning.

"I am in a hurry," Bellami looked up at the man's face. It was shaded by a pale tan hat with a wide brim. She had noticed most of the men wearing the same type of hat everywhere she went today. "I'm on my way back to the train station," Bellami told him, putting her usual reserve and caution aside. Another tiny piece of her armor fell away. It was, after all, broad daylight. What could it hurt? "I'd be grateful for your help."

After he took her packages, Bellami fell into step beside him. His legs were long, and she found herself having to trot to keep up. When she'd said she needed to hurry, he must've taken her at her word, she thought to herself.

"I'm sorry, I don't even know your name, Mr. . . ." She waited for him to supply it.

"O'Bannion, ma'am. Flynn O'Bannion. I'm a U.S. marshal," he said as he released her arms and tipped his hat. His lean face creased into a charming set of dimples when he smiled.

"My, isn't that a coincidence! I'm on my way to a ranch to take care of a child named O'Bannion."

"Is that a fact? Are you a nurse?" He had a nice deep voice.

"Not really. I train blind children," Bellami told him as they approached the depot.

The tall man stopped abruptly and looked hard at Bellami's veil with penetrating brown eyes. She bit her lip when she felt his attention riveted on her face. She knew he couldn't see through the veil, yet his searching gaze made her uncomfortable. His brow creased into a frown, and he seemed a little less friendly all of a sudden. She wondered if she'd made a mistake by allowing a total stranger to escort her.

"What is this child's name, ma'am?" His tone clearly indicated he expected an answer.

"Trace O'Bannion." Bellami said, somewhat puzzled.

He quickly started placing the bundles back in her arms, one by one. He stepped back and looked at her again with agate eyes. Then he let out a long, low whistle. "Well, I see Pa has been keepin' secrets again," he said cryptically.

Bellami wondered if he could be dangerous, but suddenly the dimples returned. His brown eyes sparkled in the sunlight. He pushed the hat back on his forehead with one lean index finger and grinned wider.

"Sorry, ma'am, didn't mean to frighten you. Let me help you up the steps. You have a safe trip." He placed his hand under her elbow and practically lifted her into the train in his haste. Then he turned and left without another word.

Bellami peered through her packages to see where he went, but he was nowhere in sight. A gust of wind whipped up a tiny dust devil in the street. She retreated into the shelter of the train to avoid the flying dust as she puzzled over her unusual encounter. The man had said his name was O'Bannion. Maybe a relative of Trace's—an uncle, perhaps? She made a mental note to ask about him as soon as she reached San Marcial.

Flynn strode across the street to the board sidewalk. A muscle in his jaw twitched. On her way to the O'Bannions'! That had been more than enough to take the wind out of Flynn's sail! There wasn't another O'Bannion family in the territory.

It had to be his family. She said she was there to take care of a blind child! A shiver ran up his spine. What the hell could his father be thinking of? Hugh O'Bannion must've lost his mind. That little slip of a woman was no more going to be able to handle Trace than she could handle a team of wild horses. The whole thing became crystal-clear. Hugh had intentionally let everyone believe Trace would have a man teaching him.

Flynn clenched his jaw a little tighter and hopped into the saddle. He'd been headed to see Trace, anyway. Now he had one more reason to go. The muscles in his gut tightened up as he thought back to that day last October. Trace didn't even have the hate of revenge to sustain him. The bastard who'd shot Trace had died a split second later, after Flynn's bullet hit him between the eyes. It was an even heavier burden to bear, knowing that his brother had been blinded by a bullet meant for another man. The lone gunman had been after Elfego Baca, not Trace.

That little lady said she trained blind children. Well, Trace O'Bannion was a long way from being a child. How his father expected a lady to handle Trace O'Bannion's frustration and fury was anybody's guess. Flynn kicked his horse, and the big bay broke into a ground-eating lope. He didn't know what was going to happen, but he intended to be there when it did. The train would reach San Marcial long before he could. He hoped the woman would be all right until he spoke with Hugh and found out what the hell was going on.

Hugh O'Bannion entered San Marcial at first light. He'd taken great pains to see that Missy, Shane and Logan were busy elsewhere. Missy had put up one hell of a fight, nearly getting her own way, as usual. In the end, though, Hugh had managed to keep his three youngest busy. He shook his head, and his hair whispered along the collar of his heavy coat. Imagine, having to cut his own fences, just for a bit of privacy. He wondered what the hell the world was coming to. Stepping into Brewster's Hotel, he decided to enjoy a quiet breakfast, for a change. The train wasn't due for another hour. He didn't want to stand around waiting at the empty station.

"Howdy, Mr. O'Bannion. What'll it be?" the freckle-faced girl asked as she filled a cup to brimming with strong coffee.

"Steak and eggs, and burn 'em," he replied, and settled back in his chair with a sigh of contentment. He wrapped his lean hands around the cup of black coffee. Allowing his eyes to roam over the street outside, he thought about how things had changed since he and Clell had come here.

For years, civilization had slowly inched its way across the country, but when the train came in 1880, it had thundered in with a roar. Prosperity had come right along with it.

Ranchers didn't have to drive their stock for hundreds of miles anymore. They were able to load them on stock cars in Magdalena. This meant bigger profits to the rancher. Cattle didn't run off the fat they worked so hard to put on them. It also meant fewer losses from raiding Apaches. The mines in the area were also booming. Transporting the ore quick and cheap was easy now. Of course, cheap labor still had to obtained, so the mine owners started bringing in men. First Negroes from the South, and now Chinese. Hugh watched a group of the newcomers passing the restaurant window. They walked together with their heads bowed. Some of the locals treated them with contempt. Mine owners and investors only cared about getting the ore out as cheap as possible; they gave little or no thought to those men, especially those with different customs and religions.

The territory was experiencing a real population boom. Now, instead of families coming to settle the land and raise children, the newcomers were mostly men. Men looking for a quick buck. Gunslingers, cowhands, gamblers, saddle tramps and worse. Hugh sipped his coffee, thinking about the problems in Lincoln and now here. As more and more "Anglo" settlers came in, they did everything possible to drive out the Mexicans.

A muscle in his jaw twitched. Hugh's second son would be permanently blind because of a stupid attempt on Elfego's life, and only because he was Mexican. He took a deep breath and tried to control the frustration he felt. He'd been here long enough to realize they were all nothing but newcomers.

The Spanish had come in the 1500s. When they'd arrived, the Apache and Comanche were already here. No one knew who'd been here before that. Shootings were inevitable, but he wished his son hadn't been in the line of fire. Hugh wasn't particularly happy Flynn was still wearing a badge, either. More trouble was bound to come. He didn't want to lose more than he already had. One son's blood in the dirt was enough for the damned territory.

Pulling out a letter from his shirt, he opened the worn envelope. The paper was tattered at the edges from frequent handling, but he read it once more. Hugh smiled at the spidery scrawl. It almost sounded like old Doc Malone had a special fondness for Miss James. Hugh wondered what she'd be like. He envisioned a kindly, stout woman with iron-gray hair and soft eyes. Yep, that was the type of female Doc Malone would think capable of caring for his son.

"Here ya go, Mr. O'Bannion. Charlie fixed 'em just like you like 'em," the girl said as she set the steaming plate on the checkered table cloth.

"Tell him I said thanks." Hugh looked at the charred piece of meat, as big as his fist.

"I'll do that, sir." She filled his cup once more, then disappeared through a door toward the back of the building. While he was drinking his third cup of coffee, the train whistle screamed. Pulling on his heavy sheepskin coat, Hugh paid for his breakfast and stepped outside, into the cool March air. He saw the dark trail of smoke in the distance.

Bellami changed into a blue traveling suit made of heavy cotton and carefully arranged her hair. Her excitement made it difficult to manage her combs. Finally, with a trembling hand, she managed to pile her hair up and secure the veiled hat with a long hat pin. It was important that she make a good impression on the boy's father. Smoothing her skirt, she pulled the matching cape over her shoulders. The mirror in the sleeping car was a small one, but she wiggled until she had one last look. With shaking hands, she pulled on her kid gloves.

The brakes screeched and the car shifted when the train came to a jarring stop. The porter walked down the corridor, announcing San Marcial, New Mexico Territory.

Taking a deep breath, Bellami stepped off onto the platform, getting her first look at the rustic town. Cows and cowboys were milling through the street. As she watched, Bellami realized just how far she'd come from New York.

Hugh quickened his step and went directly to the platform at the train station. Several people got off, but he didn't see anyone who looked remotely like the matronly woman he was expecting. The conductor and porter were busy unloading a passel of trunks farther down the rails. He intended to speak with them, but they finished and boarded the train. A feeling of dread crept up his spine. Maybe something had happened to delay her departure. Hugh wondered if he should send a telegram to New York City.

"Well, hell . . ." Hugh muttered to himself as he paced back and forth. He noticed a fashionable woman standing by the trunks. She, too, seemed to be awaiting the arrival of someone. From the cut of her clothes Hugh knew she wasn't from around here. She was tall and slim and was wearing a hat and veil, which completely obscured her face.

Bellami knew Doc had told the O'Bannions she'd be on this train. Why wasn't somebody here to meet her? Pacing up and down the walk near her trunks she allowed herself to consider the worst. Maybe they had changed their minds after she'd left New York. She saw a tall, auburn-haired man pacing nearby. Occasionally he would look her way and frown. Plucking up her courage, she walked over to him.

"Excuse me, sir? Can you tell me where I might send a telegram?" She wrung her gloved hands together when he turned in her direction. His looks were stern, but when he smiled his face creased into a pair of deep, weathered dimples. He reached up to sweep off his hat, the same kind the men wore in Socorro.

"Ma'am. Are you waiting for someone?" His brown eyes sparkled.

Bellami sighed. Disappointment lay heavy in her chest. "Yes, but evidently the O'Bannions have changed their minds." Her voice quavered a little, and she adjusted her veil out of nervous habit.

Dark brows rose a bit. He squinted his eyes and looked her up and down once. "Ma'am, you wouldn't be Bellami James, would you?" He sounded as if he hoped she were not.

"I am. Are you, Mr. O'Bannion?" Bellami asked hesitantly, extending her gloved hand. She wasn't sure what expression she hoped to see on his craggy face, but it certainly wasn't the one she received. Fear of rejection loomed. Bellami sucked in her breath, bracing herself for the worst. Just before she despaired completely, the man grasped her hand.

"Well! It is a pleasure to meet you. Doc Malone didn't tell me... That is, I expected an older person...." Hugh stammered.

Bellami felt her stiff-necked James pride take command. "I assure you, I am quite qualified, Mr. O'Bannion."

"Oh, I'm sure you are. Come, let's get your trunks loaded, and I'll give you a ride out to Trace's." Hugh took her by the elbow, and they walked into the depot. He managed to get a couple of burly men to agree to load the baggage, but when they saw how many trunks were lined up, the men balked. Hugh offered more money quickly, not wishing to delay a minute. The sooner he got her out of town, the better off he'd be. Soon they were rolling down the hard-packed trail on the edge of town, trunks piled high and tied precariously. He hoped they wouldn't topple off in the middle of the rutted dirt road.

Hugh was mute with shock. Doc hadn't really *said* the teacher was an older woman, but he'd certainly implied it. What the hell could Doc be thinking of? "And what the devil can I be thinkin', taking her to Trace's house?" Hugh asked himself under his breath. "But what choice do I have?"

An uneasy tension sizzled between them as the wagon rolled down the dirt road. If Doc had left out a few particulars about Miss James, exactly what had he told her about Trace?

"Miss James, what did Doc tell you about my son?" Hugh tried to keep his voice light. He kept his gaze locked on the rump of the horse, afraid to betray how nervous this situation was making him.

Bellami had been concentrating so hard on the stark, rugged countryside that she jumped when he spoke to her. She cleared her throat and tried to recover her poise. "Not much, I'm afraid. Just that your son's been blinded in some sort of an accident. I train blind children, you see."

Children—blind *children*. Yep, Hugh saw a lot, all of it bad. "Miss, did Doc tell you the ages of Trace and my other children?" Trace needed a teacher, and he needed one now. There wouldn't be enough time to find another if this one bolted and headed back to New York. Hugh didn't want to spook her by telling her what lay in store at the end of this road.

"No, Mr. O'Bannion, he didn't. He said you have five children, and Trace is next to the oldest. Is that correct?" The conversation kept taking funny twists and turns.

"Yep. That's about it, I guess." Hugh looked at her out of the corner of his eye as he spoke. It would be a damn sight easier to know how she was taking all this if he could just see her face. A small breeze ruffled the cloth of her veil as he watched her.

Bellami squirmed uncomfortably. Something about Mr. O'Bannion bothered her, but she couldn't put her finger on it. He seemed to be hinting around at something. She took a deep breath, trying to steady her nerves, and forced herself to concentrate on the job ahead, and the little boy involved.

Hugh hated to do it, but he had no other choice. The woman would have to stay—that was all there was to it. He cursed Doc silently once more and took a deep breath. He'd never been much good at small talk. Clell took care of that department. Hugh could see her tension. She had her gloved hands clenched together so tight the stitching across the fingers looked like it might tear out any minute.

"Miss James, is this your first trip to the West?"

Bellami started a little when he spoke, but she managed to answer. Her voice was steady, and it belied her anxiety. "Yes it is."

"Well, I guess I better be a proper host and show the sights to you, then," Hugh said pleasantly. He pointed to a bird hovering overhead. "That's an eagle. We've got a few nestin' near my ranch."

Bellami tipped her head upward, to follow the line of his finger.

Hugh caught sight of pale, creamy skin on the curve of her jaw beneath the veil when she moved. A pang of guilt gripped him when he realized she was, indeed, young, but he reminded himself of Trace's troubles. He had to do what was necessary, and he couldn't allow himself to get sentimental—not now, not over a stranger. The trip passed pleasantly, with him pointing out a coyote loping through the mesquite, a hawk circling overhead. Her earlier uneasiness seemed to be almost gone. Hugh noticed her hands were now lying sedately in her lap. He sighed in relief when they reached his ranch and turned toward Trace's house.

A fork in the road drew Bellami's attention. A large one-story house sat at the end of a long road, surrounded by trees. It looked nearly as peaceful as the mission in Socorro. Mr. O'Bannion urged the buggy past it.

"Trace's place is about five miles farther."

Bellami was about to ask why he kept referring to it as "Trace's place," when four antelope broke out of the juniper and bounded across the road. She stood up in the buggy to watch. Their white rumps disappeared quickly from sight. She stared at them until they were no more than specks on the horizon. A shiver of excitement ran through her. When she turned back to Mr. O'Bannion, he was watching her with an odd expression on his face. He coughed and turned his attention to the road ahead, as if he didn't wish to have any more conversation.

Soon they drove through a large gate. Bellami saw a pretty two-story house with an incredibly steep roof at the end of the hard-packed dirt road. The breeze picked up and the blades of a windmill began to move. Water gushed into a huge wooden-staved tank, spilling over the sides. It all looked quite charming and bucolic to Bellami. An older man stepped out onto the porch. He was shorter than Mr. O'Bannion, and lean to the point of looking gaunt. His weathered skin looked hard and brown as leather. Bellami noticed the look he gave her, but he turned away and started unloading her trunks.

"Come this way, Miss James." Hugh took her by the elbow and guided her to the large wrap-around porch. Bellami waited as Hugh opened the sturdy front door, expecting him to enter with her. She was a little surprised when he stepped back out of her way.

"Aren't you coming in?" A premonition of danger crept up her spine. Her voice sounded shaky, and too high.

"No. I'll help Clell. You go ahead. Trace's probably upstairs, first door on the right. Why don't you go in and introduce yourself?" He turned and walked back to the wagon.

Bellami stepped inside. She stood in the parlor of a lovely, rustic home. The furniture all appeared to be very new. Not at all how she expected a house where five children lived to look. The hardwood floors were covered by some sort of woven rugs with geometric patterns on them.

Pulling off her cape, hat and gloves, Bellami touched the shiny curved and turned banister. Someone had put a lot of love into the furnishing and care of this house, she thought. She climbed the stairs and stopped on the landing to get her bearings. The first door on the right, Mr. O'Bannion had said. Bellami turned and focused on a closed bedroom door. Another shudder of foreboding gripped her. Shaking her head to clear away the feeling, she lifted her chin and took a deep breath. She reached out to open the door. Faint sounds, like someone moving around inside, held her attention. Bellami turned the knob and pushed the door open.

At first she couldn't see anything. Heavy, dark drapes were drawn against the daylight. Slowly her eyes began adjusting to the dim room. She let out a squeak of surprise when she saw what was inside.

No child waited in this room. No angelic face with soft brown eyes stared in her direction. No innocent boy greeted her. Bellami James looked into a pair of emerald-green eyes under a tangled mass of dirty ebony hair. She could, with some difficulty, distinguish a face beneath the heavy beard. A tall, heavily muscled man with nothing on but a pair of dirty Levi's stood amid heaps of discarded clothing.

"Clell? Is that you? Answer me, damn it! Who the hell's in here?" The hard voice was full of menace.

Bellami staggered back against the door. "Oh, I am sorry, I must have the wrong room." She stumbled toward the landing as she timidly apologized. "I'm looking for Trace O'Bannion."

The man groped along the furniture toward the open door. "I'm Trace O'Bannion. Who the hell are you?" He took a slow, shuffling step forward.

Bellami's head spun as his words registered. Trace O'Bannion wasn't a little boy at all. He was a filthy, wild-eyed madman who was stalking slowly toward her. Panic welled up in her chest. She turned, hesitating only long enough to grab a handful of her heavy long skirts before she ran down the stairs. Her only thought was to reach Hugh O'Bannion and return to the train in San Marcial immediately.

Behind her, the man raved and cursed, demanding to know who was in his house. He shuffled barefoot behind her. It seemed strangely quiet outside as Bellami opened the front door. She stepped out onto the porch and nearly fainted dead away. All eight of her trunks stood in a neat row on the porch. The buggy was gone. Looking out across the New Mexico desert, Bellami couldn't see another human being. She was alone.

Well, not exactly alone. A raging lunatic was slowly making his way down the stairs. Bellami turned, nervously watching the man grope his way toward her. The deranged creature was obviously blind as a bat—and angry. His eyes looked like green flames as he bellowed.

"Who the hell's in my house?" He stopped when he reached the bottom stair.

Bellami was torn. Should she move away, or should she stand her ground and speak? Even if he couldn't see, he knew there was someone else in the house. His house.

She swallowed hard. "My—my name is Bellami James." She managed to stammer the words out, hoping her voice sounded steadier than it felt. Her hand was shaking like a leaf in the wind.

Confusion played across the man's face. He blinked his blind eyes three times in quick succession. Suddenly he erupted into a string of obscenities that would have stripped the hide off a mule skinner. "James? Mr. Bellamy James? You're the one my father sent for? Son of a— When I get my hands on that old man's neck, I swear, I'll—'' He turned away from her, then suddenly spun around to face in her direction. "What the hell kind of a name is Bellamy for a woman, anyway?" Green eyes blazed from beneath the camouflage of tangled hair and dark furrowed brows.

Bellami dug deep inside herself to find a bit of courage. She pulled her shoulders back and stood a little straighter. He took a step toward her. "It happens to be a perfectly nice name, as a matter of fact, Mr. O'Bannion. It's spelled *B-e-l-l-a-m-i.* It's French."

The man stopped abruptly no more than two feet in front of her and blinked again. He seemed to be assessing the situation.

"Well, Miss Bellami James, please do me the very great favor of getting your French ass out of my house!" He folded his arms across his bare chest.

Bellami felt fire burn along her cheeks and ears. Anger flooded through her. "I'd like nothing better, believe me, but your father has seen fit to strand me here!" She blinked back the tears of anger that welled up in her eyes. Bellami would not let this great unwashed oaf make her cry.

Trace opened his mouth as if to speak, then slammed it shut. He whirled away from her again. "Clell!" He yelled the name several times. With a snort of disgust, he turned around and inclined his head in Bellami's general direction. "Well, Miss James, it appears we've both been abandoned." He frowned and rubbed a brown, work-roughened hand across the tangled beard. "Can you ride?" His tone was slightly more civil.

"Yes. I ride sidesaddle rather well," Bellami said confidently, although she still felt very threatened. His conversation seemed to take so many twists and turns that she had trouble following his train of thought—just like his

sneaking father's. She retreated one more step away from
him.

He barked out a short, bitter laugh. "Well, I guess
you're stayin' right here until someone decides to come
back for you. Ghost sure as hell wouldn't let you ride him
sidesaddle, even if I owned one, which I don't!"

"Ghost?" She repeated the word. She wasn't sure she
really wanted him to explain. This flesh-and-blood person
was bad enough. Dealing with someone or something
called Ghost would really be more than she could handle.

"My stallion. I don't have any other saddle horses
penned up right now. As you can plainly see, there isn't
anyone here capable of handlin' a horse." His caustic
words stung her ears as much as his epithets had earlier.
"Come on, I'll point you in the direction of an empty
room." Trace's voice was rife with hostility.

Bellami didn't move an inch. She sucked in her breath
sharply. "You don't mean you expect me to sleep here,
with you, alone?" The idea was preposterous. Not even
this brute could conceive of such a notion.

Trace stopped in his tracks and tilted his head a little to
one side as his lip curled into a nasty sneer. "Miss James,
in case you can't tell, I'm totally blind. If you were God's
gift to mankind, you'd be completely safe from me." A
bitter note punctuated each word as he spoke. When he
finished, he turned his back to her and began shuffling
away.

His reference to her looks cut Bellami to the quick. So,
word of her disfigurement had preceded her. "Well, as we
both know, Mr. O'Bannion, I am not God's gift to mankind!"

He continued to the stairs. Bellami realized he was
completely absorbed with the task of feeling his way along
the smooth banister. He groped along until he reached the
landing, then pointed to a room at the end of the hallway.

"You can use that room, for tonight. You'll be leavin' in the mornin', one way or the other. The privy is out back. Follow the path from the kitchen door." He turned toward the room she'd found him in. He stopped in the doorway and turned toward her once again. "I don't suppose you can cook?" He cocked his head to one side again, listening for her voice.

"Yes, I can cook. Why do you ask?"

"Because, my dear, I can't. Not now, anyway. I guess we won't starve before Clell gets back," he said evenly as he stepped inside.

Bellami closed her eyes, drawing in a shaky breath. "Doc, how could you do this to me?"

Chapter Four

Hugh and Clell were halfway home before either of them spoke. "Do you think what you just did was right?" Clell's voice had an edge to it. He looked at Hugh with something like accusation in his eyes.

"Maybe not, but I've got to do what's best for Trace." Hugh said, trying to justify an action that left a bad taste in his mouth.

"Well, what about the young woman? Trace hasn't exactly been what I'd call a gentleman lately."

Hugh pulled up on the reins, stopping the horse to look his oldest friend square in the face. "Do you mean to tell me you think Trace would hurt her? My son may be a lot of things, but one thing for sure, Tom McClellan, he'd never hurt a woman! And you damned well know it."

Clell shifted in the seat. It was true, of course. Even in his present state of mind, Trace was too decent a man to take out his anger on an innocent female. Still, he'd been yelling like a wounded bull as they left. Things wouldn't be too pleasant for Miss James. Clell hoped she had the grit to take it.

Doc seemed to think so. He'd sung her praises in letter after letter. Letters that only one other person in the territory knew about. "When do you plan on goin' back?"

Clell asked, in a less judgmental tone. He didn't want to be pushing too hard—not just yet, anyway.

"I figure you and I can ride over every day and take a look from that rise by Trace's house." Hugh grinned, and dimples formed in his lean jaw.

Clell chuckled. "Oh, so you plan on making sure things don't get out of hand, without them knowin' it, huh?"

Hugh nodded and slapped the reins against the horse's rump. He hoped this would work. Lord knew the rest of them hadn't been able to do much with Trace up to now. Maybe being stranded with that little lady would be the best thing that happened to Trace in a long while.

Bellami woke in a cold sweat to the sound of thunder. Her cotton chemise clung to her skin. The room felt hot, oppressive. It was like being buried alive, and she gasped for breath. Trembling, she couldn't remember where she was. On the train? No. With a groan, she remembered.

Throwing back the blankets, she put her feet on the smooth wood floor. She walked to the tall window, curious about the noise coming from outside. She hadn't explored the room earlier. Now, in the sliver of moonlight, she could clearly see a balcony running along the entire second floor. Pulling the heavy curtains back, she saw walk-through windows that could be opened from each room, on the second floor leading to the balcony.

The thunder seemed to be getting louder, more rhythmic. Bellami frowned. It didn't sound like thunder at all. She looked down at the scene below.

Bathed in a silvery blue light, she saw a corral. In it was a horse, but he could have been a phantom of the night. His body was the same color as the pale moonlight. His smooth body glistened as he ran the length of his enclosure. When he reached the end, he would slide to a stop, whirling to turn and run back again. He did it over and over.

Bellami watched, totally mesmerized, as he reared on his hind legs tossing his head. The horse's hot breath escaped his flared nostrils in a little cloud of vapor that drifted slowly away.

Her heart seemed to be beating in cadence with his hooves. She imagined herself as that animal. Confined. Restless. Trapped.

Bellami James stood in a stranger's house, with no way of leaving. She'd never faced anything like this before, never been without her family's support and protection. Bellami didn't believe she possessed the strength to handle this situation. Yet she must. Taking a deep breath, she tried to calm her fears. After all, someone would surely return soon. All she had to do was manage to stay away from Mr. O'Bannion until then.

Trace woke with a jolt, his pulse pounding as it did nearly every night. When he swallowed, his throat felt as dry and hot as the desert. Ghost was at it again. The steady vibrations of the heavy hooves hitting the ground flowed through Trace's body. Sitting up, he held his throbbing head in his hands.

"Damn your sorry hide, Ghost. I ought to sell you," Trace moaned. No, he couldn't do it. Just knowing the gray devil was out there gave him a sort of bittersweet happiness.

If he could just ride. Of course, riding was just one more thing he'd never be able to do again. Never ride, never shoot, never know the love of a woman. He held his pounding head and tried to make order from the chaos of his thoughts.

Right now he faced a more immediate problem than Ghost. What was he going to do about this damned woman? Trace knew his father was capable of something like this, but Clell? That really surprised him. Clell must've been in on this all along. Now Trace knew why the old man had offered to bring him home.

He hadn't ever known Clell to be dishonest—until now. It seemed every single person he counted on had betrayed him in one way or another. Self-pity and bitterness welled up in his chest.

"Fine, if that's how you all want it! You'll see just what a bastard I can really be," Trace snarled into the darkness of his room. "When you come to pick up this Eastern spinster, she can tell you what a worthless son of a buck I am," he vowed aloud. "I intend to make her regret every minute under my roof. I didn't ask the old biddy to come here in the first place." He'd enjoy sending her back home with her tail between her legs.

Bellami woke early, with the first rays of morning sunshine blazing across her face. After watching the horse last night, she'd forgotten to close the drapes on the window facing east. The horse had been like a living dream. His thundering stride had excited and depressed her all at the same time.

How awful it must be, so full of life, so eager, yet locked away. Bellami grimaced. She could be describing herself.

Dressed in the same suit she'd arrived in, she crept downstairs. If she could avoid the volatile Mr. O'Bannion for a few hours, until someone returned for her, so much the better.

Bellami opened the heavy front door quietly. She found the trunk with her work dresses in it. Taking out a plain brown cotton, and one of the full aprons she used when working at St. Michael's, she tiptoed back to her room.

She put on the sturdier clothing and brushed her long hair. With it coiled around her hand, ready to pin in place, she suddenly decided to wear it down. Wondering what possessed her to break such a long-standing habit, she braided her hair. Quickly she tied it with a small blue ribbon as her stomach growled noisily. She hadn't had anything to eat last night. If she was hungry, then *he* must be ravenous. Picturing him as a starving animal with wild green eyes, Bellami shivered. That image made her none too happy.

Him. That horrible man. She felt like such a fool, being duped into this situation. Child, indeed—the man was the devil incarnate.

Once in the kitchen, she began searching for coffee makings. When she had everything together, she put the granite-ware pot on the black cast-iron stove. A box full of kindling sat next to it. A tin of matches lay on the tiny shelf built into the stovepipe. She managed to get a good blaze going, thanks to the dry, seasoned wood.

The kitchen was well equipped, if a little primitive, compared to the kitchen in New York. A hand pump brought water into the house. Bellami was grateful she had never had to carry water, and she didn't want to start now.

Opening the back door, she looked outside. She needed to go in search of the privy Mr. O' Bannion mentioned. By following the hard-packed path in the dirt, she found the small outhouse. It was constructed from rough pine, with a tiny growth of some odd bush beside it. Dusky pink sprigs of flowers were beginning to bloom. After attending to her needs, she looked around the yard on her way back to the house. A lean-to built of wood joined the kitchen. Inside, several metal buckets were stacked near a huge wooden tub. On the rough wood wall, a well-used washboard hung on a bent nail.

On the opposite side of the kitchen, she found a smokehouse stocked with meat. The smell of hickory and pungent smoked hams made her mouth water and her stomach rumble.

Reaching up, she took down a slab of bacon from a wire hook. Bellami was glad she'd spent so much time visiting with Tilly and the cook in the kitchen. Tired of her sitting idle, Mrs. Wiggins had encouraged Bellami to learn how to cook. Her skills were limited in comparison to those of most women her age, but she could manage four or five different meals. Thank God for Mrs. Wiggins.

A cock's boastful crow brought a smile to her lips. Roosters meant hens, and hens meant eggs. Bellami said a silent thank-you to her father.

When Bellami and Brooks were twelve, Donovan had taken the entire family to a rustic farm in upstate New York for the summer. At the time, they'd all thought it was charmingly eccentric. Playing in the hayloft, milking the cows. Now Bellami realized what he'd hoped to accomplish. He'd wanted to teach his children about country life. Thanks to that summer, Bellami knew which end of a cow milk came from.

A woven basket sat on the floor by the back door. Swinging it over her arm, Bellami stepped inside the lean-to. A rough brown gunnysack full of chicken scratch, stood in one corner. Bending down, she scooped up a good-size handful. By following her ears, she located the chicken coop.

It was sturdy and covered on top, to foil the hawks and eagles Mr. O'Bannion had pointed out, she supposed. Lifting the wooden latch nailed to the gate, she stepped inside. She clucked to the hens while she threw the feed. Scratching chickens immediately clustered around her full skirt. While the hens were occupied, Bellami located half a dozen nests and eight beige eggs. Gingerly she laid them in the basket and went back into the house.

After mixing up biscuits, she slid them into the hot oven to bake while she sliced the bacon. The sizzling meat filled the room with a rich aroma. The odor mingled with the smell of strong fresh coffee. The familiar scent of breakfast made Bellami feel less apprehensive.

Trace woke up to the smell of coffee and bacon. For a minute, he felt happy. He stretched and put his feet on the floor to get up. When he rubbed the sleep from his eyes, it all came flooding back. Reality.

He was blind. Impotent rage boiled up inside him. Having no focus for his anger, he chose the nearest target. Miss James.

"Well, she isn't going to be here another night! She can walk, I don't give a damn, just as long as she leaves," he railed as he searched for a shirt in the wreckage of his room. He'd been sleeping in his Levi's half the time, and the last shirt he'd worn was tossed on the floor, somewhere.

Bellami poured herself a cup of hot coffee and took an appraising look around. The bottom floor of the house was well-ordered and clean. What a contradictory picture this all made! Such a pleasant house, owned by such a wild, rude, filthy man. Bellami wished that Samuel Richards had come instead of her. He'd fit right in with the maniac upstairs!

Taking a sip of hot coffee, Bellami sat down at the table. She frowned, thinking of the hostile Mr. O'Bannion. He deserved the kind of treatment Sam Richards meted out. How she wished Doc had asked him to come. Sam Richards was a difficult taskmaster. Still, he'd been extremely successful with some very difficult patients. In fact, she remembered one a lot like Mr. O'Bannion. Bitter, mean, uncooperative. Dr. Richards had been almost cruel in his treatment of the man. He'd gotten results by goading the patient to his limit. The poor bitter creature had finally decided to live, just to spite Richards.

Narrowing her blue-gray eyes, Bellami wondered. Was that it? Did Mr. O'Bannion hate life? Had he always been bitter and mean, or had he lost his will to live after the accident?

Trace made his way slowly down the stairs, and with each step he became more curious. What kind of a woman would come all the way out to the territory? Why on earth would a spinster leave New York to accept a job as nursemaid to a blind man?

"Who gives a damn?" Trace muttered to himself. He didn't care, he just wanted her out. Life continued to deal him one bad hand after another, and he didn't deserve it. The sooner he got the meddling woman out of his house, the sooner he could go back to his disillusioned half-life. The smell of food cooking made his gut growl. Clell's bad cooking kept his appetite honed to razor sharpness.

"Damned nice of her to cook breakfast, before I throw her out," Trace whispered under his breath as his foot touched the last stair.

Bellami heard shuffling on the stairs behind her and swallowed hard. *Oh, Lord, please, I'm not strong enough to handle this. Please help me find the courage.*

Entering the kitchen, he turned more or less in the direction of the stove. Trace assumed she was standing before it, cooking.

Sitting at the table holding a coffee cup in her hands, Bellami watched him enter the room. He stopped not a foot from her, looking toward the hot cookstove. Gripping the cup so hard her fingers hurt, she realized he didn't know where she was—yet.

"Lady, I want you out of here! Now!" He yelled so loud she jumped. The legs of her chair screeched across the wood floor. Trace whirled toward the sound, aware she'd been right beside him all the time. Embarrassed by his mistake, he felt his temper flare to life. His face was a mask of pure rage.

Bellami gasped as he reached out to grab her. She tried to evade him, but didn't move quite fast enough. By luck and instinct, his hands found her arms. He gripped her hard, dragging her up from the chair. Cruel fingers bit into her skin. He meant to hurt.

"Mr. O'Bannion! You're hurting me! Let me go!" Bellami's voice shook with fear. What kind of a man acted like this?

He frowned, and for a moment his face softened at the sound of her voice. Then it turned hard again. His grip relaxed, but Trace didn't let her go. He couldn't release her, not now. Knowledge flowed from her arms through his fingertips toward his brain. "Miss James?" His tone suddenly sounded more inquisitive than hostile.

"Yes, Mr. O'Bannion?" She tried to use her most professional voice. Not an easy feat, with him half-naked, holding her captive.

"Why are you here?" His voice was soft, yet powerful. His deep green eyes stared, unseeing, at her face.

Bellami's first instinct was to be self-conscious about her scar, but of course that was silly—he couldn't see it. "I'm a teacher of the blind." Her voice quavered.

His face darkened with rage, and his body tensed again. "Bullshit! I want the reason, not a list of your lofty accomplishments. No woman would take a job like this without a damn good reason. Now tell me, why are you here?" A little vein in his temple pulsated as he yelled.

Bellami blinked. Why was she here? Simple enough question. What was the answer? She allowed her thoughts to race back over her actions from the point when Doc had first spoken to her about this job. She saw it play out before her, like a scene at the theater.

Why am I here? A little voice in her head repeated the question. Taking a deep breath, the words tumbled out unbidden.

"Because I'm ugly, Mr. O'Bannion I'm ugly, and I had very little life to leave behind. Satisfied?" Bellami spit the words at him.

Trace felt the shock down to his bare toes. Of all the reasons in the world, this was one he could never have expected. Women didn't ever say they were ugly, not even if it was true. It just wasn't in their nature. A kind of shame washed over him, as if he'd caught a glimpse of some inner part of this stranger—a part no man was ever meant to see. Trace was sorry he'd forced her to bare herself to him. This woman's critical assessment of herself was something he wasn't supposed to hear. It had been a private thing, and he'd bullied it out of her. He was ashamed. Trace O'Bannion belittled a woman for his own twisted pleasure. His actions disgusted him, but instead of admitting it he fought to deny the truth.

Since he felt guilty, he did what was becoming a habit— he lashed out to hurt. "Are you butt-ugly, or just sort of everyday common ugly?" He heard her sharp intake of breath. It made his gut twist with regret. What the hell was wrong with him? Trace didn't know himself anymore. It scared the holy hell out of him.

His lips twisted into a cruel imitation of a grin. Bellami wanted to hit him. Nobody had spoken to her like that since the day Rod had beaten the bullies for calling her ugly. She fought the urge to hit him, believing he would hit her back. Bellami was afraid of this man. All her life her brothers and the rest of her family had protected her; she'd never had to be brave or strong or deal with a brute like this alone. A lump formed in her throat, unshed tears burned her eyes. She stiffened, then she made a decision. She would not let this bully—this bastard—break her. Let him fling insults. One thing Bellami James had learned was how to endure. She'd been through much worse than what this uncouth man could dish out. Straightening her shoulders, she stuck out her chin defiantly.

"I will be brave," she muttered under her breath. Images of Rod and Brooks floated through her mind. That gave her the courage to hold her head a little higher.

Trace realized she wasn't going to cry. She also wasn't going to give him an answer. He felt defiance telegraphing up his arms. The more she resisted, the madder it made him. Why was she doing this? If the silly bitch would just shed a few tears, he'd have a little mercy on her. Wouldn't he? A nagging little voice inside his head told him no. The truth of that only served to infuriate him further.

"Well, Miss James, I'm waitin'. Were you born ugly? Is that why your parents gave you such a god-awful name?"

It happened so fast Trace hadn't even realized what he was going to do. He gave her a good hard shake. He'd never had the urge to throttle a woman like he did this one. But was it really her he wanted to shake some sense into, or was it himself?

Bellami saw red as her teeth hit together with a sharp clack. She clenched her jaw and wrenched her arms out of his grip. Leaning toward his unshaven face, she shouted so loud her throat hurt. "No! I was *not* born ugly! I had an accident!"

Horror filled Trace as he realized how cruelly he was treating this poor spinster. What in God's name was he doing? He'd never spoken to any woman like this. He'd never acted like this with Becky, who deserved it. Not even when she'd turned her back and walked out on him. This woman hadn't done anything, except fall for his father's deception. He felt the blood draining from his face. Trace came dangerously close to breaking down and bawling like a baby at Miss James's feet. He took a deep, ragged breath and tried to regain some control. It was frightening to think that he had just shaken her like a rag doll. Trace clenched his jaw. He didn't want to hurt Miss James. It was his own weakness he wanted to attack and kill—being blind and helpless and half a man. Trembling with fear and rage, he grabbed her slender arms again, but gently this time.

Bellami felt him shaking all over through the hands on her arms. He'd gone so pale, she thought he might faint dead away. Never in her life had she raised her voice like that. What in God's name was she doing?

Slowly her rage diminished and a deep resolve took over. Bellami decided she would teach this man a lesson. Many lessons, in fact. He wasn't going to bully her, and she certainly wasn't leaving. She'd been hired to do a job, and she intended to do it. The James family members kept their word. She pulled free and whirled away from him. Her long braid lashed out like a whip across his bare chest. Bellami grabbed the back of a chair to steady herself.

Something heavy and soft, almost silky, hit Trace in the chest. Burning curiosity grabbed his attention, shaking him from the unreasonable rage of a moment ago.

"What was that?" His words were barely above a whisper. Bellami thought maybe she imagined he spoke. She looked at him trying to read his expression. She couldn't, mostly because she wasn't able to see enough of his face beneath his tangled beard and wild dark hair.

"What was that?" He repeated the question a bit louder.

Bellami frowned and tossed her braid across her shoulder. "What was what? I don't understand what you're asking me." He's exasperating, maybe he's even mad, Bellami told herself, watching Trace warily.

"Something hit me, in the chest. What was it?" His eyes blindly scanned her face.

Bellami squirmed unconsciously under that intense stare. A tiny smile curved her lips when she understood what he meant. As she turned away, her braid had whipped out, touching his chest.

"My braid." Yes, the man was obviously quite mad, completely unhinged. Probably a result of his injury. Of course, it might run in the family. His father certainly displayed some of the same deranged characteristics.

"A braid." He pronounced the word softly, almost reverently, as if the mysteries of life had been explained for him. Sighing heavily, his face softened. Some of the tension left his body.

Her simple answer left him oddly content. A braid. A woman's braid. Such a plain, ordinary thing. He didn't have the slightest idea why, but suddenly Trace wasn't the least bit angry with this strange woman. He felt spent, almost numb. He didn't have any anger left in him, just a dull sort of emptiness where rage had burned only seconds before.

"Somethin' smells awful good. I could eat a bear, raw," he said, and grinned in her direction. Not a cruel, distorted twist of his mouth, like before, but a real honest grin. Straight white teeth flashed from the tangle of beard and unkempt mustache.

Smoothing her apron, Bellami ran her hand over her hair to capture what had been shaken free of the braid. "Well, sit down. I'll fix you a plate. Tomorrow we will begin your lessons." Her voice rang with control and authority.

She left him sitting at the table, struggling with bacon, eggs, biscuits and a cup of steaming coffee. She could see he'd learned nothing about eating since he'd been blinded. Bellami marched up the stairs, her back ramrod stiff, to his bedroom. She pushed the door open and stepped inside.

It was still as dark as a bear's den inside, and she wondered if a bear smelled any worse. She jerked open the drapes, and sunlight flooded through the tall window. Filth surrounded her. The linen on the bed badly needed changing, and a thick layer of dust covered every surface in sight. Clothes lay in untidy heaps all around her.

Vowing to have her revenge, Bellami stripped the bed and gathered up the soiled clothes. Soon a large bundle sat on the landing outside Trace's bedroom.

Rough wool rugs with strange designs, like the ones downstairs, covered the floor in his room, as well. She puzzled over what they were; she'd never seen anything quite like them. The room was stuffy and full of dust from her labors. She struggled to open the walk-through window. Stuck from lack of use, it finally came free with a creak. Bellami breathed deeply of the clear, brisk air. She gathered the rugs and took them to the railing to air out in the spring breeze. The windmill pumped water steadily. Its metallic screech was the only sound, apart from the occasional cry from a hawk overhead.

As she carried the bundle of dirty sheets and clothes to the front porch, she saw Mr. O'Bannion standing by the horse's corral. She watched him for a moment. He seemed to be speaking to the animal, but she couldn't be sure.

What an odd, confusing man. He had been so openly hostile to her, yet now he gently stroked the animal. He looked almost human. No doubt a trick of light, or too much fresh desert air. She found a broom and went to finish cleaning his bedroom. Bellami had no idea where a man would keep sheets, if he even had extra linen, and she wasn't about to ask Mr. Trace O'Bannion. God knew what reaction a simple question like that might cause!

She retrieved her own bedding from another trunk on the porch. Tilly had been sure nothing as civilized as sheets would be available in the New Mexico Territory. Lavender sachets lay in the bottom of the trunk. She picked one up, holding the cloth to her nose. Bellami smiled, comforted by the familiar smell. It reminded her of home.

Standing in the doorway a good while later, she surveyed her work. Nothing short of a miracle. It was really a nice room, masculine and simple. The style of furniture was unlike anything she'd ever seen before. She ran her hand over the pale wood, fascinated by the intricate, primitive designs. She'd been surprised to find handsome leather-bound books on a shelf. Bellami wondered if they belonged to Mr. O'Bannion, or someone else. Had he read before he was blinded? The more she saw, the more she discovered contradictions about the man.

Bellami decided one other matter would have to be attended to before the sun went down. Anyone but a blind man could see by the set of her jaw that she was a woman with a mission. Of course, Trace was a blind man. He was blissfully unaware of the gal who had set her mind and energies to transforming her surroundings.

Several hours and many buckets later, the big wooden tub, full of steaming water, sat in the middle of the kitchen. Bellami found a shaving cup, brush and razor in Trace's room. Clean toweling was neatly stacked on a chair near the tub.

As if on cue, Trace shuffled up the steps from the stallion's corral. Bellami watched his slow approach, her arms folded across her bosom. When he stepped through the door, she spoke sharply.

"Mr. O'Bannion, I do not intend to suffer another meal in this house with your... fragrance."

One dark eyebrow shot upward. He hated the way she said "Mr. O'Bannion." It sounded more like a curse word than a name.

"Really? When are you leaving?" Trace sneered.

Bellami couldn't help herself—she smiled. His caustic wit was really quite entertaining, once you got used to it. He could also think fast on his feet, she'd give him that. She felt something like admiration for the surly man. Bellami forced the grin from her face. "No, you misunderstand, Mr. O'Bannion. There's a tub full of water two feet in front of you. Now, will you undress and get in, or do I remove your clothes for you?"

His eyes narrowed menacingly. He couldn't believe his ears. Who the hell did Miss New York think she was talking to? He wasn't some damn shirttailed boy. Undress him? When hell froze over! "Miss James, it would take somebody a helluva lot bigger than you to undress me," he replied dryly, folding his arms across his chest and bracing his bare feet apart.

"Fine," she said, and picked up a bucket that she'd earlier placed near the pump. With a flourish, she threw the cold water straight into his face. He gasped out of surprise, and because it was very cold water.

He dropped his arms and clenched his fists at his muscular thighs. Bellami watched in horrified fascination. His body was coiled, as if he meant to lunge at her. Water ran over his bearded face and trickled off the ends of his shaggy black hair. His tall frame nearly vibrated with the effort he exerted in order to restrain himself.

"Well, Miss James, it seems you win this round." His mouth twisted into a tight line as he prepared to deliver one of his insults. Bellami braced herself for the assault.

"Miss James, will you stay to watch?" He moved his hand down to unbutton his Levi's. A dark wet spot formed along the waistband, where the water had soaked in.

Bellami saw the dark hair on his chest growing downward. It entered the wet waistband, like an arrow, from his flat stomach. Her view of the dark growth of hair and his flat pelvis widened as he unbuttoned the denim, opening his pants farther. Heat flooded Bellami's face, but she clenched her jaw, determined not to give ground.

"Mr. O'Bannion—" she tried to sound totally unimpressed "—I worked in a hospital for twelve years. I can't imagine you have so much less than any other man I've seen." She saw him tense at the implication that he might be lacking in his manliness. Thank God her brothers had been so open and frank about the things men were sensitive about. Satisfied she'd given as well as she got, she turned and walked away smiling.

Damn her! Every fiber of his male pride recoiled when she delivered her sharp retort. The sound of her departing footsteps sounded like gunshots in the quiet house.

"Sharp-tongued bitch! Probably never even had a man, dried-up old prune!" Trace snarled into the empty kitchen. He pulled off his clothes and groped around until he found the edge of the tub. Trace stuck his fingers in the water and found it pleasantly warm. Slowly, he eased his lanky body into it. The water rose slightly, but still only reached the lower portion of his rib cage. His knees stuck out uncomfortably. It felt wonderful. Trace sighed. It had been a long while since he enjoyed a bath. He shut his eyes and tried to relax. He almost managed it, even in his nearly doubled-up position, but then he heard someone moving around in the kitchen.

He sat bolt upright in the tub, water splashing over the edge. "Miss James? Are you in here?"

"Yes." Bellami smiled at the disbelief she heard in his question.

"God, woman, what do they teach you in New York? You don't come into a room, with a man, when he's bathin'!" He spread his hands, trying to cover his groin with his palms.

Bellami grinned at his discomfiture. "I'm gathering up these stinking clothes, and they teach us quite a few things, actually."

He could hear laughter, barely under control, in her voice. "What?" Trace snapped.

"You asked me what they teach us in New York. I'm going to show you some things I've learned, Mr. O'Bannion."

His face was a mask of shock. She smiled as he colored and fidgeted in embarrassment. Let him squirm for a while! Mean bully! He deserved much worse; now he'd learn what it felt like to be humiliated.

Trace listened while she moved around the room. He wanted to ask what she was doing, but he stubbornly refused to give her the satisfaction. Something cool touched his head, and he jumped at least a foot, nearly clearing the tub before he caught himself. Small fingers probed, massaging rhythmically in his hair.

"What in Sam Hill are you doin' now?" he bellowed, pushing her hands away from his hair. They returned almost immediately and he impatiently swiped at them again.

"I'm going to wash your hair. Now be still." She gave his long hair a spiteful tug.

Trace bellowed like an enraged bull. "Ow! What did I ever do in my sorry life to deserve you, Miss James?" His deeply resonant voice dripped with self-pity and sarcasm.

She smiled again, involuntarily. "Clean living, I guess, Mr. O'Bannion." She finished lathering his hair and picked up another bucket of water to pour it over his head. She didn't give him a single word of warning.

When she tipped up the bucket he gasped and sucked in his breath. The sound of his teeth grating together pleased Bellami immensely. She was still smiling when she grabbed a handful of the thick beard. She pulled on it, not quite as hard as she yanked his hair, but just enough to get his full attention.

Trace heard the unmistakable sound of metal rasping against metal at the same instant he felt cool air against his cheek.

"Now what?" His eyebrows rose in exasperation.

"I'm going to shave you." Bellami clipped away the long hair on his face with the scissors.

"Oh, the hell you are," Trace was half-out of the water as he spoke. This had gone on long enough. It was humiliating enough when his own sister tried to shave him. He'd be damned if some New York spinster would do it. He'd had enough of being treated like a boy in need of a sugar-tit.

"Would you like a towel, Mr. O'Bannion, or will you dry in the air?" Bellami asked sweetly.

Instantly Trace sank into the water, his face flaming with heat. Damned woman riled him up so much, he hadn't realized he was standing buck-naked in front of the old crone. He groaned in frustrated humiliation.

Neither one spoke for the remainder of the bath. Trace sat in the water, sulking, while Bellami clipped and pulled his hair. She was glad Trace had no way of knowing that she had quickly averted her eyes when he stood up in the water. She tried to will herself not to be embarrassed, or curious, about his body. After all, he was only a man.

She worked the soap into a heavy lather with the shaving brush. Frowning in concentration, she generously dabbed it against his cheeks, creating a white, frothy sculpture. His scowling face made him look like a rabid dog, and she tried to ignore his frightening appearance.

Bellami hadn't actually shaved anyone before, but she had watched Rod and Brooks do it many times. How hard could it be?

She didn't hesitate an instant. She picked up the straight razor with a confidence borne of total ignorance. With a flourish, she made a great swipe across his lean jaw. Immediately, pinpoints of blood sprang up in the swath across his face.

She sucked in her breath, and her eyebrows rose. Bellami held her breath, waiting for him to kill her. Dozens of bright red, bloody dots began to trickle amid the white foam. It looked very painful. She bit her lip. Any moment now he would strike her, she was sure of it.

The muscles in his jaw tightened, and the skin on his midriff rippled. He expelled a long heavy sigh. She could see that he was fighting for self-control. For the first time, Bellami really looked at him.

All of a sudden, swallowing became difficult. His skin looked like velvet stretched over hard bands of steel at his ribs. Bellami felt the heat of a blush rising to her face when her eyes lingered on the dark triangle of hair beneath the water. Her train of thought was broken by his voice, steady and low.

"Miss James, if you plan on skinnin' me alive, an inch at a time, get on with it. The damned water's gettin' cold."

Bellami finished shaving him in mortified silence. Her hand shook so much, she barely managed to finish trimming his hair. When she poured the last bucket of frigid water over him, she tried not to notice how his nipples contracted at the shock of the liquid. Dark tufts of hair floated around his slim waist. He never said another word to her.

Bellami's voice squeaked and broke. "There is a towel on the back of the chair. Your clean clothes are on your bed upstairs. While you dress, I'll clean this up. I hope you're hungry. We'll eat as soon as you're ready."

She turned on her heel and left him sitting in the tub of water. She didn't like this man, not one little bit. He was rude, obnoxious, and wallowing in self-pity. The sooner she trained him to get along by himself, the sooner she could leave. Bellami prayed it would be soon.

Chapter Five

Hugh O'Bannion took a deep breath and shut his eyes. When had he lost control of his children? He opened his eyes to find three O'Bannion faces staring at him. He couldn't say exactly when it had occurred, but it certainly had.

For a quarter of an hour now, Missy had been instructing him on how he should deal with Trace's new teacher, and the hell of it was, none of them even knew yet the teacher was a woman!

The minute Missy started her speech, Clell gave Hugh a questioning glance, encouraging him silently to make a clean breast of it. Hugh knew he was going to have to tell them, but did it have to be right now, in the middle of breakfast? If only Missy would take a breath. Lord, how that girl could run on.

Hugh expelled a deep sigh and rubbed a rough thumb at his temple. The whole situation was giving him a pain in the head. He decided to just do it—let the chips fall where they might. After all, when everybody knew the whole story, they'd agree with what he'd done.

The front door slammed with enough force to jiggle the glass in the windows. Spur rowels jingled in rhythm to the steady footfalls of a long-legged man. The steps grew louder as they came closer. Hugh recognized the stride without looking up.

"Hello, Flynn," he said wearily. "When did you get in?"

"Just now, Pa," Flynn said, glowering from the doorway.

Missy jumped up to fling her arms around Flynn's neck but he didn't seem to notice. He just kept boring a hole in Hugh with those deep brown eyes.

"Pa, I want to know what the hell you've been up to. Why didn't you let us know the teacher was Miss Bellami James?" Flynn pushed his hat back on his head with his index finger.

Clell groaned, while a gasp of shock came from the rest of Hugh's assembled offspring. Well, the fat was in the fire now! How the hell had Flynn gotten wind of this? Hugh prepared himself to be roasted over the fires of hell. Now, instead of telling them the story in a reasonable, calm manner, he was going to have to defend what he'd done.

He took a deep breath and looked up at Flynn. "Coffee?" Hugh intended to act like this was the most natural occurrence in the world.

Flynn pulled out a chair and sat down next to Missy. He took off his hat and set it, crown down, on the table before he gave her a kiss on the cheek. Daggers flew from her eyes as she watched Hugh. Not one word had been spoken since he'd greeted Flynn, and the silence was becoming mighty strained.

Clearing his throat, Hugh took a breath. "I was going to talk to all of you this mornin'." Hugh's voice was low and steady, leaving no doubt as to who was in control. When he used that tone, his children knew it wouldn't be too smart to interrupt or argue. He could be a patient and indulgent father but he had a breaking point, and it sounded like he had finally reached it.

"Flynn, did you just ride in?" Hugh had a few questions of his own. Enough was enough.

"Yep, I rode all night. Where is Miss James, Pa?" Flynn wasn't going to let the question go.

Hugh looked his son straight in the eye. "She's at Trace's."

"Alone?" Flynn's voice was hard, and he gave Clell an accusing glare.

"Yes." Hugh still met his son's steady gaze straight-on.

"Why, Pa? The teacher is a woman. What you're doin' just ain't proper. Why all the mystery?"

Taking a sip of coffee, Hugh grinned ironically. "If I'd told any of you the teacher was female..." He looked at each one and raised an eyebrow. "Well, look how you're reactin' now. Besides, Trace would've got wind of it, and he'd never get the help he needs."

Missy squirmed a little in her chair, and a faint stain of pink rose to her cheeks. Hugh grinned a little wider, and his dimples appeared. "Isn't that right, Missy?"

"Probably." She kept her dark eyes averted, not wanting to face Hugh.

"Tell me, Flynn, how did you find out about Miss James?" Hugh leaned back in his chair and crossed his long legs. The toe of his worn boot twitched up and down, like a cat's twitching tail.

"Ran into her accidentally, in Socorro." Flynn took the cup of coffee Lupe had quietly set beside him. He watched her full skirt swish around her brown ankles as she silently left the room.

"Look, I know you are all curious, so I may as well tell you the whole story." Hugh said. All eyes turned in his direction. Clell propped his chair back on two legs and balanced precariously, his eyes bright with interest.

"Clell, Doc Malone and I were in the army together. When we got out, Clell and I came here, as you know. Doc went to New York and started workin' with blind soldiers.'' Hugh looked out the window, his eyes unfocused, remembering. "We keep in touch, one or two letters a year. I got a letter from him a few weeks after Trace was shot. He kept talkin' about this woman who was a wonder at trainin' the blind.''

Clell coughed behind his hand and shifted in his chair. It nearly fell backward, and he jerked to recover his balance.

Hugh's brow furrowed as he continued. "That letter comin' like that, when it did, it was like a sign from God. I sent a telegram askin' him to send her to us, right away.''

Logan choked on a sip of coffee, and Flynn hit him a couple of times sharply on the back. "Easy, little brother." He grinned as Logan blushed crimson.

Hugh shrugged his shoulders and took a sip of coffee. "That's it. You know the whole story.''

Flynn chuckled dryly. "Not quite, Pa. Why is Miss James at Trace's alone? It ain't proper.''

Missy perked up and looked at her father. Clell gave Hugh a glance that clearly said "I told you so.''

"Well, for pity's sake. I was expectin' an older woman. I figured ol' Doc would have a steady old spinster workin' with him. When she arrived, and I found out she was a young single woman . . .'' His face flushed as the reality of what he'd done hit him. "Trace would have never agreed, and I didn't figure she would have, either. So, I left her there. Alone.'' His voice sounded flat and remorseful.

"Pa, did you see her?" Flynn leaned forward, trying to read his father's expression.

Now the others found their voices. Shane looked at Flynn, beginning to realize what they were saying. "What does Miss James look like, Pa?" Green eyes much like Trace's sparkled with curiosity.

Rolling his eyes toward heaven, Clell moaned, "I knew it. Now here it comes!"

Missy's black eyes narrowed suspiciously. "What does she look like, Pa?"

Hugh shifted in his chair. He made a feeble effort to be evasive. "Well, I never saw her face."

Clell let out a low, long whistle as Flynn snorted impatiently.

"Pa?" Missy pressed.

"Well, from what I saw of her, she looks like a real nice lady," Hugh finally replied.

Flynn rose from his chair like it was on fire. "Pa, she's a little slip of a thing. She's never goin' to be able to handle Trace without help, and you know it," he continued, blushing slightly. "And she is unmarried, Pa. What can you be thinkin' of? I know this ain't New York City, but this kind of thing ain't exactly done here, either. I'm goin' to go get her—now!"

Before Flynn finished clearing his chair, Hugh stood in front of his son, a look of pure stone in his eyes. "Flynn. Sit down. You're not goin' anywhere."

Flynn stood as tall as his father and outweighed him by forty pounds, but he knew when to back down. Hugh O'Bannion had tangled with about every tribe of Indian and lived to tell the tale. The look he wore now told Flynn he'd tolerate no more argument.

"It's time you all shut up and listen! I'm only goin' to say this once. Trace needs help, and he needs it now—not in a month or two. None of us have been able to do anythin' for him. If somethin' doesn't change soon, well, you might as well put another bullet in your brother's head!" Hugh's voice cracked with emotion.

"The good Lord saw fit to send a woman, and I pray she is the answer! No one is goin' near that ranch until I say so. Do you understand? Clell and I'll keep an eye on things from a distance." He took a long, hard look at each of his children. They could see he meant what he said.

"Pass the biscuits, please," Logan said, grinning from ear to ear. He hadn't seen so much excitement since he and Missy had turpentined the mules' rumps last spring!

Chapter Six

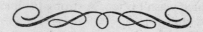

Dinner was a complete disaster. Bellami managed to accustom herself to Trace O'Bannion's sharp tongue, only to have him change tactics. The man was tricky and inconsistent. First he bellowed at her, then he sat in stony silence and endured her peeling the skin off his face with a razor. Now she agonized as he first struggled, then flatly refused, to eat.

He acted like a petulant child. He would sulk one minute in silence, then burst into a noisy fit of temper in the next. Every suggestion she made only seemed to frustrate him more. She wondered if maybe he wasn't just dull-witted. Not mad, just stupid.

The concept using the image of a clock face to help him find his food seemed quite beyond his grasp. Bellami finally found herself staring at him in exasperation. Even the youngest child had been easier to teach than this man! Unconsciously she scrutinized his pouting face. She looked at him dispassionately, trying to assess his rigid features, searching for some clue to his complex personality.

Thick, jet-black hair curled across his forehead. Bellami could see that even it had a tendency to be unruly. Striking emerald green eyes under black eyebrows that cut straight across his forehead. A tiny tuft of hair on each brow, near the middle. Yes, decidedly impish in nature,

Bellami caught herself thinking. Belligerent, stubborn, too handsome. Used to getting his own way, and not above using those looks to do it. She narrowed her eyes and continued her evaluation.

A long, straight nose, with just a little bump on the bridge. The full bottom lip in a defiant pout. His lean face had character—at least it did when he wasn't scowling or sneering, which wasn't often. A strong jawline tapered to a determined chin.

Bellami winced involuntarily at the raw spots scattered across his face, where she had shaved him. Maybe shaving was just a bit trickier than it looked, after all.

She still didn't understand why he didn't scream at her, at the very least. He was a walking mass of contradictions, no doubt about it. She didn't have a clue as to what made him tick. He fought her at every turn, when she was only trying to help him. Then he went and did something unexplainable, like enduring her clumsy attempt to shave him in silent forbearance—like a gentleman. It just didn't make any sense. She scanned his rugged face once again. He was really quite handsome in an unpolished sort of way. She felt heat in her face as she shook her head to clear away the muddled thoughts.

Every muscle in her back and arms cried out. She wasn't used to working like this. "I'm just tired," she whispered under her breath. If he noticed, he didn't give her any indication. Trace scowled as he continued to jab his fork into the plate. Sometimes, by accident, he hit a piece of meat.

Bellami rubbed the back of her neck with her palm, trying to relieve some of the tension. Tilly made it all look so easy at home. Her mind drifted over the whole tiring day. First she'd heated the water for his bath, then she'd struggled to empty the huge tub. It had to be done a bucket at a time, until it was light enough to drag outside.

Cleaning his room took most of the morning, and then there were the meals to cook and the cleaning up. She began to see the sheer enormity of the task before her. How long would it take Mr. O'Bannion to come to his senses and come to give her some help with this impossible man?

"Miss James." His deep voice sounded loud as cannon fire in the quiet room.

The fork in her hand clattered to the table when she jumped. "Yes, Mr. O'Bannion?" She squirmed a little, preparing herself for one of his verbal barbs.

"What color is your hair?" He wasn't looking in her direction. Instead, he was moving food around on his plate by feel.

He's mad as a hatter, she thought to herself. His family should have him committed. Bellami wondered if perhaps he might be truly dangerous. "What color is my...hair?" she repeated incredulously.

"Yes, the color." He cocked one ebony brow.

She'd heard it was better to humor people who were mentally unbalanced. "Brown," she said flatly.

"Brown? Just plain brown?" He frowned. Evidently that was not the answer he wanted to hear.

"Just plain brown. I told you before, Mr. O'Bannion, I'm no beauty." Bellami narrowed her eyes as she watched him across the table.

"It must be very long.... I mean, for your braid to hit me like that, it has to be long." His voice had a wistful, inquisitive sound to it.

Bellami shifted uncomfortably in her chair. His unpredictable nature had just thrown her for another loop. She decided to change the subject. "Mr. O'Bannion..." Her eyes slid to the neck of his shirt. Several dark, coarse curls of hair peaked out. She chided herself for noticing these little things about him.

"Yes, Miss James." He sat a little straighter.

She suddenly visualized how he must've looked as a young boy. She could picture him speaking to his schoolteacher, calling her Miss James. Very proper, very polite.

"What are those strange rugs all over the floors?" Bellami frowned as she asked the question. Only after the words left her lips did she realize how stupid it sounded.

Trace smiled. An honest, genuine smile, a hint of a dimple showed in his cheek among the razor nicks. He looked younger, more vulnerable. "Those are Navaho blankets. I use the prettiest ones for rugs, but they have a thousand other uses," he explained, his voice deep and resonant.

She couldn't help but smile out of gratitude at the way he'd answered her question. It was a silly question, but he hadn't laughed at her; in fact, he'd sounded quite gracious. Bellami found herself appreciative of his small gesture of kindness. "Please tell me about them."

Leaning back in her chair, she continued to watch the transformation taking place on the man's razor-ravaged face. He spoke softly, using his hands as he talked. He made expressive little gestures in the air. His hands were strong and lean, with long, well-formed fingers. There were calluses on them, too. Evidently he was used to hard work. She wondered what work he'd done before.

"They are woven out of wool by Indian women. Each different design tells a story. We also use them for horse blankets. There isn't a better pad under a saddle," His voice trailed off suddenly, and she saw an odd, faraway look in his jewel-colored eyes.

"Tell me about the horse, Mr. O'Bannion. Why does he run at night?" Now that Bellami had found the courage to ask her first question, they burst forth like a rain-swollen river. She wanted to know about the territory, the people, this man. Her natural curiosity was slowly overcoming her fear.

Trace's eyebrows rose in unison. A deep furrow appeared across his forehead, under the lock of black hair. "Ghost? What can I tell you about Ghost? I raised him." Pride rang in his simple statement. "He's a stallion, Miss

James. Comin' from the city, uh, I don't know how much you know about stallions and mares." A stain of color rose from his shirt to highlight his prominent cheekbones.

"Not much, I'm afraid," she admitted, feeling quite awkward and ill at ease.

"Well, ol' Ghost can smell a mare in heat, in season, for over five miles. He'd do just about anythin' to get to a mare."

Bellami was grateful he couldn't see the hot flush on her own face. She touched her hand to her forehead, surprised to find it wasn't burning with fever.

"That's the reason his corral is so high. I've seen stallions jump over fences that would hold an antelope." He stopped for a moment, and a frown appeared on his face. "But, to answer your question, he raises hell at night, I believe, because he wants to be ridden." His voice sounded melancholy.

"Why isn't he?" she inquired innocently.

The expression on his face spoke volumes. He looked both shocked and disgusted. "Miss James, I can barely get around in my own house. How in blazes do you think I can ride?"

His change in tone stung her feelings. Instead of letting the question pass, she blurted out a curt response. "I can't imagine it'd be very difficult. If you didn't leave the corral . . . well, he can still see, after all. It's not like you have to show him where to walk." Men could be so arrogant. Did he really believe his sight was necessary for the horse to get around?

"Miss James, you have a lot to learn—about horses." He rose from the table abruptly. The chair scraped on the bare wood floor, and his feet made a shuffling noise as he turned to leave the kitchen. He slowly inched his way up the dark stairs.

Trace opened the bedroom door. For a moment, he thought he was in the wrong room. The window stood wide-open and the room was cool, he felt the breeze as it flowed over him. A smell hung in the air. Lavender. The room smelled of lavender.

Thinking he must've walked too many steps from the landing, he felt for the banister, then approached the door again. He was definitely in his room, all right.

"What the hell?" His voice echoed through his empty room. "Miss James! Of course. How stupid of me to think she'd confine her attention to my body alone." Unconsciously he rubbed his palm over his raw, but relatively hairless, jaw. He moved to the window and started to slam it shut, but suddenly he stopped, allowing the clean, crisp breeze to wash over him.

"Naw, I'll leave it open. If I get too cool, I'll sleep under the blankets for a change," he muttered to himself.

Turning away from the window, he shuffled to his bed. He stripped off his shirt and pants and nearly dropped them on the floor. Instead, on impulse, he tossed them over the end of the footboard.

"Damned woman! She's already makin' changes in my house and me." For an instant, he thought about throwing the clothes on the floor just for spite, but changed his mind. It rankled him to realize that he actually cared what she thought about him. *Why should I? All she's done since Pa dumped her here is act like an iron-assed drill sergeant.* He wished Clell would come back; they'd have a lot in common. Both of the old fools seem to enjoy chewing his ass off. With a snort, he threw back the covers and climbed into bed.

Trace lay on his back with his arm curled under his head, listening to the night sounds. A bullbat swooped by and he heard the distinctive sound of its mouth closing as it captured insects. A pack of coyotes yipped somewhere in the distance. The clean sheets were stiff, and the smell of the lavender made him nervous. It was such a female smell. Unwelcome thoughts of Becky made him clench his jaw

until it ached. He forced himself to think of something
else, but thoughts of Miss Bellami James made him cuss
under his breath. He tried to concentrate on something
that didn't upset him—something not having anything to
do with females. Slowly, his eyes drooped closed.

The night silence settled around her after Mr. O'Bannion slammed his bedroom door. It was late, very late.
Tomorrow would probably be worse than today. Bellami
grimaced involuntarily at the thought. When she allowed
her eyes to scan the wreckage of the empty kitchen, she
groaned.

"Oh, Tilly, I wish I'd packed you in my trunks," she
wailed. "I promise, when I get home, I'll be more appreciative of what you do." It seemed at least a century had
passed since she'd been in the comfort of her home.

Rolling up her sleeves, she poured hot water from the
reservoir of the wood-burning stove. After she washed and
dried all the dishes, she put them away. Several trips later,
she had stacked enough firewood for tomorrow morning.
Finally she picked up the kerosene lamp to light her way to
her room.

Bellami was completely exhausted by the time she pulled
off her stained, dirty work dress. The smell of lavender
clung comfortingly to the clean cotton gown as she slipped
it over her head. When she slipped between the cool sheets,
a contented sigh escaped her lips. Never had a bed felt
softer. She closed her eyes and breathed deeply, pretending she was home. Visions of a hot, steaming bath flitted
through her fantasy.

"Tomorrow," she vowed aloud, "I'll find the time to
take a bath if it kills me." She couldn't remember ever
having gone so long without a bath or washing her long
hair. Bellami decided the worst thing about this place—
even worse than Mr. O'Bannion himself—was the fact she
couldn't take a hot, comforting bath. With a sigh, she

turned over on her side and pulled the blanket up to her chin.

The sound of Ghost's piercing scream jarred Bellami awake with a start. Trembling from the abrupt waking, she lay still and listened for a moment. Her heart pounded loudly in her chest, as it could only in a strange, dark bedroom, in the middle of the night. Finally, her curiosity forced her from the warm security of the bed. She tossed the covers back, with a snort of disgust for her weakness. Her bare feet squeaked on the smooth wooden floor as she approached the window. Peering into the darkness outside, she beheld an eerie sight.

In the moonlight, the gray horse's body seemed to flow like liquid. Instead of moving, he appeared to evaporate from one position to another in the crisp night air.

She was so mesmerized by him that she wasn't immediately aware of the figure standing on the balcony several yards away, until a slight movement caught her eye. She turned her head and saw Trace standing at his own window. He'd been listening to the horse while she watched.

Bellami stepped back inside her room quickly, but something pulled at her. Almost against her will, she allowed her eyes to return and focus on the man's form. His body was stiff with concentration. Except for the steady rise and fall of his chest as he inhaled, he could have been carved from stone. Her eyes followed the dim but definite outline of his body. Heat flooded her face.

He was naked. She couldn't make out any specific details in the muted light. Only patches of light and dark were discernible. She could, however, see the paleness of his legs and narrow hips where the sun had not browned him. Dark hair, fanning out from his flat stomach, shimmered in the silvery light. Against her better judgment she allowed herself to become more and more curious about the sullen man. He was almost as intriguing as the restless horse below her.

When Ghost unexpectedly shattered the silence with an eerie scream, the muscles in Trace's chest and shoulders bunched up.

Bellami almost felt sorry for him at that moment. Almost, but not quite. She wasn't about to forgive his abuse that easy.

He had problems, but no more than anyone else. She stepped back inside the bedroom as she reminded herself that Trace O'Bannion was spoiled and cruel—and her pupil.

Bellami gritted her teeth against the morning sun. It seemed like she'd just gone to bed. Would she ever feel rested again? She recalled hearing, somewhere, something about the West being great for men and dogs, but hell on women and horses. Rubbing her sore back, she was positive she knew what it meant.

With stern resignation, she put on her soiled work dress. Ignoring her aching muscles, she walked down the stairs. Her thighs burned and protested with each descending step.

The fire in the stove caught easily, and as she had yesterday, she put the coffee on to boil in the graniteware pot. While it boiled, she gathered the eggs. Only four this morning—but still enough for breakfast. She cast a wishful gaze at the big wooden tub in the lean-to, making herself a promise. She'd have that bath, later.

Trace heard her get up and go downstairs. "Damned industrious little ant." He wanted to lie there and ignore her, but he couldn't. Why he let her needle him so much, he didn't know. "Miss High-and-mighty Spinster. Cool, efficient—yep, like a piece of old crusty snow," he muttered while he rose from the bed. He reached for his clothes on the footboard of the bed and dressed quickly. It made it much easier to dress, not having to search through piles of discarded shirts and pants.

"Hate to admit it, but her neat-as-a-pin ways do help," he mumbled, chaffing at his brief spell of neatness. He grinned in satisfaction when he discovered, quite by accident, that holding the bottom of his shirt together and buttoning from bottom to top, he finally got it straight. "Much better than the other way." He always seemed to end up with three extra buttonholes hanging on one side.

The room still held the faint clean fragrance of lavender, of *her*. Trace wanted to grumble about it, but actually, he'd slept well. The odor hadn't bothered him nearly as much as he'd thought it would. The smell of coffee hit him as he shuffled noisily down the stairs. His stomach growled, and the noise sounded loud enough to bring down the roof. He sensed the room was empty the moment he entered. Being alone smoothed his ruffled feathers, a bit. He shuffled to the hooks on the wall and located a cup. Clumsily he found the pot. He'd just started pouring coffee for himself when she walked in.

"Good morning," she said crisply and she scooted past him, scrunching up her body to avoid any physical contact with him. Positioned near the door as he was, she had to turn slightly sideways to keep from brushing against the back of his thighs.

He winced involuntarily at the sound of her voice. God, did she always wake up in a good mood, or did the prospect of torturing him make her happy? Trace grunted in response to her greeting, concentrating on the cup he was balancing.

He didn't fill the cup till it ran over. She took that as a good omen. Bellami also saw he was fully dressed, wearing Levi's and a shirt—a vast improvement in his morning attire. If she had about a century to work on him, he might actually begin to look civilized.

"Miss James." His voice overflowed with exasperation when he finally spoke.

"Yes, Mr. O'Bannion?" Bellami was wary; he'd had that sound in his voice again.

"Tell me, who do you pattern your behavior after? Napoleon or Caesar?" He leaned against the table with one lean hip and cocked a dark, impish eyebrow as he sipped the hot coffee.

"I knew it! I just knew it!" She exploded without warning, like a shot from a rifle. She slammed the basket of eggs down on the table with a dull thud. One broke, and the clear liquid oozed out. Her control shattered as easily as the fragile shell. "I knew your civility last night had to be my imagination. Obviously, I was correct. I see you have returned to normal," she hissed.

Trace turned a little in her direction. His mouth curled up in an expression of amusement. "Damned if you don't have some spunk," he said, and choked on his next sip of coffee. It took some effort, but he managed not to bust out laughing. He really couldn't say why he enjoyed baiting and badgering her so much. Maybe 'cause she was so goldang entertaining. He suddenly felt almost cheerful this morning. Probably the fresh hot coffee.

"Miss James, for a spinster, you make a dang good cup of coffee." With a quiet chuckle, he threw a leg over the chair he found with his free hand, and sat down at the table.

Breakfast proceeded quickly. Bellami slammed and banged her way through bacon and eggs. She barked at him, in a tone any brigadier general would've envied, as she gave him an outline of his schedule of instruction.

"The first thing," she said in a voice that brooked no argument, "is for you to learn to walk. Not shuffle, but walk!"

Trace shoved food in his mouth to keep from grinning. "Yes, ma'am. Anythin' you say, ma'am."

"Oh, you are—" Bellami never finished her sentence. She slammed out the back door muttering under her breath.

Trace walked and walked, until he was ready to kick Miss Bellami James's ass right out the back door. His boots scraped and thudded on the bare wood floor. Often he caught the toe of one under the edge of a rug and stumbled. Several times he caught himself on a piece of furniture. More times than that, he barked his shins on the furniture and spent the next several minutes spewing a string of oaths.

"I feel like a Missouri mule kicked me. How much longer?" He rubbed the front of one long leg. "Miss James, hasn't anyone told you? Men out here don't walk if they can ride." His lips twisted ironically. "'Course, I can't ride, so maybe this is justice." He snorted.

She could stand it no more. She sat down heavily in a soft, comfortable chair in the parlor and looked at his face. A thin sheen of sweat glistened above his brows. A lock of ebony hair had fallen forward.

"Mr. O'Bannion, did you have this house built?" For some strange reason, she had to fight the urge to brush the hair away from his sightless eyes.

"Yes, I did, Miss James." There was a melancholy sound in his voice. He rubbed at his leg unconsciously.

"Do you have any recollection of the dimensions of the rooms?" She bit her lip, willing her hand to keep away from his forehead.

"What the hell kind of question is that?" He stopped rubbing his shin and stood up straight, staring blindly toward the sound of her voice. He brushed impatiently at the strand of hair.

Bellami sighed in relief when the ebony lock was back in place. She looked to heaven for guidance and took a deep breath. "Mr. O'Bannion, if you know how big the rooms are and where the furniture is, why on earth do you stop walking four feet from the wall? Didn't you ever come downstairs in the night, in the dark?'' She spoke louder and louder with each word, and by the time she finished she was yelling at the top of her lungs.

Trace opened his mouth, then shut it and opened it again. He blinked twice and rubbed his hand through his hair. "Yeah, I did.''

Bellami smiled. At last. She'd finally made a breakthrough. Maybe there was hope. "Mr. O'Bannion, that will be enough for this morning.'' She dismissed him curtly. Best not to tempt fate too much. He might find his vile tongue again if she persisted.

Trace felt like a schoolboy. And her general's voice was getting mighty tiresome. He wanted to give her a sharp retort, but before he could think of something cutting to say, she left.

"Damn little general. Well, fine,'' he yelled at her retreating footsteps, "I'll go talk to Ghost!'' He turned and took three confident strides, then hesitated and slowed to a shuffle.

Bellami filled all the buckets and put them on to boil while she dragged the heavy tub into the kitchen. She would have a bath and wash her hair if hell froze over, as Mr. O'Bannion would no doubt say. Trace had gone to the corral, and she expected he'd stay there sulking until dinnertime. She hoped he would, anyway. She needed some peace.

She dug deep into her trunks until she found her favorite scented soap and a pair of clean drawers. It occurred to her, with no little measure of chagrin, that she would have to wash clothes soon. The thought brought an involuntary groan to her lips.

She brought her brush and comb down from her room. When she had everything laid out neatly on the kitchen table, she filled the tub with the hot water. By the time she had heated and filled the tub, all her muscles were crying out in rebellion at the strenuous task being done twice in as many days. As quickly as she could manage, she stripped off her clothes. She eased herself stiffly into the water. It felt so good.

Eagerly she unbraided her hair, watching it float down into the steaming water. She fit fairly well into the big tub. The water covered nearly all of her breasts, and only a tiny bit of her knees stuck out above the water. She savored the feeling of peace. Rubbing her sore muscles, she felt the tension leaving her body.

Cupping her hands, she scooped up water and wet her long hair. Then she vigorously soaped it. Scrubbing hard at her scalp with her fingers, she quickly produced a good lather. A froth of bubbles surrounded her face. Round bubbles slithered down her cheeks, dripping off her chin.

She wiped the suds away from her cheeks. No doubt about it, this had to be sheer heaven. Before she knew it, soap was running into her eyes. It stung like the very devil. The more she wiped at it, the worse it got. She had so much soap in the water, she sat surrounded by white froth and bubbles.

"Oh, damn," she whimpered aloud, using uncharacteristic profanity. Mr. O'Bannion was having an unpleasant effect on her already.

"Is there anything I can do, Miss James?" The voice came from the doorway, dripping with sarcasm.

Bellami jumped, splashing water over the rim of the tub onto the wooden floor. "What are you doing here?" she gasped.

"I live here, remember?"

Bellami opened her eyes enough to peek at him. Trace stood in the doorway between the kitchen and the parlor with his arms folded across his chest. She wanted to keep an eye on him, to see what he was doing, but more soap ran into her eyes.

She squinted them shut against the burning sting of strong soap. "Ouch! Oh!" She wriggled around, trying to find a towel, but she couldn't reach the things she'd brought down.

"Miss James, will you please tell me what's wrong?" Genuine concern rang in his deep voice.

"I have soap in my eyes, that's what." She hated to admit something so stupid to him. Now he'd think worse of her than he already did. No, it would be impossible for him to do that.

"Please, let me help you, Miss James," he purred as his boots hit the floor in determined, steady strides.

She knew. She heard him walking toward her, and heard the rasping sound of the hand pump, and she knew. She knew exactly what he was doing and why. But he was faster than she'd expected, faster than she'd thought he could be. Before she could rise from the tub, cold water flowed over her head and down her body. Her nipples contracted at the shock of the cold water.

Trace heard her astonished gasp and the sharp intake of breath. A chuckle bubbled from his chest. He was quite pleased with his revenge. "Would you like a towel, or will you dry here in the air?" There was laughter in his deep voice as he repeated her own blunt words back to her.

"A towel would be nice. *If* you can manage," she snapped sarcastically.

Trace stopped chuckling, and his back stiffened. A grim line replaced the playful curve of his lips. He felt his way along the backs of the chairs. When he located the towel, he thrust it out roughly, toward the sound of her voice. "Damn you! Don't you ever miss an opportunity to remind me I'm half a man? I know it—you can save yourself the trouble," he bit out bitterly in the direction of the small sloshing sounds. Towel in hand, he shot out his arm and brushed his knuckles across Bellami's full breast and hard erect nipple. He froze, and a half-uttered word stuck in his throat.

At first he didn't realize what had happened, but the soft flesh against his hand became recognizable almost instantly. He heard her gasp and he felt her tremble as he turned his wrist slightly palm up. Then he rubbed the back of his hand all along her breast as he took his hand away.

Bellami shuddered, and grabbed the towel.

He slowly allowed his hand to drop away, holding it at his thigh. Curiosity flamed to life within Trace O'Bannion. He had formed a mental picture of what Bellami James looked like, based on ... what?

That she said she was ugly? Yes. That she was a spinster? Yes. The fact that she acted like a domineering witch? Hell, yes!

Still, something wasn't right. Trace had good instincts. A lawman had to. Right now, his instincts were screaming at him, and he couldn't figure out why. But he was damned sure going to find out!

Trace went to his room, where he paced back and forth like a penned-up cougar. Miss Bellami James invaded his thoughts, and he couldn't get her out of them. The moment he touched her, his slumbering senses sprang to life. Some dormant part of him had been roused. A keen awareness had crept from his hand to his brain, and now it gnawed at his gut like an insatiable hunger.

Frustrated, he realized he knew absolutely nothing about her, save the fact she had worked for twelve years in a hospital in New York City. He'd smugly assumed she was a dried-up, old spinster. Her tongue was as sharp as an ax blade; he'd reasoned it had been honed on lonely nights and unfulfilled dreams. Frowning, he stopped his pacing near the open window. The night air washed over his burning body. Trace wasn't a man who liked to make mistakes; he hated being wrong. When her warm flesh touched his hand, he knew he'd been wrong, all right, dead wrong!

The flesh his hand connected with had been anything but dried-up and old. It had been soft, warm, yielding. Inviting.

Trace felt something hot expand within his chest and his groin. For the first time in many months, Trace O'Bannion felt the drives of a man—a whole man. The fact that he was surrounded by darkness didn't do a thing to curb his lust or dispel the image of firm, warm flesh. Running his long, lean fingers through his hair, he laughed. The irony of the situation tickled him. Damned if this wasn't funny, in a twisted sort of way. A woman he couldn't stand, couldn't see, who openly declared she was ugly, made him hard and hot as a poker!

His worn Levi's felt tight and uncomfortable on his turgid sex. He tugged at his pants, and tried to accommodate the swelling, without success. With razor-sharp awareness, he opened his door and stepped out onto the landing.

Bellami wiped the water from her face. She was alone, but his presence hung in the air as surely as if he were standing right in front of her. She'd never felt anything like that before in her life. His touch was unsettling, to say the least. When the accident happened, Bellami had just started noticing boys, and they her. When she left the hospital and came home, all of that had changed. Forever.

No one had looked at her with that kind of interest ever again. She'd had no experience in her life to prepare her for the kind of physical shock Trace O'Bannion's touch gave her. The innocent contact had been so intense it was almost painful. She wondered what it would be like if she touched him back. Bellami wondered about the magical ingredient between men and women. Brooks seemed to have a devastating effect on women, and she'd seen the way Ross looked at her sister Claire sometimes.

Was this why? Did something as chaste as a simple touch of the hand bring such pleasure? She puzzled over it for a minute, then pushed the thought away.

Bellami James would never know the answer to that mysterious question. She'd resigned herself to that many years ago, and she only invited pain and frustration by allowing her mind to conjure up such images.

Mr. Trace O'Bannion was a job, nothing more, nothing less. To begin questioning her place in life could only invite disaster and heartache. Bellami took a deep breath and pushed the questions to the back of her mind. She locked them safely away with all the painful memories she kept stored there. For many years she'd refused to examine her thoughts and feelings about herself—about the scar—and she could continue to do it for many more.

Wrapping the towel around her wet body, she picked up her clean drawers and chemise. The soft white lawn felt good against her skin. She'd picked out the frilliest ones she owned, embroidered and trimmed with narrow pink ribbon. Bellami felt less ugly when she wore pretty underthings. Her hair and her frilly feminine underthings were the two little vanities she allowed herself. She wasn't quite sure why, but she needed to feel less ugly right now—needed it badly. A niggling question tried to form in her mind, but again she closed herself against it.

Dressed in her soft clean underclothes, she looked at the mess in the kitchen. Water dripped from the ends of her long, wet hair. It dampened the front of her chemise, making the fabric cling to her skin. With grim resignation she started the whole laborious process in reverse.

First she scooped bucket after bucket of water from the huge wooden tub until it was light enough to drag out the back door to dump. Then she used the damp toweling to sop up water from the floor. Each time she wrung the cloth out, she cursed Trace O'Bannion for startling her. If he hadn't done it, she wouldn't have such a mess to clean up.

It gave her some comfort to be able to lay one more black sin at his feet.

By the time she restored order to the kitchen, at least two hours had passed. She felt fatigue deep in her body and her mind. Her long hair was only slightly damp but the breeze from outside chilled her. Gooseflesh rose on her arms, and she shuddered. She sat down in front of the cookstove and opened up the heavy iron door. Pulling a chair as close to the stove as she could get, she started working out the tangles in her hair while it dried. The heat from the fire dried the chemise quickly, leaving it plastered to her body like a second skin. Working her fingers through her tangled mane, she absently watched the flames dance and sway through her dark veil of hair.

Trace felt different, like a great ravenous beast on the trail of wounded prey. He felt the stairs beneath his boots, the smoothness of the banister. The familiar odors of his house filled his nose. Along with a new smell, the smell of *her*.

Lavender wafted up the staircase, and he stopped for a moment to close his sightless eyes. He allowed the sensation to drift over him, cover him. He smelled her, felt her, sensed her being—as if she were with him on the stairs. Miss James might be an ugly spinster, but the feeling her presence gave him right this minute affected him like warm summer sunshine. Trace gloried in it. He let it surround him and lift him. He opened his eyes and continued down the stairs toward that unseen radiance.

Bellami flipped her hair over her head. The day had been warm, but tonight was chilly. Her hair dried quickly, and she enjoyed the play of light across it from the open stove. A thread of electricity sizzled up her spine. She felt him before she ever heard him. He wasn't shuffling tonight. For the first time, she felt truly fearful of Trace O'Bannion. Not in the usual way—this was not fear of his insults, but something quite different. She could see him out of the corner of her eye through the strands of hair. Shock rippled through Bellami, hit her like the bucket of cold water. He might be blind, but Trace O'Bannion was still a man. Ruthless, selfish and probably dangerous. Bellami shrank from him, trying to make herself small, so small she might just disappear. She pictured the great gray stallion outside. She saw a certain cunning grace in Mr. O'Bannion's movements, like that stallion's.

What had he said? Ghost would do *anything* to get to a mare. She didn't like this man one bit, and now she saw him as a threat of a totally different kind. He had proven to her how strong he was when he grabbed her by the shoulders. Bellami vowed never to make that mistake again. She was going to make sure Trace O'Bannion never got close enough to put his hands on her again.

Rising from the chair, she made sure she kept it between them. Since she was barefoot, he didn't hear her. A tiny, predatory smile teased the corners of his mouth.

What a fool I am, she thought to herself. What did she really know about this man? Nothing, and what she'd learned since she'd come here didn't speak well of his character at all. The memory of his accidental touch made the pit of her stomach drop like a stone.

Trace listened for her breathing. She was moving away from him. The room nearly crackled with her fear and her tension.

Why? Did she fear him? Maybe he had been a little hard on her—a little rude and nasty. All right, damned hard on her, but he hadn't done anything to make her truly afraid. Had he? A cold knot of disgust formed in Trace's chest. Weeks of self-pity and whining flashed through his mind. What had he allowed himself to become?

"Miss James?" He made a real effort to sound friendly, not threatening. Instead, he thought with chagrin, he only sounded hungry. Like a wolf, closing in on a newborn lamb. The image filled him with more self-loathing. He deserved it, after what he'd been putting his family through.

Bellami went stiff. He was trying to sound nice. Dread crept up her spine. "Yes," she answered softly.

His head turned a little more in her direction. Narrowing in on her like an eagle on a field mouse.

She shivered.

Trace didn't know what to say. He really only wanted to hear the sound of her voice, maybe talk with her awhile. Actually, he'd hoped he might discover some clue about her age. Something about her, anything, to help dispel this burning curiosity, to quench his burning lust.

"Did you want something, Mr. O'Bannion?" Bellami saw him hesitating, but instead of reassuring her, it made her more wary.

"No. No, I just wasn't sleepy. I'm sorry I bothered you." He frowned as he turned to leave the kitchen. His boots thudded as he steadily climbed the stairs.

When he was gone, she sagged into a chair. Bellami knew she was near the end of her strength. It had been a long day, and she was more than ready for sleep. She picked up the kerosene lantern and gathered her things into her arms. It was awkward, with brush, comb, soap and dirty clothes, carrying the lantern.

When she was directly outside his bedroom door, the silver-backed brush fell out of her hands onto the floor with a noisy clatter. Instantly his door flew open.

"Miss James, are you all right?" Trace had been in the processing of undressing. He wore only his half-buttoned Levi's and socks. The moonlight silhouetted his lithe body in the doorway. Light from the lamp danced along the hard planes of his chest. Dark, silky hair shimmered as cold night air from his open window rushed past him.

Bellami's nipples contracted at the sudden change in temperature. She felt vulnerable and self-conscious and entirely too aware of him. "Yes. Yes, I'm fine. I'm sorry

I disturbed you," Bellami snapped shortly in her distress. Her voice sounded so shrewish. His eyebrows knit into a frown at the sound of it. He brought out the worst in her every time.

Gathering up her fallen brush, she turned to go to her room. He remained in the doorway. She wished he would go inside and shut it. Bellami took another step toward her room.

"Miss James, tell me about your accident." Trace didn't know where the request had come from.

The whole world began to tilt in front of Bellami. The breath whooshed from her lungs. She couldn't breathe. Sweat beaded across her forehead, even though she'd been cool a moment before. A huge lump had grown in her throat, and she thought she might faint. Clumsily she grabbed for the banister and dropped everything but the lamp. Her grip around it tightened as she struggled to remain on her feet. Memories and unwanted feelings tried to break through the barrier she'd kept up for so long. Suddenly strong hands grabbed her around the waist.

"Miss James." His voice was soft and compassionate.

"Don't! Don't touch me," she said, wrenching her body free and stumbling back a step to look him in the face. He had frozen where he was on the stairs.

The force of her words hit Trace like a fist. God! He disgusted her! He dropped his hands from her like they'd been burned. Trace had never imagined it was possible to elicit such revulsion from a woman. "Sorry, I was only tryin' to help. I should've known better. Please, rest easy, I won't touch you again." He stomped back to his room, slamming the door with a bang.

Bellami relaxed instantly. Well, at least things were back to normal. This she could deal with. His verbal abuse she could handle. Just as long as he didn't ask about her accident. She must not allow herself to think about the accident and the guilt and the pain.

Trembling, she took the lantern into her room, then went back to the landing to retrieve her things. She could hear the rhythm of pacing footfalls coming from inside his room.

Bellami imagined he would look just like his horse. Silver moonlight falling across his lean chest. He would appear more liquid than solid, like something in a dream. She shook her head to clear away the thoughts. This was a bitter, unbalanced man. She had to remember that. Yet his voice had sounded so full of compassion and pity for her, only moments ago. Bellami James knew with every fiber of her being that Trace O'Bannion was dangerous to her. But just how dangerous, she couldn't have said.

Chapter Seven

The horses pawed the ground impatiently. Bright light sculpted three weathered faces shadowed by wide-brimmed Stetsons.

"Gettin' warm early for March, ain't it?" Hugh remarked to no one in particular. A meadowlark sang nearby.

"Yep. How long are we goin' to sit here watchin' this house, Pa?" A large-boned hand reached inside a shirt pocket and pulled out a small bag. Flynn took a thin paper out of it, then made a crimp down the middle. Holding the paper steady, he shook a bit of tobacco into it, tapping the paper with one free finger to settle it in the middle. White teeth pulled the yellow drawstring on the bag closed. With deft precision, he rolled the cigarette and licked it along the edge to seal it. After he put the makings back in his shirt, he struck a match on the cantle of his saddle.

"We're stayin' as long as it takes, and I don't want to hear any more about goin' down there and takin' Miss James to the train." Hugh glowered at Flynn and shifted his weight in the saddle. The mare he rode snorted as a long-legged jackrabbit sprinted from behind a clump of sage.

"That's a nasty habit, boy." Clell never took his eyes off the house below them as he spoke to Flynn.

"Well, you ought to know. You're the one taught me how to roll 'em." Flynn laughed. Dimples creased his weathered face. The smoke curled around the brim of his hat.

"Look, there she is." Hugh raised up in his stirrups to get a better look. All three men concentrated on the figure moving around the yard below.

"Look at her hair. I never would've guessed it'd be so long," Clell said, with unabashed admiration in his voice.

"At least she is still kickin'. You suppose Trace is doin' as well?" Hugh asked. He wrinkled his face in concern.

Flynn didn't answer as he continued to watch the woman. The morning breeze lifted the edge of her skirt as she walked. She tossed scratch to the chickens as she neared Ghost's corral. For a moment, she stood touching the gray stallion's nose, and then she went back inside. The door reopened almost immediately, and she reappeared carrying something in her arms.

"Now what do you suppose she's doin'?" Clell found himself growing mighty curious about the woman. Bellami walked from the corner of the house to the chicken coop and paused. It looked like she was tying something, but again she returned to the house. This time she came out carrying a large bundle heaped in a basket. The men watched while she placed wet clothes across the makeshift line she'd just made.

"Canny little thing, ain't she?" Hugh chuckled, mesmerized by her ingenuity. He was beginning to see why Doc Malone thought so highly of her.

"Pa, I still say this ain't right," Flynn said. "Besides, looks to me like she's doin' the chores. How can you be sure Trace is gettin' all the trainin' you're so hell-bent to give him?"

The kitchen door opened, and Trace stepped outside into the sun. Blue-black highlights glimmered in his clean, relatively neat hair.

"I'll be damned," Clell said with awe, "she's managed to get him cleaned him up! That's a damn sight more than I'd been able to do. I wish I knew how she did it," he mused, rubbing his hand pensively over his own scruffy chin.

Hugh felt relief and a slight lessening of his own guilt over what he'd done. It had been three days since they'd abandoned Bellami James, and he'd been almost afraid to hope.

Flynn's eyes narrowed thoughtfully as he watched Trace speaking to Bellami. Flynn couldn't tell what he was saying, but his brother appeared to be mad. "Looks like he's givin' her a piece of his mind, don't it?" he drawled, with a slight smirk on his face.

Turning on his heel, Trace stomped back to the house, stumbling once. He slammed the door hard enough for them to hear it from their vantage point on the little hill.

"Appears she's got him a bit riled," Hugh said, his eyes widening. "Wonder if she'll go after him." His dimples creased his clean-shaven cheeks for an instant.

If Bellami James cared a bit, she didn't show it. She kept on hanging wet drawers, wet Levi's and shirts across the line.

Flynn liked this Bellami James and, as much as he hated to admit it, Hugh seemed to be right. Trace looked healthy enough, and if she was making him mad, then she was probably making progress. Reining his horse around he put out his cigarette with his thumb and forefinger.

"I am goin' to Magdalena, Pa. I may be gone for several days. You two can keep an eye on this without my help. She looks fine to me."

Hugh looked at his son for a minute; Flynn troubled him. He might be giving in right now, but it wasn't like

Flynn to let go of a notion so easily. He needed to be watched carefully. "Shane and Logan are goin' to move some cattle, end of the week. You be back to help?"

Flynn grinned at his father, he was so easy to read. They didn't need his help. Hell, Missy alone could outrope two seasoned cowboys, Hugh just wanted him around so he could keep an eye on him for a while, but didn't want to come right out and say so.

"Sure, Pa. I'll be back in plenty of time." Flynn put his spurs to his big gelding, and the horse moved out.

Flynn was well out of sight when Clell turned to Hugh and narrowed his brown eyes. "You know, I think he feels real protective of that lady down there."

"I know," Hugh said, sighing, "but I'm countin' on him leavin' things be for a while. You know, what he needs is a woman of his own to fuss over. I sure thought he'd be married before now."

"He does seem to be kinda slow. You had Flynn and Trace both by the time you were thirty." Clell agreed as he watched a crane settle awkwardly on the water near Trace's house.

"You know, Clell. I blame you for Flynn bein' such a mother hen," Hugh stated accusingly.

"Me? Just 'cause I let those boys know how a proper lady is supposed to be treated?" Clell declared indignantly.

"Proper lady? You never spent time with a proper lady in your life!" Hugh guffawed as he turned his horse and kicked her into a gallop.

"In this country, any woman is a lady, as I've heard you tell them boys more 'n once," Clell said as his horse passed Hugh's.

Trace was fuming. This morning Miss Bellami James had given him the usual instructions, then made herself scarce. As he fumbled around the parlor, she'd been busy doing something. What he didn't know, but she sounded like she might be tearing down the kitchen. The hand pump screeched furiously. The steady gruff humming sound grated on his nerves. Finally he realized she was washing. Washing! Was the woman trying to kill herself? All she did was work, day in and day out. Besides, wasn't she supposed to be helping him? She hadn't been any help to him at all. If his family had brought her here to train him, then that was what she should be doing. He barked his shins on a large chair.

"Damn," he moaned as he bent over to rub the smarting leg. "Little general, that's all she is. If she keeps doin' all the chores, and insists on regular baths and clean clothes, she'll be dead before the week is out." He ranted in rhythm to his unsteady steps. He stopped in the middle of the parlor and rubbed his sore, razor-nicked jaw. Maybe if she did drop stone dead, he'd have some peace. The thought brought a brief flash of a smile to his lips. As quickly, a dark scowl descended.

"Then what good will she be? The sooner the little general gets me trained, the sooner she can get back to New York. Got to see she stays healthy," he muttered as he slumped in the chair. Something had to be done. But what?

Until Clell or somebody from the ranch came by, they were totally alone. Cold fear gripped Trace from out of nowhere. What if something really did happen to her? His wish of a few moments ago was now forgotten, as cold reality settled over him. The little general might act like an iron-ass, but she was flesh and blood. Warm flesh and blood, as he well knew.

"God, Pa, what on earth can you be thinkin' of? You've got a damn sight better sense than that," Trace muttered. "Clell or somebody should at least be keepin' an eye on her. Hell, what if she broke a leg or somethin'." Suddenly a grin softened Trace's grim countenance. The sly old fox!

Of course they'd be keeping an eye on her! He rose from the chair and took two quick steps before he connected with the corner of a small pine table.

"Son of a—" he moaned, grabbing his smarting shin.

By lunchtime Bellami felt like she was going to fall over. So much washing really should have been a two-day job, but she'd done it in four hours. Her knuckles were red and scraped raw from the washboard. She grimaced as she touched the broken nails on her right hand. Breakfast, dishes, gathering eggs and cleaning had chapped her hands.

"Tilly, if you could see me now," she muttered as she rubbed the small of her back. A muscle twinge made her purse her lips. She was feeling light-headed when she slumped into a kitchen chair. Her head felt so heavy. She laid her forehead on her arms on top of the scrubbed pine table. She promised herself she'd rest—just for a minute.

Trace stumbled out the front door to the porch, trying to visualize the lay of the land around his house. If he was spying on his own house, where would he do it from?

The rise.

It hit him like a bolt of lightning. They were probably up there right now, the crazy old coots!

He starting walking up the little hillock overlooking his house. A small growth of yucca caught his boot and sent him sprawling to the ground.

"Pa, when I get my hands on you . . ." Trace didn't finish his threat. A picture of how he must look flashed through his brain. It tickled him. Why, he couldn't imagine, and that tickled him, too. He laughed heartily at himself as he crawled up off the ground. He chuckled while he brushed the dirt from his pants.

"Guess I'll have to take the little general's advice and pick up my feet when I walk."

About a quarter of a mile away from the house, Trace caught the familiar smell of leather, horse sweat and tobacco.

"Clell? Pa? I know you're there." He stopped and slipped a thumb into his belt loop, cocking one hip.

Leather creaked as the man shifted in his saddle. If Trace had still had his sight, he would've appreciated the look of pride shining in the old cowboy's eyes.

"Come on, answer me. Quit tryin' to act like some damn Apache, sneakin' around spyin' on people, and come to the house." He heard the unmistakable dry cackle and knew it was Clell, not his father.

"Smart ass," Clell growled. "It's good to see you beginnin' to use some of your God-given horse sense, agin'." Clell noticed the network of tiny nicks on Trace's smooth face. "What shaved you, boy, a bobcat?" he asked, trying to suppress the side-splitting guffaw threatening to erupt.

"Miss James. Same as a bobcat," Trace said, shifting his weight a little in embarrassment.

"So, you figured out I was up here, huh?" Clell leaned comfortably on his saddle horn. The little brown mare grazed contentedly.

"Finally dawned on me, you wouldn't leave that woman at my mercy without keepin' an eye on things."

"I knew you weren't stupid. If you'd showed up sooner, you could've spoke with your pa. He left for the ranch a bit ago." Clell watched Trace with interest.

"I'm sorry I missed him. I'd like to know what the hell he thinks he is doin'—with Miss James, I mean."

"Figures she can teach you what you need to know. Also figures if he gives you any kinda choice you'll be too damned hard to manage." Clell was grinning broadly. "So, he didn't give you a choice."

Trace thought about that for a minute. His father's logic made a lot of sense. Still, she needed to go. If she stayed, something might happen. Something beyond Trace's control. The memory of warm, wet flesh made him squirm for a minute. No, she had to go, that was all there was to it. Trace cleared his throat and raised his chin in the direction of Clell's voice. "Well, I'd like for you to get her out of here."

"No can do, Trace. Your pa would have my hide." Clell watched Trace closely. He sure didn't act like Clell's refusal bothered him all that much. In fact, he almost looked relieved—mighty relieved, in fact.

Trace frowned. He was happy Clell had refused. Now why would he be happy? He wanted that woman out of his life and his house—didn't he? "I'll tell you one thing, Clell, if she keeps goin' like she is you won't have to worry about it—we'll have a dead teacher on our hands. She needs some help."

"You almost sound like you care, Trace." Clell frowned as he watched the conflicting emotions flicker through Trace's sightless eyes. The boy was fighting a war within himself, plain as day. Clell did see a change in Trace, the way he moved and acted, but he wasn't convinced it was anything permanent, not yet. This could be a sly trick. Hugh was probably right. If Trace could find a way out of this training, he would. Miss James would have to stay, whether either one of them wanted it or not. Funny thing, though, Trace didn't act all that disappointed she was staying.

Clell hated being a part of this whole deception, but if it helped Trace, then he guessed it was worth it. Still, pangs of conscience bothered him every time he thought about all those letters he'd sent to Doc in New York. If he hadn't persuaded Doc to suggest Bellami James to Hugh, she wouldn't be here now. He hoped Hugh wouldn't find out about his meddling. "What needs done?" Clell asked with a little sigh of resignation.

Trace frowned. He looked like he was thinking awful hard about the answer. "Just little things. Firewood, meals, the laundry. She never stops. Hell, she near worked herself to death just to empty the damned bathtub."

Clell rubbed the grizzled stubble on his chin. "Now, after all the money and fuss you went to installin' that fancy porcelain tub in the house, why would she have to do that, Trace?"

The smile on Trace's face was genuine and mischievous. "Well, I ain't told her there's a tub. Don't intend to, either. Not yet, anyway."

Laughter boomed across the prairie. Clell would love to be a fly on the wall when those two were going at it! Yes, indeed he would. Looked like Miss James was all they'd hoped for—and more. Trace was coming back, all right, or at least his sense of humor was.

"I'll see what I can do about those little chores," Clell said when he finally quit chuckling.

Trace walked beside Clell's horse as they came down the hill. The older man noticed he was moving with more confidence.

"Come on down to the house. You haven't met my angel of mercy, have you?" There was a tone of sarcasm in his voice, and something else—something elusive.

"No, I haven't met her. Your pa got me out of here so fast, I never even got a good look at her. She was wearin' the damnedest hat I ever laid eyes on!"

"Hat, huh? She says she's ugly. Maybe her face is truly a fright." Trace felt the burning heat of curiosity taking over again. He didn't want to be curious about the little general. He didn't like her, he didn't need her. He damned well didn't want to, either. She was a tyrant, and he wanted Clell to get her out of there. Didn't he?

Clell hesitated, pulling his horse to a stop. "Trace, I can't meet her. She'll expect me to take her to the train. I can't do it."

Trace's eyes narrowed, and he turned his head, listening for some sound at the house. "Clell, it's quiet in there. Too quiet." His voice was barely a whisper.

Clell leaned forward on his horse, listening as intently as Trace.

"You got no choice, Clell, you've got to see if somethin' has happened to her." Trace said flatly. Cold dread filled his chest.

They reached the house, and Clell swung out of his saddle silently. He tied the brown mare to the railing and slipped up to the door. It was quiet—deathly quiet.

Trace walked to the back door warily. Years of being a deputy had honed his survival instincts. Clell pushed open the door as they stepped inside. Both men walked on tiptoe in their boots. Clell took care to keep his spurs from jingling. Trace cocked his head, listening. He could hear steady breathing.

Clell smiled and let out a sigh of relief. "Guess you weren't exaggeratin' none. She's sound asleep at the table."

As Trace turned to Clell, he felt the older man's hand on his shoulder. Clell leaned close to whisper in his ear. "I'll take a quick peek at your angel, and then I'm leavin'." He moved a little closer on tiptoe. Clell bent toward her face. Her head lay nestled in the crook of her arm. The thick braid spread across her work-reddened hands on the table. Her right cheek was against the smooth wood. Smiling, he again admired the heavy hair against her cheek. Then he saw it. A trick of the light?

His eyes widened as he made out the lightning-bolt shape of a jagged raised scar. It cut a path from just below her eye to the jawbone. Understanding coursed through Clell. The hat, Trace's remark about her telling him she was ugly...working with the blind. Doc had mentioned it—more than once, in fact. His letters had been vague about the accident, but he had written something about a scar and how self-conscious the woman was. Clell just never quiet expected it to look like that.

He turned and with gentle pressure escorted Trace back outside. "I'll come by from time to time, but I don't want you to tell her anybody has been around. This will be our secret."

Trace thought about putting up an argument. He really should just reach over and give her a shake. If she woke up now and found Clell here, it would solve all his problems. She'd put up a fuss and catch the first train back to New York, and he'd be rid of her. Yep, that was what he should do. The same relentless flood of curiosity seeped into his bones. That was what he should do, but he didn't do it. Instead, he felt the question forming on his lips.

"Clell, is she— Is she, real ugly?"

"That's a damned funny question, comin' from a blind man." Clell said evasively as he moved away from the sleeping woman. They were still whispering. "Why would a man who can't see, care what the hell his teacher looks like?" Clell asked with amusement. He didn't wait for Trace to say more. He slipped out the door and grabbed the reins. With amazing agility for a man his age, he leapt into the saddle.

The sound of leather stretching while he adjusted his boots to the stirrups told Trace he was leaving. "Where are you goin', you old desert rat?" Trace was not through with this conversation yet.

"Back to the ranch. Maria and Lupe have been killin' and pluckin' chickens for a couple of days. They're gettin' ready for the roundup. I bet I could scare up a pretty nice spread for you two. I need to talk to your pa about somethin', anyway."

Clell put the spurs to the horse. Trace smelled the fine dust the hooves kicked up in his face as they whirled. He stood for a long time, just listening. It was still quiet inside. If he went in again, he'd probably wake her, and he didn't want to do that. Of course, he told himself, it wasn't because he thought she deserved the rest. No. The little general would probably get all worked up because of the peace and quiet he'd enjoyed while she was asleep. Well, he wouldn't give her the satisfaction. He could find things to keep him busy outside.

Ghost enjoyed being curried. It had been too long, Trace admitted to himself grudgingly. While he stroked the horse he had a long, one-sided argument with himself. He didn't *care* if Miss James was ugly. If Clell had given him a chance, he would've explained that. He was just curious, that was all. Wonder and amazement had filled him when he accidentally touched her, and it hadn't left yet. How could he explain that to Clell? How could he possibly tell the old codger that his brain burned with questions about the mysterious woman? How could he explain that being near her made him feel like a man again?

Ghost snorted and tossed his head. Strands of long, coarse hair brushed Trace's cheek when the horse nudged him in the shoulder.

"Glad you liked it, fella. I'll do it again tomorrow, promise," Trace said as he felt his way along the rail to climb through the corral.

He slowly brought wood from the pile to the back porch. He didn't bother even trying to stack it, but at least it was closer to the kitchen. As much as he hated to admit it, even to himself, he wanted to do something nice for Miss James. He wondered if the little general would even notice his efforts.

Clell rode the little mare hard. He was anxious to speak with Hugh. The woman had looked near tuckered out. She couldn't hold up to that kind of work alone for long. Her hands had looked close to bleeding across the knuckles. A pang of conscience hit Clell, and he urged more speed from the horse.

Trace could help some if he wanted to, damn him. Clell knew Trace could do a lot more than he realized, but then, it wasn't Clell who needed convincing, was it? It was Trace himself.

Clell was already swinging out of the saddle before the mare even stopped. He stripped the saddle off and led the sweaty horse to the corral. He removed the bridle as he patted her rump to send her in. Again he grimaced at the way he'd ridden her and at putting her up wet, but talking to Hugh had to come first.

Stomping inside, his jangling spurs announced his arrival at the same time he bellowed. "Hugh, where are you?" Clell hollered as soon as he cleared the doorway.

"What in tarnation's wrong?" Hugh said, coming from the kitchen with a slice of hot corn bread in his hand. Melted butter dripped off the side, plopping on the clean wooden floor.

Lupe frowned in aggravation and bent to wipe it up with a corner of her apron.

"Me and you got to have a talk, now." Clell said.

Hugh and Clell had been friends the better part of their lives. When the old cowhand used so few words, it was serious.

"Let's go in the parlor. No one's home right now. Missy and the boys are out movin' cattle," Hugh said, shutting the door behind his back as they stepped inside.

It was a sunny room, and Maria had left a window open for the spring air to clear away the mustiness of winter. A white curtain billowed into the room occasionally as a light breeze caught it.

"Okay, Clell." Hugh swallowed the last piece of corn bread.

"How much did Doc tell you about Miss James?" Clell's brow was furrowed deep.

"Only what I told you. Why?" Hugh lowered his tall frame into a rustic chair. "Is there some problem with her helpin' Trace?"

"No, it's not that. You remember the hat she wore the day you picked her up in San Marcial?"

Clell put his boots up on the cold hearth in front of their chairs.

"Yep. Funny-lookin' thing, wasn't it, with that veil and all?" Hugh grinned while he shook his head in amazement.

"Yeah, well, there is a reason why she wears that veil." Clell's voice was ominous.

"What reason?" Hugh wished he'd get to the point. Clell could drag out a story till a body near dropped.

"The little lady has a scar on her face." Clell's voice rang with pity.

Hugh frowned. A strand of auburn hair fluttered in the breeze. "How bad?" he asked quietly.

"You and I seen lots worse, when the Comanches were raidin' heavy, but it's bad enough. In a place like New York City, I kin just imagine how bad it'd be to a young gal like that." Clell raised a bushy gray eyebrow. "That's probably why she wears that contraption to cover her face. She's sorta hidin'."

Hugh closed his eyes and took a deep breath. "You mean to tell me that I may have done the right thing? I mean, by just droppin' her at Trace's place, it may have saved her from havin' to be uncomfortable?"

"Don't go pattin' yerself on the back, Hugh," Clell snapped.

Hugh sighed and shifted in his chair. A pale stain of color rose from his denim shirt collar to his hairline. "You think that's why she works with the blind?" Hugh asked softly.

"Yep. We got a problem too, a big one. She's workin' herself to death, keepin' up the place and teachin' Trace.

The problem is, I doubt she'd welcome someone comin' to stay and help. And if anyone comes around, she's gonna' be caterwaulin' to catch the first train outa here. What are we goin' to do?'' Clell narrowed his pale eyes.

Hugh grimaced. ''Guess I didn't think any of this through, did I?'' His dark brows rose in a frown of consternation.

''Maybe none of us did,'' Clell whispered as he rubbed his stubbly gray jaw.

''I feel plumb foolish. I don't know what womenfolk do all day to keep busy. So what can we do about it, Clell?''

''Well, hell, I don't know. For now, I'm goin' to take some food. Have Maria get everything that's cooked already packed up. Use the fancy basket Missy takes to the church picnics. I can chop some wood easy enough, on the sly. I guess we'll just have to be damn sure we keep a close watch without her knowin' or seein'.'' Clell seemed genuinely afraid of what Miss James's reaction would be if they ran into her face-to-face.

''Do you really think she'd insist on goin' back?'' Hugh asked.

''Hugh, you've never been a stupid man. Now, what would you do if your best friend and doctor lied to you, had you come all this way, and then you got dumped off with a strange patient. Especially when the patient is a mean-tempered cuss, not some dogie boy like everyone said?'' Clell cocked his head to the side.

''I see your point.'' He coughed gruffly. Hugh could have kicked himself for not asking more questions of Doc. He rose, patting Clell on the back. ''You're a softhearted cuss aren't you, Tom McClellan?''

It sounded sort of strange to Clell to hear his real name used twice in one week.

''I guess I am. It's a shame. She's a pretty little thing, 'cept for that scar.'' His eyes grew misty and soft.

"I'd like to believe you're wrong about the scar botherin' her that much, but when I think of what Doc said—or didn't say—in his letters, and the way she acted, well, I'm thinkin' you're right."

They left the parlor, heading for the kitchen. Neither of them was aware of the tall man in the Stetson just stepping onto the porch. At the last minute, Flynn had decided to go to Magdalena another time. He'd only gone halfway before he turned around. The change in Trace at his ranch this morning had haunted him all day. Seeing his brother on the road to recovery had brought a grateful smile to his lips.

Flynn had an irresistible urge to go visit Trace, to see how he was getting along, but now he hesitated. How could he do that? He promised his father he wouldn't interfere. There had to be a way. Flynn stepped off the porch, striding toward the barn. He'd find a way to see how Trace and Miss Bellami James were doing. The trick would be for them not to know about it. Hugh had made it real plain that none of the O'Bannions were to come around until Trace and Miss James had settled in a bit. As Flynn tossed the folded blanket up on the back of the bay, a mischievous smile curved his lips.

Clell got a fresh horse and loaded bundles of food in back of the saddle. After it was tied on, he mounted and wheeled around. It bothered him to be riding another horse just as hard as he'd ridden the mare earlier, but he vowed he'd take it real easy coming home. The sun was dipping low in a brilliant red sky when he saw Trace's windmill. Clell used all his Indian savvy to sneak up to the house unnoticed. He was about two yards from the back door when he heard Trace.

"She's still asleep. I guess she was near dead on her feet. You can quit stompin' around," Trace said dryly from his position behind the smokehouse.

Clell knew he'd been quiet. The way he'd been coming in could hardly be what anybody could call "stomping around." He wondered if the old myth was true, about blind people having better hearing than other folks. "Here's a basket of food, and some extras. Don't know how you'll explain where it came from, but that's your problem. I got to be gettin' back." Clell turned and started walking to his horse, taking little care to keep his spurs from jingling.

Trace's voice stopped him cold. "Clell, you ignored me earlier. I want an answer, now. What does Miss James look like?" Trace stood with his feet braced apart, his sinewy arms clasped across his chest. Clell knew the posture well. It meant Trace had dug in like a mad badger and wasn't going to give any ground.

"You're gonna hang on like a dog with a bone, aren't you, boy?" Clell growled.

"Yes. Is Miss Bellami James ugly?"

Chapter Eight

Clell let out a long sigh. He walked a couple of feet to the pile of wood, upturning a length of piñion. The old cowboy sat down on the edge and cleared his throat. "Well, now... Pretty or ugly, those words mean different things to different people."

"Clell, quit stallin'," Trace hissed.

"I can answer you better by tellin' you a little story."

Trace groaned. He knew it'd be a long one—they always were. He fanned the air with outstretched hands until he located the side of the chicken coop and leaned against it. He brought one leg up to put the heel of his boot flat against the wall. Relatively comfortable, he prepared himself for a big windy.

Clell saw Trace get settled and took it as his cue to begin. "Back before your pa and I mustered out, we had to bring a herd of cattle from Sedalia to Fort Craig. I'd been occupied in town, longer than I should've been. By the time I showed up, the others already had their mounts picked for the drive. I got stuck with the leavin's, you might say." Clell tilted his hat back on his head and narrowed his eyes to look back in time, remembering.

"Well the others, your pa included, had picked the pretty, flashy horses. The only things left in the pen was a mule and a little mare. Now, that mare was a sorry-lookin' little thing. She had a roman nose, spavined legs, a U neck. Looked like a strong wind might blow her over." He took a deep breath, pausing for a minute. "I had half a mind to pick the damn mule, but I hate mules. So, I finally took the little mare. The first day or so, I sulked and pouted and thought about how unfair life is, you know how a young man does. Then about noon of the third day I began to notice the little horse. No matter what I asked of her, she seemed willin'—almost eager—to please. About a week out, the other horses were beginnin' to get downright cranky. But not my little mare. The farther we went, the worse those other mounts got. Pretty soon them other soldiers were gettin' downright envious."

Trace heard the smile of satisfaction in Clell's voice.

"In fact, I had several offers to trade, you know, for one of them bigger, pretty horses. But I wouldn't do it. No siree, that little mare, she'd carry me all day long and be ready and fresh in the mornin' to do it all over agin'. My plain little mare had a lot of heart."

Trace leaned his head back against the wall, frowning. As the silence stretched on, he realized Clell was through with his story. "Clell, you've told me this story about a dozen times. Every time you do, it's supposed to have a different meanin'. What're you tryin' to tell me this time? Just say it straight out."

"Just this, boy. Pretty or ugly means something different to all men. That little mare, to some she might have been ugly, to me she was downright beautiful. That's a decision you got to make for yourself. Ain't no one can tell you how to feel about somethin' you see. Like a sunrise or a sunset. Whether you see it pretty or not so pretty, that's strictly up to you. So don't be askin' me what a woman looks like."

"You are a mysterious ol' bird, Clell. I suppose that's all I'm goin' to get out of you, isn't it?" Trace said as he put his foot down and leaned away from the wall.

"Yep, it is. Now I got to go before that lady wakes up and demands to be taken back to civilization." Clell walked to his horse and hopped into the saddle.

"Trace, just remember one thing. There's been lots of people in this world hurt as bad as you've been hurt. Don't ever get the notion you cornered the market on pain. Savvy?"

"Yep. I savvy, and you know I'm gettin' just a little tired of you tellin' me these stories like I was a ten-year-old."

"Well, to my way of thinkin', that's exactly how you been actin' lately!" A dry chuckle punctuated the statement.

The sound of spurs hitting horseflesh made Trace clench his jaw against the truthful words that dug into him just as deep as the Spanish rowels dug into the horse's belly. Trace felt the rush of air as the horse trotted past him. He was alone, with the echo of Clell's words hanging heavy in the air.

Turning toward the house, he wondered if Miss James was awake yet. Trace felt around and picked up the basket from the back porch, where he'd left it, and opened the door quietly.

He found Bellami still sleeping. He thought about waking her, but his mischievous side took over. How it would devil her to wonder where the food came from. He placed the heavy picnic basket on the cold cookstove, taking care not to make any unnecessary noise. Then he tiptoed out to Ghost's corral.

It seemed like an eternity passed by while he waited. A tiny grin teased his mouth. Would the little general be surprised and pleased?

She woke with a jerk. The position she'd slept in had made a cramp in her neck, and she rubbed the sore muscles as she tried to clear away the cobwebs in her brain. Bellami immediately noticed a large basket that hadn't been there when she sat down. Had Mr. O'Bannion put it there, or had someone come? Her hand flew to her cheek instinctively to cover the scar. Someone had seen her face. Who? Bellami's worry over her vanity quickly evaporated as she realized that whoever might have seen her had left, and she was still stuck here with Mr. O'Bannion. She approached the mysterious basket.

Bellami had never smelled anything so good in her entire life! The closer she got to the basket, the more her stomach growled and the less she thought about being stranded here. Golden fried chicken had been wrapped in a blue gingham cloth. It was wonderfully brown and crunchy outside. A crock of fresh-churned butter with a hinged wire lid, and two large rounds of corn bread, were stuffed into one corner of the basket. Bellami had no idea who her benefactor could be. Maybe they hadn't seen her clearly. The basket had been set on the stove. No lantern burned, and the room was dim. Maybe they hadn't noticed her at all, asleep at the table.

Her mouth watered as she stood looking at the food. A tiny frown creased her brow. No one was in the house now, not even Trace. Bellami moved to the back door. The setting sun bronzed Ghost's gray body as Trace brushed him.

Bellami bit her lip, wondering if she should ask *him* where it had come from. *No.* Obviously, whoever it was had come and gone without Mr. O'Bannion knowing, also. If he had been aware of someone's presence, he would've sent Bellami packing in all possible haste. "The beast has probably lazed around all afternoon," she said to herself. A tiny, devilish smile touched her lips. The smile broadened to a grin. "Well, Mr. O'Bannion, I believe I'll just let you think I worked like a slave in this hot kitchen all day. It will serve you right to have a moment or two of guilt."

Bellami put the food out on the table as if it were the most common thing in the world to find dinner in a basket. She placed the fried chicken in a bowl, next to the hot corn bread and butter, then went to the back door.

"Mr. O'Bannion, would you please wash up for dinner?" Bellami called.

Trace moved across the yard without a moment's hesitation. Bellami frowned, trying to remember exactly when he'd quit shuffling his feet. He brushed passed her as he entered the kitchen.

"'Scuse me, Miss James," he said when his arm brushed her shoulder.

Bellami tried not to suck in her breath at the light contact. He went straight to the hand pump. One lean brown hand grabbed the red handle, and he began to pump vigorously up and down. Cold water gushed out. He ducked his head to splash the stream of water on his face. She couldn't stop herself from watching. Dark, wet hair curled at the nape of his neck. He made an altogether too appealing picture. She told herself to remember that this was strictly a business arrangement.

Trace felt his way to the chair and swung one leg over the back, plopping down. He breathed deeply, savoring the aroma, as she had done.

"Somethin' smells mighty good, Miss James." He felt along the table until he found a plate. Without a word, they both began piling food on their plates. In their haste and hunger, they reached for the chicken simultaneously. Trace's fingers closed around Bellami's wrist, instead of a piece of chicken.

She gasped in surprise, but she didn't pull away. Trace felt the tension travel down her arm to his fingers. He knew he should release her, but he didn't. He simply held her while his sightless eyes stared across the table into the unrelenting darkness. It wasn't a hard grip. He exerted just enough pressure to keep her, the way he'd hold a baby bird. She didn't struggle or try to pull free, but every muscle in her body tensed. Trace's brain absorbed messages from his fingers, picking up bits of information not available to him before.

Bellami felt his flesh touch hers, and it was like being burned. Tingles of white-hot fire shot up her hand to her arm, and a prickly warmth flooded her whole body. She watched his eyes while he held her hand over the fried chicken.

This is ridiculous. Yet while Bellami admonished herself for not pulling away, she gazed deep into his blind green eyes. It was her first big mistake. Bellami felt a powerful heat rise. It began somewhere deep in the pit of her stomach and spread out, to fill her whole being. The strength of the feeling jolted through her.

Trace spoke, and the enchantment of the moment was broken.

"Miss James, I'm afraid I'm bein' greedy. Perhaps I want too much." His voice was low and husky.

There was the slightest change in his eyes. A tiny grin crept across his chiseled face. Only then did she realize there had been a double meaning to his words. Bellami felt more heat. This time it rose to the roots of her hair.

Trace knew she was blushing; he could actually feel the heat of it. The effect she had on him was nothing short of stunning. Her hand was warm and soft and nice to hold. Instantly his curiosity and interest sparked, again.

This woman was a mystery, drawing him in. Yet, while he felt himself being drawn to her, he wanted her out of his life. He wanted her closer and he wanted her gone. Gone from his home and his life. He couldn't remember having such conflicting emotions about anything or anyone before this.

Dinner was riveting. Bellami and Trace plowed into their food. Neither one said a word to the other about where it had come from. They ate with a ravenous hunger—a hunger not just for sustenance.

Bellami was pleased with herself for fooling Trace so easily. Especially after his remark earlier, as he held her hand. His innuendo had both aroused and embarrassed her. He had the ability to make her uncomfortable, yet at the same time she enjoyed being near him. Confusion flowed through Bellami's head. She was so busy thinking about Trace that she completely forgot about someone being in the house, probably seeing her scar, and leaving her here. The only thing occupying her mind was the magnetic pull of her pupil.

It tickled Trace to the bone, realizing this paragon of virtue had feet of clay. He'd never enjoyed spending time with Miss James more than he was this evening. The knowledge he gained with every tiny intentional touch was greedily absorbed into his brain. She made his senses sing with newly awakened interest. He felt a gladness and sense of well-being that had eluded him for months. Trace pondered the mysterious woman and her many contradictions.

"Mr. O'Bannion?" She buttered another piece of corn bread.

He hastily swallowed a mouthful of chicken before he could answer. "Yes, Miss James."

"I wonder, well, if you wouldn't mind, could you tell me about your accident?" she asked timidly, her voice dropping slightly when she remembered her own reaction to a similar question.

"Accident!" he snapped. "Is that what they are calling it? My *accident?*" His eyebrows rose, and a hard glint replaced the warm glow in his eyes.

Bellami was shocked by the tone of his voice. "Well, yes. Dr. Malone said an accident took your sight."

"I was shot, Miss James! Pure and simple. It was no damned accident. I was shot in the head, by a stupid Texas cowboy." His voice rang with bitterness.

"When?" Her voice was little more than a whisper. She knew she shouldn't pursue this. He was obviously very upset, but she couldn't hold the words back.

''Back in October.'' He sighed heavily. A sad, haunted look flitted across his face.

''Why?''

Trace thought about it a moment. Good question. Had anyone ever asked why before? ''Miss James, you're without a doubt the most unusual woman I have ever met,'' he said, leaning back in his chair, smiling. He knew she was blushing again. ''All right. I'll tell you about my, uh, accident.'' He squinted as if trying to focus while looking through a mist.

She watched as different emotions washed over his jaw, and cringed again as she noticed the healing nicks in his uneven whiskers.

''My brother and I went to get Elfego Baca. He's a deputy, too. There'd been some shootin'. Molo Armijo rode to Socorro. My brother and I had just gone for breakfast.'' His eyes clouded over. ''I ordered steak and eggs.'' He chuckled at the memory.

Bellami focused on his face, trying to read his expressions.

''A group of men from town had Elfego pinned down for a day and a half. We got him out easy enough—too easy, I guess.'' Trace frowned and rubbed the slender white scar on the side of his head. The cowboy, they tell me, was aimin' for Elfego. Just my bad luck he was such a poor shot.''

Trace's eyes had gone cold and hard. No feeling at all showed in them now, not even hate. Then he laughed. Bellami couldn't believe it, but he actually laughed out loud. She wondered again if he might be slightly mad. ''Why did the cowboy want to shoot Mr. Baca?'' she asked, in all innocence. She'd been trying to follow the confusing story and his mercurial emotions—but neither task was easy.

''Because the cowboy was a Texan,'' Trace replied simply.

"I'm sorry, Mr. O'Bannion," Bellami said, shaking her head from side to side, "but I still don't understand. What does being a Texan have to do with shooting people in the head?"

"Elfego arrested another cowboy from Texas for murder. In the process he had to shoot a man," Trace said.

"But you said he's a deputy. That's his job. Why would this other man want to shoot him for doing his job?"

Trace couldn't understand how such a smart woman didn't understand a simple thing like the conflict between white and Indian, Mexican and Texan, farmer and rancher.

"Miss James, people out here have been shootin' each other because of the color of their hides for a long time," he replied. What did they teach them in the city?

"Well, I still don't understand." She laid her fork down with a clank.

"Miss James." Trace sighed heavily. "Don't you have any kind of racial intolerance in New York?" Trace was genuinely interested in her answer.

"Yes, I suppose we do. Tilly told me the Irish and Chinese were treated badly in some places."

"Tilly? She a friend of yours?" Trace leaned back in his chair, looking thoughtful and curious.

Bellami didn't know why, but she didn't want to tell Trace that Tilly was her maid. For some silly reason, and she couldn't possibly understand why, she didn't want him to know how easy she'd had it—before coming to the territory and meeting *him*.

"Yes, Tilly is a friend." She felt a little guilty, but it wasn't an outright lie, it just wasn't exactly the whole truth. Tilly was one of the few people Bellami did consider a friend, one of the very few who ever saw her without the veil.

"Well, you can tell your friend about the kind of prejudice we have here in the territory when you get back home. Elfego is Mexican, and there are some Texans—a lot, in fact—who feel that's reason enough to shoot them."

"That's the most ridiculous thing I've ever heard in my life!" Bellami said with complete conviction.

Trace just sat there and let her words sink in. The sincerity of her outraged statement surprised and pleased him. Truly, she was the most puzzling female he'd ever met. He hadn't really studied women up close, not like Flynn, but he knew enough to know that she was sure different from most. Without any good reason for doing so, Trace found himself comparing the little general with Becky Kelly.

Becky had beauty and charm. Now, what did Miss James have? Character—without a doubt. And something else. Trace couldn't quite put a name to it, but she possessed something, some elusive, powerful quality that he couldn't name. Trace frowned, trying to decide what the commodity could be.

Bellami saw a subtle change come over Trace. While he was talking about his friend Elfego, for the first time she'd seen him show real concern for another person. But when she spoke, his scowl returned. Evidently she'd said something to offend him again.

"Well, I'm stuffed," he said. "I'm goin' upstairs." Trace abruptly pushed himself away from the table. His words took her by surprise, and she jumped. Evidently their conversation was over, by his decision. She felt hurt.

"Good idea. Tomorrow we need to begin some new exercises for you. I'll just clear up here, and then I'm off to bed myself," Bellami agreed quickly. Obviously he didn't intend to suffer her presence any longer.

As he walked up the stairs, Trace found himself thinking a lot about Miss James. Why he'd given the little general so much information about the shooting, he didn't know. Maybe it was because he hadn't really spoken to anyone about it, till now. Funny thing, too—he felt better. Just the simple act of putting the whole mess into words seemed to leave him somehow more at peace about the whole thing. Or was it his sudden, unexplainable urge to measure Becky against Miss James? And why on earth would any sane man want to compare a young single woman with an old spinster? He rubbed his forehead, wondering if maybe the bullet had addled his brains. As he stepped inside his room, it dawned on him.

The little general wasn't going to say a word about the basket. She intended to act like she'd cooked it all. "What a fraud!" Trace nearly laughed aloud at the little cheat. Oddly, though, he found her deception kind of endearing. For the first time since Bellami James had shown up, he felt something akin to understanding for her. Maybe she was human after all.

Bellami knew she should've said something about the mysterious basket, but it was so darned nice to have the upper hand with him, for a change. He'd been so belligerent and rude since she'd gotten here. And it was such a tiny thing, really—who would it hurt? Yet the more she congratulated herself on fooling him, the smaller she felt. By the time she trudged upstairs to bed, she felt horribly guilty. It weighed heavily on her. Basically an honest person, she couldn't remember ever telling anyone an outright lie. Bellami felt bad about deceiving Trace, even if it was a small and very well deserved deception. She also felt a deep compassion for him, something she would never have believed possible a few days ago. Knowing how he'd lost his sight suddenly made him seem less selfish and a lot more human.

Before she retired, she thought about writing to her family and Tilly—but how could she send a letter? As she lay in her bed, thinking about his story, the image of Trace being shot played over and over in her head. The shot rang out across the prairie, and he fell to the ground. Then she envisioned a man rushing to his side, his brother. Bellami's eyelids fluttered and drifted closed.

Trace woke with the thundering of hooves in his ears, as usual. Swinging his legs to the floor, he started to rise. Then, without warning, every star in the sky exploded inside his head. The room tilted crazily and began to spin. A pain, so intense he nearly lost his dinner, gripped his head. Trace gasped and dropped to his knees in agony. Breathing brought on waves of excruciating pain. He held his fragmenting head in trembling hands. "God..." he moaned softly. When he thought he was going to pass out—actually hoped he would pass out—the pain disappeared as if it had never happened. He sat on the floor, weak and shaking like an aspen leaf in the wind.

Since the shooting, he hadn't suffered any side effects. Except, of course, being stone-blind. The doctor in Socorro had told him he was very lucky. He certainly hadn't thought so at the time. The bullet had passed between the scalp and his head, traveling along his skull, just creasing him. After he regained consciousness, the doctor had told him there'd been some swelling. He'd warned Trace that if the swelling resumed, he could die.

Now, how am I goin' to break this to the general? he mused. *What am I sayin'? The woman tears into me like a cougar as it is, last thing I need to do is give her more ammunition....* Trace laughed, or he tried to laugh. It was a bitter, hollow sound in the empty room. *Hell will freeze over before I give her any more reason to think I'm less than a man, than she already does.* Besides, she'd kept the food a secret. Trace grimaced as he tried to justify his need to keep this most recent weakness a secret of his own. He conveniently forgot that he and Clell had started keeping secrets with the basket in the first place. All that mattered to Trace right now was salvaging one tiny shred of his battered pride. And that meant keeping this episode from Miss James.

Crawling back to his bed exhausted him. When he finally got off the floor, he climbed stiffly to the edge of the mattress. Breathing hard, like he'd just ridden hard all day, he fell into bed. Every muscle in his body cried out from the strenuous bout of pain. He marveled at how it could twist a man into knots—a lot like a woman.

Flynn hadn't really planned to go to Trace's house, but here he was. For hours after dark he sat on his horse watching the house. He could see them clearly through the kitchen window. How he'd teased Trace about buying a picture window. That enormous piece of glass and the porcelain bathtub had been the hot topic of conversation between the brothers for six months, at least. Now he found himself grateful. The kerosene lamp cast pleasant shadows across the table while they ate. He recognized the basket instantly as the one Missy took to church socials.

When Trace took hold of Miss James's wrist, Flynn smiled. The lady had made some quick and damned near miraculous changes in his brother. A tiny glimmer of hope flamed in Flynn's chest. He shifted his weight in the saddle and watched them talking quietly. A couple of times Trace actually smiled. As much as he hated to admit the truth of it, Hugh and Clell were right. Trace was getting better, and Miss James seemed to be the reason for it. Light played on both heads of dark hair.

"They make a damn fine-lookin' picture, don't they, Jack?" Flynn muttered to his horse. The bay's ears moved back and forth in the moonlight at the sound. He rolled a smoke, thinking about it. A small burden of guilt lifted from his shoulders as he watched the simple scene through the big window.

Flynn just sat there, watching the house. Even after they both went up the stairs and the house got dark and quiet.

He reined his horse around quietly. "A trip to Magdalena is what I need. I've definitely been without a woman for too damned long," he said aloud, kicking his horse into a gallop.

Chapter Nine

Flynn woke to the harsh, bellowing voices of mule skinners, and the pop of their cracking whips. He rubbed the sleep out of his eyes and turned over onto his stomach. A groan issued from the other side of the bed when he moved.

"What the hell?" He growled and threw back the sheet, surprised to discover a heart-shaped set of buttocks. A little blonde, buck-naked, grinned up at Flynn.

"Who are you?" he asked in surprise.

"Clara. Don't you remember me?" Half-closed eyes regarded him suspiciously.

Flynn squinted his eyes. A cloudy recollection of holding a beer in one hand and a woman in the other came to mind. After that, it got kind of vague and fuzzy. She smiled seductively as he looked her over. Morning light shone into her face. Her hair glowed like a ring of flame around her head.

"Get dressed, honey. How much do I owe you?" he asked bluntly. He wasn't one to worry about the details of what went on—he just hoped he'd enjoyed himself.

"Two dollars," she said, rising quickly from the bed.

"Two dollars! Magdalena is gettin' kind of pricey, ain't it? Are you tryin' to get a bigger reputation than the Varnish Queen?" he said, teasingly, watching her gather up clothes from scattered, haphazard piles. Flynn frowned, wishing he could remember more of the evening. The girl was pretty enough. No reason to be tightfisted with her because he'd forgotten most of the night. Reaching for his pants on the bedpost, he dug deep in a pocket.

"Who's the Varnish Queen?" Clara asked, and pulled on her skirt.

"You ain't never heard of the Varnish Queen? Hell, she's famous. She runs a real nice place up in White Oak. Calls herself the Varnish Queen 'cause she says there ain't a cowboy she can't shellac!" Flynn slipped the two dollars into Clara's hand, slapping her on the backside as she scampered out the door. Flynn cursed himself as he rose from the bed, "Damn fool, ought to be old enough not to drink so much that I can't recall my fun." Sunlight warmed his nude body as he walked barefoot to the window overlooking the street.

Magdalena was bustling in the spring sunshine. Wagons of ore from the Kelly mine, eight miles away, were coming and going at an amazing pace. Cattle in the holding pens lowed while they waited to be loaded onto the stock cars. Magdalena was a booming metropolis. Flynn touched his aching head, grimacing. He must've drank a goodly amount of beer. Another thing Magdalena could boast lately was Hammel Brothers Beer. The Hammels' brewery in Socorro supplied the territory with beer by rail.

Flynn squeezed his eyes tight against the throbbing of his head. The shrill train whistle picked that exact moment to shatter his already splitting head. He felt the vibration of it to the marrow of his bones. His teeth hurt, he felt the sound so far down inside him.

"Coffee. I got to have coffee," he moaned as he pulled on his Levi's and boots.

Flynn walked down the carpeted staircase to the street. The rowels of his spurs jingled, sounding like Lupe ringing the dinner bell, he noted with a grimace. Carefully ad-

justing the Stetson on his head, he managed to shade his
eyes from the morning sun.

It wasn't often he drank so much. In his line of work,
you couldn't enjoy such frivolities. A man with a fuzzy
head and slow reflexes was a sitting duck. He kept the hat
low and gritted his teeth as he negotiated the crowded
street. Weaving around yelling teamsters and horses'
rumps, Flynn finally put his boots on the threshold of the
restaurant. The smell of cooking bacon wafted through the
air. For a moment, he felt a sickening feeling, and his
stomach churned. Swallowing hard, he scanned the room
quickly. It was a habit developed by years of wearing a
badge. One empty table, in one secluded corner, caught his
eye. It seemed to be the only one not occupied this morning. Flynn pulled out a chair that afforded him a view of
the street and lowered his tall frame to the seat with a sigh.

"Howdy, Flynn," an entirely too loud, too cheerful
voice said as the waitress plunked down an empty tin cup
and sloshed steaming coffee into it. He replied with little
more than a grunt, never looking up, as he tipped the cup
to his lips. A moment later, his Adam's apple bobbed, and
he smiled gratefully. "Mornin'. Bring me the usual."

She giggled at his obviously sore head. Flynn gave her a
wink. The freckle-faced waitress blushed, giggling prettily
as she scurried to the kitchen. Gingerly he took off his hat
to lay it on the table opposite him. Passengers from the
train were beginning to filter in. A few more sips of coffee
made their low rumble of conversation nearly tolerable.

Flynn occupied himself by trying to guess what they did
and where they all came from. Soon he had them lumped
roughly into two categories. East, and the rest of the
country.

East was easy. They were soft-looking men with pasty
white faces and smooth hands. The women had creamy
skin and wore clothes that would be in shreds by the end
of one day in the territory.

The rest of the country consisted of hard men, work-worn and tough, with restless eyes that scanned the room. The women's eyes held a sad, haunted, slightly hungry look. One gaunt older man with a thin mustache, carrying the black bag of a physician, held Flynn's attention. The man was pale to the point of looking unhealthy. While Flynn watched, he doubled over in a racking fit of coughing. The handkerchief he dabbed at his mouth was spotted with flecks of bright crimson. Flynn had heard tales of people coming here for their failing health. This was obviously one of them. He frowned, doubting a change of climate would be enough to cure the man's ills. Flynn's gaze traveled over the group, but kept returning to a tall, well-built man about Trace's age. He was well dressed and definitely Eastern, but that wasn't why Flynn watched him. He seemed vaguely familiar. Not so much his face, but the way he moved, or something. The marshal sipped his coffee, frowning. His head still hurt, and not being able to remember where he'd seen the man worried him. Maybe a wanted poster? He prided himself on being able to recollect faces and names.

The young Easterner strode across the room and spoke to the pretty freckle-faced waitress. She looked around the room, then shook her head. Disappointment was written all over the man's face. The blushing girl walked away with the speckled coffeepot in hand. She had a red-and-white checkered rag around the wire handle, and steam rose from the spout.

"Honey, what does the dude want?" Flynn drawled, inclining his head in the direction of the traveler.

"He wants to eat, but there ain't no empty tables," she replied succinctly.

Flynn looked back at him. Again the vague sensation of recognition nagged at him. "Tell him he's welcome to share my table." Maybe a close-up view would clear the cobwebs.

The waitress's eyebrows rose, surprised at Flynn's uncharacteristic display of generosity so early in the day. With a high-pitched giggle, she swayed back toward the group of passengers standing near the door. After a brief moment of giggles and mumbles, Flynn saw the stranger look in his direction. A pair of blue-gray eyes narrowed momentarily, and then the stranger smiled in gratitude. White teeth flashed in a clean-shaven face. For a split second, while the man walked toward him, Flynn almost knew why the dude was so familiar. Then the answer evaporated into the fog of his hangover.

"Hello. I thought I'd stand there until I starved to death," a deep voice with a slight accent said in crisp, educated tones. The man was definitely from the East.

"Pull up a chair, mister." Flynn gestured as the waitress brought a cup and filled it to the brim with coffee. She smiled shyly at the man, who pulled out a chair opposite Flynn.

"Is it always like this?" the Easterner asked, looking around the room, which was rapidly becoming more congested as people waited for a table.

"Since the Kelly started shipping ore, it has been." Flynn leaned back in his chair, sipping his coffee. He studied the man with suspicious eyes. The nagging feeling of having met before returned.

In a remarkably short time, the young woman placed two huge plates of ham and eggs in front of Flynn and the stranger. The man attacked his with a vengeance. Flynn couldn't help but grin at his obvious hunger. He chuckled silently as the gentleman polished off his food, and several more cups of strong black coffee.

"You always eat like that?" Flynn asked with a broad grin on his face. He hadn't been able to finish his own breakfast, but his headache was gone. He'd started to feel almost human.

"No, not usually. It's been a long trip." A lopsided grin appeared.

"You mind me askin' where you're from?" Flynn couldn't believe the words even as they left his lips. His curiosity had driven him crazy. The idea that they'd met before just wouldn't give him any peace.

"No, not at all. I'm from New York," the baritone voice replied pleasantly. Flynn didn't doubt that for a minute. Any man around here asked that question would've been mad as hell. Most residents of the territory resented being asked where they came from, or what they'd done before they arrived. It was considered the height of bad manners, like asking somebody what his name was in the East. Flynn's curiosity prodded him further. Since his companion didn't seem to mind his rude interrogation, he might as well find out what he could. "What are you doin' here?" he blurted out.

"I came for a visit. I have a relative out here."

Flynn narrowed his eyes and searched the man's face. The hair on the back of his neck bristled. It only did that when he wasn't going to like something. The man was still talking companionably, explaining his answer.

"She's staying near here, at a ranch." Blue-gray eyes met Flynn's steady gaze unflinchingly.

The man didn't act like somebody on the run. Still, Flynn knew something wasn't right. His nerves were taut.

The dude smiled, sipping his hot coffee. "My twin's out here, doing a job. Maybe you've met her. Bellami James?"

Flynn nearly spewed a mouthful of coffee clear across the table. Choking, he swallowed the hot liquid, trying to regain his composure. "Bellami James!" he sputtered loudly, choking slightly on the name. All other sound in the restaurant came to a screeching halt.

The man across the table blinked in surprise at Flynn's reaction, and then his sky-blue eyes narrowed. "Yes, Bellami James." His voice took on a dry, flinty sound.

"What's this all about, Mister? And I don't believe I got your name." He stiffened and sat more erect.

"O'Bannion, Flynn O' Bannion. My brother is the 'job' your sister is out here to do," Flynn replied dryly. He sighed heavily and leaned back in his chair again. Now the vague familiarity, the odd sense of having met the man before, made sense. Bellami James had a brother—a twin brother.

"Oh? Doc led us to believe all the O'Bannion children were much younger. My name is Brooks, Brooks James." He smiled again, but it was not nearly as friendly a smile as before. He rose, politely extending his hand across the table.

Flynn stood to shake hands with the young man. Now he saw the resemblance. It was the way he moved. Brooks and Bellami had the same smooth economy of motion. A sort of natural grace. Since Flynn hadn't seen her face, he couldn't say if they looked alike or not.

"So, you and your sister thought the job would be takin' care of a passel of children, huh?" Flynn started grinning, then began to chuckle. Within a second, he was laughing heartily.

Brooks rose from his chair. A hard frown creased his no longer amiable-looking brow.

"Please, Mr. James, sit down," Flynn suggested. "We've a lot to talk about. There are some things about your sister's employment here you should know. I doubt you're goin' to like it very much." Flynn wiped the mirthful moisture from his eyes. He'd laughed so hard his eyes were beginning to tear.

Brooks's cold eyes told Flynn humor was the farthest thing from his mind.

"I'm sorry to laugh, but you see, it appears your friend Doc was just as dishonest with Bellami as my pa was with Trace." Flynn took a deep breath. "Trace is near to your own age. He's the reason my pa sent for a teacher."

Brooks's frown turned to a deep scowl. Once-clear blue eyes now looked like Southwestern thunderheads. "Why would they lie about such a thing?" he questioned as the waitress refilled their cups.

"Maybe they had sense enough to know she would probably refuse the job," Flynn said without a hint of his previous humor.

Brooks sat still and digested that for a moment. His face began to feel sore from the steady pressure he kept exerting on his jaw. He was furious. With himself, with Doc Malone, and mostly with Trace O'Bannion for being a grown man, and not an innocent little boy. As he continued to watch the man opposite him, his anger rose to a fever pitch.

Finally, Flynn stopped speaking. He stared across the table expectantly at Brooks. It was obvious he expected some kind of response. Brooks opened his mouth to speak, then slammed it shut. He closed his eyes tight for one brief moment and rose from his chair. He placed his palms flat against the table, his vision clouded with barely controlled anger.

Flynn's instincts prickled at Brooks's posture. At that moment, the pale passenger from the East bumped Flynn's chair, and was seized with another fit of coughing. Flynn allowed his eyes to flick over the hacking man for only a second. It was just long enough. He felt Brooks's fist connect with his jaw as he heard a resounding thud. His headache came back. All motion around them ceased as the patrons froze in midthought, midsentence. Every person waited, expecting bloodshed. It looked like the whole room had taken a deep breath and was holding it. Flynn blinked once and clamped his jaw tight as a vise. Very quietly, he spoke.

"What was that for?" He was a bit stunned and amused, but not angry. He rubbed his jaw. Brooks had a hell of a good right.

"Well, I can't very well go beat up a blind man! Let's just say you took that one for your brother." Brooks's voice dropped to a low, controlled timbre. As he spoke, the dining room suddenly abandoned its vigil. Obviously the men weren't going to brawl or draw. Relief flooded through the crowded dining room.

Flynn's entire appearance changed suddenly when he heard Brooks's words. He raised his head slowly and locked on to Brooks's cool blue-gray eyes. "I wish to God I could take more than that for him." Flynn's voice cracked with emotion.

The anguish in Flynn's voice diffused any remaining fury in Brooks. He sat back down, stunned by the conviction of the other man's words. With a jolt, he realized they shared a bond. Neither of them spoke for a few minutes, each lost in his own private world—a world of guilt and remorse.

A heavy sigh escaped Flynn, and he lowered his eyes, staring at his cup as he swirled the dark liquid around and around. "If I'd been payin' more attention, talkin' less, or if I had drawn faster—anythin'..." He seemed to be speaking to someone who wasn't there at the table, or perhaps to himself. He raised his eyes to regard Brooks darkly. "Mr. James, I'm responsible for my brother's blindness, just as surely as if I pulled the trigger. Can you understand how that feels? To allow a thing like that to happen?" A long silence answered his question.

Brooks felt the cold tentacles grip his chest. He knew what it was, of course—guilt, pure, hollow guilt. How many times had he said nearly those same words to himself? He knew he should say something, something polite and casual, but his throat felt tight. A perfect stranger sat across from him, saying things he'd said over and over to himself since the day of Bellami's accident. He wanted to rise, to leave, to flee. He felt exposed, vulnerable. Guilty.

"I'm not in the habit of askin' favors from any man, but I'm goin' to ask one of you, Mr. James. Your sister was brought here without my knowledge. If I'd known what my father and his friend were up to, I would've put a stop to it. But I didn't. Now your sister is here, and I've seen with my own eyes she is helpin' my brother. I'm askin' you to wait. Wait awhile before you go see her." Flynn spoke quietly, but his words sizzled with emotion.

Brooks wanted to refuse. He intended to refuse. Even as his brain groped for the right words to say no, he knew he couldn't do it. He couldn't refuse this hard, proud man. Even if it meant leaving Bellami alone awhile longer with Trace O'Bannion—a full-grown man, not a helpless child. Lord, what would his family say? Rod would have a fit. The connection between Flynn and Brooks was strong, too strong to ignore. Brooks looked across the table and saw himself. Flynn O'Bannion was, in a sense, his perfect counterpart. They had failed to protect the people they loved, and now those people were suffering for their inadequacy.

"All right, Mr. O'Bannion," he sighed heavily. "I'll wait for a while." His voice was low.

Flynn smiled. It wasn't the kind of smile he usually wore; it held none of his usual flashy bravado. This smile was one of pure gratitude. "Thank you, Mr. James. I owe you." He said it easily, but Brooks felt the deep meaning in the words.

"Well, I guess I better go find a hotel and arrange for a room if I'm going to be here for a while." Brooks rubbed his hands across his eyes and sighed.

Flynn crinkled his dark eyebrows. "That won't be necessary. Since my family has snarled your life up with our problems, it's only fair you come stay at the ranch. There's enough room, Lord knows, and it's only five miles from Trace's place. I think you'd feel better, I mean about the arrangement, if you were closer."

Brooks nodded mutely and finished his coffee. He knew what he'd just agreed to, but the why of it puzzled him. Conversation between the two men seemed impossible as they finished the last dregs of the coffee.

Flynn picked up his Stetson, placing it on his head, and rose from his chair. As he turned toward the door, he heard a familiar voice. A jolt of anger coursed through him.

Brooks stood up, watching the lawman stiffen.

"Why, Flynn, it has been just ages," the feminine voice declared. Brooks heard the rustle of petticoats as the woman swished forward. Morning sun caught her hair, setting it ablaze. She looked like a tiny, bright flame standing before Flynn's dark glare.

Flynn had never hit a woman in his life, but he considered it now. "Hello, Becky," he said, his voice flat as Magdalena Mesa. The tension did not go unnoticed by the girl. She looked at him thoughtfully for a minute. Flynn had the impression of a snake focusing on a mouse before devouring it. He clenched his jaw tighter.

"How is Trace? I've been intending to stop by, but you know, it's so painful for me." Her voice dripped with feigned sympathy.

Flynn watched as she cast a sideways glance at the tall man standing at his side, obviously curious. He shifted his weight, and one spur jingled. "Yes, I've seen just how much pain it's caused you in the last few months."

She flinched. For a moment, Flynn thought she might retreat in fear, but she didn't. Instead, she raised her chin and lowered her lashes coquettishly. "Aren't you going to introduce me, Flynn?" She smiled up at Brooks.

"Becky Kelly, this is Brooks James." Flynn said, without one shred of enthusiasm.

Brooks looked at Flynn, trying to perceive what was between the two. "Miss Kelly." He grasped her hand and brought it close to his lips, stopping just short of the back of her hand.

Her body tensed in anticipation. Flynn tasted something sour in his mouth, and his head started pounding again. She disgusted him. He'd never known what Trace saw in her. He thought Trace was actually better off without her, saved from God knew what, but how did you convince somebody in love of something like that? It rankled him, knowing his brother suffered even one moment of pain because of her cold indifference.

"Will you be with us long, Mr. James?" Becky asked in her most flirtatious simper.

Brooks hesitated, for only a moment, but Flynn saw it. He saw it and realized Mr. James wasn't taken in. He knew the grasping, manipulative female for what she was. Flynn's respect for the Easterner rose another notch.

"Perhaps," Brooks replied noncommittally. He released her hand, narrowing his eyes at her, as his face changed ever so slightly. He took on a predatory look of his own. "I'm going to be a houseguest at Mr. O'Bannion's ranch." He gave a brilliant and completely treacherous smile to the woman.

"Oh? Well, I really have been meaning to get out there. I haven't had a good visit with Missy in ever so long. Perhaps we will see each other soon." She turned back to Flynn, trying her very best to look sincere. It didn't work— she still looked like a cold-blooded reptile. No wonder the Indians compared liars to snakes. It wasn't their tongues, it was more the cold, flat eyes.

"Please tell your father and Missy that I will come by this week."

"Oh, I'm real sure Missy will be lookin' forward to that." Flynn quipped sarcastically. Yeah, she'd probably be sharpening a skinning knife in anticipation. He nodded curtly, touching the brim of his hat. Even that small gesture of courtesy seemed too good to waste on Becky. She made him want to throw up.

Brooks looked at Flynn, seeing the hard set of his jaw, as they left the building. "Are you going to enlighten me?" he asked lightly.

"Trace fancied himself in love, with her." Flynn pronounced *her*, like a vile word. "When he was blinded, she couldn't get away from him fast enough."

"A loyal one, eh?" Brooks raised one eyebrow. Flynn got the impression Mr. Brooks James might have seen a few Becky Kellys in his life. They walked side by side toward the baggage area of the train depot. Occasionally they sidestepped to make room for groups of people claiming valises and trunks.

"You didn't fall for all that flutterin' and sashayin'. Why not?" Flynn was curious again. Becky had never interested him—so few women really did—but he'd seen the effect Becky had on most of the unattached men in the territory.

"I guess I'm just immune. Her kind is all I ever see in New York. One thing about it, though, once you have that kind of sickness, you'll never catch it a second time. One dose and you're immune for life," Brooks said, sounding jaded and old. "I look at Claire and Bellami, and I know that another kind of woman exists, somewhere."

Flynn felt another kind of kinship with the man. He usually felt the same disappointment in the women he met. "Who's Claire?" he asked quietly as they gathered up Brooks's baggage and walked toward the livery.

"My older sister—she's married. Claire James Cooper, very proper—upper crust of New York society." Brooks made a dour face, joking, but instantly he turned serious again. "Bellami and Claire are quiet different. Claire likes the social scene." He acted like he was going to say more, then stopped.

Flynn prodded him. "Go on. You were fixin' to say Bellami doesn't, right?"

Brooks looked puzzled as they stopped at the door of the livery and set the baggage down. "Well, you've seen Bellami. She shuns groups of people, because of it." Brooks said quietly, turning his face away from Flynn.

The marshal had seen the pained expression on Brooks's face as he turned away. He frowned. "It? Mr. James, I don't quite catch your meanin'." Flynn wanted to know what *it* was.

Brooks turned back to Flynn, seeing genuine ignorance there. "The scar, of course, Mr. O'Bannion," Brooks snapped impatiently.

"What scar?" Now Flynn was really intrigued.

"Mr. O'Bannion, have you met my sister or not?" Brooks was feeling apprehensive. What kind of joke was this? Was Bellami here, or wasn't she?

Flynn shifted his weight and used the toe of his boot to dislodge a pebble in the dirt. He looked at Brooks for a moment, then lowered his eyes. "I met her, but I didn't see her face. She was in Socorro, wearin' a hat with a veil." Flynn spoke softly, a wistful quality to his voice.

Brooks could feel the curiosity issue from the man. "I see. Exactly who has seen my sister, Mr. O'Bannion?"

Flynn frowned, looking thoughtful for a moment. He turned toward the cornflower-blue sky, squinting. He thought about spying on Trace and Bellami through the big picture window.

"Trace. As far as I know, the only person she's been around, without the hat, is my brother Trace," he finally replied.

Brooks raised one eyebrow, and a tiny, sardonic grin tugged at his lips. "I see—and your brother is completely blind."

Flynn waited for Brooks to provide more of an explanation, but he turned, entering the livery. Evidently the answers to his many questions would have to wait. Flynn glanced at Brooks a couple of times while they loaded the rented buckboard. Brooks picked up the reins as he climbed in. He handled the two-horse team expertly, and that surprised Flynn. "You know how to drive a team?" Flynn asked, and raised his dark eyebrows.

Brooks grinned, pleased with himself. "Escorting ladies around Central Park has many advantages." He chuckled as he slapped the reins against the horses' rumps.

Mounting his big gelding, Flynn moved out in front to set the pace as the two left town. Each man pondered what the other had said, and not said, as they rode toward the O'Bannion spread.

Chapter Ten

The sun highlighted the austere terrain of the New Mexico Territory. As they approached the outskirts of town, Flynn pulled up his bay and wheeled him around. With one lanky hand he directed Brooks's attention to a mountainside.

"Look up there," Flynn said as the gelding danced, anxious to be on his way again.

Brooks squinted up at the side of the mountain, not seeing anything out of the ordinary. "What?"

"Do you see her?" Flynn asked, hardly concealing his mischievous grin.

"Her? I don't see anything but the side of a mountain." Brooks suspected Flynn was having fun with the "tenderfoot." He'd been warned on the long train ride that hard-bitten cowboys could be ruthless in their humorous exploits.

"Look, see the outline of a woman's face, the hair?" Flynn said as he continued to point. He drew an imaginary line with his outstretched hand.

Brooks began to distinguish the image of a woman's face in profile. He nodded slowly at Flynn, a frown appearing between his brows.

"Our Lady of Magdalena. Folks 'round here say the Apache won't attack within sight of her. Funny thing, too, those bushes never change, never grow, never die. The outline never gets bigger or different in any way.'' Flynn looked pensive for a moment, then turned to Brooks with a totally innocent smile shining on his face.

''Of course, it's all superstition, right?'' Brooks didn't really believe all that Flynn said. Yet something in those brown eyes bade him believe it. This man was a difficult puzzle to put together.

''This is one of those things you got to decide for yourself.'' Flynn chuckled as he let the bay have his head and move out again. Brooks continued watching him as he rode beside the wagon. Meadowlarks sang to each other from the shelter of cacti and sagebrush. Soon Brooks was lulled into a pleasant drowsiness. The steady creaking of wood and leather made his eyelids heavy. The team automatically matched their pace to keep up with Flynn. There was little for Brooks to do except watch the broad-shouldered man ahead of him.

Flynn stopped and took a relaxed position, draping his reins across the saddle horn. He drew a pale cloth bag from his shirt pocket. Brooks watched, fascinated, as the man produced a narrow, thin paper and proceeded to roll his own cigarette. It was no easy feat, especially on the back of a horse, but Flynn made it look like nothing at all. He drew a long puff on the stubby cigarette, allowing the smoke to escape his nostrils in a slender tendril. Brooks used the idle time to look at the countryside. They lingered beside a flat, grassy plain, where a well-worn trail intersected the rutted wagon road. Brooks stared out over the grassland, his brown eyes narrowing as he picked out a large dust cloud moving slowly but deliberately toward Magdalena.

Flynn lifted his Stetson and ran his long fingers through his hair. The sun caught the auburn color for a brief moment, haloing him in light. Brooks saw by the direction of his gaze that he was watching the dust cloud. Brooks stared

at it until shapes started to take form. Cattle, hundreds—
maybe thousands—of them, moved across the flat plain.
Long, heavy curving horns sprouted from their lowered
heads. They reminded him of sabers, sweeping forward,
then spiraling down and inward.

"What's this place?" Brooks asked as he stood up in the
buckboard to get a better look at the mass of animals.

"The Plains of San Augustin. Folks say it was a lake bed
long, long ago. It's near forty-five miles long and fifteen
miles wide. Makes it real easy for the cattle." Flynn finished his smoke, setting the hat back on his head. He
kicked his horse lightly, and Brooks realized it was time to
move on. He allowed himself one last look at the cattle and
the dusty cowboys moving toward him across the still
plain. Settling back on the seat, clicking to the horses, he
followed Flynn. Brooks was beginning to like the harsh,
untamed country.

By noon, Brooks had shed his suit coat. Using the sleeve
of his shirt, he dragged it across his forehead, wiping the
sweat away. He wished he'd bought better clothes in town.
Silently he chided himself for being so ill-equipped. Riding around Central Park was a far cry from what he was
doing now. He felt small and insignificant in the vast
openness. Bright blue sky and endless prairie stretched as
far as he could see. They'd been traveling for hours, and
the only noises had been the creaking of leather and wood
and the breathing of the horses. Brooks felt a kind of
hypnotic lethargy. Flynn's voice took him totally by surprise. He jumped, and Flynn grinned broadly.

"That's Trace's place over there. If you look, you can
see the top of the windmill from here." Flynn pointed with
his chin.

Brooks squinted, just making out the small, dark circle
atop the wooden tower. He could see the outline of a fairly
large house. He thought about just turning the wagon,

leaving Flynn sitting there, but of course he didn't. He'd promised Flynn he'd wait, and he intended to keep his word. Brooks took a deep breath and held it for a moment.

"Thinkin' about your promise, aren't you?" Flynn said curtly, looking out toward the spinning windmill.

Brooks released his breath as he nodded.

"Well?" Flynn said.

"Well what? I promised. Do you think just because I'm from the East I can't keep my word?" One brow rose indignantly.

Flynn's gaze never wavered or changed. The bay pawed the earth, showing his irritation at yet another stop. The horse was used to a much quicker pace than the one he'd had today.

"I expect you'll keep your word." He let the horse have his head. Before the bay took two steps, a shrill scream, sounding almost like a whistle, floated to them on the breeze. Flynn's body vibrated in the saddle as his horse answered the call, his body jerking rhythmically as he nickered toward Trace's ranch.

"What was that?" Brooks eyes widened.

"I guess Ghost can smell us," Flynn said with a wistful look in his brown eyes.

"Who or what is Ghost?" Brooks wished his companion could be just a little more generous with his explanations. Pulling teeth would be easier than getting any kind of complete answer out of him.

"Trace's stallion," Flynn said.

Brooks grimaced. Flynn acted like releasing the tiny scrap of information hurt him physically. The name Ghost meant nothing to him. He raised both eyebrows questioningly.

"A stallion can smell and hear things you wouldn't believe," Flynn supplied, catching Brooks's expectant look.

"How much farther did you say your ranch is?" Brooks asked as they resumed their leisurely pace.

"Around five miles."

"Tell me something, Flynn—" the wagon lurched to a stop as Brooks pulled back on the long reins.

"Hmm?"

"Is everyone in your family as talkative as you are?" Sarcasm rang across the prairie.

Flynn chuckled. Soon it erupted into side-splitting laughter. He convulsively slapped his hand down on his denim covered thigh, several times in quick succession. He was soon pulling off his Stetson, brushing his hand through his hair again. The man on horseback completely mystified Brooks.

"Whee, you're entertainin', by thunder," Flynn said. "Now that you mention it, I suppose I ought to tell you what to expect when you reach the ranch." Flynn was still grinning. "Pa's an old soldier—he can be cantankerous, but usually he's pretty easy to get along with. Clell, he'll talk your leg off if you're not careful. He's like an uncle to all of us. Shane is the ripe old age of twenty, cocksure of himself. Logan's the baby, fourteen now, wantin' to grow up fast, be a man—watch it if you play cards with him. And there's Missy." He studied Brooks.

"Your sister?" Brooks asked, hoping he might again prompt an unusual flood of words. Flynn had spoken more in the last few minutes than the whole long trip combined.

"Yep. My baby sister." Flynn frowned, taking an appraising look at Brooks. "I don't quite know how to say this, except to just spit it out."

Brooks felt uncomfortable. Obviously something was terribly wrong with Flynn's sister. He could see how the man hesitated to talk about it. It must be something dreadful.

"Missy is nearly seventeen. Our mother died when she was just a kid, around five or so. We boys raised her." His eyes lost their sharp focus as he stared out across the endless grassland. "We've kinda taught her to be a little rough. She can ride like a Comanche, rope a steer, shoot fast and straight. She can skin a deer better than most men." He shifted in his saddle, causing the leather to groan softly. The big gelding's ears twitched back and forth.

"What're you trying to say, Flynn?"

Flynn smirked at him. "She just hates tenderfeet. Missy is more of a man than most men. I hope you are up to it, 'cause I have a feelin' she might make life interestin' for you! She can be...sort of opinionated sometimes." Flynn was chortling again, and Brooks felt his irritation growing. Flynn appeared to be highly amused by the look on his face.

"Flynn, I seriously doubt that a sixteen-year-old girl is going to bother me much." Brooks snorted. A sixteen year old girl—why, the very idea!

"Just remember I warned you, she don't take to strangers, and she really don't cotton to dudes."

Clell continued to eye the slow progress of the buckboard, as he'd been doing for over an hour. From his vantage point above Trace's ranch, he could see for miles around. Several times he'd seen Flynn pull up his horse and speak to the other man. He was mighty curious, but he wasn't going to leave, not just yet. The argument he'd been having with himself for two days wasn't over yet, and it was a toss-up which side was winning.

Whimpering sounds escaped the leather saddlebags. A fluffy ball of gray and tawny fur wriggled at the open flap. By twisting in his saddle, Clell was able to reach in and extract a good-size lobo pup. It made a low growling sound in its throat when Clell lifted it by the loose scruff around its thick neck.

"Settle down, you li'l devil." Clell had found the she-wolf poisoned outside her den, near Trace's house, two days ago. She'd died trying to reach her pups. Only one had survived—this one. Now Clell found himself sitting above Trace's ranch, trying to make a decision. Wolves, even baby wolves, weren't looked upon with benevolence in the territory. Bounty on their hides was leading to wholesale slaughter, and it sickened Clell. All the mindless killing. Any idiot could see how the smaller animals and rodents were multiplying, damaging the range, since they weren't being kept in check by wolves or other predators. Even hawks and eagles were being regarded as enemies of the rancher all of a sudden.

"Stupid, just plain stupid, to my way of thinkin'," Clell muttered to the pup as he rubbed his gnarled hand through its fur. It growled and tried to sink needle-sharp teeth into his hand. He chuckled, but a deep sadness came over him, and for one black moment he feared man might actually kill every last one of the wolves living in the territory.

"Surely not. That'd be insanity—they got to have more sense than that," he said aloud, squinting his eyes and looking back toward Trace's house below.

Amber eyes looked up at him as a rough tongue licked across his wide thumb. The trusting cub was the source of Clell's dilemma. He couldn't keep the cub; Hugh would have a fit—after all, he was a prominent member of the local cattlemen's association. Still, Clell couldn't bring himself to abandon the helpless creature.

He'd considered ending its life—mercifully. Then he'd been so revolted by the idea, he growled and skulked around the ranch in a fury. The old soldier's attention turned back to the ranch below him. The sun was going down, bathing the entire yard in a rosy glow. Bellami was moving around inside the kitchen. He could see her through the big window.

He'd managed several furtive trips to the ranch over the past couple of days while he pondered the question of the lobo pup. Once, he'd left a blueberry pie, still warm. Another time, three loaves of freshly baked bread, along with a couple of tins of piñion nuts—Trace's favorites.

Last year had been extra good for the nuts, and Clell hoarded them away selfishly, like one of the local squirrels. He hadn't examined his reasons for leaving the nuts too closely. If he had done so, he would've had to admit he'd left them out of guilt. He'd been avoiding Trace on his visits lately, and he felt bad about it. He was still watching the woman inside the kitchen when a thought hit him.

Grinning like a fox in a henhouse, Clell tucked the large pup inside his shirt. He tried to rebutton it, but finally had to content himself with leaving the pup's head sticking out the front between the bulging buttons. The hefty ball of fur fidgeted for only a minute, then settled down comfortably.

Clell shifted the reins on the horse's neck. The last rays of sun burnished the hillside to a coppery red as he turned toward the back of Trace O'Bannion's house.

Stopping his mount well away from the house, he tied the reins to a salt cedar, crouching down low. Using the skill learned from years of Indian-fighting, he moved toward the house.

A scant yard from the back door, he took the animal from his shirt. Very carefully he deposited the pup on the gray, weathering step at the back door. He rapped sharply on the door and melted away into the shadows. When Clell reached his mount, he allowed himself one last look back. A little warning voice in his head said he might someday regret this decision. He noticed the trunks still sitting on the porch as he rode away.

"Somethin' will have to be done about those damned trunks," he told his horse as they topped the rise and turned toward Hugh's spread.

* * *

Clell heard an unfamiliar voice when he stepped through the back door of Hugh's house. Lupe scurried past him with a basket of tortillas. He placed his index finger on his lips.

"Shh . . ." He winked at her as she brushed passed him.

She nodded, smiling. Clell came and went frequently, sometimes not letting the family know he'd even been there. Quietly Clell followed her to the door, taking a peek around the corner at the group seated at the table.

At the head of the table, Hugh was smiling. Shane was laughing at some joke or other, and Logan looked downright jolly. That in itself usually meant trouble. Flynn was watching his father with mild amusement shining in his brown eyes. Missy sat glaring at somebody, or something, just beyond Clell's view. The look in her black eyes was pure steel.

He'd seen that look only a few times before. Once when she'd taken a horsewhip to a man for kicking a cur dog, and once when she'd killed a rattler in the henhouse. Clell couldn't help being curious about the critter causing such a reaction in her now. Taking another step, he craned his head around to see the far end of the table.

There sat a young man with his back to Clell. He didn't even have a pair of horns or cloven hooves. His hair was silky and dark as— Clell let out a low whistle, realizing immediately where he'd seen hair like that before. Only once had he seen hair that precise color.

The sound of the whistle halted all conversation. Everyone turned to look at Clell, including the young man. Feeling mighty embarrassed to get caught sneaking around, Clell managed a timid grin. "Sorry," he said sheepishly.

Hugh rose from the table, happy to see his old friend. "Clell, please, sit down and eat with us. We have company. Flynn brought this young man home. Allow me to introduce you."

"No need. I'm Clell, and you must be related to Bellami James." Clell grinned, taking a step toward the man with his right hand outstretched.

Brooks smiled. "Was it so easy to figure out?" He shook Clell's hand eagerly.

"Real easy. I've seen hair that color only once. On Bellami James. Not to mention a certain resemblance." He colored slightly and let his words trail off. He breathed a sigh of relief when nobody commented on his slip of the tongue. Explaining how he knew what Bellami James looked like could be a bit tricky.

"Well, you're right, of course. I'm Brooks, Bellami's twin brother."

Clell cast his eyes around the table. The boys seemed to accept the young Easterner completely...but Missy...Clell was surprised to see so much hostility in her. "Missy, is somethin' botherin' you?" He pulled out the chair beside her and sat down, never taking his eyes off her face.

She didn't answer. Instead, she shot another venomous glare toward Brooks. Flynn watched her from under partially lowered lashes. Clell saw the slightest twitching of his lips, as if a grin wanted to burst across his face.

Brooks James looked at Missy for a moment with deep intensity in his light eyes, then turned to face Clell. White teeth flashed in a dazzling smile. "Miss O'Bannion is not very happy to have me here, I'm afraid."

Clell raised a gray eyebrow. "Oh? Why is that?" Clell could see none of the O'Bannions were going to explain anything to him. Brooks would have to supply the details.

"She's afraid I'll persuade Bellami to return home with me to New York. Actually, Miss O'Bannion has told me if I so much as try to speak to my sister she'll shoot me. 'In my black heart,' I believe was how she poetically put it." Brooks turned his full gaze on the pair of black eyes examining him intently. For a full minute they held each other's gaze. There wasn't any backup in either one of them. This could be a problem, Clell mused.

Flynn coughed once behind his hand. Clell knew he was fighting to keep from busting out laughing.

"Well, if this isn't the damnedest thing I've ever seen," Clell whispered under his breath.

Logan, ever the diplomat, broke the silence. "Pass the tortillas and chili, please." His cocky smirk quickly withered as two sets of eyes drilled him. One pair was black as night, the other dove gray, and both full of defiant strength.

Chapter Eleven

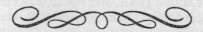

Bellami touched the pup affectionately. He made little growling noises in his throat, and his whole body vibrated. The pup stuck his nose deeper in the pan, smacking his jaws as he braced his paws, jealously protecting his food.

Bellami giggled. "Little pig." She'd been feeding him a concoction of corn bread, eggs, bacon drippings and whatever scraps were left from dinner. He looked bigger already. His head was wide, topped by petite pointy ears with black tufts of hair. She didn't know what kind of a dog he was. Nothing in New York looked quite like this. She'd been calling him Tip, for the tips on his ears.

For the past week, she'd been hurriedly finishing the evening meal in order to go to her room. Mr. O'Bannion had been more sullen and pensive lately, anyway. He didn't even seem to mind her early departures. She suspected he enjoyed his solitude, since it appeared he barely tolerated her presence most of the time. There'd been a subtle change in him recently. He seemed to be losing some of the restless energy that plagued him. He acted calmer, quieter. She didn't know if that was a good sign or not. Maybe this new attitude signaled acceptance of his situation.

Bellami shuddered at the thought. Trace O'Bannion was by far the rudest, most self-pitying man she'd ever met, but it made her sad to think he might be settling into a safe, undemanding life. A life where he'd have no challenges. She felt color drain from her face. She realized she didn't want him to do exactly what she'd done so many years ago.

She'd withdrawn into a safe, insulated world, where her limits had never been challenged—until now. Her quiet soul-searching was interrupted by a determined tugging on the hem of her cotton gown. She looked down into amber eyes that caught the light from the kerosene lamp and reflected it back. Never had she seen such odd eyes.

"Tip! You little scamp. Are you ready to go to sleep?" Squatting down, she ruffled his neck. She picked up the heavy pup and took him to the corner of her room to put him in a basket filled with soft cloth. Bellami's best flannel gown now made a bed for her new pet. When she placed him in the basket, he regarded her for a moment with serious eyes. His head plopped down between outstretched paws. She smiled as a contented sigh escaped his body.

"Happy?" she asked, giving him one last stroke through his thick ruff. The cub blinked a couple of times at the sound of her voice.

When the hoofbeats began, low and regular, as they did every night, Bellami moaned and turned over. She squeezed her eyes tight, refusing to leave her warm bed and dreams. It was just too difficult to break the bonds of sleep and walk to the window. She slipped back into the dream. Brooks called to her from a distance. She knew she must seek him out, but in her dream she couldn't move. A gentle force kept her firmly rooted. She couldn't break away, and she really didn't want to. The hoofbeats quickened as she slipped further into the velvet softness of her dream.

Trace reached the bottom of the stairs and sat down, pulling on his boots and shoving his arms into his denim jacket. The spring nights still were cool enough to frost sometimes. Every night it seemed to take longer and longer until he didn't hear any sounds coming from Miss James's room. He grinned, thinking about the little charade he'd been playing the past couple of weeks. Ghost had been prancing and pawing, anxious to get started for a while now.

Opening the back door and screen, Trace crept to Ghost's corral. The huge gray stallion whiffled his nose against Trace's cheek in greeting. Trace leaned his face against the horse's head affectionately.

"Hello, old boy. So you've been waitin', too, have you," Trace whispered as he felt the stallion's ears working back and forth. Trace didn't open the gate. Instead he folded his muscular body and squeezed between the rails of the fence. Once inside, he ran his hand along Ghost's neck, feeling for a handful of mane at the withers. Giving the beast one loving pat, he vaulted up onto his back. Trace braced himself for the customary dizziness as it predictably swept over him. It passed, as usual, within a minute or two.

Firmly planted on the stallion's back, he shifted his weight almost imperceptibly, and the horse moved. There was no bridle, no saddle, only horse and man. Both of them reveled in the newly discovered freedom of the night. Trace rode in the large corral, animal and man exploring, learning together. The subtle knee commands, the shifting of his seat. Ghost never faltered and, so far, Trace had only fallen once.

He thought back to the first night, and his clumsy attempt. It made him chuckle. He had tried to ride immediately after one of his "spells." That was how he thought of them now, as spells.

Trace had had trouble sleeping that night. He'd been pacing his room when the pain came blazing through his head, bringing him to his knees in a cold, gut-wrenching sweat. He'd bitten down on his lip until it bled to keep from crying out. He hadn't wanted to alert Miss James.

For what seemed an eternity, he'd lain on the cool wood floor, paralyzed—in too much shattering agony to move. When the pain abruptly left, he'd heard the horse nickering to him, calling to him to try, just once more. Trace had felt like a small boy sneaking out of the house that night.

The episodes of pain were becoming more frequent and more severe. He knew he had only a short time to live. Death lay just around the corner. The doctor had warned him—he knew what to expect. He was going to die, and he was damned well going to ride again before he did. It was that simple. Now Trace grabbed for all the life he could and held on to it with both hands.

They'd settled into a pattern, he and Miss James. As soon as dinner was over, he discouraged any conversation with her so that she'd go to her room. Funny, she hadn't seemed to mind too much, either. She seemed almost eager to climb the stairs each night.

Ghost changed leads, and Trace shifted his weight and regained his balance. He intended to show Miss James what he'd accomplished, just once, before he died. The thought of how impressed she'd be brought a silly grin of vanity to his lips.

The memory of his first attempt returned. Trace chuckled out loud, thinking of what a fool he could be at times. He'd been so excited to be riding again, he'd vaulted completely over Ghost's back. He'd hit the ground, laughing like an idiot.

When he finally got up and back on the horse, he'd felt better than he had in a long, long time. Now, only a short time later, he had regained the grace and strength lost during his long period of inactivity. He was developing senses that he'd never relied on before.

The stallion felt the slight change and stopped on command. Taking a deep breath of the clear air, Trace prepared to dismount. Then, from nowhere, came another keen stab of pain. A sensation like someone cleaving his head from his shoulders seized Trace. He sagged forward, onto the gray's neck, holding the mane with quivering hands. Cold beads of sweat broke out on his face and upper lip while he groaned in agony. Incredibly, for a brief instant, Trace saw a glimmer of light. Like the first weak ray of sun in winter. He wasn't really sure his impression of sight was real, he was in so much pain. But for an instant there did seem to be light, or at least less darkness, as if someone had raised a curtain in a darkened room. Then it was gone. With the vanishing beam went the pain.

He slid weakly off Ghost. His knees buckled when his feet touched the ground. Moaning, he held on to the thick neck for support, waiting for the weakness to pass. Finally he was able to make his way to the house. He crept up the stairs, exhausted.

He had just placed his hand on the doorknob to his room when he heard a sound. "I must be goin' crazy," he whispered to himself. He could've sworn he heard soft whining coming from inside Miss James's room. "Fool," he said, shaking his head.

He closed the door behind him and pulled off his boots, dropping them easily to the floor. He stripped off his clothes and climbed stiffly into bed. Soon he was dreaming of riding Ghost across the New Mexico Territory.

Bellami woke to the smell of freshly brewed coffee. "Impossible," she muttered to herself as she flopped over. Pulling the blanket over her head, she tried to shut out the bright light. She'd had dreams all night long, and this was obviously just one more. But the persistent smell lingered, and finally she opened her eyes and sniffed suspiciously. It was coffee!

Dressing hurriedly, she kept glancing at Tip. Now how on earth could she get him outside without Mr. O'Bannion knowing? The man had become extremely perceptive—even if he was sightless.

Bellami worried her lip with her teeth while she tried to find an answer. Silently she cursed herself for being so timid. She'd been afraid he would object to her keeping a dog, so she'd kept her new pet a secret—and now she didn't know how to tell him.

Amber eyes scrutinized her somberly from inside the basket. Tip raised his head, moving his pointed ears back and forth, but he remained silent. Bellami marveled at how quiet he could be. She remembered the strays she and Brooks had dragged home in New York. Their noise had kept the whole family awake all night long.

Not Tip. He would obligingly lie quiet as a mouse until Bellami came to take him outside. She tried to find some way to hide him as she came downstairs.

Bellami adjusted her long skirts again. With luck, this just might work. The pup had been stuffed inside the oversize pocket sewn within her skirt. Mr. O'Bannion would think she was on her way to the outhouse. Surely even he wouldn't ask any questions about that. Feeling like a little girl, she tiptoed down the stairs. Mercifully, none of them creaked under her feet.

Trace sat at the table drinking coffee. His head came up with a snap of awareness when she entered the room. His scrutiny never ceased to unnerve her. The haunted, probing look in those emerald eyes as he looked toward her face. His jet-black hair was neatly combed back, and little damp curls of dark hair showed at his temples and the nape of his neck. His beard was beginning to grow scruffy again. She grimaced, remembering the time she'd shaved him. Considering what a mess she'd made of his face, Bellami felt certain that first attempt would be the last.

"Good mornin', Miss James," he drawled lazily. Again Bellami detected a subtle difference in his demeanor.

"Morning," she said crisply as she slipped past him, out the back door. As she shut the screen she thought she heard him chuckling. She hurried toward the outhouse, slipping Tip out of her skirts as she went. He hit the ground running, ready to begin his usual daily routine. She watched him investigating the yard with his customary thoroughness. The silly pup put his heart and soul into the morning's diversion.

He spent a lot of time at the little stream, each day. Giggling, she allowed herself a peaceful moment to observe his antics. He laid his ears flat against his broad head, lowering his body. With precision he placed one foot in front of the other, creeping up on his intended victim. Today it was a large, grayish goose with a black head. It was considerably taller than Tip, but that seemed of little importance to the mighty hunter.

She saw the dog recoil quickly when the bird's long neck snaked out menacingly toward him. The goose made a hissing noise that sent shivers up her spine. Bellami watched for a few minutes longer, then decided she needed to get back inside. The time had come to accelerate Mr. O'Bannion's training.

"Miss James, I think you are crazy!" Trace's voice was deep and rich. Bellami felt the timbre of it as he spoke.

She had expected him to be a little stubborn, but this was ridiculous. "Mr. O'Bannion, I assure you I'm not crazy. Blind people do read using Mr. Braille's system." She sighed heavily as she started explaining for the fifth time this morning. They were not going to get much done today if he continued to be so obstinate. "In New York, this has been in use for some time. Now, if you'd try to be a little less..."

"Pigheaded?" he supplied thoughtfully, grinning happily in her direction.

Bellami felt the color rise in her face. "Yes! Pigheaded, bullheaded, muleheaded, whatever animal you feel like today!" She slammed the book against the table in frustration. The room shook with the force of it.

He laughed. A rich, hearty sound. When he turned sightless yet compelling eyes in her direction, she saw that they twinkled merrily. Today he wore a plaid shirt with pearl buttons. A sprig of black chest hair curled over the top of the first buttonhole. When he moved, the material stretched over his abundant chest and shoulders. Such a handsome brute, the way his dimples threatened to show as he laughed. She just couldn't find it in her heart to get angry with him, not today.

"Miss James, sit down," he ordered softly. "You work too hard. You certainly work me too hard! Don't you ever want to do anythin' else? Tell me about yourself. Tell me about New York City." He adjusted his long legs, and she couldn't help but notice the softer, lighter blue denim at the juncture of those long legs. His muscular thighs bulged against the fabric as he moved to find a comfortable position.

Bellami swallowed hard, obediently sitting down. "What would you like to know?" Her voice was almost a whisper. Her throat felt tight and funny. This happened every time she let her guard down lately. Every time she looked at Mr. O'Bannion as a man, instead of as her student.

"Everythin'," he said huskily, throwing his head back. He closed his eyes. Jet-black lashes, curly at the ends, lay against his finely sculpted cheekbones. Except for the scar where the bullet had creased his head, he was flawless, even with the now almost healed razor nicks in his chiseled chin. She hadn't noticed until now how utterly perfect his features were.

She could see the pulse in his neck. A sharp pang of regret gripped her. The man was beautiful! What kind of a woman did he desire? Certainly someone who could match his physical perfection, not some pitiful flawed creature like herself.

"Miss James? Tell me about your family." The silence had slipped by as she momentarily lost track of time.

"All right." She swallowed hard. With great determination, she tried not to be mesmerized by his face and his jewel-colored eyes. "I have two brothers and one sister. My father retired a few years ago. Now he spends all his time doting on my mother. I—I don't know what else to say," she stammered apologetically after another moment of silence passed between them. Her fingers worried on the edge of her bodice.

"Tell me about you. What do you do in New York, besides work with blind children?" His voice was hypnotic.

Bellami searched her mind for an answer. What did she do? The cloth knotted and twisted as she wrung it between her fingers.

Trace could feel her panic rising. He knew it as surely as if he could see. He knew her. He had learned her every mood, and yet he didn't know her at all. The flame of curiosity blazed to life again. She was the strangest woman. Always his little general, in control, commanding, the master of every situation. Except one. The few times Trace had shown any interest in her private life, he'd felt her sudden alarm, felt her fragile veneer of control crumbling. He knew he should back off and leave her alone, but something inside urged him on. He continued to press her. "Surely there are lots of things to interest you in New York. Tell me about one of them. What is it you do for fun, Miss James?"

Bellami could feel her face going pale. Fun? Fun? When was the last time she'd had fun? Her mind raced like a runaway horse. Bellami was being drawn back to that day, against her will. That terrible day.

A carnival. Brooks and Bellami had been going to the carnival. Bellami stood up quickly. Her full skirt caught on the edge of a chair, causing it to tumble backward and hit the floor with a crash. Her head was spinning. All her emotions spun out of control, as well.

Trace felt her fear and panic, and his need to comfort her surged forward. He reached out for her as he stood up. He could hear her muttering something incoherent. She started to sway, stumbling. She was going to fall—he sensed it.

"Miss James?" Instantly he regretted questioning her. He realized too late how much it upset her. But why? What could have happened to her? The need to protect her bloomed inside him.

A cold, sick feeling gripped Bellami's stomach. The memory of that day washed over her, and she felt as if she were suffocating. She fought for control. She tried to push the memories back into the recesses of her mind, where they'd been safely tucked away for years, but they refused to obey. Her vision blurred, and she couldn't seem to find her center of gravity. She was flying away, slipping, losing herself. Then, somewhere in all the confusion of her senses, she felt strong arms and hands.

Trace took hold of her shoulders, steadying her. Even though she was still gasping for breath, she felt comfort in that steely grip. Closing her eyes, she leaned into his chest, panting. The room still tilted crazily, and a sick dizziness threatened to make her spill the contents of her stomach, but she sucked in great gulps of air.

"It's all right, Miss James. I'm here, it's okay, just relax. Lean against me. There, that's the way." He spoke to her like he would a scared animal. He felt her breath coming in short little gasps against his chest. She shuddered and continued to cling to him.

To him.

Trace felt her small hands on either side of his ribs, clutching his shirt. Twisting her hands and squeezing tighter, until the pearl buttons started to pop open. One by one, they broke off and hit the floor with a hollow clink.

He felt the cool air on his bare chest. An unreasonable sensation of satisfaction flooded his body. He knew she wasn't aware of her actions; she just kept clinging to him as if she were too terrified to let go. But still, he felt so good holding her, offering comfort and solace to the little general. He took a deep breath and filled his lungs with the sweet scent of her. She shivered within his grasp.

What was happening to her? This had never happened before. Even when she came home from the hospital, there'd been a calm about her. She didn't understand. Why was this happening? At this moment, the only thing sensible, realistic Bellami James could be sure of were the strong arms holding her. A small, anguished cry escaped her lips as she struggled to master her terror.

Trace heard one muffled sound of utter pain and desolation leave her. It went ripping through his heart like nothing had ever done before in his life. The need to protect the frail woman within his arms surged through him. Bending his head toward her, he caught the unmistakable smell of her. Lavender and woman's smell. Soft, sensuous, powerful.

Holding her tighter, he whispered things he wasn't even sure made sense. Trace didn't know what else to do. His experience with women was somewhat limited. He'd certainly never tried to comfort one before. Even as a child, Missy had been less vulnerable than this woman. Miss James's sorrow ripped a hole in him as wide as the San Francisco River, and he didn't know how to help her. Gently kissing the top of her head, he could feel the silky strands of hair against his lips. In a heartbeat, the urge to comfort her became something different. He felt the blood heavy and thick in his veins. She felt so warm, so soft, so totally helpless and feminine in his grip.

Trace released one arm, slipping his hand around her back, pulling her closer. Now he squeezed her form against him all the way down from his bare chest to his thighs. He could feel the heat of her through the fabric of his Levi's. A sensation of pleasure rocked him from head to toe. Tightening his grip, he appreciated the smallness of her waist. The end of her long, heavy braid brushed the back of his hand. It was so long and soft. He tried to guess the exact shade of brown. Not brown, like she said, not just plain old brown, but dark, like the velvety night.

Feeling her growing still and calm in his arms, he suddenly was afraid she might shove him away. The fear of rejection squeezed his chest. Fear and his instinct for self-preservation chilled the warm feelings growing within his heart.

Foolish, foolish man. Foolish, blind man, he chided himself. What would any woman, even an ugly woman, want with half a man? Still, he couldn't release her. His body had a will of its own. He continued to hold on to her as if she were the essence of his life, warm and fragile. Closing his eyes, Trace breathed deeply, wanting to cherish and memorize every scent, every curve of her warm body—before she shoved him away.

Bellami became vaguely aware of her surroundings. A warm firmness pressed against the entire front of her body. For a moment, her mind refused to accept the situation. She simply could not believe it—Mr. Trace O'Bannion was holding her. Holding her as if she were something precious to him. She knew she should remove herself from his arms, but she felt so safe, and yet at the same time so vulnerable. She felt at this moment more a woman than ever before in her life.

Without realizing it, she moved closer to that wonderful, hard warmth. His arms felt like a haven from the world. With a deep sigh, she relaxed against his chest, content and calm. Finally, Bellami forced herself to lean away from him, just a little, so that she could see his face. His expression was beautiful. Utterly, painfully beautiful. She marveled at the kind of wonder surrounding his face.

His eyes were closed, and he was breathing deeply, as if he'd been chopping wood all morning. Fascinated, she continued to look at him with her head tilted back. Then, slowly, he started bending his face toward hers. She watched for a moment, but then the image became too achingly magnificent for her to watch, and she allowed her eyes to flutter shut.

When his lips brushed hers, something primal and strong exploded inside her. Bellami felt as if she had touched hot embers. She worried she might faint away from the force of it. Some instinct in her wanted more, wanted to explore and taste him. Parting her lips, she felt a shock ripple through her as his tongue invaded her mouth. He outlined the inside of her lips. She let her tongue meet his and tentatively touch.

Bellami had never been kissed before. The feel of his stubbly beard against her face was rough and exciting. She caught a taste on his lips. It was unlike anything she had known before, and it whetted her appetite for more, much more.

Trace wanted to devour her. He wanted to hold and kiss and lick every part of her. She tasted sweet, like nectar he'd once sucked from a honeysuckle blossom. The taste and feeling of her imprisoned him like a spider's web. He raised his hand to touch her face, and allowed his fingers to caress her neck and along her cheek. He immediately felt her stiffen in his grasp.

Bellami pushed herself away from him. The magic moment had ended the minute his fingers neared the scar on her face.

For long moments they stood apart, but not apart. Not touching, yet each feeling the other intimately, as if they were skin to skin.

Taking a deep breath, Trace tried hard to tamp down his passion. He had never felt anything like it before. There was no reference point for the power this woman had over him. She scorched him, and yet she refreshed and cooled him, all at once.

Bellami could see his jaw tightening. Suddenly she saw him tense every muscle in his body. His shirt hung open, and she watched the muscles in his stomach ripple with hidden strength. Something told her touching him would feel so good. If she just trailed her fingers over that chest, downward . . .

The dark hair growing in a line down his flat belly looked damp. She followed it with her eyes. A tiny gasp escaped her kiss-swollen lips when she saw the hard bulge within the soft, pale denim. Blood heated her cheeks as she snapped her eyes back up to his face. He had opened his eyes, and a tiny grin teased his mouth. Emerald eyes smoldered with some secret emotion she couldn't fathom.

"Miss James?" His deep, husky voice made her stomach contract.

"Yes."

"Would you do somethin' for me, please?" He was still breathing deeply.

"Of course, Mr. O'Bannion." If she could just remember she was his teacher. He was her student. He needed her to teach him.

"Would you give me another shave?" The dimple appeared in his cheek, along with the impish grin.

Trace decided he could endure any amount of torture, just to have her hands on him again—even if it meant being peeled alive.

Minutes later, her fingers trembled as she worked the brush along the contour of his jaw. Bellami swallowed hard as she lathered his face.

Closing his eyes, he ordered his body and mind to memorize the feel of her. Again he cursed himself for being such a fool. This was pointless torture, and he knew it. Still, while his mind told him that he was a cripple, with no right to hope and dream, a tiny seed of want and hope grew valiantly in his chest.

He heard her heavy sigh and felt the cold edge of his own razor skim along his jaw. No sting or burn accompanied the feeling this time.

She hesitated.

"It's all right Miss James. I survived your first attempt, remember?" Trace clenched his fists, forcing them down into his lap. God, he wanted to reach out and grab her. He wanted to hold her, to cover her slim body with his.

Bellami couldn't stop her hands from shaking, and yet he seemed so calm. He actually acted as if nothing peculiar had taken place. She watched his face for a moment, and suddenly it dawned on her. What had happened wasn't anything extraordinary for him at all. Fool! Silly little fool, she told herself. A man as handsome as Trace O'Bannion had probably been kissing girls like that since he was a half-grown boy. With a feeling of bitter disappointment, she chided herself again. Bellami had spent many years telling herself she had no right to expect love and romance like other women, and yet the first man to treat her like a woman made her forget all that. Suddenly she felt a resentment so deep it hurt. She turned that resentment toward Trace. How could he have taken such liberties? How could he do that to her? The kiss had been nothing, had meant nothing. It was such a small, insignificant thing to him, yet he'd never begin to know what it cost her.

Now she knew. And the knowing was like bitter poison to her. What had been a mystery before now had shape and substance and form. She was no longer ignorant of what she was missing—would always miss. She cursed him silently. *Damn you, I wish I hadn't found out.*

A dam of emotion inside her broke. All her pent-up hopes and dreams suddenly poured out, engulfing her senses, flooding her judgment with painful awareness. She wanted to shout at him, to beat her fists against his chest. To make him hurt the way she was hurting now. Why, oh, why? Now she'd go through all the rest of her lonely nights remembering the feel of his embrace, the touch of his lips, the pleasant scratch of his beard.

Gritting her teeth, she somehow forced her hand to be still. She began sliding the razor across his chiseled jaw.

I wish I'd never laid eyes on you Trace O'Bannion.

Chapter Twelve

Trace tried to calm the vortex of thoughts swirling through his brain as he rode the stallion. He felt like he was going to explode, shatter into a thousand little pieces. This situation with Miss James nibbled away at him like some strange disease.

He caught himself thinking of her at least a hundred times each day, and a thousand more at night. When she leaned over him to place his fingers on the odd little raised dots that she said would make words, he felt himself falling into a bottomless pit. Just the touch of her hands or the scent of her near him drove him into a hot frenzy of passion. He'd been adjusting his pants to accommodate his swollen tumescence with amazing regularity lately. Did she know how often his face burned with embarrassment? How could she not know. He was the blind one, not her. He was as randy as a mustang stud all the time, and it was Miss James that made him that way.

Trace knew his tenuous grip was slipping. He knew he was losing the battle being waged within himself. Persuading her to shave him had been both torment and euphoria. Each time she came near, his sex rose and burned with unrelenting heat.

Ghost picked up his pace, changing leads. Nearby, a coyote yipped mournfully. Trace patted the side of the stallion's neck appreciatively. "Good boy."

If he didn't have this outlet for his frustration, he didn't know what would happen. The past three weeks had been a sort of delicious hell. Since he'd kissed her, she'd never left his thoughts for very long.

Trace had shocked Miss James mightily by insisting they have lessons twice a day, instead of one, as they been doing since her arrival. She'd been damned hesitant at first. He squeezed his eyes shut in misery. She didn't want to be with him any more than was absolutely necessary, that was obvious. He didn't care. He had no pride left when it came to her. If enduring the slow, complicated process of learning braille kept her near him, then he'd do it. He'd willingly walk through fire if he could hold her once again. Just thinking of her now in the still night brought on another painful erection. Snorting with disgust at his weakness, he swung his leg over the horse and slid to the ground. Standing in the open corral, he pointed his face toward heaven.

"Please, God," he whispered into the night.

No answering voice came. His plea floated on the night air, lost amid the whispering wind and the chirping of crickets. Walking back to the house, Trace took long, deep breaths, trying in vain to calm himself. He opened the door with the stealth of long practice and stepped inside. Finding a chair, he sat down and quietly pulled off his boots so that he could tiptoe up the stairs like he had every night. When he reached the top of the landing, he heard it again. A low sort of whining noise. Taking a step closer to Miss James's door, he listened. He strained for a sound of her.

Just thinking of her lying in bed, sleeping, made his heart beat faster. Clenching his boots to his chest, he turned to his own room. Then he heard her cry out. Without even thinking about it, he dropped his boots to the floor with a thud, and burst through her door. For a moment, and only a moment, he was disoriented. Then he took a deep breath, and knew exactly where she was. He knew by her sweet lavender scent. She was standing in the middle of the room. Immediately he sensed the same panic issuing from her body, the same as before.

"Miss James?" he asked softly, "are you all right?" He kept moving slowly toward her as he spoke. She didn't answer.

Trace lifted his right hand and brushed his fingers against soft fabric. Her whimpering moans and his breathing were the only sounds he could hear in the room. He closed his fingers gently around the warmth of her upper arm. She started to make more of a sniffling noise.

"Miss James?" Stepping to her side, he felt her trembling all over. It tore right through him. He wrapped his arms around her, and he experienced such a powerful rush of pleasure, it was almost obscene. Trace cursed himself for feeling so happy to be holding her when she was locked in some nightmare of pain.

The firmness of her breast under the thin gown caused liquid fire to burn in his veins. He was glad she wasn't really awake. If she knew how much lust was coursing through his body, she'd recoil in horror. Trace knew he'd die if she rejected him.

He held her head gently, and she suddenly leaned against his chest. Smoothing back her loose hair, he allowed himself a wild moment of indulgence. He wrapped a length of it around his fist, savoring the feel and weight of it. He smiled because of the sheer pleasure embracing her gave him. Then he heard her voice.

"Oh, Brooks. Brooks, it hurts." Her voice was full of anguish and pain.

Pure, cold jealousy filled him. Trace clamped his jaw so tight it throbbed. He didn't know who Brooks was, but he loathed him. Whoever he was, Bellami cared for him, and from the anguish in her voice and her words, it was plain he'd hurt her. He continued to hurt her now, in her nightmarish prison. Trace kept stroking her back, trying to comfort her while visions of her caring for another man wrenched his gut.

Bending down, he slipped an arm under her firm buttocks. He lifted her slender body and took a step. Pushing the sensation of the way it felt to hold her to the back of his mind took a monumental effort. Crossing the room with her in his arms was the longest and the shortest journey of his life. Gently he laid her down and pulled the blanket up over her legs. He smoothed the long hair back from her face. She never woke up.

Determined to curb his primal desires, he remained a moment by her bed. He allowed his fingers to touch her softly. His hand moved down her neck with a will of its own—down her chest. Feeling the nipple firm beneath the fabric, he sucked in his breath. Then he felt the outline of her body. She felt utterly perfect beneath his rough fingers. He wanted to stroke her face, cover her body, bury himself deep within her.

Knowing that if he stayed his control would evaporate, Trace sighed heavily and moved toward the door. He stopped at the door and listened to her even breathing. She started to whisper again.

"I love you, Brooks."

Trace blindly stumbled to his room in a jealous rage. He closed the door and leaned against it, squeezing his eyes shut, forcing the images into the darkness that was his world. Her words echoed in his head, more powerful than the kick of a mule. His breath came in short, painful gasps. Miss James was in love. It explained a lot.

Trace had wondered why she had consented to take this job, way out here, so far from her home and family. Now he knew—she was obviously not a woman happy in love.

His hurt feelings busily constructed the entire situation. He could see the innocent Miss James being lured to destruction and ruin by a more worldly man. Then, in another scenario, he saw her wiping tears from her face, waiting at the altar for a bridegroom who never came.

Brooks. His rival had a name.

She'd been ridiculed. She'd given her heart to someone who played her false. That was why she called herself ugly. Had he left her for a prettier woman? Feelings of hate assaulted Trace as he sought an explanation for Miss James's torment. Balling up his fists, he pushed himself away from the door, cursing as he walked toward his window. He raised it roughly. The clean, crisp air rushed across his face.

The intensity of pain that engulfed him was the worst so far. He felt his knees turn to water as he grabbed for the railing on the balcony, but it was too late. He fell heavily, as if he'd been clubbed from behind. This time he feared he would lose consciousness. Clamping his jaw down, he fought to master the anguish with all the strength he possessed. With one shaking hand, he finally found a purchase on the railing and slowly pulled himself up. Panting with effort, he opened his eyes a crack.

Below, Trace could see, through a milky fog, the distinct outline of a corral, and inside it a pale horse. Ghost.

Disbelief gripped him. Then, when he allowed himself to believe it might be true and not the wishful image his tortured mind conjured up, it started to dim and rapidly disappeared.

Trace understood! Laughing, bitterly disappointed, he knew what lay in store for him. He'd see again, all right, and then he'd die. A few months ago, even a few weeks ago, Trace would've welcomed death. Now a tenuous little flame struggled to burn within him. Trace clung tenaciously to his life, limited though it might be. He wanted laughter, sunshine. He wanted to ride Ghost and feel the sun on his shoulders. But most of all he wanted Bellami James.

Waking early, Bellami smelled coffee again. Wincing, she threw her hand over her eyes. Her nights had been one torturous nightmare after another lately, and her lack of restful sleep was beginning to wear on her. When she turned over, her hand slid from the mattress and her knuckles came to rest against the floor. A soft nudge was followed by a rough, wet tongue licking her hand.

"Good morning, Tip." She turned her head and looked into somber yellow eyes. His large head was nearly level with the bed now. In a matter of weeks, he'd grown so much he no longer looked like a pup. Tip was reaching the gangly stage of puberty. He stood as tall as the shelty she and Brooks grew up with in New York, and he was growing more every day. She grinned at the serious canine face, wishing she could read his mind. The answer to some mysterious secret seemed concealed in his amber eyes.

Nudging her again, he indicated how anxious he was to escape his confinement. Grudgingly, Bellami got up. After she smuggled him outside each morning, she watched him lope off across the prairie, wondering where he went and what he did all day. Carrying him downstairs had become impossible in the past couple of weeks. Now she was forced to wait until Trace went to brush Ghost every morning, then slip into the parlor and let Tip out the front door. He was always quiet, so it had worked thus far, but how long would her luck hold?

Sticking her head out her door, she listened carefully. No sound came from the kitchen. She assumed Trace had gone outside. He'd developed the custom of rising before her over the past several weeks. She saw him at lesson time and at meals. The rest of the day he kept busy here and there outdoors. He still insisted they work double-time on his training—probably in an effort to send her packing as soon as possible. She puzzled over his changed attitude.

He'd become almost fastidious in his appearance, too. Now he insisted, rather forcefully, in fact, that she shave him regularly. His beard barely had time to grow at all before he would begin badgering her about needing a shave. In fact, only her pleading fatigue and exhaustion kept it from being a daily event.

When she lied and told him how tired she was, he quickly consented to being shaved every other day. The look of concern on his face seemed almost genuine. She allowed herself to feel flattered by it, for a brief moment, until her better sense prevailed. Trace O'Bannion's mind was changing daily, right along with his appearance, as if he were being driven by some unseen force. Bellami made a quick slicing motion with her hand, and the lanky animal fell into step beside her. They made their way downstairs quietly. She crossed the floor on tiptoe. As she opened the heavy oak door, she whispered softly to Tip. He froze in midstep. His amber eyes glowed. His ears lay flat against his head.

"What is it, Tip?" Bellami frowned. She'd never seen him act like this before. Turning back to the doorway, she gave a startled little yelp of surprise. Trace stood no more than six inches from her face.

"Miss James, did I startle you?" They both heard the low snarl behind Bellami in the parlor. She glanced back. Tip crinkled his flews across the top of his broad muzzle. White fangs flashed against rose-colored gums. A deadly look blazed within his eyes.

"What have you got in there, Miss James?" Trace asked her mildly. He slowly moved into the doorway, positioning himself in front of her. Broad shoulders rested against the frame of the door. He crossed his arms at his chest.

He had his shirtsleeves rolled up, and Bellami chided herself for noticing the knotting muscles in his forearms.

"It is, er, that is…I found… Oh, drat—it's a dog," she finally blurted out in disgruntled embarrassment.

"A dog? Sounds more like a mad badger." One dark eyebrow rose, as if to emphasize his point.

Tip was not moving. He held his body in a low crouch. Bellami could see the muscles tightening in his body, as if he were readying himself to spring. The change in her beloved pet was uncanny.

She felt a soft whisper. Trace's breath fluttered across the hair on her neck. An involuntary shudder immediately traveled down the length of her body. Tip's eyes darted from Trace to her and back again. A vague worry that Mr. O'Bannion might be in jeopardy nagged at her.

"Does this dog have a name?" Trace leaned in closer toward her as he spoke.

"Tip. I call him Tip. I hope you don't mind. He's very quiet. I found him at the back door. I should've told you. I apologize." She frowned, trying to will her body to stop trembling with excitement. When she looked up at him, she was struck by the manly picture he presented. His eyes were half closed, in a lazy, sensuous expression. He seemed to be contemplating something. Her heart flip-flopped as it always did when he was near her. Memories of his searing kiss returned, unbidden and unappreciated.

It was almost enough for Trace, being this close. Almost. He kept talking, allowing his senses to enjoy her nearness. Each time he inhaled, lavender scent floated to his nose. He could feel the heat from her body. When she spoke to him, soft puffs of her breath tickled his lips. He wanted to kiss her.

He'd been aware of the animal for a while now. Actually, he'd expected to find she'd smuggled in some sort of a cat, or a baby coon. The soft padding of the paws didn't sound like any dog he knew of. He'd been a little surprised to hear the deep, throaty growl coming from inside the parlor. The critter sounded big and mean. "I don't care a bit about the dog, Miss James. If you like it, keep it. Keep as many as you wish. Keep a dozen, if you want. I'd like you to feel at home here." With a sigh, he pushed himself away from the doorframe and sauntered away.

Tip relaxed immediately. He moved nearer to Bellami, sniffing, as if to assure himself she was well. Then, with one last glance of his oh-so-wise gold eyes, he padded off the porch into the sunshine. She watched him go. With a grin, she noticed that he traveled using a lazy gait similar to Trace's own.

"Men." She sighed as she shut the door.

Trace leaned against the corral and listened intently to the sounds of life around him. He could identify geese flying overhead, and a meadowlark on the fencepost of Ghost's corral. The chickens were scratching the dirt, and Bellami was moving around in the kitchen. He felt her presence even at this distance. He wanted her. His mind and body ached with wanting her. Each time he found himself thinking about the way her soft voice sounded in the night, blood boiled in his veins.

"Damn you." He cursed no one in particular. He felt his body grow rigid with frustration and want. Then a thought came to him, and he sucked in his breath. Bellami was in love with another man, but she was here, and the mysterious, fickle Brooks wasn't. Trace didn't have much time left—he knew that. But what time he did have, he wanted to spend with Bellami James. With a renewed sense of purpose, he walked to the kitchen. He heard her stand up quickly when he entered the room.

"Mr. O'Bannion, are you ready to begin your braille lessons?" She sounded a bit breathless.

"No, Miss James, I'm not. Today we're goin' to do somethin' different." His voice rang with authority.

She watched him and felt slightly perplexed when he cocked one eyebrow. Bellami wasn't sure she trusted him when he acted like this. He could be so unpredictable at times.

"What are we going to do today?"

"We're goin' on a picnic." Trace was grinning like a happy boy.

"A picnic?" Disbelief echoed through the kitchen.

"Yep. You pack the basket. We can go on Ghost. Of course, you'll have to sit astraddle. I'll ride in back." He moved away from her and turned his back so that she couldn't see his face.

She started to protest—to say she couldn't possibly ride—but what could it hurt? There wasn't anyone around. Hugh O'Bannion had never shown his face or sent word, and the mysterious benefactor who'd left the fried chicken and the other things remained a mystery. Who could possibly know or care? The idea of getting away from the ranch was appealing beyond belief. "Fine, I'll pack a lunch. Can we take Tip?"

Trace heard the gentle appeal in her voice as he headed toward the stairs. His heart soared. "Sure, but he has to walk!" A deep bass chuckle wafted down the stairs, the sound of a closing door punctuating it.

She smiled and shook her head. Trace O'Bannion had a sense of humor. She never would've thought it. Bellami started collecting things and packing them into the basket. She smiled again when she realized she was humming.

He took the stairs two at a time. She'd said yes! He felt relief and hope beyond anything he'd even imagined up to now. He told himself she just wanted to get away from the ranch for a few hours. He warned himself not to make too much of this. She'd been little more than a prisoner here. Still, he wanted to believe it might be more. Hoped it might be more. He went to his closet and felt around for his saddlebags, in the back, on the floor. Pulling the heavy Indian blanket off the rail at the foot of his bed, he rolled it up as small as he possibly could and stuffed it in one of the leather bags. He opened up a tin and poured his shirt pockets full of piñion nuts.

Trace knew Clell only shared his piñions when he owed someone a peace offering. Funny thing, though, he honestly didn't know why Clell had left them for him. He forced his shirt pockets shut and was barely able to button them over the bulging nuts. By feeling along the closet wall, he located a pile of clothes. When his fingers touched the cold metal of round silver conchos, he knew he had the right bundle. Missy had left a pair of chaps, gloves, some Levi's and an old plaid shirt at his house before the shooting. He could only hope they'd fit Miss James. Both her looks and her overall size were vague mysteries that nagged at him constantly.

Thinking he might learn a little more about her by giving her the clothes to wear sparked his curiosity even more.

She met him coming up the stairs when he stepped out of his room. He nearly allowed himself to touch her when he sensed her so close to him. The thought of pretending to bump into her accidentally made his cheeks burn with embarrassment.

"Ma'am, here's some clothes that you may be able to use—for ridin', I mean." Trace's mind reeled with exquisite awareness of her essence. Every nerve ending in his body longed to reach out to her. "See if they fit." He thrust the bundle out quickly before he weakened and crushed her to him. Then he hurried down the stairs.

Bellami turned and watched him descend the stairs. It was like poetry, seeing the play of the muscles in his back and legs beneath his clothes. Her heart ached with a desire she didn't dare indulge. Bellami kept telling herself it was futile to hope. Why would such an incredibly handsome man ever want an ugly woman? With a deep intake of breath, she turned toward her bedroom. She started unbuttoning her dress before she shut the door behind her. It surprised her, but she was anxious to go.

Bellami tried using the small mirror to look at herself, but it was next to impossible. The pants seemed obscenely tight, and the chaps hugged her like her own skin. Only the shirt was roomy and soft. Evidently whoever wore these things liked to be able to move their arms without binding. She had brought a pair of her own riding boots from New York, and she slipped them on.

The effect couldn't be called high fashion, but she decided it would serve the purpose. A tiny smile tugged at her lips when her eyes fell upon her long-unused veiled hat. She realized how much freedom she'd been enjoying while in the presence of Mr. O'Bannion. His blindness allowed her a measure of freedom from the bonds she'd created for herself long ago. It was silly, but she felt a debt of gratitude to him for it.

A pair of leather gloves to protect her hands was the last thing left in the pile Mr. O'Bannion had given her. She pulled them on and flexed her fingers. They fit perfectly.

She found herself wondering if it was a woman who owned these things. Who else would have such small hands? What was the woman to Trace O'Bannion? A hollow sadness crept into Bellami's heart when she thought about the faceless female.

She went outside and found he already had the horse saddled, bridled and ready to go. Without her asking he helped her into the saddle, then climbed up behind her. She felt the pull on her heart when he settled himself against her. The gentle fluttering in her stomach turned into a million beating wings when he wrapped his arms around her waist.

"Well, it's up to you—lead the way," he purred pleasantly in her ear. His soft breath made tingles run down her arms. He squeezed her a little tighter around the waist. She tensed her body and tried to steady her breathing. "So I won't fall off, Miss James. Don't think I could stay on, otherwise. You understand, of course. I hope you don't mind."

"Oh. No, of course not, not at all, Mr. O'Bannion." She was instantly sorry she had reacted. She was acting silly. He was only holding her because he needed to—he wasn't enjoying it. What a change. A few weeks ago, his pride wouldn't have allowed such an admission of weakness. The least she could do would be to behave graciously about it.

Grinning like a fox in a henhouse, Trace signaled Ghost to move. Bellami couldn't even guess, but he was about as helpless on Ghost's back as the gray-and-cream shadow that fell unseen into step beside them. From one bush to the next, from shadow to shadow, the animal loped silently, keeping amber eyes on the woman.

Clell rolled a cigarette and waited patiently until they were well away from the ranch before he came down. The wolf had grown, a lot. He stubbed out his cigarette and tied his horse to the railing around the porch. The sight of Trace on Ghost's back, riding like a Comanche brave, made a lump stick in his throat. That made all his meddling and scheming worth it. The man was going to be all right. "I guess I'd better hurry and move all these damned trunks," He muttered grudgingly to himself as he opened the heavy oak door to the empty ranch house. He dragged the back of his hand over misty eyes and said a prayer of thanks for Miss Bellami James.

Chapter Thirteen

Brooks tried to catch his breath and spit out the dirt and manure in his mouth at the same time. When he rolled over on his back, his muscles cramped in protest. "Tell me again, Clell," he said, letting his head fall back into the dirt and closing his eyes for a moment.

"All right. There never was a horse that couldn't be rode and there never was a man who couldn't be throwed." Clell's singsong voice recited the old saying for the twentieth time this week.

"Yeah, that's it," Brooks said. "Now tell me again, why am I doing this?" He leaned forward on one elbow, frowning at Clell. The chaps he'd purchased two weeks ago no longer looked new. Dirt and manure covered nearly every inch of his body, and his lean face was brown from the sun.

Clell chuckled as he thought back to the first day Brooks had worn his new finery. Missy had been determined to shame the young tenderfoot. Day after day she'd goaded him, until finally he'd taken the bait. She started out by gracing him with some Western wisdom she'd learned. Whenever he was around, it seemed, she'd tossed out one of those salty little sayin's old cowboys were so fond of. Sort of "outhouse logic," Clell called it. Brooks had taken it all in stride, showing remarkable restraint—for a while.

Brooks shifted his position on the ground. It seemed like a hundred painful years had gone by since he and Flynn had gone to Magdalena so he could send a telegram to his family. It had been short and to the point.

MAY 19, 1885
BELLAMI WELL AND BUSY STOP TERRITORY EXCITING
STOP STAYING LONGER STOP
LOVE BROOKS

He'd told himself it was the truth in the strictest sense of the word. He hadn't been so convinced, however. Before they left town, he'd bought some new clothes, something more practical for his stay. Levi's, shirts, chaps, boots and a good wide-brimmed hat. When Brooks appeared at dinner that evening wearing his new clothes, Missy had given him an appraising look. Then she'd announced in a tone that would have singed hair, "It's the man that makes a cowboy, not the riggin' he wears."

Shane and Logan had watched with wry amusement as Missy kept digging her spurs into the New Yorker. All through dinner, Brooks had ignored her vicious swipes at him. When Hugh and the boys suggested he come and help with the roundup, she'd snorted in contempt—and that was all she wrote!

The man had stood about all he intended to put up with. Brooks had accepted only because she kept making it plain she didn't think he had the guts, or the stomach, for such work.

Missy had it in her head he was soft and lazy. He'd set out to prove her wrong. For two weeks now, they'd been rounding up cattle. Now the hard work was really beginning. Branding, dehorning and cutting. Brooks had his work cut out for him, that was certain.

Clell chuckled out loud from his perch on the fence. He had grown fond of the Easterner. He had grit, and he wasn't soft. Clell didn't know what young gentlemen did to stay fit in New York, but they sure did something, 'cause Brooks was as hard and lean as any range hand.

Three days ago he'd come asking for advice on picking out a mount for the roundup. Brooks had wanted something that would take Missy down a notch or two. They'd looked over the broke stock, but discounted them all as too tame. When the wranglers brought in the mustangs, Brooks's eye had gone immediately to an oxblood paint.

With considerable effort, they'd finally managed to get him snubbed up. Then Clell had started instructing Brooks on how to proceed. For two days he'd met the horse head-on, never once wavering in his resolve. He vowed to break the horse and use him for the roundup. And it appeared he was going to do it if it killed him!

Clell laughed as Brooks got up off the ground, dusted off his rump, and headed for the bronc again. In the wink of an eye, the man was on the stallion's back. He grabbed hold of the rigging, and away they went. Straight up.

Clell winced when the horse hit the ground stiff-legged, taking a few bone-jarring hops. That had to hurt like the bejesus. Riding like that made your back hurt, and usually a man pissed pink for a week. Amazingly, the horse stopped. Then he started trotting—hesitantly at first, then it smoothed out. After a few minutes, he seemed to accept his fate and to submit to the man's will.

Missy climbed up next to Clell on the top rail of the corral. Swinging one long, slim leather-clad leg over the fence, she sat down. When she pulled off her hat, the sun hit her blue-black hair. For just an instant, Clell saw something like admiration in her dark eyes. Brooks grinned, and Clell could see the unmistakable look of satisfaction on his face. He was just getting ready to tell Brooks what a good job he'd done when a feminine voice cut through the air like a knife.

"On a gentle horse, every man is a rider." Then she slid off the rail and sauntered away.

"Damn and double-damn her, Clell!" Brooks took his brand-new Stetson and slapped it across his thigh with conviction. The crown of the hat crumpled with the force of the blow.

"What did you expect? You didn't really think she'd say somethin' nice, did you?" Clell watched Brooks closely. It occurred to him that was exactly what had motivated Brooks to suffer days of bruises and pulled muscles—the idea that Missy might say a kind word or two.

"Listen, Brooks, I'm goin' to tell you somethin', and it ain't for publication, okay?" Clell stepped down and walked slowly up to the skittish horse. Reaching out a gnarled hand, he gently stroked the horse's muzzle. "There will be one way, and one way only, a man will win Missy O'Bannion." He waited a moment for the words to sink in. When he was sure Brooks was really listening, he continued. "The man that can best Missy, just like you did this horse—that'll be a man she can love. She'll never give her love away. It'll have to be hard won and taken."

Brooks frowned as he set his hat back on his head. Then he turned to Clell, grinning broadly. "If I didn't know any better, Clell, I'd swear you were looking forward to the day and the man." His bright blue eyes twinkled.

"Could be," Clell said, then turned his head and spit in the dirt.

"Will you do one more thing for me, Clell?" Brooks grew serious again.

"Sure, boy. What?" Clell wiped a dribble of tobacco juice from his lips with the back of his hand.

"Teach me some of those damned irritating sayings!"

Clell couldn't help but laugh at the look on the young man's face. He didn't have the guts to tell Brooks Missy'd learned every damned one of those irritatin' sayin's at his knee, before she was even old enough to go to school. "All right, boy. All right," he replied, and turned away from Brooks when he heard the hoofbeats of a single horse.

The old cowboy squinted his eyes against the sun. He could make out a dark man of medium build wearing a wide-brimmed hat, riding a palomino. As the horse got closer, he recognized the rider as Elfego Baca. His horse was heavily lathered around the saddle, like he'd been ridden hard.

"*Amigo.*" Clell greeted him as he stepped up to take the tired horse. Elfego dismounted, and Clell led the thirsty horse to the trough, letting him drink. Then he began walking him out to cool him down.

"*Gracias, amigo,*" the man said gratefully. "Where's Flynn?" Clell saw signs of fatigue in his face.

"Here he comes now," Clell said, and motioned with his chin toward the tall figure walking from the ranch house.

"Flynn, it's good to see you looking so rested," Elfego said. He smiled and shook the larger man's hand vigorously.

"*Que paso, amigo?*" Flynn grinned. "What brings you here in such a hurry?"

"Trouble. You've heard about Señor Curtin? He has a new plan to get Socorro out of debt. He's been fining the gamblers and whores. In the last ten days, fifteen whores and ten gamblers have paid two hundred dollars. Now Mayor Eaton is accusing Marshal Monroe of, uh—improprieties." Elfego took off his hat and wiped his shirt sleeve across his forehead.

"Just what sort of improprieties?" Flynn narrowed his eyes.

"The mayor is accusing the marshal of neglecting his duty. Not arresting enough soiled doves and gamblers. Also accusing him of allowing opium dens to continue undisturbed—and for trading favors to obtain a railroad pass for himself."

"Damn," Flynn said flatly. He hated to have to get involved in politics. The bad blood between Monroe and Eaton was common knowledge. Getting involved in their squabble would be serious enough, but these new laws and all this fuss over morality, well, it went against Flynn's grain.

At the first of the year, the new city government of Socorro had taken bold action. Wanting to pacify the families of the socially prominent, they'd passed an ordinance outlawing "bawdy houses, houses of ill-fame, houses of assignation, or places for the practice of fornication, or for the practice of smoking or otherwise using opium." When Flynn read the new ordinance, he'd nearly guffawed. He had no love for the opium trade, but damn, trying to outlaw whorehouses seemed downright barbaric, almost uncivilized. What was the territory coming to? All this change made him damned uncomfortable. There'd even been some talk of a skating rink and something called baseball teams. It was too much, too fast, as far as he was concerned. This kind of thing made him itchy to saddle his horse and take off for parts unknown.

"I've been sent to get you, Flynn. There are going to be formal charges filed, and an investigation. The committee wants you there, just in case." Elfego smiled apologetically at his friend.

Sighing in disgust, Flynn said, "I'll get my horse." He turned toward the barn, and Clell noticed the deeply etched lines on his face. He knew Flynn wanted to stick around awhile longer. His trips to Trace's place had become a lot more frequent lately. Clell was pretty sure Flynn had been keeping a close eye on Trace—and Miss James, of course.

Brooks dismounted, then went to put the paint stallion away. He walked over to the trough to join Clell and the Mexican deputy. He listened, fascinated, as the two old friends discussed family and friends. Baca laughed at some silly joke of Clell's, then turned serious again.

"The bullfights are scheduled for the Fourth of July. Only a few weeks away. Say you will persuade the O'Bannions to join me in my box," Elfego cajoled, his black eyes sparkling.

"Bullfights? I've never seen one," Brooks said enthusiastically.

"Well, personally, I don't care for it," Clell said as he regarded the toe of his boot, "but I guess it'd be rude to decline such a generous invitation. I'll talk to Hugh and Shane. Logan will go along with whatever they decide."

"What about Missy?" Elfego asked.

Clell shrugged noncommittally. "Who knows? That's a lady that makes up her own mind—'bout everythin'." He slanted a sly look toward Brooks.

They all turned when they heard Flynn approaching. His saddlebags were slung over his broad shoulders, and he was leading his favorite gelding, Jack. He shook Brooks's hand, then had a word with Clell before he swung his body into the saddle. Clell and Brooks watched them till they were completely out of sight.

They'd just started washing up at the trough when the sound of buggy wheels singing on hard-packed earth caught their attention. Their shirtsleeves were damp at the cuffs.

"Damn, I don't recall so much company in nigh on to a year," Clell said, rolling a smoke as he waited for the buggy to come to a stop.

Brooks slicked back his wet hair with the palm of one hand. His face darkened when he saw a blaze of red hair and yellow ruffles emerge from the covered buggy. He heard a distinct groan come from Clell as Becky Kelly swayed up to the men, a ruffled parasol twirling in her gloved hand.

"Well, now, don't the both of you look cool," she exclaimed. "I think it's mighty unfair that you men can dunk yourselves whenever you wish. I'd give anything to be able to do that.'' She lowered her lashes and fluttered them expertly.

''Why don't you, then? I'd be glad to help you into the trough.'' Missy had come up on them as quiet as any Apache. She looked as deadly as one, too. There was pure loathing in those jet eyes skimming over the visitor. ''What are you doing here?'' she asked without ceremony.

''Flynn and Mr. James invited me. Isn't that right, Mr. James?'' She'd lost some of her color and she seemed to be tearing the lace off her parasol under Missy's level gaze.

Brooks neither confirmed nor denied her statement. It made him furious to be put in the middle of two spitting wildcats, but he had been raised to be a gentleman, even if it hurt.

''Actually, I came by to ask Mr. James if he'd like to escort me to the bullfight at the Fourth of July celebration,'' Becky said sweetly. She smiled seductively while she waited for Brooks to accept. She stood twirling her parasol, completely confident of her carefully practiced charms.

Brooks couldn't resist. It had never occurred to the little tart that he just might refuse her. First he grinned, almost shyly. Then he put on one of his most devastating phony New York society smiles. The kind guaranteed to reduce any feminine creature to pliant jelly in his expert hands. When he was sure it was having the desired effect on Becky, he took a step forward.

Toward Missy.

She'd been leaning against a post, with one shapely leg hitched up on the rail behind her. He noticed how her shotgun chaps hugged her thighs as he neared the dark-eyed beauty. When he was less than a yard away from her, he suddenly reached around her waist and pulled her into the crook of his arm and against his hipbone. He held her there, feeling the heat from her firm thigh against his leg. She tensed, but refrained from sticking a knife in his ribs—

yet. Probably because he'd surprised her, he thought with wry amusement.

Brooks turned his cool stare back to the little vamp, who now showed signs of tension in her rehearsed smile. "I'd love to, Miss Kelly, I truly would, but I already asked Missy, and she's consented. After all, what man could pass up the chance to take the prettiest girl in the territory?"

It worked. On both of them.

Becky paled and began making excuses why she couldn't stay any longer, and Missy remained mute. In a remarkably short time, Clell was helping Becky into the buggy. Raindrops started pelting the ground as the buggy disappeared from sight. A sharp crack of the whip indicated she was leaving quicker than she'd arrived. Discreetly and very wisely, Clell made himself scarce.

"I'll be at the barn. Never could stand bloodshed," he quipped as he left.

"What in the Sam Hill is this about?" Missy threw his arm off as soon as Clell was out of sight. Then she drew herself up to stand on tiptoe to shout up into Brook's face. Several raindrops landed on her upturned nose and eyes, spiking her long black lashes. Brooks was totally captivated by the sight of her. She threw sparks at him from her dark eyes while the rain made her skin dewy and soft.

"I guess it is kind of playing dirty, isn't it?" he mused as the rain fell harder. His hat shed water down the back of the brim as it was intended to do. Soon a dark, wet stain plastered the wet cloth to his body. He was oblivious of everything except the snapping black eyes before him.

Brooks bent down to pick a blade of wet grass, glancing briefly away from the vixen before him. He bit the end off, tasting the tart liquid. It mingled with the sweet, warm summer rain trickling into his mouth. "I really do want to take you to the bullfight. Besides, I couldn't pass up an opportunity to shame her."

Missy was still furious. She didn't know what to make of Brooks, and she was unsure of his motives. Clamping her jaws shut with a click of her teeth, she frowned at the man towering above her.

"Why?" She regarded Brooks warily, like someone observing a coiled rattlesnake.

He shrugged his muscular shoulders, still looking down into her damp face. "I dunno," he said. "I don't like her. I heard what she did to Trace."

Missy felt something—not pride, but something warm and satisfying—for the man who looked at her with pale, probing eyes. She could see her reflection in those remarkable eyes while he studied her intently.

"Besides, you *are* the prettiest girl in the territory."

She turned and walked away, shaking her head in amazement. What could she say to him? Missy had never met anyone like Brooks James, and she wasn't quite sure she was happy to have made his acquaintance now. His presence was having an odd effect on her.

Clell materialized from the shadows near the barn. The old cowboy casually walked up beside Brooks. "Boy, I'm goin' to start teachin' you some territorial wisdom right now. Are you ready?"

Brooks inclined his head slightly, waiting.

Clell cleared his throat, speaking solemnly, as if he were a Baptist preacher on a Sunday morning. "Never marry a woman with the kind of looks you'd like to see on another man's wife." Then, with a mischievous chuckle, he turned and left.

Standing alone in the rain, Brooks realized he should've known it wouldn't be simple. Now, every time Clell said something to him, he'd be searching for some hidden meaning in the old man's words. What a place this territory was. He walked toward the ranch house thinking hard about tomorrow. The roundup would begin at dawn. Hugh said they'd be gone for a couple of weeks. Brooks set his jaw, determined to be up to the task ahead.

Chapter Fourteen

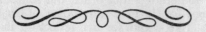

"Mr. O'Bannion?" Her voice sounded soft and shaky and too hopeful.

"Yes, Miss James." His breath fluttered across the back of her neck.

"Have you ever been married?" Bellami blurted out the words. The heat of a blush rose on her cheeks a second later.

"Nope." He smiled, happy to hear her curiosity, and more than a little surprised by it. "I was makin' plans to be married before I got shot."

Bellami noticed there was no bitterness in his voice, only a wistful, dreamy sound. "What happened? If—if you don't mind my asking?" she stammered.

"I don't mind. Guess it's the least I can do—I mean, to tell you about it. Seein' how all this is why you ended up out here."

Bellami let the horse pick his own way. There didn't seem to be any hurry, and she was completely content to let the animal guide her. Being away from the ranch and feeling the sun on her exposed face thrilled her.

"I was fixin' to ask a girl by the name of Becky Kelly to marry me. I built that house for her." Trace paused for a moment, and Bellami felt his arms stiffen around her waist. "That's not exactly true. I built the house for a wife and family, but truth to tell, I can't say it was Becky I pictured in that house.''

A tiny flame of hope, or something like it, flared within Bellami's breast. She trembled slightly.

"Miss James, are you troubled?" Trace asked.

"No, not at all. Please go on, Mr. O'Bannion."

"Not much to say. When I got shot, she hightailed it out of my life. Told me how she had expectations." He chuckled dryly, thinking back. "Sounds pretty stupid now. Expectations. What the hell is that supposed to mean, anyway?"

"Was she pretty?" Bellami asked in a whisper.

"I thought she was the prettiest girl in the territory."

Bellami frowned, trying to decide if his voice was quivering from pain or something else. He fell silent then, and she asked no more questions for a few minutes. Ghost moved steadily onward, seeming to respond to her commands before she even gave them. She'd never ridden astraddle before, and the sensation was not altogether unpleasant. She loved the smell that drifted up when the horse rubbed against a stubby bush. A sweet odor filled the air each time a twig or branch broke under his hooves. She hated to break the comfortable silence, but her curiosity was up again. She finally decided to ask Trace what the aromatic plant was.

Before she had a chance to speak, he shifted his weight behind her. Then he exhaled softly. She felt his breath, warm and intimate, on her neck. He moved her heavy braid aside with one hand. His nearness had a most disconcerting effect on her. The area in her lap where he gently rested his free hand had steadily become hotter and more moist. She shifted her body a bit, but his hand only seemed to sink deeper into the cleft between her legs. She wondered if he could feel how warm she was where he touched her.

"Mr. O'Bannion?" The catch in her voice embarrassed her.

"Yes," Trace replied, and grimaced when he heard the deep huskiness in his voice. He'd been mighty grateful that the cantle of his saddle stood between him and Bellami. If it didn't, his sex would be pressed up against her hips. He didn't think he'd be able to stand it. As it was, he'd been fighting for hours to keep from opening his hands and rubbing her. He could feel the heat at the juncture of her legs. She was deliciously warm at the open spot in the chaps where only denim separated his hands from her flesh. A pitiful poor barrier between them—a flimsy scrap of cloth, and the leather cantle. Her soft voice shook him back to reality with a jolt.

"What's that wonderful smell?" It was hard for her to focus on what she'd wanted to ask only a moment ago. Bellami's entire concentration seemed to keep drifting back to a pair of lean brown hands.

"It's sage. It does smell nice, doesn't it? Miss James, what is the wonderful smell on you?" He inhaled deeply, and waves of passion surged through him.

She squirmed uncomfortably. His question was so personal, so unexpected. Color flooded her face. She knew it because of the heat in her cheeks.

Trace felt her blush. There were times, like now, when his blindness almost seemed an asset. He had become so attuned to her. If he could see her, would he still be as aware of her shifting moods, of her very spirit? He doubted it.

Bellami tried to clear her throat. She knew that if she didn't, it would squeak and break again. She didn't want him to know how much his innocent conversation affected her.

"It's lavender, Mr. O'Bannion. Tilly packed my clothes in it for the trip." She felt awkward discussing this with a man. With *him* particularly.

Trace smiled. He liked feeling her feminine mortification. He had no way of knowing for sure, but he imagined that all women guarded their little secrets from the prying of menfolk. A tiny wave of satisfaction washed through him. He liked being the man who knew those little details about her. He wanted to be the only man who knew them. It made him feel somehow more connected, more intimate. More like she was *his*.

It gave him pleasure each and every time he managed to get her to reveal some mysterious woman's thing to him.

He allowed himself to imagine what it would be like to know all her secrets. To know all the little things that made her uniquely her. A fantasy of spending countless hours and days learning why she was so special floated through his brain. Trace wanted to discover everything about her. He wanted to know things like what would make her writhe and moan beneath him.

He tried to push the pleasant vision from his mind before it was too late. His Levi's were already becoming painfully tight, again. He shook his head in amazement. Just the thought of her sent his blood to the boiling point.

Bellami was determined to find the perfect picnic area. There wasn't anything like the beautiful spot in Central Park where her family went. Of course, this wasn't New York.

She scanned the area again and dismissed every possibility. Too rocky, too brushy, too hilly—no shade. After another hour, she heard her stomach growl loudly, and nearly died of embarrassment. There was no way Mr. O'Bannion couldn't have heard it.

"Miss James, are you havin' trouble decidin' where to stop?" he quizzed.

"Well, yes, as a matter of fact, I am. I'm sorry." She squirmed, and his fingers brushed her groin.

"Please, don't apologize. I'm perfectly content to keep ridin'." Trace meant what he said. The ride wasn't bothering him in the least—not that way, anyhow.

"You do seem fairly comfortable," she mused as a tiny finger of suspicion snaked up her back. If he was ill at ease or felt awkward riding blind, it didn't show. In fact, when the stallion jumped over a small trickle of water earlier, Trace had expertly kept her in the saddle with his strong, sure hands.

Bellami saw it then—the perfect spot. Smooth, no rocks, a satiny strip of ground in the middle of the vast prairie.

"There it is, Mr. O'Bannion, our picnic spot," Bellami declared. "Let's eat."

Trace held Bellami securely while she swung her leg over Ghost's neck. He sat immobile on the horse as he lowered her to the ground. She was light as a feather, and he held her suspended above the ground for a second longer than necessary, just enjoying the feel of her in his hands.

When she touched the ground, she started chattering pleasantly about the color of the sky and the rocks and silly things. Her voice soothed him. He liked it, the pleasant way she chatted about little things he'd never noticed or thought of before. A tiny smile teased the corner of his mouth. He slid off the back of Ghost's powerful hips. Feeling inside the saddlebags, he pulled out the Navaho rug. He shook it out with a pop of the heavy wool fabric, then dropped to one knee and felt the ground. With a flick of his wrists, he spread it out. She was still talking a mile a minute. It seemed perfectly natural, the sound of her voice against the quiet of the prairie.

"Miss James?" he inquired.

Bellami looked in his direction. He had such a nice voice, mellow and deep. The sound of it struck some chord deep within her.

"Yes. I'm right here, Mr. O'Bannion. Are we ready? Oh, how wonderful, you brought a blanket." She felt very touched, the way he'd thought of this little outing. Bellami sniffed back little tears of emotion that threatened to fall as she brought the basket to Trace. He'd flopped his lanky body down to recline comfortably on the rough wool of the blanket.

When she looked at him, an arrow of feeling whistled through her. She encountered his total maleness. For the first time, she allowed herself an uninhibited appraisal of him.

His long legs stretched out in front of him, crossed at the ankles. He reminded her of a young male lion she'd seen at the zoo in New York. So powerful, sensual, in control, potent. So very male. He was grinning toward the sky, at nothing in particular. He let his head fall back, and the hat toppled from his head, but he didn't seem to notice. It was almost too much for her to abide. The sun shining on his handsome face, his look of utter contentment. Suddenly he sat up. His movement jolted her.

"Where's the grub? I'm starvin'!" he bellowed.

She laughed; she couldn't help herself. Being with him like this was so far from what Bellami had ever imagined her days in the territory would be like. Even though the little voice in her head cautioned against it, she permitted her little fantasy to rush forward, beyond her control, with a life of its own.

In her fantasy, Trace loved her, totally—without reservation. He coveted his privacy with her so much that he brought her here so that they could be alone, with their love. She smiled at her foolishness as she prepared their picnic lunch.

"Miss James, do you miss New York?" he asked in a soft voice.

"No, not too much. I really didn't have much of a life there," she answered truthfully.

"Funny, isn't it, how me gettin' shot has made so many changes for so many people," Trace said dryly.

They talked quietly for some time, finally letting an easy silence settle over them. Bellami was content just to watch him.

Trace was content just to feel her near him. She radiated a force so strong, it was almost painful to him. He knew every breath, every sigh. When the wind moved her silky long braid, he knew it. If she smiled, he felt it—deep inside him.

Bellami thought he looked ten years younger than the first day she'd seen him in that dark bedroom. So happy, so relaxed, so at home in this rugged land. She felt a powerful emotion ripping through her at the sight of him. In that moment, Bellami faced her greatest fear and hopes. She was falling in love with Trace O'Bannion.

He could perceive her deep concentration, and then a ripple of something passed between them. He didn't know what, but he sensed a deep change in Bellami. It was like an invisible obstacle suddenly drifting away from them, a barrier that suddenly disappeared, leaving her presence to engulf him. It was like a door being opened to let in a strong breeze.

Gently he reached out to touch her hand. He didn't grasp it. Instead, he simply laid his fingers on hers. He felt her quake.

Abruptly he turned in her direction. "Would you like to take a walk?" His thick, dark brows were raised quizzically.

"A walk would be nice."

"Good." Grinning boyishly, he rose from the blanket. Bellami watched with appreciation as the muscles in his thick thighs rippled.

"Now don't go steppin' on a rattler," he teased gently as they fell into step beside each other. His easy banter filled her heart. Ghost grazed idly nearby. His head came up abruptly and his tulip-shaped ears worked back and forth, trying to identify some sound too faint for the humans to hear. He blew softly, pawing the ground. Then he put his head down and began to clip grass again with his teeth. Every few seconds his head would come up and he'd blow softly.

As Trace and Bellami were walking, Tip watched them from a short distance. His yellow eyes never left Bellami. He, too, raised his wide nose into the air, periodically sniffing, trying to identify some unknown smell.

Bellami saw Trace stop in midstep and inhale, like the animals. He frowned darkly. "Miss James, where are we?" His tone of voice made her heart plummet. She thought she must've done something to displease him, and that ripped at her soul.

"We are out—here," she answered, allowing her hands to flutter in the air, unseen by the man at her side. She had no idea where they were in this vast open plain.

"No. What I mean is, what's the land around us like?" Trace asked. His frown deepened, and he sniffed the air again like Tip. A raindrop fell, then another. One hit Trace's hat with a noisy plop.

Bellami looked around. "Well, the ground is flat, and it's sandy and smooth," she began, trying to find the proper words to describe the little path they'd been walking on.

"Miss James, is the land around us higher than where we are standin'?" Now Trace's voice sounded really concerned, and he spoke in a quick rush. Fear grew inside her.

Tip had started to pace back and forth in agitation. Ghost screamed out one of his shrill nickers from the hillside above them.

"Yes. We are on a sort of path." She could smell the rich, loamy fragrance of wet earth as the rain fell harder around them.

"Run!" Trace roared.

It happened so quickly that she didn't really have time to be shocked at his fierceness. Trace grabbed her wrist so hard she knew it was going to break—snap right in two. He began running full-out, at a right angle from the direction they had been walking. Bellami scrambled to keep her feet as he jerked her along.

The sandy path was wide and flat, and it seemed as if he'd been running for hours, dragging her along, pressed hard against his hip. His legs pumped with powerful strides. Bellami knew he was running as hard as he could. She just didn't know why.

When they were halfway across, she looked up and saw it coming toward them. Rumbling and frothy, like fresh milk being squirted into a pail, but brown, carrying sticks and boulders. A wall of water crashed down upon them.

"Oh, dear God!" Bellami croaked. As she was sucked under, she heard one word.

"Bellami—"

Of course, it could only have been her silly imagination. Trace had never called her by her first name.

Chapter Fifteen

Through the veil of pain and returning consciousness, Bellami distinguished two things simultaneously. A rough tongue licking her cheek, and a callused hand smoothing the hair from her forehead. A silly giggle escaped her lips.

"My champions," she croaked out. Her mouth was full of grit and the taste of blood. As she put her teeth together, they crunched most unpleasantly, as if she'd been eating dirt.

"Thank God." Trace's voice sounded like it might've cracked with emotion, but Bellami was sure it must be a trick of sound. She opened her eyes a little wider. Looking up, she saw a velvet-black sky above her. It was pitch-black, with a thousand jewels sparkling in it. The most magnificent night sky she'd ever seen.

Bellami tried to rise, and doubled over with a stabbing pain in her chest. She moaned and sucked in a painful breath. The more she tried to breathe, the more the raw stinging took her breath away. She let her body slump back, taking short breaths. There wasn't one spot on her body that didn't scream with pain.

"Don't try to get up. I think you've cracked a rib. Your breathin' has been soundin' all wheezy." A wide, splayed palm pushed gently on her shoulder, forcing her down. There was authority in his quiet voice.

"What happened?" She was dimly aware that Trace's hands were traveling over her entire body. Why? Was he searching for broken bones?

He stopped his exploration of her form. He seemed satisfied with her battered, sore body. She heard his deep sigh in the still night. "Flash flood. I should've warned you, happens out here all the time."

"Will we be all right?" Fear tinged her words. A long moment passed.

"Miss James, I'll get you back safe. I promise." His deep, throaty answer rang with conviction. He had moved away from her, and she was dimly aware of him picking up small sticks and branches in the darkness.

She felt a little better, and slowly raised up on her elbows. But when she maneuvered around and tried to stand, her knees buckled beneath her. She collapsed with a cry of pain. The hot, stabbing fingers radiated through her ankle.

"What? Miss James, what is it?" Trace was beside her in a heartbeat, dropping an armful of broken sticks and wood in a heap at her feet.

"My ankle. I can't stand on it," she said, trying to steady the quiver in her voice. "Mr. O'Bannion, how will we ever get back? I can't walk."

The despair in her words slashed him to the bone. There was real terror in her voice. Did she think he'd let anything happen to her? "I'll carry you," he said simply. Rising to his feet, he turned away from her. Slowly, methodically, he went about picking up the discarded wood.

She could perceive him feeling around on the ground until he located a piece. Then he would move forward and repeat the process. Somehow he managed to get a fire going. Bellami never knew how, but she was certainly grateful for the golden flame.

Tip sat just outside the glow of the fire, watching intently. Ghost was nowhere to be seen.

"Do you think the horse is hurt somewhere?" Bellami cracked open one of the small nuts Trace had handed her. Piñons, he called them. He'd not only managed to get them warm and dry, now he had supplied a dinner of sorts.

Trace knelt down beside her. He squatted back on his strong calves. The flickering light of the fire played across his face. Small bruises were beginning to show on the ridges of his cheekbones.

"No, I imagine he's headed for home by now," he said, and touched her lightly on the arm. "How are you feelin'?" His deep voice rumbled through her.

"Better, thank you." Bellami felt unworthy of his careful attention. She should've had more sense. She was supposed to train him, care for him. Now, because of her stupidity, she had placed them both in jeopardy.

"You know, Miss James, there's somethin' very odd about your dog," Trace said softly. Between words, he cracked the smooth brown hulls of the piñon nuts with his teeth. He spit the shell out between words.

"Really? What?" She spit out a piece of broken shell, chewing the white meat.

"I never would've found you if it hadn't been for him. He clamped on to my wrist—pulled me to you."

Bellami looked at the marks on her own wrist, visible just above her leather gloves. In the light of the campfire, she could see them clearly, encircling her wrist. Black-and-blue bruises, which outlined the shape of a perfect canine maw. Tip had dragged her to safety.

"Just as I reached the bank of the arroyo, you slipped from my grip." There was a sound in Trace's voice she'd never heard before.

Fear.

"You must've been unconscious," he continued. "I felt along the bank, called your name, but I couldn't find you. Then the dog brought me to you."

She looked across the small fire at the glowing amber eyes. Her protector, ever vigilant. Then her eyes fell upon the hard, determined man next to her, and she knew. They'd die before they'd let anything happen to her. Bellami had never felt more protected or loved than she did right now.

Sitting on the cold ground, battered and bruised, she knew she was safer here in this desolate location than she'd ever been in the drawing room in New York. A warm feeling washed over her.

Trace felt the cold grip of terror. He'd never been so scared in his entire life. Not for himself, but for Bellami. If it hadn't been for that dog— A shudder ran through his body.

"Will anyone find us out here?" she asked.

"Maybe. I'm pretty sure Ghost will head straight for the ranch. There's a chance Clell or one of the hands might see the stallion saddled and come lookin', but we can't count on it." Trace shifted his weight on his calves. "Do you know what direction we rode in, Miss James?"

She swallowed hard, feeling a painful lump in her throat. "No, I don't."

"I felt the sun on my right cheek, so tomorrow we'll keep it on the left." He sighed. He hoped he was right. It seemed simple enough, but could he navigate blind? Tomorrow they'd begin the walk home. A long shot, to be sure—but the only one they had.

Trace listened to her steady breathing. She was sleeping peacefully. It made him feel good inside to know she trusted him to keep her safe while she slept. The nights were fairly warm in May, but when he touched her forehead she felt too cool. He scooted his long frame closer to her and put his arms around her. With infinite tenderness, he tightened his hold on her slightly, until she stirred. He stilled instantly. She'd been different lately. Bellami seemed warmer, more open, but he still feared her rejection.

So far, Miss James was mercifully unaware of Trace's clumsy efforts to get closer to her. Each time he held her or touched her, she'd been asleep, locked in one of her nightmares. Except for that one kiss. He closed his eyes, remembering, and immediately felt the heat rise within him. He hugged her tighter to his body, savoring the sweet hell it put him through, having her so close, yet so totally out of his reach. Sighing heavily, he shook his head.

"Only an idiot would hold a woman this close and try not to want her," he whispered softly to himself. Exhaustion overtook him quickly, in spite of his intention to enjoy the painful pleasure of her nearness.

Soon he was dreaming. Not of riding Ghost across the prairie, but of holding Bellami—making love to her. He could see her body clearly in his dream, but no matter how hard he tried, he couldn't see her face.

Bellami woke to the first light of morning, pink and gray and fresh after the rain. She couldn't move. Panic gripped her. Then she realized why she was firmly rooted to the earth. At her back, a hard chest rose and fell in a steady rhythm. In front of her, pressed against her belly and thighs, a thick coat of gray and cream snuggled against her tattered, filthy Levi's. The warm objects surrounding her were immovable. She grinned. A bushy tail covered everything except her furry companion's glowing gold eyes. What a silly group they made. Had any woman ever been cared for by a more unlikely pair? A blind man and a half-tame dog of unknown parentage. She giggled at the sheer absurdity of it all.

The animal rose without a sound and gracefully stretched. His rump stuck up in the air as he placed his front paws out in front and executed a graceful bow. Bellami marveled at the sheer size of him now. He'd grown tall, and had filled out with hard muscle. His wide head held almond-shaped amber eyes. His paws were wide and fleshy, his tail full and bushy, with a diamond-shaped dark spot centered about six inches from where it joined his sinewy flanks. He gave the two humans one last glance before he loped off into the breaking dawn. He was out of sight before Bellami felt Trace stir behind her.

Trace adjusted the woman in his arms. He'd been walking steadily all morning. At first he'd stumbled frequently, unable to avoid rocks and small yuccas, but now he seemed more aware of the brush and rocks.

"How are you doin'?" he asked as he maneuvered over a small gully.

"Fine, just fine." Bellami seemed shy and uncomfortable. The arm around his neck held him stiffly, and Trace wondered if she was afraid he might drop her. An involuntary grin curled the corners of his mouth.

"What's so funny, Mr. O'Bannion?" As usual, she was completely mystified by his behavior. The man was as changeable as the weather in this place.

"It's silly." He seemed embarrassed to tell her. She realized he hadn't been aware of the smile on his face or the deep dimples flashing in the sun.

"Please tell me," she cajoled.

"I was just thinkin'. I've walked more in the time since I met you, than in the rest of my life put together. At the ranch, I thought of you as a little general. Always makin' the troops drill." He chuckled softly to himself as he shook his head, obviously astonished.

"General, am I? Once you did ask me who I admired more—Napoleon or Caesar, wasn't it?"

"I did? I asked you that? Funny, I don't remember doin' that," Trace said as he negotiated a gravelly hillside.

All morning long, the closeness of him had made Bellami uncomfortable. She couldn't move her head without getting a close-up view of his magnificent profile. The sun gleamed off his face. Purple-and-black bruises colored his finely chiseled jawline, and spots of blood had dried on his forehead. Now she noticed the length of his beard.

"You need another shave," she said wistfully. She hadn't intended to speak her thoughts aloud. Heat rose to her face when she realized what she'd done.

"Yes, I expect I do." He sounded pleased.

When he spoke, she could feel the deep vibration of his voice through his chest. He was altogether too masculine, too handsome, too appealing. She felt hot and itchy and out of control with awareness of him.

"Mr. O'Bannion, could we stop? I mean, you must be tired." She had to get out of his grasp before she lost all her composure. The urge to touch his brow, stroke his lips with her fingertips, was becoming almost unbearable.

He frowned for a moment. Suddenly he seemed embarrassed by her request. Color began to rise from the collar of his shirt. "Oh, I'm sorry. Miss James, if you need— Well, I'll leave you alone for a few minutes," he said, and cleared his throat as he gently placed her on the ground. Quickly he walked away from her.

She realized with embarrassed distraction that he thought she needed to heed the call of nature. Actually, that wasn't a bad idea. It had been a long morning. She hadn't had any privacy since they'd started their trek, shortly after dawn.

With some difficulty, she hobbled to the nearest bush to relieve herself. Bellami was horrified to see that nearly every inch of her smooth skin was starting to color. Bruises were showing up everywhere. Her thighs and belly were mottled with dark spots. Trace wasn't the only one wearing marks from their ordeal.

The water must have beat her against brush and debris. If she hadn't been wearing the protective leather chaps and

Levi's, there was no telling what she would look and feel like.

She finished quickly and hobbled back to the spot where Trace waited.

"I'm ready now, Mr. O'Bannion."

He grinned as he slipped his arm under her legs and crushed her to his chest.

"Would you tell me about— What was it you called it? A flash flood?" Bellami was searching for a topic, any topic, to keep her mind off his chest and the pulse throbbing in his neck.

"A small rain up high turns into a torrent in the lower, flatter country. By the time it has rushed down the hillsides, gatherin' speed and brush, tons of water can come plungin' through the arroyos in a matter of minutes." He turned his face toward her, and her heart skipped a beat. "It was my fault for not warnin' you. I'm sorry, Miss James."

She listened in awe as he spoke her name. It flowed over her like a kiss.

"We're lucky to be alive. Many newcomers die each year." In his strong arms, Bellami had to agree she was indeed lucky to be alive.

Later in the afternoon, they stumbled upon a little stream of water. Evidently left over from the storm, it was cold, but muddy and dark as coffee. Even so, Bellami was tempted to take off her boots. She finally gave in to her desire. After some painful maneuvering, she managed to bathe her sore ankle and wrist in the frigid liquid. She sat at the edge of the water, watching Trace scan the horizon with his beautiful sightless green eyes. He seemed to be trying to get his bearings without the benefit of vision. The thought came to her that they were hopelessly lost. They would wander around to end up dying alone. She shuddered at the thought. Then she looked at the tall man with the scruffy beard and felt totally at peace.

She trusted him.

When he came to the stream, he crouched down near her. She watched with fascination as he dropped down on his hands, with his entire body outstretched on the ground. Then he submerged his head in the muddy stream. She smiled with pleasure, just watching his power and grace.

After a minute or two, he pulled his face from the cold water. Droplets of water arched up and out as he shook his dripping head. He gasped for breath, filling his lungs with air as the muddy water dripped from his beard and face. He looked like Tip. Feral, strong, indestructible, and painfully beautiful to watch. His resourcefulness was endless and bountiful.

"Let me have your gloves, Miss James." Trace sat by her side, water dripping off the ends of his hair.

He took the gloves and filled them both with water. Then, by feel alone, he tied off the tops with the little leather strings made for tightening the tops. He had created makeshift canteens for them. It wasn't a lot, but it would keep their lips wet through the long day. Trace allowed Bellami to trickle a few drops down her throat every hour or so. It tasted so good, mud and all!

The next time they stopped Trace took a few minutes to instruct Bellami on what a prickly pear looked like, then left her alone. She painfully maneuvered her body from one bush to the next. It was murder avoiding the long thorns, but she was determined to help forage for their food. Earlier he'd given her another handful of the wonderful piñon nuts he carried in his shirt pocket. She was terribly hungry, and she wondered how he felt. He'd been carrying her all day long without one word of complaint. If he felt tired or weak, he didn't show it. Bellami was overwhelmed by his sheer physical endurance. It occurred to her now that she'd seriously underestimated the man.

Since she'd been hired to teach him, she'd discounted his abilities. She flushed with embarrassment at her mistake.

When the fire was going, Trace sat near Bellami and used his knife to cut open the prickly pears. The flesh had a flavor that took some getting used to, but Bellami was so hungry she didn't care. When they were finished with the fruit and the piñon nuts, they each took a sip of water from one of the leather gloves. The wet leather had a pleasant acidic odor. It was slightly metallic, but as with most everything lately, she got used to it quickly.

Bellami saw Trace tense and turn his head a little, listening intently. She looked in the direction of his interest and saw a large gray-and-cream form loping toward them.

Tip went to Trace, instead of Bellami, and dropped something at his feet. Then the animal lowered his head, laid his ears back and dropped onto his back, with all four legs sticking straight up in the air.

"What in the world?" Bellami said with some distress. She'd never seen Tip act like this before.

"It's Tip, isn't it?" Trace said, knowing the answer without having to hear it.

"Yes, but I don't know what's got into him. He's lying flat on his back, staring at you, with his legs up in the air. He's dropped something in front of your boots."

Trace felt the ground in front of him and knew what it was the minute his fingers touched the fur. A cottontail. Tip was providing dinner. "I'll be damned! There's somethin' mighty strange about your dog, Miss James." He opened the pocketknife he pulled from his pocket and began dressing the rabbit by feel alone. Again she was impressed.

He spitted the rabbit on a stick and thrust it toward Bellami.

"Can you hold this over the fire? Not too close, though. Never did like my rabbit burned," he chuckled.

The smell of the sizzling meat made her mouth water.

"Is Tip still here?" Trace had a curious look on his face. Bellami looked at Tip out of the corner of her eye. He was still in his strange position.

"Yes."

Trace crawled on his hands and knees toward the sound of the animal. When he reached him, he gave Tip a playfully rough shake. Tip leapt up immediately with a look of satisfaction on his face. His tongue lolled out one side of his mouth. Bellami could swear he was grinning as he jumped from side to side in front of Trace. After a moment, he loped off, disappearing into the falling darkness.

They finished the rabbit, licking their fingers clean.

"I better make sure and save this last piece for Tip, since he was nice enough to provide the meal," Trace said to Bellami.

She sat staring up into the sky again, captivated by the sheer size of it. Everything seemed bigger out here, the land, the sky, and *him*. She looked at Trace and at the piece of meat he held for Tip. She remembered another benefactor, and heat flooded her cheeks. Guiltily Bellami remembered how she'd let Trace believe she'd cooked that meal, baked the corn bread. She felt very small sitting under the massive Southwestern sky.

"Mr. O'Bannion?" She saw his head come up and his sightless green eyes turn toward her.

"Yes." He had that husky sound in his voice, the one that always made her breath catch in her chest and her heart beat a little faster.

Instantly he was beside her. "Are you all right? Do your ribs hurt? Maybe we pushed too hard today." The concern in his voice touched her. "Is there anything you need?"

"No. It isn't that. I need—" She couldn't find the right words. "I have to tell you something."

Trace heard the strain in her voice, and his blood ran cold. Here it comes, he thought. Rejection. He'd been such a fool to hope. She'd no doubt seen the desire in his eyes, been disgusted by his notions. He hadn't hid it from her well enough. She'd felt his lust. Now she'd set him straight, just like Becky had. "Go ahead." He tried to harden his heart against the pain he was sure was coming.

Bellami swallowed. She could hear the coldness and contempt in his voice. She didn't blame him one bit. She didn't deserve to be with this kind, honest man. "Do you remember the night we ate chicken and corn bread?"

He felt his stomach knot. How could he ever forget it? That night he'd first felt her warm flesh. That night he'd started to compare her with Becky. He remembered he couldn't put a name to that special something about Miss James. Suddenly Trace knew what unnameable commodity Miss Bellami James possessed. The question that had nagged persistently at him since that night was suddenly answered in a blinding bolt of knowledge.

He could put a name to it now. Now, when she was going to crush any hope living in his heart. Why did he have to realize at this precise moment? Why did he have to face the truth now? Worthless as it was Bellami James boasted something Becky Kelly never had and never would. Miss James possessed his respect. And—he realized with a painful sense of wonder—his love. Bellami James had Trace's love. All of it, every flawed bit of it, and she always would. He had fallen head over heels in love with Miss James. He hadn't heard half of what she'd said.

"I should've told you, but, well, I was mad and a little hurt," she said softly.

"What? What did you say?" He shook his head, trying to clear away the bewildering knowledge that he'd fallen for the little general.

"I said, someone left a basket of food. I allowed you to think I cooked it. I'm sorry."

Trace blinked. "Basket of food? That's the terrible thing you wanted to tell me about?" He started to laugh. Deep, rich, booming laughter echoed across the land.

Bellami frowned. This wasn't quite what she'd expected.

"Oh, Miss James," he said, slapping his thigh, "I knew all the time."

"What?" Her voice was rising.

"Yes. I knew. Clell brought it out. You were workin' too hard." He held his sides, collapsing clumsily on the ground near her.

She observed his mirth with growing aggravation. "Mr. O'Bannion," she said sharply. There was anger in her words.

"Yes." He wiped the smirk off his face. He still chortled, sputtering a bit, not quite in control.

"You mean you knew all along and you said nothing? You let me think I had deceived you?" Her tone was sharp.

He knew she was angry. Sheepishly he nodded. It had never occurred to him she'd be upset. He was just so damned happy it wasn't what he'd thought. The tiny flicker of hope still burned stubbornly in his heart.

"Well! I think that's the meanest thing anybody's ever done!" she snapped at him.

He listened to her agitated breathing, and he loved her. He adored her. Trace O'Bannion let the May breeze caress his face as he sat on the open ground with a stupid grin on his face. He didn't care if Miss Bellami James looked like the south end of a northbound bear. Actually, he wasn't even curious about her looks anymore. He loved her. With all his heart. She could be the ugliest woman in the world. Hell, he didn't care. He had fallen hopelessly in love with the little general! Now he had a reason to live, and finally he had the will to live, as well.

All he had to do was get her home safe and keep her with him. Teacher, general, whatever she needed to be—all he had to do was keep her by his side, and it would all be fine, just fine. He made a determined vow to himself—he'd keep her with him no matter what.

Trace's eyes showed signs of fatigue, but that was the only indication of his weariness. At sunrise he picked up Bellami, ever so gently, and without a word started walking again.

As the day wore on, she began to feel a sort of selfish pride in him. He'd learned so much in such a short time. A deep sense of accomplishment, and a deep sadness, enveloped Bellami.

Trace felt her stiffen in his arms. For a while now she'd been thinking hard about something that made her sad. He could feel her pulse through his fingertips. Finally he could stand the worry no more. "Miss James, is somethin' wrong?" He stopped and bent over to set her on the ground. Then he knelt down beside her.

She looked at his face. Tiny lines of worry showed at the corners of his eyes. The urge to reach out and smooth them with her fingers was so very strong. "I was just thinking what a good student you've been," she said softly.

He grinned, and some of the strain in his face eased a bit. She felt intensely relieved.

"I owe it all to you, little general. All that drillin' of the troops really paid off," he teased her gently. "When we get back, I'll really apply myself to the braille, I promise." He touched the back of her hand gently, and Bellami felt fire in his hands. A fire that burned without flame.

"Maybe braille isn't as important out here as I thought," she whispered.

"Sure it is, and all the other things you want me to learn, too." He grinned and hefted her in his arms again.

Trace had been quiet all afternoon, his thoughts straying to his childhood and his upbringing. When his mother was alive, he'd known the softness and laughter of a woman. It was probably the best part of him. The tenderness he'd learned from her was what he had tried to show Missy and Logan when they were babies. Maybe they knew what was in his heart, maybe not. Lord knew he'd never gone so far as to actually tell them.

Trace and Flynn had been taught from the cradle that men showed no tenderness. Men asked no favors, and they gave none.

He realized he'd been taught to never, under any circumstances, allow himself to need someone. He'd never said "I love you" to another human being since his mother's death—not even Becky. He'd never said "I need you" to anyone in his life—never considered that he even could. Now, forcing himself to ponder the question of how much he might actually need Miss Bellami James made his gut twist into knots. This thought was a new and slightly discomforting concept. It brought up questions he'd never thought about before.

Bellami felt the sadness so deep in her heart it hurt. There wasn't anything left for her to teach him. The truth of it had been shown to her, hour after hour, while he carried her.

He could do more than just manage with his blindness. He'd saved her life, and he continued to do so now. The time for her to leave had come.

The very idea seemed incomprehensible to Bellami. She'd come here expecting to stay through the summer with a little boy. Instead, she'd found Trace. She'd spent one turbulent spring finding out that he didn't need her now and he probably never had. She looked at his lean, hard face and saw the strength etched on every plane.

Trace O'Bannion was a man. A strong, willful, independent man who no longer needed a teacher—or a general. She wondered if he ever really had. All he had ever needed was some time to heal and come to terms with the reality of his life. He had every skill he would ever use, and then some.

Now, as she faced painful truths, Bellami didn't think she'd really taught him anything. He'd finally just started to use what he already knew. But what he had taught her—now that was something else again.

Through Trace, she had learned of her own inner strength. A strength she had never had to call upon back in the city. And then there was his kiss. The kiss had awakened her sensuality, and a hunger she had never known existed. The thought of his lips on her own sent chilling shivers down her spine and a bittersweet smile to her lips.

She'd never be the same. Bellami could never go back to being the kind of woman she'd been before. She would never be able to hide behind her hat and veil. Now, for better or worse, she'd have to face life, meet it head-on. The excuse of sparing the rest of the world her scar wouldn't do.

It was funny, really. A blind man had opened her eyes.

Trace could feel the conflict within her. Damn it, what was wrong? She was hurting deep, he could feel it. A metallic screech carried on the wind as he struggled to feel what was causing Bellami pain.

"What is that, Miss James?" He snapped his head up to catch the slightest sound. Each muscle in his body tensed. He was wary of any danger that might harm the precious cargo he carried.

Bellami squinted her eyes into the setting sun. It blazed orange, and its brilliance momentarily blinded her. At first she couldn't see anything at all. Then, slowly, a familiar silhouette took shape. A small round circle atop a wooden spire. The windmill.

"Oh, Mr. O'Bannion, you did it, we're home!" There was a little catch in her voice. The sound of it nearly brought Trace to his knees. Home, with Miss Bellami

James safe in his arms. With renewed energy, he shifted her in his grasp and put one foot doggedly in front of the other. Getting her home safe was the only thought left in his mind. The rest of it could be sorted out later.

Thank you, God, He prayed over and over, silently.

Chapter Sixteen

Bellami felt like kissing the ground in relief, but at the same time she was horrified. She wanted to beg Trace to never take her back. The emotions warred within her. He had been so quiet the past hour, she'd been almost afraid to speak to him. The lines of concentration and fatigue were etched deep in his face. He was operating on sheer strength of will alone as he topped the rise and trudged toward the sound of the windmill. Bellami tore herself apart each time she knew it was time to leave. Her silent agony was interrupted by a well-known squeal. Snorting playfully through flared nostrils, Ghost trotted to Trace and Bellami. He nipped at Trace's shirt and shook his head. Then he wheeled and ran back toward the empty corral. The last few paces toward the back door brought a lump to Bellami's throat.

"Can you get inside?" Trace asked.

"Yes," she whispered.

"Ghost, you gray devil, come here," he called to the animal as he opened the gate to the corral. The horse nipped at Trace on the way by. The saddle was still on him, but the bridle was gone. Bellami stood leaning against the door, watching. Again she forced herself to acknowledge how accurate Trace's intuition had been. He said the stallion would go straight home, and he did. Wiping impatiently at a blurry wetness in her eyes, she crept painfully to the lean-to for the buckets.

Bellami had just finished bringing the last of the buckets inside when she heard the screen slam shut.

"Miss James?" Trace spoke softly, as if he were afraid he would disturb her. He took slow, tentative steps in her direction. The mud-caked boots left little outlines on the wooden floor.

"I'll put some water on. We need baths," she said wearily.

"You're not goin' to do anythin' right now." He reached out to her. "Sit down, please, Miss James." He gently forced her shoulders down until she sat in a chair at the long pine table. Then he turned and groped for the buckets.

One by one he unbuttoned what was left of his ripped and filthy shirt and stripped it off. Without hesitation, he let it drop at his feet. Then he stepped over it.

She smiled sadly. Just another bit of evidence that he hadn't learned anything from her. Had never needed to. He was a man to the bone, and picking up his dirty clothes seemed inconsequential.

"After a nice long soak, you'll be back to your old self again," he told her as he grasped the pump handle.

Bellami knew her old self was gone forever—regardless of what Mr. O'Bannion thought. Even though she promised herself she wouldn't do it, she watched him fill the buckets. Warmth flowed over Bellami as his powerful arm worked the hand pump up and down. A funny hollow place grew in the pit of her stomach as the muscles in his back rippled beneath satiny skin. When he picked up the heavy buckets full of water and moved to the stove, a little moan escaped her lips.

"Are you all right?" He frowned as he lit the stove, put the round black lid back into place and set the buckets of water on to boil. "Does your ankle hurt much?" A lock of ebony hair fell across his dusty brow when he raised his head in her direction.

"I'm fine," she managed to croak out. She touched the pool of sweat that had formed in the hollow of her throat. It mingled with dirt and made a tiny spot of mud on her fingertips.

Trace frowned when he heard the lie stick in her throat. He could feel her pulling away, withdrawing from him. The door that had opened between them was slamming shut. She was leaving. He knew it as surely as if she'd told him flat out. Trace clenched his jaw and realized with absolute certainty when she'd made the decision to go. A change had started taking place when she said he didn't need to learn the damned braille. His gut twisted into a hard knot. Trace felt like he was walking in a den of rattlers. One wrong move, one misstep, and it would all be over. Forever.

The room crackled with the tension between them. When he picked up the buckets and heard the little sound she made, he had to fight the impulse to throw her on the table and plunge into her right then and there!

Some vague notion of pounding all thoughts of leaving out of her head occurred to Trace. An ironic smile touched his lips.

He knew, or he thought he knew, what might keep her with him. But even though his heart knew, his mind fought against it. He fought a dual battle. One against the terror of being rejected, and the other with the value he placed on being an independent man.

Could he do it? Could he say the words that might keep her with him? Was it possible for him to ask her to stay? It went against everything he'd been taught, all his twenty-eight years.

Hard country made hard men—men like him. Men who'd sooner end up alone and lonely than acknowledge weakness or need of any kind. Was he ready to face that? Was he ready to spend the years ahead without her?

The hair on the back of his neck bristled. She slipped a little farther away, and he felt powerless to prevent it. The dirt in his teeth made a harsh grinding sound as he clenched his jaw against the thought of losing Miss Bellami James before he ever had her.

Dinner was agony for them both. Trace managed to find some dry biscuits, barely edible, but better than nothing. He brought in a ham from the smokehouse. Bellami seemed content to allow him to hack off a few pieces with a knife. There were times when Trace thought she might admonish him for his clumsiness, but she didn't. She simply accepted the jagged pieces of meat in polite silence.

That was the worst part. The quiet. An absolute hush seemed to have fallen over the ranch. Even the usual chirping of crickets and frogs from the stream were quiet. It sounded like the world was holding its breath. They ate in total silence.

He wanted to hold her again. When she was in his arms, at least he could feel her thoughts, could tell what she was thinking. Now, with the distance of two feet between them, he felt her shutting the door. Bellami was locking him out of her heart.

God, I'll die without her! a voice in his head screamed silently, but he couldn't form the words in his throat.

Bellami could barely swallow the food. Even after she'd drunk her fill of cold, fresh water, her mouth was dry as dust. She didn't think it was the food. Each time she looked at Trace a huge lump seemed to form in her throat.

He'd been so quiet and tense. Any minute now she expected him to announce it was time for her to go. Now that he knew he was capable of fending for himself, all pretense of a reason for her staying was gone. He didn't need her, and he'd made it plain from the first moment that he'd never wanted her here. Even his father had known it would be necessary to trick him.

Oh, God, I'll die without him! Her heart cried out.

"Can you make it upstairs by yourself?" he suddenly asked. So it was beginning—his dismissal of her from his presence.

"Yes." She rose awkwardly from the chair. Her back and legs were stiff, and her ankle still hurt when she put too much weight on it, but that pain paled compared to the rending of her heart. Bellami limped up the stairs to her room. When she was inside, she shut the door and leaned heavily against it. She had been drained of energy. Her will to live was ebbing away.

Hot, dry tears stung her eyes, but she wouldn't cry. She hadn't cried for thirteen years. Why start now?

She didn't know how long she'd been standing there in abject misery—maybe a long time. Time had seemed to fly by since they'd gotten home. She jumped when she heard a soft knock on the door. When she opened it, a tiny breeze from the open window ruffled a strand of inky-black hair that had fallen across Trace's brow. How she wanted to reach out and push it back from his bruised face.

"Miss James, I have a surprise for you," he said simply as he turned away from her. She hobbled along behind him quite numb.

He walked past his own room, farther down the landing. She hadn't ever been in this part of the house. She really didn't even know the stairs went this direction. He stopped in front of a door that he pushed open with one wide hand. Then he stepped back, out of her line of vision.

A very large white porcelain bathtub sat squarely on ornate lion's-paw feet. Steam rose in swirling tendrils from the water filling it three-quarters of the way. The empty buckets were stacked beside it.

She laughed; she couldn't help it. How stupid she'd been! Using that big wooden tub, killing herself to empty it. What a fool!

"Go ahead. Take as long as you want." His words snapped her back to the present. "When you're done, just pull that little chain. It drains out back, in the garden. I'll heat water for my own bath, later." He turned and left her.

Bellami closed the door behind him. She felt very dim-witted indeed. A dry, ironic chuckle escaped her lips as she unbuttoned her ripped shirt.

The bitter sound of her laugh touched him all the way to his toes as he put his boot on the stairs. What was she thinking? He paced back and forth in the parlor like a caged animal. Visions of her wet, naked skin kept flashing unbidden through his head. He could feel her, taste her.

"Please, God," he said in anguish. He pushed the heels of his palms hard against his eyes.

Then it hit him.

This time was the worst by a long shot. He fell to the floor like a poleaxed steer. Waves of nausea buffeted him. Bile rose in his mouth, and his stomach churned. A cold sweat covered his face as he writhed in pain on the Navaho rug. Trace groaned incoherently when a flash of blinding white light seared his eyes. It was identical to the brilliant light he'd seen when the bullet hit him. It took every shred of strength he possessed to open his eyes and look at it—but he did it.

Dim light surrounded a huge furry head. Golden eyes regarded Trace without emotion. Trace tried to unsnarl the jumble of thoughts tumbling through his head. Was he dying of the bullet wound, or was he about to have his throat ripped out by a lobo? Nothing made sense in the crazy blurring vision before him.

A numb lethargy settled over Bellami, and she reveled in the luxury of a long soak. Her limbs were heavy, and she allowed her bruised body to sink into the water. Only when it became uncomfortably cool did she find the motivation to get out. As she pulled the little chain, the sound of draining water gurgled through hidden pipes somewhere in the recesses of the quiet house. An ironic smile curled her lips as she dripped on the wooden floor. A tiny puddle formed around her feet. No towels had been brought in. She hadn't even noticed, she'd been so dumbfounded when Trace showed her the tub.

She cautiously peeked around the half-open door and saw nothing. A little trail of water on the wood floor marked her path as she padded quietly to her door. A blur of gray fur caught her eye when she glanced downstairs toward the parlor. Tip. He slipped out the heavy oak door, which stood ajar. Trace must've let him in, Bellami thought to herself. At least when she was gone they could keep each other company.

She slipped on her prettiest gown, of soft white lawn, and then it dawned on her. Her room looked different. She gasped in surprise. Eight trunks neatly lined the walls.

Trace wondered how long he'd been unconscious. He sat up and tried to clear the cottony feeling in his head. A cold panic gripped him when he thought about Bellami finding him weak and vulnerable like this. He'd die first! Hell, he probably would die next time it happened, if this was any example of what lay ahead.

Struggling to his knees, then shakily to his feet, he managed to stand. His teeth ground so hard together they made a screechy grating sound. It occurred to him that water was gurgling through the pipes. She'd finished her bath. A tender smile touched his lips. Sucking in deep breaths to ease his pain and weakness, he staggered toward the kitchen.

Laboring under the weight of steaming buckets, he managed to climb the stairs. Several times he stopped on the landing to catch his breath. He felt like he'd run halfway to San Marcial. His muscles strained with effort—the usual effect of the crippling pain. While he was recovering from the effects of being unconscious on the floor, the water had reached a boil. He was forced to carry up two extra buckets of cold water so that he wouldn't be cooked alive. With each step, he cursed his weakness, and the frailty of his body. Finally, with a sigh of relief, he poured the last bucket of water into the white tub.

Trace lowered his bruised form into the bath. A thousand points of pain radiated from his legs and back. He couldn't see them, of course, but he'd been battered enough in his life to know that if he could see it, his body would be colored black and blue.

One rib felt so tender to the touch he could barely wash it. All down his right thigh the muscles felt soft and squishy under his gentle probing. Soaping his left shoulder caused him to suck in his breath and wince.

"Funny, while I held Miss James I felt fine," he muttered into a handful of soap. He scrubbed his face and beard, wondering how he hadn't noticed any of these complaints before. It felt so good just to hold her, protect her, keep her safe, he mused as he ducked his head under the water to rinse the heavy lather.

He leaned back, trying to relax a body that was wound as tight as a spring. He was on the edge. He could feel all reason and control slipping through his fingers like grains of sand.

"Maybe I'm goin' loco," he mumbled under his breath, "seein' a wolf in my parlor. That country doctor probably didn't know how much damage the bullet did to me." He rubbed his hand over his scratchy beard, as if to wipe away the thoughts.

A pang of deep regret seized his heart. He'd probably never again feel the touch of Bellami's soft hands as she shaved him.

Fool. Soft, blind fool, he thought with contempt for himself. Trace jerked the little chain to drain the tub as he rose from the water. Without any hesitation, he opened the door and walked down the hall to his room. Water sheeted off the hair on his legs. He opened his bedroom door, and a cool breeze hit his chest. Only then did he realize he was naked as the day he'd come into this world.

Trace moved like a man in a dream, like a man sleepwalking. The only thought in his head was Bellami. Her name was like a chant. Over and over the cadence repeated itself—*Bellami, Bellami...*

Groaning against his feeling of desolation, and battling against a weakness he could not control, he stepped out onto the balcony. With a cry of torment, he gripped the railing so hard his knuckles hurt. He wanted them to. Maybe the pain would drive her from his brain and his heart.

Damn it, I'm a man. A man is supposed to be strong. Trace groaned. He felt anything but strong. He'd been raised to ignore weakness, to fight against frailty—to acknowledge need was to succumb to it. This feeling he had for Bellami was like the thing he'd been taught to deny. How could he live with the void her absence would leave behind?

Bellami turned toward her open window. She stood looking around the room, *her* room. This would be the last night she spent in this house—Trace's house.

She stumbled to the balcony, trying to see through the blur in her eyes. A pitch-black sky, and the same thousand enchanted jewels, twinkled above her head. The sheer beauty of the velvet night tore at her soul. How could the sky that had felt so safe and warm a day ago now make her feel cold and alone? Then she heard the sound. A mournful thing. An inhuman, tortured tone. She turned her head toward its source, but the blackness engulfed her.

Trace. Her only thought was that something had happened to Trace. Groping toward his section of the balcony, Bellami prayed, *Please let him be all right.*

Trace felt her presence like a summer breeze. His head snapped up as he turned toward her. She was no more than a foot from him, and coming closer. The heat from her body stirred his emotions like he was being stroked with her silken fingers.

He was afraid to move, afraid to speak. He stood on shaky legs, afraid to take a step. If this was just one more mad delusion, then so be it. He'd gladly lose his mind. After all, his heart was already gone. He welcomed the illusion, groped for it, blindly—willingly.

Bellami hesitated for a moment, listening. She could hear his ragged breathing. Something wasn't right. She took one more tentative step, then halted.

"Trace?"

Trace heard her say his name. Not his surname, but his first name. Groaning deep in his chest, he wrapped her in a hungry embrace. Her body felt like all the good things he'd ever known in his life. She was here, and she was calling to him. For the moment, at least, she was his.

He bent his head in surrender, covering her lips with his. He crushed her mouth. Then he clenched his jaw, taking control of his lust, and forced himself to be tender, gentle. She grew warm, soft, more yielding in his grasp. Wildly he thrust his tongue in her mouth. It was so inviting. He invaded her softness, as he would invade every inch of her. Tomorrow would come, but tonight, in the darkness, she was his. All his.

Bellami felt a rush of power and passion flowing through her the instant his arms folded around her. This was what she'd feared and wished for. Twenty-six years of female longing poured out into the night. She had no restraint, no inhibitions, no thought of tomorrow. Holding nothing back, she met his lust and matched it, measure for measure.

He bent and took her into his arms. She bit his earlobe. While he strode to his bed, she suckled his neck, licked his nipples.

Trace thought he'd burst into flame when he felt her mouth on his neck. He'd constructed fantasies of her, but this was far beyond anything he'd ever imagined! Grabbing the thin material of her gown, he ripped it cleanly down the middle.

Suddenly she was fighting. Not to stop him, but to help him tear it from her body. She wanted to be naked against him, and that knowledge fanned his blazing passion like the wind across a range fire. Trace wanted her like he'd never wanted any woman in his life. He ran his hands over her shoulders, down her body. His wide palms skimmed her waist, the flare of her hips, down over the luxuriant thighs, to the tips of her toes. He felt her shudder beneath his caress. With deliberate slowness, he nibbled at her feet. He tasted her sweet flesh. Palms open, he committed to memory every valley, every mound, every inch of her body.

If all he could take was one night, then it would be a night that would live in his memory forever. He vowed he would know her, even if he couldn't see her. Trace's brain painted her picture in his heart as his hands discovered her, inch by inch.

Bellami felt his soft, warm mouth on her instep. It was the most incredibly sensuous feeling she'd ever experienced. A rush of moist heat began between her legs. The feel of his firm palms on her skin awakened each delicate nerve ending. His touch brought her to life.

As Trace moved up her legs, his warm chest touched her own, rubbing against her susceptible nipples. She became aware of his flesh against her flesh. First her shins, then her thighs. His skin rubbing against her own created a sensual friction. The moist excitement started changing, to become a dull, aching need. She reached out and grabbed a handful of his thick, tousled mane.

He nearly exploded when she tugged on his hair. Never in his life had he known that a woman could be so passionate. Biting down on the soft inside of his mouth, he tried to control the wild fires of desire and need. Her soft whimpers drove him nearly mad with turbulent passion. Like a feral animal, he closed his mouth over her spicy, damp mound, tugging at her with his lips, gently, persistently.

Bellami writhed.

"Trace, oh, Trace..." she whispered. Each time she said it, he sucked harder. She jerked hard on his hair.

Trace couldn't tell if she wanted him to continue, or if she wanted him to stop. It didn't make much difference. It would've been easier to move a mountain than to check the yearning he felt for her.

She thrust her pelvis hard against him as he licked deep within her. He sampled her wetness. Suddenly she arched her back, slamming her pelvic bone hard against his chin. At the same time, her nails dug into the skin on the top of his shoulders. Warm trickles of blood seeped from under her fingernails. Some part of his mind, a tiny part still capable of rational thought, wondered why his body no longer hurt.

Bellami rocked in rhythmic shivers as Trace continued his persistent exploration up her stomach. He nuzzled the downy softness above the hot triangle he'd just abandoned. When he reached her rib cage, the part of him that hadn't succumbed to the madness of lust told him to be gentle. Mindful of her ribs, he delivered feathery kisses and nibbles up to her breasts.

When he found a hard nipple, he encircled it with his tongue, and she wrapped her long, slim legs around his waist. The squeeze of her muscles against him was so pleasurable, it almost drove him wild. A deep growl started somewhere within his chest, rumbling out.

She bent her head to his chest, nuzzling within the soft whorl of hair there. They lay locked against each other, rubbing their palms against each other's nipples. If she continued to do that, Trace knew, he'd be completely lost.

He forced her down to the mattress gently, hearing the deep intake of her breath. Little beads of sweat had formed on her skin. He slid his hands over the slippery moistness as he sculpted her smooth skin with flat, splayed palms. He knew her body now as well as he knew his own.

Bellami begged Trace for some kind of release. She didn't know what it was she wanted, but some instinct told her Trace knew. He knew exactly what she wanted, and how to give it to her. If only he would hurry!

Suddenly he left her. As the cool breeze washed over her body, she cried out in frustration and reached for him. Then he came back to position himself over her hips. She reached out and wrapped her fingers around his hard shaft. It jerked within her hand. So hot and firm—that part of him she'd wondered about so many times, when it was beneath his Levi's.

He jerked convulsively as her fingers stroked him. When he moved toward her, her hand slid up the length of his manhood, coming to rest against the coarse hair there. It couldn't have been better if he'd planned it that way. A satisfied sigh escaped his lips as he touched her mouth with his tongue.

She bit down on it gently, drawing his tongue inside her mouth. He placed his hand over hers on his pulsing tumescence. As one, they positioned themselves together, and he plunged deep—as deep as he could get. Bellami gasped and arched her back, tensing. Then he rocked against her rhythmically. She shuddered uncontrollably as he withdrew, slowly, sensually, nearly to the tip. Her legs entwined around him in an effort to restrain him, to keep him close and deep within her. He thrust again, harder than before. A cry of ecstasy bubbled from her mouth.

She understood now. He covered her mouth with his. Again he pulled out, nearly all the way, but not quite. With exquisite slowness, he undulated his hips in a circular motion. So good, it felt so good.

Bellami felt her mind leaving her body. Something within her fragmented as her soul exited and shattered into a million little pieces. In the protective black-velvet night, the pieces that had once been her floated among the stars.

He thrust against her again, and his roar of primal pleasure mingled with her cries of ecstasy. Somewhere, out in the darkness, a wolf howled, and a stallion's triumphant cry pierced the silence of the night.

Chapter Seventeen

The acrid odor of singed hair and searing flesh combined with sweet burning sage in the clear morning air. It created a picture so vivid in Brooks's mind he knew he'd never forget it.

He doubted he ever could forget one moment in this dynamic environment. The thought of going back to the dissipated way of life awaiting him in New York made a deep ache in his gut.

Shane roped, threw and tied the young bull. When he lay relatively motionless on the ground, Brooks picked up a red-hot branding iron and pressed it against the animal's flank. Moving quickly, he then went to the head to mark one ear and dehorn, while Logan cut the bawling calf. As soon as the piggin' string was jerked loose, it hit the ground running. The healthy calf bled only slightly, running to join the hundred or so they'd already cut and branded since sunup.

When Shane said the Circle B ran fifteen hundred head of shorthorn crosses, Brooks had thought it was a joke. Now, as the herd was being brought in, he realized the cowboy had been completely serious. The sheer mass of milling, dusty, cattle was mind-boggling to behold.

As Brooks watched, Shane reined his dun back and forth. Then he expertly cut out a large bull calf, delivering it to Logan and Brooks.

"Here you go, boys," he said, and grinned cockily, bringing his horse to a sliding stop. The dun was lightning-quick. Some of the other hands had made the mistake of racing with him—once.

Shane tried to coax one more race out of the men drinking coffee by the cook wagon, but had no luck. Brooks had noticed that as these men worked they always managed to find time for fun.

He looked at the rangy, long-limbed cattle called longhorns mixed with the stockier, beefier shorthorns. Clouds of dust swirled amid the animals' hooves. Their constant lowing created a steady hum around the camp. Hugh explained that the tough, disease-resistant longhorns bred stamina and endurance into the meatier shorthorns. Pride rang in Hugh's voice as he talked of the hearty longhorn's calving ease. He looked possessively out over the herd of animals, and over his children, working them.

"It's a nice sight, ain't it, Brooks?" Hugh said. "Same time each year, all the stock is brought here. That's when we do the branding and cutting. Then they go to the stockyards in Magdalena for sale back East." Hugh's face clouded. "This is the first year Trace hasn't brought his stock to the roundup."

Brooks remained silent, allowing the man to speak his thoughts. "Day before yesterday, I sent a couple of cowboys to Trace's, to round up his three hundred head. They're due back anytime now." He took off his Stetson and wiped the sweat from his face. Both men turned to scan the fence line, expecting to see a telltale cloud of dust on the horizon. Nothing broke the vista.

Missy had been watching Brooks for the past half hour. She just couldn't figure the man out. He didn't have to do this. He could've sat at the ranch house, comfortable and clean. "Bet he never got dirty like this back East," she speculated aloud. The kind of life he led in New York was a source of irritation and curiosity to her. It made her feel deeply inadequate, imagining how he probably looked on a normal day... dressed in fine clothing, a pretty woman on his arm. She gritted her teeth and slapped her gloved hand against her leg in irritation. Missy wasn't really sure, but she figured all the women in New York were beauties with pale delicate skin, always fashionably dressed. "Doubt any of those girls ever did a day's work," she grumbled to herself.

The nagging fear had always been with her that she'd never learn how to be a proper woman—that she'd never be enough of a lady to attract a man.

As she remembered the smile Brooks had given Becky the other day, it became almost a certainty to her. That dazzling smile had left a sort of raw, hollow feeling in Missy's stomach. Mainly because she'd never been on the receiving end of such a smile and didn't see any change likely in her future. She sighed wistfully. Up until now, she hadn't minded so much. Being raised by men, she'd never had a woman around to teach her about the complicated contraptions young ladies were supposed to wear.

Usually, like now, she ended up wearing knee-length union suits, Levi's, and shirts that barely fit. They were the cast-offs of some older brother. The Mexican women working at the ranch had tried to give her some brief instruction, but they didn't go in for the more formal attire of fashionable society. They wore traditional full skirts with low-cut blouses. Missy had tried that kind of clothing on once, but she'd looked scrawny and awkward. Her body was more slim and willowy, not full-figured, like Lupe's.

Frowning in bewilderment, she continued looking at the confusing Eastern dude. Sweat made a dark V down the front and back of his shirt. His dark hair hung in sweat-dampened strands. Her heart leapt when he took off his hat. It made her squirm uncomfortably, just looking at him. She'd noticed the same thing happening when she closed her eyes at night and thought about him. What the devil was wrong with her lately? Maybe she was coming down with the grippe, or some awful disease.

The bawling of a calf made her jerk around in wide-eyed surprise. A longhorn cow stood nervously watching her calf while it struggled to free itself. The silly creature was tangled in somebody's discarded lariat.

"Now what fool left a rope layin' around?" Missy cursed under her breath. "If I find out, I'll tear the hide right off him." Disgusted, she walked to the thrashing animal. He managed to snare himself up good and proper. His terrified, soulful eyes were rimmed in white. She felt sorry for the little fool.

Reaching down, she patted him, trying to give him some reassurance. He bawled all the louder as Missy started unsnarling the heavy rope, his struggles increasing with heartfelt intensity. Missy laughed at the animal.

"Just like a bull or a man, aren't you, fella?" Bending down on one leather-clad knee, she tried to heft him up to loosen the rope. Suddenly her name rang on every cowboy's lips. She jerked her head up, and her eyes widened in fear.

Brooks rammed his hat back on his head when he heard all the commotion. The calf sounded like someone was skinning him alive. When he saw Missy bending near him, he wasn't surprised. Frankly from what he'd seen, she was capable of tearing the hide off most any living thing. She grappled with the large bull calf. For some reason, Brooks mounted his stallion. He didn't have any real reason for doing it, but he did. For once—in fact, for the first time—the horse didn't crow-hop for twenty minutes before deciding he'd already been broke. Instead, he moved out like a seasoned cow pony who'd been on a dozen drives or more. Brooks felt momentary pride for the sudden act of obedience, and he glanced toward Missy to see if she had witnessed his small victory over the animal. That was when he caught sight of the longhorn cow as she started her charge. If not for the silly little vanity on his part, he'd never have seen it.

Missy watched the big cow, running hell-bent for leather, right at her. For one brief moment, she considered fleeing, but only for a moment. Missy knew she'd never regain her feet and outrun the cow. Nothing, but nothing, could move like a mad longhorn. And, from the white-eyed rage in her eyes, this cow was mad as all get-out. Missy swallowed hard. The morning sun glinted off the animal's horns.

"Nice Texas twist," she mumbled absently, admiring the graceful shape of the lethal horns that would soon gore her to death. "Never really thought I'd die before my first real kiss," Missy commented to the squirming brown-and-white calf.

Brook's mind flashed instructions to his legs and hands so fast he wasn't even aware of what he was doing. If his horse could catch up to the cow, maybe—just maybe—he'd reach Missy at exactly the same time.

A sickening vision of himself and the stallion being gored and trampled into the dust flashed before his eyes. Then the image became a slender feminine body lying in the dirt, bloody and broken.

No. Brooks gritted his teeth and dug in his spurs. When the rowels touched the stallion's ribs, the mustang exploded in one huge leap. His legs pumped with hidden strength, and he gained precious ground. Brooks leaned low over the right side of the swells of the saddle and crooked his arm. He took a deep breath and braced his body for the impact. When his forearm connected with her rib cage, it felt like his shoulder was being ripped from his arm. A searing pain opened up an eight-inch gash just below his shoulder at the same moment, but he held on. With a grip of iron, he carried her. They still leaned precariously out over the side of the horse.

The mustang made a full circle with his nostrils flaring as he tried to evade the charging cow. The wicked horns swiped viciously at his flanks.

Missy smelled the grassy breath of the cow while she was being hammered against a solid, lean hip. The vibration of the horse's feet on hard-packed earth jarred her teeth, and she tasted blood. If she'd been gored, she wasn't feeling it. Maybe that kind of wound stays numb for a while, she thought to herself.

Looking through her tangle of hair, she could just make out the color of the horse, but little else. She watched out of the corner of her eye as the enraged cow's head came up, just missing the heavy muscle in the horse's rump by inches.

They circled the camp once more and came near the cook wagon. Cowboys mounted quickly and tried to head off the enraged creature. The horse of her unseen rescuer came to a sliding stop. Missy felt herself held tightly against that mysterious body for just a split second, and then she was deposited safely on the ground. She looked up, into the face of her salvation. The last thing she expected to see was a pair of blue-gray eyes.

Missy didn't say a word. She just stared at Brooks while the blood trickled down his arm and ran between his fingers. It made a little puddle on the ground by her boot. She blinked twice, trying to clear her thoughts. He just sat there, staring at her with a dumb sort of expression on his face.

"All right. I'll go with you to the bullfight. But I ain't wearin' a dress." Missy turned and walked away.

Brooks watched her tight little butt framed by the worn chaps as she stalked away. What the hell had she said that for? When had he ever asked her to wear a dress? The bullfight was the farthest thing from his mind at this moment. Brooks watched the saucy sway of her hips as she disappeared behind the cook wagon.

"She's the damnedest female I ever met," he said aloud. "She didn't even bother to say thank-you, or go to hell, or kiss my ass. Does somebody save her from sure death every day?" he asked his horse as it eyed him warily. He found himself completely at a loss with her. He just didn't know how to reach her, couldn't figure out what she wanted. If he'd been in New York, he would've simply bought her some expensive bauble and taken her to the most expensive restaurant available. But she didn't seem to want anything from him.

Maybe that was why she baffled him. She really didn't want anything from him—anything at all. She also didn't need him. It drove him to distraction. There weren't any cabs to hail or doors to open or invitations to accept out here. He couldn't get her an audience with a Duke or a Vanderbilt. Women here didn't *need* men in the way they did back East. The thought was more than a little sobering.

Well, maybe I just proved she needs me, a little bit, he thought, grinning. *After all, I did manage to keep her from being trampled into the dust.* A cocky smirk replaced the grin.

Clell was right. If Missy ever came to him, it would have to be as a complete equal. Not for his protection or his wealth or his position or because he was well connected in society, but simply because she wanted to be with him.

For some ridiculously mad reason, Brooks found the prospect damned appealing. He shook his head in amazement.

She's a banshee! Anybody with a lick of sense would pity the poor man who got tangled up with Missy O'Bannion, he warned himself. The blood was soaking farther up his shirtsleeve, and he really looked at the wound for the first time. It didn't hurt, but just sort of stung, like being caned with a fresh hickory branch.

He looked around the camp, feeling kind of neglected and ignored. Then he spotted Hugh and Logan approaching him. The older O'Bannion carried what appeared to be a half-empty bottle of whiskey.

"A drink would be greatly appreciated at this particular moment," Brooks said to the men with wry satisfaction. "'Bout time somebody had the good sense to thank me properly." He chuckled. Hugh never uttered a single word as he turned the bottle upside down and poured the amber liquid over the bloody gash. He wore a taciturn expression while Brooks did a little dance in protest against the flames licking at his wound.

The young hero blew on the bloody slash in little short puffs, trying to cool it off. "What in hell did you do that for?" he cried while he rocked and jumped. He held his arm and looked at Hugh in disbelief. The whole damned family was crazy!

"That stuff is supposed to go in me, not on me!" He fanned at the wound with his hat.

Hugh pulled a hair out of the mustang's tail, then ran it through the eye of a needle he drew from his shirt pocket. A stifled growl erupted from Brooks's lips when Hugh pushed the whole thing through the raw edges of his tender skin. Hugh never smiled, but his eyes winked with humor. When he was done sewing the gash, he gave Brooks a slap on the back and went back to whatever he'd been doing before all hell broke loose.

Logan stood there grinning at Brooks with his usual crooked smile, his eyebrows raised. "Being a hero ain't all it's cracked up to be, is it, Brooks?" he drawled.

Both men looked up to see the wranglers bringing in Trace's cattle. They ran them in with the rest of the herd. Without dismounting, they headed straight to Hugh. After a moment of wild gesturing and raised voices, he bel-

lowed to his children. In a move so smooth it looked
rehearsed, Shane, Logan, Missy and Hugh were mounted.
Brooks watched them with curiosity as Hugh reined his
mount over to him. The older man's face held none of the
benevolent humor he customarily displayed. His look was
dark and full of concern.

"You better mount up, too. Trouble at Trace's."

Brooks was in the saddle before the patriarch even finished speaking.

"What kind of trouble?" he asked as they broke into a
lope, side by side.

Hugh frowned and settled his hat on his head, preparing for a hard ride. "Don't know for sure, but the boys saw
Trace's gray stallion saddled and running loose on the
range. They tried to catch him, but never came close.
Damn horse always was fast as lightning. Still saddled..." The old man's voice trailed off ominously.

Brooks knew a loose horse with a saddle was a portent
of disaster. He asked no more questions, but his mind
played out a variety of imagined problems, all of them including Bellami.

He couldn't picture a blind man on a horse. That meant
Bellami had been riding. If something had happened to her
again because of his lack of protection... This time he
would never be able to live with himself.

The silent group rode hard. They reached the O'Bannion ranch house in record time. Clell rode out to meet
them.

"What's wrong?" He knew this was no pleasure ride.

"Wranglers saw Ghost on the range, day and a half
ago." Hugh told him.

"I'm afraid it may have been Bellami riding," Brooks
told the old cowboy.

Clell's face darkened. The grizzled man cleared his
throat and looked guiltily at Hugh and Brooks. "They
were both on the horse. I saw them three days ago. They

were goin' on a picnic." Clell looked at the ground, his pale eyes troubled. "Guess I shoulda told you, but I couldn't see no harm in it."

Logan reached out and gave Clell a pat on the shoulder. "Trace has been ridin' that horse every night. He's as good as he ever was. They'll be all right." Logan met each surprised gaze steadily. They all looked at him with the cold glare of accusation. He stared them down one by one, showing not one whit of regret. "Now, don't go lookin' at me like that, he's my brother, too. It made me feel better, sort of keepin' an eye on him. Didn't see no need in tellin' all of you. He's watched over me for years. Now it's my turn to return the favor," he snapped.

"It don't much matter now who shoulda done what," Hugh said. "Let's just find out what's goin' on." He leaned low over the saddle horn and spurred his horse. The group followed suit. They topped a little hill, and a lone rider appeared in the distance. He sat on a big bay gelding. Only one man rode a horse like that. Flynn. With easy strides, the horse soon fell in alongside the other riders.

"What's the trouble?" He asked, keeping pace with them. The horses continued moving in unison.

"Ghost was seen on the range, saddled." Hugh gave no more explanation, and Flynn didn't seem to need any. His face creased into a frown.

Logan studied his older brother. "Why're you back? I thought they needed you in Socorro." Logan said finally.

"Hey, you almost sound like you're sorry to see me, little brother." He gave his sibling a wink. "It didn't take too long. The committee only took a couple of days to do the investigation. Monroe's been found innocent on three of the charges," Flynn said, then paused for a moment. "On the gamblin' charge, they couldn't prove he'd been gamblin' for money, but they did make it clear they didn't appreciate that kind of activity from their sheriff." Flynn smiled wryly. "Actually, I think some of those upstandin' men are findin' those laws almost as hypocritical as I do."

Logan snorted in agreement at Flynn's answer. He gave his older brother one last hard look, then concentrated on the distant horizon. No one else spoke. The steady pounding of hooves on hard-packed earth was the only sound in the early morning.

Trace woke up with a start. He knew it was morning without needing to see the dawn. Remembrance of last night flooded his brain. He touched the warm woman lying at his side, and a victorious, jubilant smile covered his face. Bellami James was the hottest, most passionate woman on God's earth. She'd met his burning desire head-on, and matched it with her own. All night long they touched, tasted and buried themselves in each other's bodies. Trace couldn't be sure, of course, since he lived in constant darkness, but he thought they'd finally fallen into exhausted slumber just before the sun came up.

He felt a sort of power and strength, a male energy he'd been lacking since he was shot. It seemed like the more he'd taken from Bellami in the heat of passion, the more manly and whole he'd felt. The more he received from her, the more he had to give back in return. Turning his face toward her, he nuzzled into the heavy blanket of her hair and smelled the mingling scents of lavender, her and himself. He sighed and rested his chin in the hollow of her shoulder. In moments, he drifted contentedly to sleep again.

Bellami stretched and found she was sore all over. By squirming a bit, she managed to move her shoulder out from under Trace's head. Slowly she raised herself to one elbow. She couldn't help looking down at him, sleeping so peacefully. In the soft morning light, she allowed her eyes to scan every inch of his male form—a luxury she'd been denied in the darkness.

A sharp gasp escaped her lips when she saw how much of his poor body was bruised. He looked much worse than she did, and she was no pretty picture. How on earth could he have carried her all that way in the shape he was in? Her eyes traveled lower, past his ribs, to the dark patch of curly hair and what lay nestled there. A hot, slightly embarrassed, satisfied quiver ran through her. Bellami was floored. If this was what men and women did together . . . If this was what it was like, how on earth did anybody who knew ever get anything done?

She'd gladly stay in bed around the clock if Trace would do that to her again. With a womanly smile, she eased herself out of bed. Returning to her own room briefly, she slipped on her worn brown work dress. Easing downstairs, out the kitchen door, she turned toward the outhouse.

It was a little surprising to see the stain of blood on her thighs and belly. She hadn't noticed it upstairs. With a smile, she realized she'd been too busy exploring Trace while he slept.

She'd need another bath now. It dawned on her then. She had yet to take him to task about that bathtub. There were many things she intended to tell that man this morning, things she'd never expected to say to any man. Words she'd thought would be denied her forever. She hummed a tune while she walked back toward the house. When she reached for the kitchen door, she heard pounding hooves and several voices. Ghost screamed in greeting to the horses.

Bellami could only make out the silhouette of riders coming toward the house. Holding up her hand to shade her eyes from the bright sun, she tried to see who they were. Her long, unbound dark hair kept blowing across her face, and she impatiently swiped at it. When they rode through the gate, she instantly recognized one of the men. A happy smile broke across her face.

Trace woke to find Bellami gone. She was probably downstairs making coffee and breakfast. For a wonderful moment, he lay there savoring the feeling of his bed and the memories of the woman who had shared it with him. Languorously he got up and found his Levi's.

"Where are you?" he called cheerfully. He had to speak to her, had to tell her of his feelings. There could be no question about it now. Whether she laughed at him or not, he had to tell her how he felt. He was on his knees, feeling along the floor for his boots, when he heard Ghost. A shiver of apprehension ran up his spine.

"Bellami?" There was no answer. Concern gripped his chest. "To hell with the boots," he growled as he straightened up. He buttoned the two lowest buttons on his Levi's and headed for the stairs. A cold premonition of doom gripped him. The floor felt cold against his bare feet. He didn't care about it, or about the blinding headache that was starting to throb in his temple. Nothing mattered but his love for Bellami. He descended the stairs, trying to identify the voices he could hear outside. When he heard Bellami's voice, relief flooded through him. Softly and sweetly, she was chattering happily to someone. The sound of her words made him smile again. He stopped to listen, enjoying the sound of her voice, the feeling of having her near and knowing how much he loved her.

Slowly the smile faded from his face. Jealously, terror, anger, all swept through him like a raging river. How could she say such things?

The riders were staring at Bellami, looking at her scar, but she didn't care. Trace had shown her that hiding was no longer necessary. She was who she was—she looked the way she looked.

In his presence, she'd found a wondrous thing—acceptance. In his arms, she'd found love. For the first time in her life, she accepted who she was. "Brooks, I'm so happy to see you!" she shouted at the top of her lungs, and ran toward her brother. "Oh, Brooks, come here and let me kiss you. Get off that horse and squeeze me."

Brooks stared down at his sister, and he hardly knew her. Her long hair whipped free around her shoulders, and she smiled, happily. What could have wrought such a change? He scanned her quickly from head to toe. A smile twitched at the corner of his mouth as he listened to her happy greeting.

Her voice sounded like a silver waterfall. She just kept telling him over and over how much she missed him and how much she loved him. He saw the heavy dark hair, her soulful azure eyes sparkling in the morning sun. The thick raised scar running down her alabaster cheek was the only thing marring her exquisite beauty. But most of all he saw that Bellami James was in love. He felt a weight being lifted from his broad shoulders. He'd prayed and asked God to give Bellami a change, something to hold on to. What better gift?

Trace opened the door, stumbling out into the warm, sunlit morning. Flynn knew immediately that Trace was in pain. It was etched at the corners of his eyes. His mouth contorted and twisted grotesquely with each faltering step.

Trace heard Bellami's excited greeting to Brooks, and his heart plummeted. She continued to chatter, about how much she loved him. The words echoed over and over in his head. He just didn't believe it. Not after last night. Bellami had been a virgin. That discovery had both surprised and thrilled him. He had naively begun to believe she couldn't have cared for Brooks as he first supposed—not if she was still pure. But now she was telling the man she loved him, she'd missed him, she was happy to see him.

His blood ran cold. He was enraged. He was devastated. He'd tell her what he thought of her. She was just like Becky. He felt used. Why had she used him? Why would she? Why would any woman give herself like that, and then, the next morning, speak affectionately to an old beau? His greatest fear was now a cold, grim reality. She'd rejected him, totally, in the most final way a woman could toss a man aside. She'd slept with him and obviously found him lacking. His heart was broken and his pride shattered. What a fool he'd been! He believed her passion stemmed from love. *Love!* Trace cursed himself for nine kinds of a fool. Only the biggest fool in the world would believe a woman like her could love a blind man.

He'd thought Becky had broken his heart, but that feeling had been nothing compared to the devastation he felt now. With a gut-wrenching realization, Trace knew just how much he loved Bellami James. He knew that if he lived to be a hundred he'd never love another woman like he loved her. Knowing that made the pain in his heart and soul a hundred times worse. He'd never be free of her memory.

Bellami heard the door and turned expectantly toward Trace. At last she could introduce him to her twin. The two most important men in her life would finally meet.

Shock gripped her. Instead of a look of affection, she saw a dark face full of rage, disgust and hatred. She sucked in her breath. The realization of what his expression meant hit her. She had touched him out of love—he had felt only lust. His need for a woman had finally overcome his dislike for her. Foolishly she'd allowed herself to hope that maybe he cared just a little. Obviously she'd been wrong. It had meant nothing to him.

From the look on his face, it was plain to see he regretted what they'd done, what they'd shared. Maybe *regret* was too mild a word. From his expression, he loathed her. His dark scowl suddenly became deathly pale. Trace staggered, losing control of his muscles. She watched in fascinated horror, unable to move or to speak.

Trace felt the spell coming on. He gritted his teeth, cursing silently, knowing Bellami would see his weakness. His knees buckled. He tried to speak, but no sound came from his lips. He stumbled forward one more agonizing step closer to the woman he cherished more than life. He was going to tell her—had to tell her—before he died. He recognized the metallic taste of his own blood. He knew he was biting his tongue but he was powerless to stop, just as he was powerless to make Bellami love him.

His body crumpled, falling heavily to the ground. This man, who had carried Bellami like a precious treasure across the prairie, fell to his knees at her feet.

"Trace!"

Digging his fingers into the dirt, he tried to drag his body forward, toward the sweet sound of her voice. The light in his head exploded. There was a blinding white flash of light, and a hundred pinpoints of fire. He was dying. He welcomed the blessed darkness. Without Bellami he had no life, anyway. Death promised relief from the pain in his head and the agony in his heart.

Hugh reached him at the same time Bellami did. The older man looked helpless as he held his son in his arms. Trace had gone limp, and blood trickled from his mouth.

"Flynn, ride to Magdalena, bring back the new doctor...the surgeon. Ruin your horse if you have to." Hugh's eyes were misty, and his face looked ashen.

"Let me go. My horse's faster," Shane said with anticipation. Hugh nodded and, in a puff of dust, Shane and his dun disappeared over the rise, out of sight.

Chapter Eighteen

"How long will he sleep, Doctor?" Bellami couldn't hide the concern in her voice. Her face showed the signs of strain and lack of sleep. Dark, sooty smudges ringed her blue eyes. She'd been sitting at Trace's bedside for twenty-eight hours without taking a break. She refused to leave his side until she knew.

The thin man with a mustache at her side seemed not to hear her. Then, abruptly, he answered, "Hard to say. The fragment of skull I removed should take care of his blindness, his loss of control, but people sometimes fall into an odd sleep after this kind of operation." His brows furrowed together as he continued to check Trace's pulse, touching him lightly here and there, as a concerned parent might touch a child.

"Will he live, Doctor?" Her voice was so soft, almost inaudible even in the deafening silence of the room. It was as if she feared that saying the words too loud might make it happen. She shuddered as she waited for the doctor to answer her.

He finally looked in her direction with eyes that had seen too much pain and death. "I can't really say—just yet. Maybe in five or six more days I'll be able to give you a better idea." He looked at her sympathetically.

Clell quietly shifted his weight and stayed in the shadows, out of sight. He listened as the doctor and Bellami talked softly. The physician had done everything he could. Now it was up to the good Lord.

Bellami never took her eyes from Trace's face, not even while she spoke to the doctor. Occasionally she touched Trace's bandaged head lightly.

Clell smiled at her gentleness. She was some kind of woman. He hadn't ever seen her like. While Shane rode for the doctor, she'd kept them all from falling apart. She'd forced them all into action—directing them like a drill sergeant. After they carried Trace's limp body inside, she'd given each one a task. The little lady knew how to make a plain kitchen into a proper operating room. She knew how to boil every piece of cloth, every last scrap of iron or steel that might touch Trace. That fact alone might be the one thing to save his life, Clell mused. He obediently followed her every direction. Not one of them had ever even seen the inside of a true hospital. No telling what they would've done without her.

When the surgeon arrived, she'd had everything set up and ready. He'd sized up the situation quickly and appointed Bellami as his nurse. She'd paled slightly but taken a deep breath and followed his instructions without hesitation.

There'd been a moment there, when she had to shave the side of Trace's head, when Clell had thought she might faint, but she hadn't. Even when the blood splattered her dress. She'd taken several shallow breaths and kept doing whatever was expected of her. Whatever Trace needed, Bellami did it. She was some kind of woman, this Bellami James. The kind of woman a man like Trace had always needed.

Her hair hung in limp, dirty strands. The brown dress she'd had on for days was rumpled and creased and stained with Trace's blood. A lost soul, if ever there was one. Her obvious love for Trace tore at Clell's heart. If Trace didn't make it, what would this little gal do?

Clell knew that if Bellami continued like this for five more days they'd be burying her for sure. Pushing himself off the wall, he started downstairs. When he passed Bellami's open bedroom door, he caught a flash of cream-and-gray fur. He paused on the landing to watch the animal disappear like a phantom, out the open window to the balcony.

"Sneaky lobo, think I don't know you keep an eye on Trace and the girl? Silly ol' wolf," he muttered as he walked quietly downstairs. His boots whispered on the stairs as he said a silent prayer. *Hope the wolf is the talisman the Indians 'round here believe him to be. We need a powerful spirit right now.*

Clell wasn't surprised to find the O'Bannions pretty much as he had left them. Flynn stood on the porch, smoking, his face drawn with worry. Clell knew how much Flynn loved his brother and how guilt had been gnawing on him for months. That was the kind of man he'd been raised to be, and Clell was mighty proud to have been a part of that raising.

Hugh, alone with his grief and his prayers, sat in the high-backed chair staring out the window. Shane and Logan were playing some card game, trying to focus on something else for a few hours. Clell saw Logan bottom-dealing, again. He made a mental note to have a talk with that boy, real soon. What a caution he was. He had a sort of quiet resolve about him the others lacked. Once the boy made up his mind about something, he was absolutely unshakable.

Clell narrowed his eyes and rubbed his hand across his chin. Maybe he shouldn't have agreed to Doc Malone's scheme, but it made sense at the time. Doc had written Hugh at just the right time. So far, it had worked out, and nobody was the wiser. Now guilt chewed on Clell. What if

Trace died? Bellami James would never be the same, and they would all share in that responsibility. "Damn my hide for meddlin'," Clell muttered aloud. "Got to do somethin' for that gal up there." The two cardplayers lifted their eyes briefly to look at him as he stepped into the kitchen.

Missy was cleaning up. Clell smiled at the picture she made, leather chaps underneath a makeshift apron. "Missy, honey, you done a right fine job of keepin' us all in coffee," he said, and patted her shoulder affectionately.

"It wasn't much. Lupe brought over some more hot soup today. It's on the stove." Her dark eyes glistened with unshed tears. Clell coughed behind his hand to hide his own tears and opened the kitchen door. The kitchen was getting too warm already. Soon the summer sun would heat the front of the house, driving them all into the shade of the cool porch.

"What is it, Clell?" Missy asked. He sniffed and turned to face her. "We've got to do something about that gal up there," he said simply.

Missy swiped at a tiny thread of sweat running down the side of her face. Grief and despair showed in every curve of her face. "I know," she said. "The last time I was up there, she nearly passed out. I guess when a lady does it, you say 'fainted.'"

"You're a lady, Missy. You just don't know it, honey," he muttered as he dragged the back of his hand under his nose. Clell knew it bothered her—there'd just been things men couldn't teach a girl. A glimmer of humor crossed his face, and his pale eyes lit up. "Missy, I have an idea, but you'll have to be the one to do it, or it won't work." Clell gave her a hard stare.

Shane and Logan entered the kitchen. They sat down at the table and listened quietly. Occasionally they would nod in agreement, glancing at Missy.

Clell narrowed his eyes as the plan took shape. "You'll ask her for help gettin' fixed up. But while she's supposed to be helpin' you, we'll really be helpin' her," he said simply.

A deep frown and a look of alarm crossed Missy's face when she realized what she'd be fixin' up for. She raised her hand. "Oh, now, wait a minute, Clell." She backed up a step. She held both slim hands in front of her, as if she could push his words away. "Brooks isn't goin' to want to go now, anyway, and I can't leave Trace!"

Shane and Logan watched Clell as he prepared to present his case to the distraught girl. "First of all, Trace's gettin' the best care possible, what with the doctor and Bellami here," Clell said, and raised his eyebrows expressively, "Brooks will go if you tell him you want to."

She lowered her face, and dark lashes covered her eyes. "I don't think Brooks will care very much about my feelings, do you?"

Clell realized Missy was unsure of herself around Brooks. He saw fear in her eyes, for the first time he could ever remember. It was a mighty big shock to him. He couldn't count how many times she had bettered seasoned cowboys. She always seemed so sure of everything. Now, suddenly, he understood her need to shame and taunt Brooks at every opportunity; Missy didn't know any other way to be sociable with the man. He chuckled to himself, realizing his plan would rope two steers with one loop, so to speak. Maybe he could meddle just one more time. "Well, Missy, the only way that little gal is goin' to leave Trace's bedside is if you trick her into it. If you go to her and ask her to help you dress real nice, ask to borrow some of her clothes, she'll do it. She's a kindhearted lady, you know." Clell didn't explain he knew that because he'd snuck a wolf cub here, one she accepted without pause. It had never occurred to the old reprobate that she had no idea what a wolf cub looked like. He simply thought it was because she possessed a large and generous heart.

He turned suddenly to face Shane and Logan, who seemed to be having a little trouble following the conversation all of a sudden. Clell's plans could be a bit complicated at times. He seemed to set great store by being able to engineer little deceptions, little mysteries, for the people around him. They squirmed a bit when they saw that look in Clell's eyes.

"Go round up the buckets, boys. We're goin' to prepare a bath," Clell said, with the gruff voice they all knew well.

A blush began creeping up both their faces, as bright as any sunrise in the territory, but they obediently moved.

Shane poked Logan in the ribs as they stepped through the door. His cheeks reddened. "If word of this gits out . . ." He grimaced.

Logan nodded. "Yep, there'll be hell to pay with the rest of the hands, if they ever found out we played the part of ladies' maids," he whispered, going pale. The brothers shivered in unison at the thought.

Bellami lifted her exhausted eyes to the window. Was it day or night? She'd been having trouble keeping her thoughts straight. Whenever she closed her eyes, she visualized the doctor showing her the area of Trace's head to shave, and then the image would blur and change. She would see his face lathered, his eyes closed contentedly, while she shaved his beard. It was getting harder and harder to distinguish between fantasy and reality.

Over and over she saw her trembling hand shaving a section of his head. Blue-black hair falling to the floor, blood dripping onto it. Bellami was transfixed and horrified as the surgeon gently lifted a thin sliver of bone from Trace's skull.

"His sight should return now," he said flatly. He might as well have been discussing the weather or the price of cattle. The conversation was so stupid, the words were so meaningless. Her heart was breaking.

She still recoiled from the knowledge that Trace hated her. Bellami didn't know what hurt her the most, though, the look of disgust on Trace's face the morning after they'd made love, or the thought of him being able to see her true ugliness.

If it turned his stomach to touch her when he was blind and didn't know what her face looked like, how would he feel when he finally saw her? She had convinced herself that he truly loved and accepted her for who she was. How wrong she'd been. A bitter laugh escaped her lips.

And after I finally decided not to run and hide from the world anymore. She closed her eyes and sighed. None of it mattered now, not with the only part of her world she really cared about rejecting her. Running her hand over her tangled hair, she tried to dispel the terrible, hurtful thoughts.

It just didn't matter anymore—nothing mattered except Trace's opinion, and he had already shown her how he felt about her, the morning after they had made love.

She blinked her eyes. The room got kind of blurry, and she felt so tired, so very tired. A dizziness swirled around her, but she fought to remain sitting at Trace's bedside.

"I'll stay until I know he's going to be all right," she whispered to herself.

While Shane and Logan poured the last bucket of steaming hot water into the tub, Missy went through one of Bellami's trunks and found some soft embroidered undergarments. As she prepared to close the lid, her eyes fell on a small glass bottle. Pulling the cork she sniffed the sweet-smelling liquid. It was lavender.

Missy grabbed a heavy flannel robe from Bellami's room. Tipping the bottle of lavender, she dropped a little into the hot water and turned toward Trace's bedroom. She had no idea how long it would take her to convince Bellami to leave Trace; it might be a while. It was obvious Bellami James was deeply in love with her older brother. Missy was pleased. She had liked Bellami the minute she laid eyes on her. Then, during the operation, her admiration had grown. Especially when Bellami had gone pale as the blood spattered her dress. For just a moment, Missy's thoughts had focused on Brooks. An image of him risking his life to save her flashed by, but she didn't know why thinking about one thing should lead to the other.

It bothered her some, this habit she'd developed of seeing Brook's face throughout the day. She'd be busy doing some little chore, and blue-gray eyes would materialize before her. Missy hadn't ever really had feelings about a man before. It all seemed a little confusing and a bit scary. When she reached Trace's bedroom, she opened the door and looked inside. Bellami was still sitting in the chair beside his bed, holding his hand.

Bellami looked up in surprise. Her eyes were the most extraordinary color, almost purple. Missy'd seen that exact color stain the sky at sundown. Bellami James was the most beautiful woman she'd ever seen. Her eyes and hair reminded Missy of Brooks. It made her uncomfortable, in a shy kind of way. She felt so awkward, so ugly.

Missy stood in the doorway, her velvet-black hair hanging past her waist in a single heavy braid. Bellami thought she looked so healthy and alive. There was a rosy glow about her skin that made her radiant. Dark eyelashes, thick and curly, emphasized the slight almond shape of her eyes. She was exotic-looking and breathtaking. Bellami grimaced at how lovely the young woman was. She moved with a grace and confidence Bellami never saw on any woman in New York. She was just a little bit envious of any woman who could be so confident and so self-assured. Lord knew she'd never felt that way—except for that brief time with Trace. She continued watching as Missy smiled, shyly.

"How is he?" the girl whispered, looking down at his motionless pale face.

"No change," Bellami said with a weary dry voice.

As Missy walked quietly up to the bedside, Bellami saw the look of adoration the girl gave her older brother. "I came to ask you a favor, Miss James," Missy said, looking at her with those bottomless black eyes.

"Please, call me Bellami."

"All right, Bellami. Brooks asked me to the bullfights with him. I need your help," Missy said flatly, never taking her eyes from Bellami's face. She didn't know if she could lie well enough to pull this off.

It surprised Bellami to hear someone as confident as Missy say she needed help with anything. A thousand assumptions about how self-confident Missy was flew out the window. "If I can do something for you, of course." Bellami whispered softly.

"Well, it's probably no secret to you, I don't know the first thing about lookin' or actin' like a lady," Missy said, gesturing with her hands at her chaps and boots. The words tumbled out in a rush. A beet-red blush crept up her face.

Bellami blinked in surprise. "Missy, I think you're lovely. But what do you want me to do?" Bellami was astounded. Maybe this was the curse of being female, the unsureness, the constant doubt.

Missy looked at Bellami and swallowed hard. This was it; there wouldn't be any turning back now. "I was hopin' maybe you'd have somethin' I could borrow to wear, and maybe you'd show me about, well, about ladies' undergarments." Heat rushed to her face again. If she ruined this by being too honest about her own feelings, Clell would skin her alive.

Bellami smiled, and the dark smudges beneath her eyes deepened. "Of course, Missy. You're shorter than I am, but I have a beautiful dress that will look wonderful on you. In fact, it would give me great pleasure if you'll allow me to give it to you." Bellami felt truly repentant that she ever envied this sweet girl. What a brave, dear heart this girl possessed—just like her brother.

Missy allowed a relieved sigh to escape her trembling lips. She didn't know if she was happy because Clell's plan was working or because she would finally begin unraveling the mystery of being a lady, but she felt deeply grateful to Bellami for not laughing at her silliness.

"Thank you, Bellami," Missy said. "I have another favor to ask. We'll wash your hair, and then would you show me how to wear—that is, how to put on—those things." Missy wrinkled her nose.

Bellami couldn't believe it. Of all the subjects to be so shy about. Missy was a charming set of contradictions. Just like her older brother. Bellami eyes snapped back to Trace's face. She couldn't leave him, not to take a bath. He might wake up. Then she realized that if he did she was the last person he'd want to see. It hurt a lot, but Bellami took a deep breath and forced herself to stand. For just a second, she felt quite light-headed. It had been a while since she'd eaten but she had no appetite.

Missy helped Bellami catch her balance. She was very near to collapsing. "Here let me help you. The bath is ready, and I found some lavender water," Missy said pleasantly while Bellami leaned gratefully against her. Together they walked slowly down the hall to the bathroom.

Bellami wasn't aware of several sets of eyes following her. One set old and wise. One pair wild amber gold.

She had had no idea she was so tired or dirty. Missy soaped her long hair and talked pleasantly of the weather.

"Really, Missy, this isn't necessary. I can show you the underthings without all this fuss," Bellami protested.

Missy ignored her. "You'll be able to show me much better if you are clean and fresh." She scrubbed Bellami from head to toe and never commented on the bruises on her body.

Later, as Bellami stepped from the soothing water and pulled on a thick robe, Missy disappeared from the room. Alone, near exhaustion, Bellami crept to her room.

A tray of food sat on the table by the bed. She touched the bowl and found the soup still warm. A wedge of corn bread dripping with butter sat by a cup of cool, fresh milk.

Trace's little sister was treating her like a member of her own family, and Bellami felt the pain of loss cut deeper. If only things were different, if only she *looked* different, this wonderful girl and she would be like sisters.

"You're in love with him, aren't you?" Missy stood in the doorway, with her arms crossed across her full bosom.

Bellami nearly choked. Of course, she'd finally been forced to admit it to herself, but hearing someone else give life to the words was like having the wind knocked out of her.

"No—I . . ." Bellami let her denial trail off. *Impossible, foolish dreamer!* Bellami braced herself, expecting Missy to tell her what a fool she was. The criticism didn't come however. She turned to look at Missy. All she saw in her eyes was deep pain and understanding. No ridicule or scorn for her ugliness, just pity. It ripped the last bit of her heart to shreds.

"It doesn't matter how I feel about him," Bellami said with sad determination. "Mr. O'Bannion doesn't have any feelings for me, except as his instructor. As soon as the doctor tells me, well, that he's better, I'll be returning to New York." She gave Missy a wistful smile and finished her soup in silence.

Bellami lifted the dome-shaped lid of one of the trunks. She started pulling yards of ivory-colored fabric from inside. Missy giggled, making out the details of a heavily embroidered dress of ecru lawn. Bellami bent nearly double, almost disappearing as she dug deep inside. When she stood erect, she produced several pieces of embroidered white lawn. As she turned toward Missy, she nearly fell to her knees.

"That's enough for now, Bellami. We can look at clothes after you take a little nap." Missy took her arm. Gently, but forcefully, she propelled the tired woman to the bed.

Bellami tried to resist, but the gentle pressure was too much for her. She had some vague idea that she would just get back up and return to Trace's room. It was the last thing she remembered that day.

Missy took one last look at the fragile woman on the bed. "Trace, you damned well better live, and you better not let this woman get away," she whispered to herself as she turned to go downstairs to tell Clell the plan was a success.

Bellami woke confused and disoriented. The events of the past several days were foggy. A familiar wet nose was pressed tightly into her palm. Serious gold eyes watched intently, bidding her to rise.

"Hello, Tip," she mumbled, rubbing the sleep from her eyes.

She dressed quickly and entered Trace's bedroom on tiptoe. Clell raised his head and grinned as she stepped inside.

"Howdy. I'm Clell. We never got properly introduced," he extended a rough, sinewy hand.

Bellami smiled and grasped it warmly. "Pleased to meet you. How is he?" Her eyes lingered on Trace's motionless form.

Clell frowned and got up from the chair. "No change. Here, you sit down a spell. Brooks gave me a message for you," he said, his blue eyes crinkling at the corners when he smiled. "He's helpin' with the cattle, and said to tell you he'd be back soon, not to worry."

Bellami smiled at his words. Brooks would assume his instructions were all she needed not to worry. "Thank you, Mr. Clell."

"Not Mr.—just Clell. That's quite a brother you have, miss."

"Yes, I've always thought so." She sighed, stroking Trace's forehead.

Chapter Nineteen

Missy twirled around again. The skirt billowed out as she pivoted in front of the mirror.

"Bellami, I've lived in this skin for nearly eighteen years, and I wouldn't know myself," she said as she gazed at her reflection.

Bellami held a medium-size looking glass so that Missy could see herself. As she turned, the full double skirt billowed out again. Missy giggled like a happy little girl, and Bellami found the sound infectious. She couldn't resist. She laughed along with Missy.

"Oh, Missy, you were lovely before, but now..." Bellami said in awe of the vision before her. She reached out to stop the spinning girl and pull her into a chair. "You'll fall if you keep that up." She gently pulled Missy's thick black hair up and caught it with a comb that held a length of ivory ribbon and lace.

"This is the prettiest thing I've ever seen." Missy plucked at the rows of lace and embroidery thread.

"It was a gift from Claire, an inducement, really. She tried to get me to attend some social affair. I don't remember what," Bellami explained absently as she finished dressing Missy's hair. None of the dances and parties in New York had ever meant anything to Bellami, but Claire never understood that. She seemed to think that if

Bellami would go and pretend to be happy, she would somehow actually make herself happy.

Bellami had never worn the dress, because she'd never gone to the dance. Seeing it now on Missy, she was very glad. It fit the young woman like a second skin. The high collar was thickly embroidered with heavy brocade and lace. The sleeves were full at the top, fitting tightly on her slim arms. A wide diamond-shaped inset of brocade and lace nipped in her petite waist. It gave her the illusion of being even smaller, as the full bell-shaped skirt flared out.

An overskirt of light, delicate material softly drifted around her like a misty cloud. When she moved, it was impossible to say whether she floated or walked. The effect was wondrous!

She turned to Bellami, her dark, sooty lashes spiked with tears. She opened her mouth to speak, but no sound came out. Suddenly she came rushing forward and reached out to hug Bellami so tight she squeezed the breath out of her.

"Thank you...." Missy whispered.

"It's nothing. You're what makes it look so heavenly." Bellami held her away and looked deep into her bottomless eyes. She felt a strong pull on her heart as she saw her flawed reflection in those dark eyes. "Don't tell Brooks, let it be a surprise, for me," Bellami said softly.

Missy nodded and blinked away her tears. There was a faraway look in Bellami's eyes. Since waking from her badly needed rest, she seemed even sadder and more distant, as if her thoughts were somewhere far away. But today she had plunged into the "great adventure of clothes," as she called it. Maybe this was the sign of a new beginning.

"Where is Brooks taking you? I seem to have forgotten." Bellami rubbed her temples with her fingertips.

"Brooks wants me to go to the bullfights, for the Fourth of July." Missy had turned back to the small mirror, where Bellami had it propped up on one of the trunks. Bellami was grateful she didn't see the color leave her face, or the hand pressing against her mouth to stifle the gasp.

Bellami had no idea what the date was. How long had it been since the flood? Two weeks, closer to three? She couldn't think—her head was spinning like a top.

"Excuse me," Bellami said quietly. Surprisingly, her voice sounded fairly normal as she left the bedroom. She was having trouble breathing, and a cold sweat had broken out on her brow. For some inexplicable reason, she went stumbling toward Trace's room. Even now, knowing how he felt about her, he promised security and safety.

It was a deep relief to find him alone. She didn't question why no one was with him as she stumbled toward the chair beside his bed. She picked up his strong, lean hand and hung her head in misery. No matter how hard she concentrated, Bellami couldn't stop the kaleidoscope of memories this time. They came unbidden, unwelcome, swirling and spinning in her head like confetti.

Fighting to regain control, gasping for breath, she squeezed Trace's callused hand, holding it like a lifeline while the ocean flood of memories took shape...

It was the Fourth of July, 1871. The Stars and Stripes blew in the breeze from every second-story window on the stately tree-lined street where her family lived.

Grand Central Station was nearly completed, being touted as the largest terminal in the world. In celebration of Independence Day and the position New York held in the world, special fireworks were being scheduled.

Commodore Vanderbilt paid for crate after crate of exploding missiles out of his own pocket. He strutted like a peacock, bragging about the display. Handbills littered the streets, and the event was on every lip.

Brooks and Bellami were unmanageable. Donovan and Patricia had indulged nearly their children's every whim all their pampered lives. The twins were growing up to be rebellious hellions. They expected to get everything they asked for, and with two of them doing the asking, they requested a lot.

With a little effort, they persuaded their parents to take them to see the stunning event.

Bellami felt the first anguished tear spill over. She thought about how foolish they'd been, how foolish *she'd* been. Such stupid children. Now she had grown to be an equally silly, foolish woman, she thought with an ironic twist of her lips.

Some of the neighbor children had been teasing Brooks, calling him a sissy, because he had to wait and accompany his parents and his sister instead of going along with the group, like the other boys.

"I should've let him go alone, but I didn't want to be left behind. I told him, 'I'll tell Father. You'll get punished.'" Bellami spoke softly, sniffling from time to time as hot, salty tears continued sliding down her scarred cheek. They fell unnoticed on Trace's pale face. They wet his forehead and trickled down his jaw. Some dropped near his closed eyes.

"We snuck down the back stairs, out the servants' entrance. It was nearly dark. I remember how exciting it was, disobeying my parents. Dangerous, wicked. I loved it." She squeezed Trace's hand tighter. Even if she'd wanted it, this time the memory would not be denied. She couldn't keep it bottled up any longer. It spilled forth. All the guilt and pain of thirteen years of denial came along with her tears.

"Brooks tried to send me home! I wouldn't go—so stubborn." A racking sob escaped her, and she wiped impatiently at her face. When she laid her free hand back in her lap, a broad, furry head was there. Bellami found comfort while she absently stroked the rough cream-and-black pattern around the yellow eyes.

She continued to speak softly. "We found the place where all the crates were stored. Several men from the docks were there. Then they left—to have their supper.

One of the boys said it would be a lark opening the crates, taking some of the missiles, just for fun. Brooks told me not to. He told me it was dangerous, but I wouldn't listen. I'm oldest, I knew best—told him so, too.'' Her shoulders were heaving with each word, while the tears fell steadily.

"Somebody struck a match, and I was holding a missile. Brooks told me not to hold it. He tried to take it from me.'' She was moaning softly, sobbing, and a moment passed before she could continue. "Brooks tried his hardest to stop me. I held it. Then the explosion. My eyes...my face.... I woke up, a long time later. Weeks. I know Brooks has felt responsible, all these years. But it wasn't his fault, really, he tried. I wanted to tell him. I didn't blame him, never blamed him. My fault. Couldn't speak of it.''

She let her head fall forward, resting on Trace's broad chest, crying her heart out. Crying until the tears wouldn't come anymore. Tip never left her side, not even when the tall, slim man with blue-gray eyes and sable-colored hair left the balcony, through Bellami's bedroom.

It was long past dark when she finally rose, leaving the man and the wolf.

Trace had been dreaming again. He'd been having the strangest dreams lately. Confusing, disjointed things. White lights and deep voices, terrible pains in his head. He even thought he'd dreamed of Missy and his father.

He kept trying to wake up, but for some reason he just couldn't seem to shake off the deep sleep. A part of him wanted never to wake up. Pain was waiting if he woke. Some part of him knew that. Not physical pain, but something else, something he couldn't quite remember, but he knew it was a horrible black pit of despair. Something about Bellami—his little general. His reason for living.

Bellami. She drifted before him like a bright, shining promise of happiness and love. He'd been dreaming of her now, sitting at his bedside. She'd been weeping. It was crazy, but he could almost feel the tears on his face. He could almost taste the salty brine of her tears.

Opening his eyes just a crack, he tried to see her. He wanted to see her face before he died, even if it was only in a dream. After all, blind men couldn't really see—it had to be a dream. He didn't care what she looked like. She had told him once she was ugly. The creature he dreamed of now was beautiful beyond description. Heavy dark hair, violet eyes, spilling heartbroken tears. She sat weeping at his bedside, this beautiful woman in his dreams, with a giant wolf at her side. What a silly dream for a man to have before he died.

Pieces of the dream floated by again. Salty tears, and words full of pain. Fourth of July. Twins. Nothing solid, nothing making sense, just sleep, safe sleep. Never wake, just drift off in your sleep. No more pain, no more hurt. No more regrets.

As long as he slept, Trace was safe. From pain, from loneliness. From . . . what?

"It will be a long recovery, but I have seen signs of consciousness. Keep him quiet, I'll be back later in the week," the doctor told Hugh, right outside her half-open door.

Trace was going to live! Bellami felt such happiness. Tears were forming again, and she sniffed and forced herself not to cry. This silly crying was getting to be monotonous.

She had things to do. Brooks and Missy were leaving for Socorro today. What was the date? Missy had patiently told her at least twice—July 2, 1885, that was it. Two days until the bullfight. Turning, she took a long look at her trunks. Impossible to take them. Not if she was going to keep her plans secret.

She packed only a single change of clothes. Then, on impulse, she found the things she'd worn on the picnic with Trace. They were dirty, ripped, really little more than rags, but she shoved them into a carpet bag with her brush and mirror.

Bellami was dressed in a plain gray dress when she stepped out onto the stairs. Her heart beckoned to her to see Trace, but she was afraid that if he woke and found her in his room it might upset him.

No. That wasn't the truth. The real reason she couldn't go see him was that she knew she wouldn't be able to stand his rejection. Bellami James was taking the coward's way out.

"You have no courage," she told herself. She felt ashamed that she wasn't more like the rest of the James clan.

Clell, Hugh, Brooks, and the whole O'Bannion brood were sitting in the kitchen with the doctor when she walked in. For a moment, she felt uncomfortable—they were staring at her again—but then she smiled and squared her shoulders.

That one night of love had meant nothing to Trace, but for Bellami it had unlocked the door she'd been hiding behind. She might not ever be able to face Trace, but she could now face the rest of the world. She was still scarred, still ugly, but it didn't matter so much anymore. Her feelings would always be with Trace, anyway. Feelings that he had brought to life and would keep with him until the day she died. Bellami could take comfort in that.

Now, when she imagined herself walking the cold halls of St. Michael's alone and lonely, she knew she'd be thinking back. Remembering one night of perfect love. It would be enough.

Setting her chin, just the way Rod would, she entered the kitchen. "Good morning," she said softly.

Brooks wanted to hold her, to tell her that he hadn't meant to eavesdrop. While Bellami was telling Trace and that huge yellow-eyed dog about the accident, he'd been standing on the balcony, weeping right along with her. Imagine, a grown man, crying like a baby while his sister talked about something that happened half a lifetime ago. All the years he'd spent thinking she blamed him, thinking that was why she wouldn't talk about it. What a fool he'd been not to understand her better.

She was beautiful, his twin, and now there seemed to be a certain radiance about her, too. There'd been a change in Bellami since she'd left New York. Brooks didn't know what it was, but he sensed in her a sort of tranquillity, a wisdom she'd never had before. She seemed to be at peace with herself, even if her eyes held a slightly melancholy look today.

"Good morning," he said to her.

Bellami poured herself a cup of coffee. Missy turned to her and winked conspiratorially.

"Did you sleep well?" Brooks asked as he gave her a kiss on the top of the head.

"Yes. Did you?" She hesitated a moment, looking deep into his eyes, but then she gave him one of her rare, dazzling smiles. While she smiled, he felt a warmth, like sunshine. Maybe at last things would be good for his sister.

Hugh watched the pair. He hadn't really seen them together before now. Brooks had stayed busy helping with the roundup, and Bellami had spent every minute these past weeks with Trace, so they'd had little time together. They were alike as two peas in a pod. It was sort of eerie. When they gave him a full gaze, it was kind of electrifying.

"Are you and Missy leavin' for Socorro today?" Hugh asked Brooks as he pulled out a chair for his twin.

"Pa? What do you mean, me and Brooks? Aren't you comin'?" Missy wore a hurt look.

"I thought I'd stay here." Hugh could see the disappointment in his only daughter's face.

"Oh. I thought since we'd gotten good news from Dr. Sedgewood, that maybe, well, since tomorrow is my birthday..." Her words trailed off.

"Hugh, go," Clell said sharply.

"Clell's right, Pa, we'll all be here. Missy deserves a nice birthday." Flynn spoke to Hugh, but he was watching

Bellami. She had something up her sleeve, he'd have bet his reputation on it. He had seen a lot of men, desperate men. He knew that look—the look Bellami wore now. It spoke volumes to him; it told him of desperation and something else. It told him Bellami was getting ready to run from something. The fewer people around for a few days, the better.

Hugh searched all their faces, letting his glance linger on Missy's. He relented. "I'll go. Get ready." What choice did he have, with his children and Clell pushing and shoving? "But if there is any change, send Shane right away," he said as the loading began. A mysterious trunk was loaded under Missy's careful supervision. Then Brooks and Missy climbed into the wagon along with Hugh. Amid waves and shouted goodbyes they left for Socorro.

Dr. Sedgewood instructed the group on how he'd been trickling broth into Trace's mouth. He planned on leaving the ranch around sundown. He seemed to think Trace would regain consciousness in several days, if not sooner. The surgeon was confident Trace would just continue to sleep until that time.

Bellami stood on Trace's porch, watching her brother until he was far out of sight. Whispering a little prayer that he'd forgive her for being such a coward, she turned and dashed upstairs. She saw Clell and Flynn in the kitchen from the corner of her eye as she snuck past.

"Please, take care of Trace," she whispered as she tiptoed up the stairs to her room.

Flynn wore a dark scowl and a far-off look in his eye. He'd been chewing on something all morning long. All through lunch he had continued to be preoccupied.

"All right, boy, spit it out," Clell said in disgust. "I can't even enjoy my corn bread and buttermilk with that hangdog look on your face. What's botherin' you, anyway?"

"What?" Flynn raised his eyebrows, feigning ignorance.

"I damned near raised you, boy. What's got under your skin? Don't try foolin' an ol' fool—it don't work on me."

Flynn looked at Clell. He might just as well try to deceive himself as to keep something from Clell.

"Damned nosy ol' coot," he admonished. "It's Miss James. She's up to somethin'." Flynn set his jaw.

"Now, what in tarnation do you mean, she's up to somethin'? What do you think she's goin' to do, hold us up?" Clell laughed heartily at Flynn and shook his head at such foolishness.

Flynn crossed his arms over his chest, letting Clell have his fun. Finally Clell shut up and really looked at Flynn, who was sitting there with a scowl on his face.

"You're serious, aren't you? Well, let's go take a look." He muttered about having to climb the stairs again as Flynn led the way. When they reached the landing, they turned to Bellami's door and knocked. After about a dozen of Clell's knuckle-bruising raps, they opened it and went inside. It was empty. The curtain billowed into the room from the open window. Flynn marched out onto the balcony. A rope of sheets hung all the way to the ground.

"Shit!" Flynn said as he spun around and bounded down the stairs.

The doctor's buggy was gone, too. She'd simply left.

"Now what do you think we should do?" Clell asked, his blue eyes scanning the horizon.

"We better find her and bring her back. Trace is so blamed in love with that gal, it'll kill him if she's not here when he wakes up." Flynn paced back and forth on the porch like a chained-up cougar.

Clell found Logan and Shane. He squeezed his eyes shut and rubbed his chin in distress when they said they hadn't seen or heard anything. However she'd managed it, she'd done it quietly.

"She must've snuck around like an Injun'," Clell said with admiration in his voice.

"Wonder how long she's been gone?" Shane asked.

Clell and Flynn looked at each other, frowning. "Last time I saw her was around noon, when Brooks left. It's nearly six now." Flynn said, shoving a battered timepiece back in his pants pocket.

"Bet she headed for the train," Logan supplied. The four men looked at each other for a moment.

"We've only got a few hours of daylight left," Shane pointed out.

Flynn raised his eyes heavenward, hoping for some sort of a sign. His brother wasn't going to like this one bit.

Trace felt the vise on his wrist. Trying to jerk it free, he winced when the pressure only tightened. He'd been dreaming of trapping wolves. Only he was the one in the trap now.

The thing on his wrist violently jerked at him. He pulled hard against it and was rewarded with a sharp pinch.

"Damn!" As he spit out the curse, his green eyes flew open.

The first thing he felt was a woeful pain behind his eyes. Then he slowly turned his head and looked down at the unrelenting pressure on his wrist. The biggest damned wolf he'd ever seen was proceeding to eat him. Evidently it had decided to start with one hand and work its way up from there.

"Help!" Trace bellowed as his eyes widened in surprise. He tried to rise, but found the wolf to be considerably stronger than he was at the moment. Misery overtook him when he was unable to remove the carnivore from the end of his arm. He slumped back, disgusted at his continuing weakness.

"Bellami!" he shouted at the top of lungs. The animal never even flinched at the sound of his voice. Instead, the hungry beast just continued tugging on his wrist. Trace grimaced again. Soon the sharp teeth would remove his hand and continue up his arm. What a way to go.

Trace heard the pounding of boots up the stairs, and then his door opened wide, slamming back against the wall with a resounding thud.

"Holy Mother of God!" Flynn shouted. His right hand moved toward his pistol.

"Flynn!" Clell shouted as he slapped Flynn's hand away from the holster.

Shane and Logan were straining to see over the heads of the two men in the doorway of the bedroom.

"Don't be trying to shoot ol' Tip!" Clell looked at Flynn like he had cussed in church or something.

"Tip? This *monster* is Tip?" Trace moaned as he warily watched the yellow-eyed vision from hell mouth his wrist some more. It looked to him like Tip was just getting a good taste before he really settled down to the business of dinner.

"You can see again. 'Bout damned time," Clell said. He sniffed and rubbed a gnarled hand across his watery eyes, and then a mischievous grin blazed across his weathered face. "Now, you boys don't go thinkin' badly of poor ol' Tip. He's Miss Bellami's favorite pet." He smiled at the enormous animal.

Trace sighed and closed his eyes. "I should've known. There's always been somethin' damned strange about this, *dog*. Bring me Bellami. I've got to talk to her." Trace finally managed to pull himself into a sitting position, but the wolf refused to let him go. It kept tugging persistently on his wrist. He was dizzy, but felt strong enough to sit up.

"Trace, your eyes...your sight..." Flynn sputtered, not sure if he should shoot the animal, hug his brother, or break the news to Trace about Bellami's disappearance.

Trace looked at his family. The four men simply stood with their mouths agape, looking at Trace with lost expressions. He knew something was horribly wrong.

"What is it? Has somethin' happened to Bellami?" Then he had a vague memory of Brooks's arrival. The words of love she'd spoken echoed through his throbbing head. "Where is she?" He tried to rise, but found it nearly impossible, wearing an eighty-pound animal on his wrist like a living, breathing bracelet.

"She's gone, Trace," Clell said sadly.

"She can't be. I have to tell her..." he felt like death warmed over, but he took a deep breath and started barking orders. "Get me some pants—and would somebody please get this damned wolf off my arm?" Trace struggled to his feet as Dr. Sedgewood entered the room.

"You can't go anywhere, Mr. O'Bannion. It might kill you." The surgeon took a step before the snarling lobo positioned his bristling body in front of Trace. Amber eyes were narrowed, and the white fangs looked lethal. The startled surgeon froze.

"I have to go, and don't call me Mr. O'Bannion. Only one person calls me Mr. O'Bannion," Trace snarled as he struggled to rise. He could see and he could walk—that was all that was necessary. He had to find Bellami.

"You have to stay in bed," the physician said, and took one more halting step as his eyes focused on the bristling, growling animal.

"Well, I'll be. Looks like Tip don't agree with you, Doc. No disrespect intended, of course." Clell grinned like a possum. He looked about as sorry as Tip did at that particular moment. Trace thought the old codger actually enjoyed watching the half-tame wolf tree the startled houseguests.

Trace looked at the animal and understood perfectly. He knew immediately what Tip wanted. Hadn't the wolf done the same thing after the flood? "He wants me to get out of this bed and find Bellami. And if it kills me, that is what I intend to do." Amber eyes looked at him for a moment, and then Tip calmly sat down at Trace's side, allowing the doctor the opportunity to move a bit closer. "Well, this is the first time I've had to face a wolf in order to check on a patient. I suppose it's safe to assume, Mr. O'Bannion, you *can* see?'' The surgeon sounded completely fed up. ''This climate might be recommended for health reasons, but the people are all quite mad,'' he muttered as he turned on his heel and stalked away.

Trace looked a little dumbfounded. He blinked twice. ''Yes, I can see you all.'' A silly collective grin appeared on five faces. He sniffed and coughed. Several sets of dimples flashed in lean, weathered jaws.

Shane finally spoke, standing on tiptoe, so that he could peek over Flynn's head. ''This is all mighty touchin', but what about Miss James?''

''Hitch up the wagon,'' Clell said, using that military tone of absolute authority they'd all learned to hate as shirttailed boys.

''I'll ride to San Marcial ahead of you. And Trace, unless she's already gone, I promise you she won't be leavin' till you get there. After that, it's up to you, big brother.'' Logan tossed an unmistakable challenge at Trace with his words. He knew Trace would kill himself to meet it.

Shane interrupted. ''Wait a minute. My horse's faster. I'll go.''

''You want to put a little wager on who'll get there first?'' Logan looked like Lucifer himself, grinning at his older brother.

''Sure,'' Shane said, completely confident. After all, nobody'd beaten the dun yet.

Logan turned to Trace with the look of a slightly tarnished fallen angel. ''Can I borrow your stud, Trace?''

''You sneaky son of a buck!'' Shane yelled as the two bolted down the stairs, shoulder to shoulder. As the front door slammed shut, Trace wondered if there was still a glass left in it.

The ride was pure torture. Every bump sent ripples of agony through Trace's head. Even the makeshift bed did little to cushion the ride. He clenched his fists until his knuckles turned a chalky white.

"You better stop this madness and turn around," Doc Sedgewood advised solemnly.

"If you don't sit down and be quiet, I swear I'm goin' to gag you," Clell threatened from the back of his horse, in step beside the wagon.

The surgeon went to the back of the wagon, opposite Trace's bed, grumbling under his breath. Trace wondered if it would do any good to tell the physician he might as well be dead without Bellami James. The thought made him feel slightly sick to his stomach.

Flynn knew Trace was really suffering. It was easy to see that some of his pain wasn't just the physical kind. "You really love that gal, don't you?" Flynn said over his shoulder.

"Guess I do." Unlikely as it seemed to Trace, the tiny flame of hope still burned in his chest. He must be some kind of an idiot. If she'd gone with Brooks, what could he possibly do or say to get her to stay?

"Well, then, hang on, 'cause I don't want you to miss her." Flynn gave the reins a flick, and the horse picked up speed. He glanced at his brother and received a look full of meaning. He knew it would hurt like the devil but he encouraged a bit more speed from the horses.

Trace gritted his teeth against the pain. "I may not even get the chance to ask her to stay, Flynn. She probably left with that son of a bitch Brooks." The wagon hit another rut, and Trace moaned.

"What?" Flynn wasn't following the conversation all of a sudden. He spoke loud so Trace could hear him over the noise of the horse's hooves. "Why are you callin' Brooks a son of a bitch? What makes you think she left when he did?" Didn't Trace realize the woman traveling with Brooks was Missy, not Bellami. Flynn wondered if Trace's vision had really been restored. At that very moment, Clell cleared his throat loudly. When Flynn turned to look at him, riding beside the wagon, he saw him shake his head from side to side. Flynn got the message loud and clear. Clell didn't want Flynn telling Trace anything—about Brooks.

Trace never even glanced up. He kept on talking in a low strained voice. "She's in love with the bastard. She knew him in New York. I heard her tellin' him that mornin' how happy she was to see him." Trace's face was bleak.

Flynn didn't know if he should laugh or not. Trace was lying in the wagon, pale as a ghost, being eaten alive by jealousy over Bellami's brother. It was a confusing muddle. And, evidently, Clell wanted Trace to keep right on thinking that way. At least for the time being. This was promising to be some reunion!

Tip kept pace with the wagon. Occasionally he would look up to give Trace a meaningful glance. Then the lanky animal loped ahead a few feet, as if to encourage the man to keep following him. None too soon—from the looks of Trace's gray, pain-racked face—they saw San Marcial in the distance. The train station sat at the far end of town, looking about a hundred miles away to Flynn at this moment.

The sun drenched the sleepy little town in a russet aura of light. Clell mumbled something about few of the population being on the streets this time of evening. Just in case, though, he moved up closer to Tip. He didn't want to see the poor ol' critter shot after all the trouble he had gone to saving his mangy hide.

Trace felt a mixture of fear, excitement and dread, all at once. He had to tell Bellami. If she still wanted to leave him after that, there was nothing he could do, short of kidnapping her. That wasn't a completely unappealing notion, he thought with a cockeyed grin. Keeping her, however he had to do it, was the main objective, after all, and he would do just about anything to have the woman he loved.

They neared the train station, where a crowd of people milled around. As they got closer, Trace recognized his brother's voice.

"I don't care what your company policy is, this train ain't leavin' till I say so. Now sit down and shut up." Logan sounded like he really enjoyed ordering the conductor around. Trace wondered if that boy didn't have a streak of outlaw in him.

With Clell and Flynn's help, Trace climbed down out of the wagon. When his boots touched the earth, he stumbled and nearly went to his knees. Then he felt the broad, furry head come up under his hand, giving him support. As he looked into the wild eyes, there was an unspoken understanding.

"All right, boy, I'll follow you. Find her, Tip. Find Bellami," Trace said. Clell and Flynn supported most of his weight, and he willed his feet to move forward.

The big wolf started moving forward through the crowd of people amid gasps of shock and horror.

"It's a damned lobo," a startled voice said. The sound of a gun being cocked made the hair on Trace's neck bristle. His blood went cold, but Flynn's voice boomed beside him.

"The first man who takes a shot at that wolf is dead." His booming voice was chilling. Trace knew why most men threw down their weapons before they dared to draw against Flynn O'Bannion.

Slowly they continued forward through the crowd, toward the station. Every footfall rang like a bell clapper through Trace's pounding head. A muscle in his jaw worked as he steeled himself against the pain. His vision was a bit blurry, but he finally made out a female form in the distance.

A dark-haired woman sat alone outside the train station. She seemed unaware of the confusion and turmoil going on around her. She stared straight ahead into the dusky evening of the New Mexico Territory.

"Bellami?" he said softly. Was this her? Tip moved
steadily in the woman's direction, but she didn't answer.
She gave no indication that the softly spoken name meant
anything to her. Still the animal walked on.

Trace's heart plummeted. This wasn't Bellami, it
couldn't be. This sad-looking woman was stunning, beautiful. Very much like the female in his delirious dreams.

He was buffeted by a deep sorrow. It wasn't Bellami.
She'd already gone. He was too late. A lump formed in his
throat.

Tip continued toward the motionless form of the lovely,
sad woman. A tiny glimmer of hope flared in Trace's chest.

"Bellami?" he said louder as Tip moved away from his
outstretched hand. The wolf walked to the woman and laid
his head in her lap. He stared up at her with golden eyes.
The lady began to stroke his fur, lovingly.

"Bellami James!" Trace practically yelled. The effort
made him sway weakly against his brother and Clell. She
finally turned toward him. He could see tears glistening in
her eyes.

It *was* her! Violet eyes, in the loveliest face he'd ever
seen, looked at him, and his heart melted.

"Damn it, woman." His temper flared along with his
feeling of overwhelming relief. "Damn it, Bellami James.
You left me before I even got out of bed. The least you
could do is give me a fightin' chance." His loud, angry
voice silenced the milling crowd. Clell averted his gaze and
cleared his throat.

"Look, if you don't want to saddle yourself with a
rough hombre like me, I understand, but you've got to
hear me out."

When she blinked, salty tears ran down her cheeks.
Taking a deep breath, Trace prepared himself to say the
toughest words of his life.

"Bellami, I love you. I need you. Please, don't leave me.
I don't care about Brooks. You just can't go like this. Give
me a chance. Stay for a while, just a while, let me show

you . . ." His voice trailed off. He didn't know what else to say. He'd played his trump card and bared his soul. What else could he do? Bellami couldn't know what it cost Trace to say he needed her. But he paid the price gladly—and would do it again if he had to.

Through her tears, she really looked at him. Everyone around them, including Clell and Flynn, just seemed to disappear. She brushed at her eyes with the back of her hand and realized for the first time that she'd forgotten her gloves. The bandage on his head was too big and bulky for him to wear his hat. Wild black hair stuck out at odd angles from between the strips of white cloth. His shirt was buttoned only halfway, exposing the hard muscles and nearly healed bruises on his chest.

He needed a shave.

The setting sun added gold flecks to his emerald eyes. Pain pierced her heart like an arrow when she caught herself thinking that just maybe he did need her.

"But my face . . ." she whispered softly.

He frowned, watching her blue eyes catch the sunlight. Blue as the deepest lake, with tiny gold flecks. He searched her face, looking for some clue, some hint.

"I know you can have your pick of men, many a lot easier on the eyes than me, but, Bellami, I love you." Trace rubbed his hand across his eyes.

"But doesn't my face bother you?" she whispered softly.

"Honey, there isn't much about you that doesn't bother me. Your face, your body, the way you smell. The way you feel in my arms." Trace grinned and felt his jaw redden.

Bellami frowned and sniffed back the irritating tears in her eyes. "Trace, what about my scar?"

"What scar?" he said. Concentrating on her words was mighty hard with her this close to him. He wanted to reach out and pull her against him. The smell of her sweet body filled his nostrils with every hopeful breath. He wished they were alone so he could show her how he felt.

Bellami watched his expression closely. He wore a somewhat befuddled look. He could see, that was obvious, but could he see clearly? Trace O'Bannion said he loved her, needed her, but what exactly did he need from her? Now that he could see, he didn't need someone like her. She was only good for taking care of the blind. She stroked Tip's head while Trace's words kept ringing in her ears, *What scar, what scar?* The light wasn't that bad. She wasn't in the shadows, after all. He could see, but had his sight been fully restored? Maybe he'd need her for just a while longer. Wasn't that what he'd said? *Stay for a while, just a little while?*

Questions and doubts swirled in her head, and she finally just gave up trying to figure any of it out. Bellami gave in to her heart as she'd wanted to do from the moment he first called her name.

"Trace O'Bannion, look at my face, look at this scar." She turned her cheek toward him and pulled the hair back from her face. She swallowed hard, baring her face and her soul.

He frowned and blinked, leaning in toward her. One eyebrow rose under the white bandage. "That little thing?" he asked, touching the scar lightly with his fingertips.

She went to him then, to lay her cheek against his chest. The crisp hair tickled her scarred cheek. He folded her in his arms as she leaned against his warm chest. The bone-crushing embrace felt so good, so safe. She felt his weight on her heavily when Clell and Flynn stepped back.

Trace nuzzled her hair, breathing deeply. Lavender. She still smelled like lavender. No other person in the world smelled exactly like Bellami James. The tiny flame of hope grew a little larger, and he felt its warmth surging through him.

"There's just one thing I have to know, little general." His eyes narrowed. "What about Brooks?" He dared not breathe, so much depended on this answer.

Bellami lifted her head from his chest and gazed into his eyes. "I think my brother will be as happy as I am—if Missy has anything to do with it," she said, and dropped her head back to the hard, loving warmth of his chest.

"Brother?" He said the word softly. Then he cast a chilling glance at Clell and Flynn. Both men shuffled their feet and looked out at the prairie, guilt written all over their faces. Trace understood, and he didn't give a good damn.

He grinned at them both and lifted her chin up so that he could gaze into her lovely face. "Bellami, would you do somethin' for me tonight?" he asked as he looked deep into her moist violet eyes.

"Anything," she sighed.

"I really could use a shave," he said with a grin.

"Oh, Trace, I'll shave you tonight and every night, for the rest of my life. I love you." Her words were lost in the warmth of his mouth.

* * * * *

MORE ROMANCE, MORE PASSION,
MORE ADVENTURE...MORE PAGES!

Bigger books from Harlequin Historicals. Pick one up today and see the difference a Harlequin Historical can make.

White Gold by Curtiss Ann Matlock—January 1995—A young widow partners up with a sheep rancher in this exciting Western.

Sweet Surrender by Julie Tetel—February 1995—An unlikely couple discover hidden treasure in the next *Northpoint* book.

All That Matters by Elizabeth Mayne—March 1995—A medieval about the magic between a young woman and her Highland rescuer.

The Heart's Wager by Gayle Wilson—April 1995—An ex-soldier and a member of the demi-monde unite to rescue an abducted duke.

Longer stories by some of your favorite authors. Watch for them in 1995 wherever Harlequin Historicals are sold.

 HARLEQUIN®

PRESENTS
RELUCTANT BRIDEGROOMS

Two beautiful brides, two unforgettable romances...
two men running for their lives....

My Lady Love, by Paula Marshall, introduces
Charles, Viscount Halstead, who lost his memory
and found himself employed as a stableboy by the
untouchable Nell Tallboys, Countess Malplaquet.
But Nell didn't consider Charles untouchable—
not at all!

Darling Amazon, by Sylvia Andrew, is the story of
a spurious engagement between Julia Marchant
and Hugo, marquess of Rostherne—an engagement
that gets out of hand and just may lead Hugo to
the altar after all!

Enjoy two madcap Regency weddings this May,
wherever Harlequin books are sold.

Harlequin® Historical

From author Susan Paul

This spring, don't miss the first book in this exciting new series from
a newcomer to Harlequin Historicals—**Susan Paul**

THE BRIDE'S PORTION
April 1995

The unforgettable story of an honorable knight forced to wed
the daughter of his enemy in order to free himself from
her father's tyranny.

Be sure to keep an eye out for this upcoming series
filled with the splendor and pageantry of Medieval times
wherever Harlequin Historicals are sold!

BRP-1

Harlequin® Historical

Gayle Wilson

**The talented new author from
Harlequin Historicals brings you
the next title in her series set amid the
sophistication and intrigue
of Regency London**

THE HEART'S WAGER
April 1995
The compelling story of an ex-soldier and a casino dealer who must
face great dangers to rescue his best friend from certain death!

Don't miss this delightful tale!

And you can still order THE HEART'S DESIRE
from the address below.

To order your copy of THE HEART'S DESIRE (HH #211), please send your name,
address, zip or postal code along with a check or money order (please do not
send cash) for $3.99 for each book ordered ($4.50 in Canada), plus 75¢ postage and
handling ($1.00 in Canada), payable to Harlequin Books, to:

In the U.S.

3010 Walden Avenue
P. O. Box 1369
Buffalo, NY 14269-1369

In Canada

P.O. Box 609
Fort Erie, Ontario
L2A 5X3

Please specify book title(s) with your order.
Canadian residents add applicable federal and provincial taxes.

HHT-2

Claire Delacroix's UNICORN TRILOGY

The series began with UNICORN BRIDE,
a story that *Romantic Times* described as
"...a fascinating blend of fantasy and romance."

Now you can follow the Pereille family's ongoing quest
in the author's April 1995 release:

PEARL BEYOND PRICE

And if you missed UNICORN BRIDE, it's not too late
to order the book from the address below.

To order your copy of the UNICORN BRIDE (HH #223), please send your name, address, zip or postal code along with a check or money order (please do not send cash) for $3.99 for each book ordered ($4.50 in Canada), plus 75¢ postage and handling ($1.00 in Canada), payable to Harlequin Books, to:

In the U.S.
3010 Walden Avenue
P. O. Box 1369
Buffalo, NY 14269-1369

In Canada
P.O. Box 609
Fort Erie, Ontario
L2A 5X3

Please specify book title(s) with your order.
Canadian residents add applicable federal and provincial taxes.

HUT-2